"Come in?" he aske in his driveway.

She didn't hesitate, which relieved him. "Sure," she said and climbed out.

His own exit took a little longer, and Ashley was waiting for him on the porch by the time he rolled up the ramp.

Nell took a quick dash in the yard, then followed eagerly into the house. The dog was good at fitting in her business when she had the chance.

"Stay for a while," he asked Ashley. "I can offer you a soft drink if you'd like."

She held up her latte cup. "Still plenty here."

He rolled into the kitchen and up to the table, where he placed the box holding his extra meal. He didn't go into the living room much. Getting on and off the sofa was a pain, hardly worth the effort most of the time. He supposed he could hang a bar in there like he had over his bed so he could pull himself up and over, but he hadn't felt particularly motivated yet.

But then, almost before he knew what he was doing, he tugged on Ashley's hand until she slid into his lap.

"If I'm outta line, tell me," he said gruffly. "No social skills, like I said."

He watched one corner of her mouth curve upward. "I don't usually like to be manhandled. However, this time I think I'll make an exception."

Home of the Brave

New York Times Bestselling Author

Rachel Lee

&

Melissa Senate

Previously published as *A Conard County Homecoming*
and *A New Leash on Love*

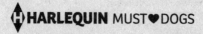

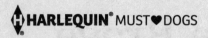 MUST ♥ DOGS

ISBN-13: 978-1-335-14733-2

Recycling programs for this product may not exist in your area.

Home of the Brave

Copyright © 2020 by Harlequin Books S.A.

A Conard County Homecoming
First published in 2017.
This edition published in 2020.
Copyright © 2017 by Susan Civil-Brown

A New Leash on Love
First published in 2018.
This edition published in 2020.
Copyright © 2018 by Harlequin Books S.A.

Special thanks and acknowledgment are given to Melissa Senate for her contribution to the Furever Yours miniseries.

This edition published by arrangement with Harlequin Books S.A.

For questions and comments about the quality of this book, please contact us at CustomerService@Harlequin.com.

Harlequin Enterprises ULC
22 Adelaide St. West, 40th Floor
Toronto, Ontario M5H 4E3, Canada
www.Harlequin.com

Printed in U.S.A.

CONTENTS

Rachel Lee was hooked on writing by the age of twelve and practiced her craft as she moved from place to place all over the United States. This *New York Times* bestselling author now resides in Florida and has the joy of writing full-time.

Books by Rachel Lee

Harlequin Special Edition

Conard County: The Next Generation

A Soldier in Conard County
A Conard County Courtship
A Conard County Homecoming
His Pregnant Courthouse Bride
An Unlikely Daddy
A Cowboy for Christmas

Harlequin Intrigue

Conard County: The Next Generation

Cornered in Conard County

Harlequin Romantic Suspense

Conard County: The Next Generation

Undercover in Conard County
Conard County Marine
A Conard County Spy
A Secret in Conard County
Conard County Witness

Visit the Author Profile page
at Harlequin.com for more titles.

A CONARD COUNTY HOMECOMING

Rachel Lee

To Ashley R. Granger, a very sweet lady
who offered to let me use her name for a character.
Thanks, Ashley!

Chapter 1

Zane McLaren pulled into the driveway after dark. Operating the hand controls of his van with the ease of familiarity, he parked so that the newly constructed ramp would be near the sliding door in the side of the van.

It was ready. His old family home had been prepped for his wheelchair existence, and only the service dog on the front seat beside him seemed happy to realize the journey had ended. Nell, a golden Lab, woofed her approval as he turned the engine off.

Arriving after dark had been a choice. By now everyone in Conard County, Wyoming, who cared to hear about it knew that Zane McLaren was coming home for the first time since his parents' funerals nearly fifteen years ago, and the ramps he'd had constructed before his arrival let them know his condition if they hadn't already heard from workmen or his housekeeper.

The fat had probably already been chewed over by those who remembered: great high school athlete in a wheelchair nearly twenty years later as a result of his military service. Heads had shaken, and curiosity had awakened.

The thought of that curiosity had brought him home in the darkness. He wasn't ready to face a parade of well-wishers, many of whom would be mostly interested in discovering how bad off he was.

He'd lost the use of his legs two years before. Rehab had followed, then adaptation to his new life. Now he just wanted to be left alone. He'd have been more anonymous in a city, but the wars had left him with other scars, too. He couldn't handle the noise, the traffic, the constant crush of people. He needed quiet and solitude, and he figured this was the best place to get it. Once everyone understood he just wanted to be left alone, they'd leave him alone. As he seemed to remember, people in this town were mostly respectful.

If it didn't work out, he'd sell the house and move on. There was nothing holding him anywhere now.

He pivoted the driver's seat and used his arms to lift himself into the wheelchair behind. Ready to go. Nell jumped off her seat and came to stand beside him, her tail swishing happily.

She was probably desperate to hit the grass, he thought with mild amusement. After locking himself in place, he pressed a button. The van door pulled open. The pneumatic lift extended itself, carrying him outside. Then another button lowered him to the ground. When he'd rolled off, Nell jumped to do her part. She nosed yet another button, the lift rose and retracted, and the door eased closed. He scratched her ears, letting him know he was pleased with her. She grinned back at him, happy.

"Go do your stuff," he told her.

She didn't need a second suggestion. She dashed immediately to the grass and began sniffing around. Apparently, the choice of where to relieve herself required some investigation.

Smiling faintly, he reached for the wheels of his chair and pushed himself toward the ramp. It felt sturdy beneath him; the slope was gentle enough, with a surface that had been roughened with outdoor carpeting to prevent slipping. Safe in the rain. Heating wires below for the snow. Perfect for his needs.

He reached the porch and pivoted, waiting for Nell. For the first time, it occurred to him that he might need to hire someone to clean up after her. He could do it unless the ground became soggy enough to bog down on, or the snow too deep. Little things. It was most often the little things that caused him problems now and often took him by surprise. He already had a handle on most of the big things.

Sitting still, waiting for his dog, he allowed the autumn chill to start reaching him. A lot of warmth came from movement, as he'd learned, and he wasn't moving much at the moment. Still, he waited patiently. Nell was on new ground and probably needed

to check it all out. He didn't have the heart to interrupt her.

At last Nell finished up and came racing to his
side. He unlocked the front door with a key that was
as old as he was, and together he and his dog entered his old home, flicking on lights as he went. He
ignored the stairway to the two upstairs bedrooms.
That part of the house was unavailable to him—not
that he needed it.

The house smelled different, but it had been thor-
oughly cleaned, and work had been done inside to
ready things for him, like a new shower and a sturdy
framework over his bed. Eventually, if he decided to
stay, he'd have to change the kitchen as well, but that
was going to be an expensive proposition. Right now
he could manage well enough with standard counter
heights and sinks. He'd had to learn.

The dog bowls were waiting, and he quickly filled
one with water and bent to place it in Nell's new feeding stand. Most things he'd been able to ship ahead, but
some had had to be replaced. This was one of them.
While she lapped water eagerly, he went to the pantry
and found that the housekeeper he'd hired had filled
it as directed. Everything was on the lower shelves or
floors, nothing too high for him to reach. The bag of
dog food in one corner was the first thing he grabbed.
Nell had been awfully patient today, and she danced
eagerly as he filled her bowl. Instead of putting the bag
away, he set it to one side for the moment.

Opening the refrigerator wasn't exactly easy, as it
was a tight space for him in his chair. He knew Nell

could do it for him if he just tied a towel to the handle, but he was jealous of every bit of independence he could protect.

Opening it, he found everything he'd requested. For now he just grabbed a beer.

Home. He wondered if he'd ever feel he was home again.

Then he heard the knock on his front door and almost decided not to answer it. He'd come here to be by himself and didn't want a tide of well-meaning or curious neighbors sweeping through. *Ignore it*, he thought.

Ashley Granger knocked on Zane's front door, a little nervous but determined. His housekeeper, Carol Cathcart, had worked with her for years as an aide at her school before taking this job with Zane, and the two had become friends of sorts. Carol had been the one to mention Zane was arriving today.

In her hand, Ashley held a warm Dutch apple pie she'd made after school as a welcoming gift for Zane. Ashley had thought a pie would be a nice gesture. Especially her famous Dutch apple.

She remembered Zane from school, sort of. She'd been five years behind him, which had precluded a friendship of any kind, but it was hard not to be aware of him. A great athlete, popular, good-looking…everyone knew Zane, if only at a distance. Then he'd left to join the military, and the last time she'd seen him had been at his father's funeral years ago. His mother had died a year earlier.

Which meant he had few ties with this town, nearly twenty years later. She was kind of surprised he'd choose to come back here, but he had, and it seemed to her that an apple pie was the least she could do.

She rapped again, but there was no answer. He might need time to get to the front door—she really had no idea how mobile he was now—or maybe he was already in bed. He must have had a long drive. Glancing at her watch yet again, she thought that nine o'clock didn't seem so late, but this was probably a different time zone for him.

Well, the pie would hold until tomorrow.

She had just started turning away when the door opened and a rough voice said, "What do you want?"

Okay, that was a pleasant opening. She had a bit of a temper, and it flared now. She faced him. "Nothing. I was just going to give you a pie."

But in an instant her mind took a snapshot of a broad-shouldered man, still wearing a jacket, sitting in a wheelchair. Beside him, a golden Lab stood watch. God, was it possible the years had made Zane more attractive? The boy had become a man, even more appealing.

Dark eyes, dark hair a little on the shaggy side, the same strong jaw, but older. Much older. The years had taken a toll, leaving his face weathered and a bit lined. Harsh suns and winds, and maybe losing the use of his legs.

"Of course," she continued stiffly, "if you don't want it…"

But then he pushed his chair back from the door. "Come in," he said gruffly.

On legs that felt rigid for some reason, she entered a house that was a clone of her own, except for the decorating. There was little decorating here except that left behind by his parents.

She started to reach for the door to close it against the growing chill, but the dog beat her to it, nosing it shut until she heard the latch click.

"What a beautiful dog," she said after clearing her throat.

"Nell. My service dog."

"Then I guess I shouldn't pet her."

"Only with my permission." Then he pivoted his chair with amazing ease and led the way to the kitchen. "No coffee," he said over his shoulder. "I didn't make any."

She hesitated. "I didn't come to stay. I just wanted to give you this pie. You don't have to entertain me."

"Good."

Well, that was blunt, she thought as her initial irritation began to give way to an unexpected, inexplicable amusement. So he was a hard case. Well, if that's how he wanted it, fine.

"I'm Ashley Granger, by the way," she said as they entered the kitchen. "You probably don't remember me."

"No."

Ah, monosyllables. When he waved at the kitchen table and its ancient Formica, she placed the pie on it. There was only one chair, and she wondered if she should even sit. But then he pointed to it, so she pulled it out and sat.

He wheeled himself closer to the table and picked up the beer that was sitting there. Then, as if suddenly remembering himself, he asked, "Want one?"

"No, thank you. Anyway, I live next door and Carol mentioned that you were arriving tonight, so I made a pie. No big deal. And I promised I wasn't here to visit. You must be tired after your trip."

She felt a poke on her denim-clad thigh and looked down. Nell was looking up at her with great interest. "Um…"

"Does she frighten you?"

"No," Ashley said. "But I'm not allowed to pet her, and I think that's what she wants."

"Sit, Nell," he said. "It's okay." Then those dark, strangely unrevealing eyes settled on Ashley again. "Go ahead and pet her, but just briefly. She's not supposed to get spoiled."

So Ashley forked her fingers into amazingly silky fur, and she could have sworn the dog grinned at her. All too soon Zane called her to heel and she went to lie beside his chair.

"So Carol mentioned me," he said after taking a sip from his longneck. "How much has she said?"

"Has she been gossiping, you mean? She's no gossip. She said she'd taken a job as your housekeeper. The only other thing she said was that you were arriving tonight. Otherwise, not a word."

He nodded slowly. "Thank you for the pie. But I

may as well be honest. I came home because I need my space and my quiet."

"A hermitage."

"Pretty much."

She nodded but felt a twinge of disappointment. She'd like to get to know him, and she didn't feel isolation was the best way to deal with his problems. Surely, he needed a community, people to spend time with, to give him a sense of belonging.

But it was not her decision. Having lived her entire life here, except during college, she was used to being surrounded by good friends and people she knew. She couldn't imagine wanting to be as alone as Zane wanted.

She had promised she wasn't here to visit, but it felt oddly wrong to just leave quickly. Maybe that was her own social upbringing, not the situation. Then he startled her, just as she was deciding to depart.

"Maybe I do remember you," he said quietly. "Your hair. It's almost exactly the color of a new-minted penny. I don't think I've seen that before."

"Strawberry blonde," she said, with a little shrug of her shoulder.

"No, it's almost unique. That's why I noticed it once. You were just a kid, but the hair was eye-catching."

"Well, thank you." Surprised by the tack he had taken, and feeling just a smidge uncomfortable over the attention to her hair, she didn't know what else to say.

"What do you do?"

"I teach fourth grade."

He nodded. "Do you like it?"

"Most of the time. It has its moments, like anything else, I suppose."

He pushed his wheelchair closer, so that it fit under the table, and rested his folded arms on it. "I'm not really good company these days," he said flatly. "I need you and everyone else to understand that. Right now I've got a bag full of stuff I need to work through, and sometimes I can flip out a little. Noise and crowding bother me. So I'm better just left alone, because I don't want to be rude and I don't want to scare anyone."

She blinked. Well, that was food for thought. "You want me to tell everyone to just stay away?"

"As many as you can. Just call me antisocial, because that's what I am."

What a change from the popular high school athlete. She couldn't even imagine what he'd been through or the ways it must have affected him. All she knew was that he evoked a very deep sadness in her heart with those words. "The detritus of war," she murmured before she realized she was speaking aloud.

"Exactly. That's me. And while I appreciate the pie, I really don't want a stream of people at my door."

"Okay." She frowned. "Except that I didn't mean *you* were the detritus. That's what you're dealing with."

"How the hell would you know?"

Her legs started to gather under her. This would be a good time to leave, she thought, but then she saw his hand gripping Nell's ruff. Clinging. This man needed more than himself, and he didn't even know it.

But it was pointless to argue. She had no background she could use to claim that she understood what he faced. What did she know, after all, about being paraplegic, or suffering from PTSD, which was what she guessed he meant about frightening people. Only what she'd read, and that simply wasn't enough.

Did he really think he could handle this all by himself? Or did he want solitude for something darker? She certainly couldn't imagine healing in a vacuum.

"I have a boy in my class who's quadriplegic," she remarked, trying to ease the tension he'd brought into the room with his confession.

"So?"

"I think he'd love to have a dog like Nell. I bet she can do almost anything."

He looked almost sideswiped by the change in direction. Maybe he'd hoped she'd get mad and walk out. But something in Ashley had stiffened. This man could be as rude as he wanted, but she wasn't just going to walk away and forget him. That seemed wrong even though he was asking for it.

"Anyway, Mikey's family can't afford a service dog. We've got a K-9 officer in the county now who trains police dogs, and he's doing a little work with service animals for people who can't afford them. Maybe, if you can crawl out of your shell long enough, you could tell him what a dog for Mikey would need to be able to do."

She was a bit startled to hear the acid in her tone, because she hadn't intended it. But there it was, clear as the words she had spoken. That did it, she thought.

He'd never want to set eyes on her again. Who was she to imply criticism of a wounded vet?

She pushed her chair back, ready to leave now, but Zane stopped her. "What's his name, this K-9 officer?"

"Cadell Marcus."

"Maybe I'll call him. I dunno." He rubbed his hand over his face.

"Sorry," she said. "You've only just arrived—you must be exhausted from your trip. I shouldn't have pressed you about anything. I only meant to say welcome home and leave the pie."

But as he dropped his hand from his face, she saw him staring beyond her. Far beyond her, as if he were seeing another place and another time. She froze, wondering if she had triggered a problem for him somehow. Maybe her being here was enough. She waited, not sure if he'd want her to just leave, not sure he'd even hear her if she bade him farewell.

God, she wished she knew what to do.

Then she learned something very important—Nell knew what to do. She rose onto her haunches, put her forepaws on the arm of his chair and stretched her head up until she could lick his cheek. Over and over again.

At first Zane didn't react. Not even a twitching muscle. His gaze remained black, almost empty. Nell continued to lick his cheek with occasional pauses to nudge him gently.

It seemed to go on forever, although it could only have been a minute or two. Then Nell barked and

Zane blinked, his eyes focusing once again. He reached out to wrap his arm around the dog, giving her a squeeze before letting her go. At once she dropped to a sitting position beside him, but she never took her attention from him.

Ashley added it all up and realized that the least of Nell's service was performing physical tasks for Zane. She was an emotional lifeline, drawing him back when he neared the precipice. Providing comfort more than physical care.

God, it was terrible to think of what had brought Zane to this point. Even her worst imaginings probably failed completely.

"I'm sorry," he said finally, his voice sounding rusty.

"No need," she answered promptly. And really, she didn't think he needed to apologize for being haunted by the demons of war. Almost nobody could escape that unscathed. At least she assumed that had been what just happened. She hoped she hadn't triggered it.

Deciding he must be uncomfortable now, considering what she had witnessed, and considering he'd already expressed his desire to be left alone, she again gathered herself to rise, opening her mouth to say good-night.

He forestalled her. "Sorry you had to see that. Did it last long?"

She settled back into the chair. "A minute or two. Don't apologize. I just hope I didn't cause it."

"There isn't always a cause. It just happens. It happens less when I'm away from known triggers, but it still happens. And I guess you've figured out that Nell does more for me than open doors and grab my socks."

"She seems wonderful," Ashley answered sincerely.

"She is. She responds immediately when I start to…slip, and she helps call me back quickly. Before Nell I could fall into flashbacks that lasted hours. Once it was even days." He grimaced. "My neighbors didn't much appreciate that last one."

She hesitated then asked because she wanted to know. "The flashbacks…they don't help you at all?"

"No."

Well, that was pretty grim. Dissociative episodes with no purpose except to make him miserable. A mind so overwhelmed that it kept trying to absorb what had happened and was totally unable to do so. Reliving horror.

"Thank God for Nell," she said finally. It seemed like such a weak response to what he had revealed.

He patted his lap, and she watched with amazement and amusement as Nell jumped up and did her best to curl up on him. The dog licked his chin, and for the first time she saw Zane laugh. Such a nice laugh. The dog apparently liked it, too, wagging her tail rapidly.

"She barely fits," Ashley remarked.

"She has to work at it," he agreed. His hands ran down Nell's furry back. "She's a lifesaver."

Somehow she didn't believe he was exaggerating.

"Anyway, I was lucky. Some of my friends got

together and gave her to me. I guess the little boy in your class could use the same kind of luck. So this Cadell guy is also trying to provide service dogs?"

"He's trying. He mainly trains police dogs, search-and-rescue dogs, but he's aware of the need. He consults with people who can help him figure out how to do it. Your advice might be very helpful."

He nodded. "Thing is, I don't know how she was trained. When I got Nell, she was on top of it all. I guess I could email one of my friends to see if they know who the trainer was. The trainer would be more helpful than I could ever be."

It was probably true, but Ashley suspected this was another way of keeping his isolation intact. Who was she to question his methods of dealing with his problems?

"Thanks," she said. "Mikey could sure use something to brighten his days. He hasn't been paralyzed long, only the last year, and he still has trouble dealing with it. The idea that kids can just bounce right back from anything... Well, it's not always true."

"How was he hurt?"

"Thrown from a horse. His mom told me his back was broken in several places and he became quadriplegic. They're grateful he's still alive, but I'm not sure Mikey always is."

"Why should he be?" Zane asked roughly. "God spare me the Pollyannas. Pardon me, but it doesn't always help to hear how lucky you are."

Ashley drew a breath. She wasn't shocked—she

knew he was right, but few people said such things so baldly.

"Count your blessings," he said. "Sure. That works. On a good day. On a bad day you just wish you'd never survived."

The stark truth rendered her speechless. Every single word that sprang to mind in answer struck her as a useless aphorism. This man was dealing with very real and very ugly memories and impulses. No words could offer any kind of succor.

"Now you know," he said. "That's why I don't want to fill my life with people. I've rattled you badly several times since you walked through my door. Who the hell needs to be around that?"

"I'm fine," she protested. Then, seeking safer ground immediately because she wanted to change the direction of his thinking as quickly as possible, "Don't you need some modifications in this kitchen?"

Startled, his head jerked back a bit. Nell jumped down from his lap and took up her watchful position. "My kitchen?" he repeated.

"Well, what else can I talk about?"

He frowned faintly. "The weather?"

"Cold and getting colder. I love autumn. What about the kitchen?"

To her amazement, a slow smile made it halfway across his face. "The kitchen has to wait. Expensive, and there's no point in doing it unless I decide to stay here."

"Ah." So he wasn't sure he was settled.

Deciding once again it was time to make her departure, she rose. "I hope you enjoy the pie. It was a pleasure to see you again, Zane. Sorry I intruded for so long."

She zipped her jacket, knowing it would be even colder outside now. "I'll see myself out. And, by the way, if you should need anything, I'm next door." She pointed. "I'm home most afternoons and evenings, because a teacher's day doesn't end when school lets out and I always have paperwork. Good night."

Then she marched out of that house with enough to think about that she'd probably be up late into the night.

She had no idea what she'd expected when she knocked on his door, but now she was deeply disturbed. Whoever Zane had become, he didn't at all resemble the young athlete she remembered.

He probably remembered that kid, though, and it couldn't make his life one bit easier now.

Zane sat in his kitchen, not moving, for a long time. The smell of the apple pie filled the room, and he clung to it as he kneaded Nell's neck.

Simple things. Good things. The schoolteacher had reminded him. Neighbors and apple pies. Running next door for a cup of sugar. Friendly faces on the streets. A world he hadn't known for a long time.

She was cute, that one. Beautiful, even, but there was no room in his hell for a woman. He'd only drag her down. Adapting to a wheelchair hadn't been as difficult as dealing with himself and the wars.

Would he like to have the use of his legs back?

Sure. Would he like to erase his memory? Absolutely. He'd trade his legs for a clean slate.

But he wasn't going to get either, so he had to find a way to make peace with himself. That was proving difficult indeed.

He'd tried group counseling with other vets. It had helped to know he wasn't alone in his reactions, feelings and nightmares, but that didn't get rid of any of them. He'd tried medications that were supposed to improve his PTSD, but he'd tossed them all because of Nell. She did more good for him than any pill. Anyway, until they invented a pill for selective memory loss, he was bound to live with himself.

It wasn't that he hated himself. But he'd been a sailor and done a SEAL's job, and inevitably horror had been etched on his memory.

Sighing, he rolled out of the kitchen, away from the enticing aroma of the pie and to his bedroom where one carved wooden box, a gift from a friend, waited on his aged dresser, set there by Carol when she unpacked the boxes he'd sent ahead. Opening it, he took out the medal presentation cases within and looked at the wages of his war.

A Purple Heart with a cluster pinned to the ribbon, the cluster for his second wounding, the injury that had paralyzed him. A Bronze Star with multiple clusters. A Silver Star with clusters. A Navy Cross. Campaign and other ribbons, but they didn't hold his attention. Those stars and the Navy Cross in particular said he was a hero.

Why didn't he feel like one? He snapped the cases

closed and put them back in the box. Once he'd mentioned that he was thinking of ditching them, but an
aging Vietnam vet had told him not to. "Someday,"
he'd said, "you'll want them. Or someone else who
loves you will. Put them away and save them. They're
the only reward you'll get."

The only reward. Yup.

He closed his eyes, remembering the kid who had
signed up nearly twenty years ago, wanting the GI
Bill, liking the promises the navy gave him of an education. Not much later he'd found himself getting
an education of a very different kind. To this day he
couldn't begin to explain to himself why he'd volunteered for the SEALs. Maybe because he was eighteen and full of hubris or too much testosterone. He
honestly didn't know.

But he'd done it, had passed all the arduous training, and had become a very different man in the process. He had been molded into a weapon.

Funny thing was, he didn't regret that choice.
Never once felt he'd made the wrong one. But now
he paid the price in memories that never left him.

One hell of an education, indeed.

Shaking his head a little, he wheeled back to the
kitchen, deciding to have a piece of the apple pie Ashley had left. The aroma was making his mouth water.

Nell sat hopefully beside him as he cut into the pie.
Treat. She had very speaking eyes, he often thought.
Hard not to read that she wanted her biscuit or a raw-
hide bone.

The pantry was still open, so he said, "Nell, get a bone."

Her tail wagging, Nell trotted into the pantry, found the plastic bag of bones and brought them out, dropping them onto his lap. He ripped off the paper label across the top and pulled the bag open. In the process, he loosened the staples holding it shut, and he made sure to gather them into a pile on the table. He'd hate for Nell to get into trouble with one while picking up the bag.

She accepted her rawhide bone with a woof and a wag then settled on the floor to gnaw happily.

And now he could taste the pie. It was every bit as scrumptious as it smelled. Closing his eyes, he savored the first mouthful, tasting its every nuance with pleasure before he swallowed. It had been a long time since he'd had a good pie, but this one was spectacular. Whether he wanted further contact or not, he was going to have to compliment the chef on this one.

Which meant making a connection he really didn't want to make. Ashley Granger was a beautiful young woman, and he didn't want to put any shadows on her face or in her heart.

While he didn't wallow in self-pity, he always tried to be straight with himself. His ultimate conclusion was that he was poison. Until he found a stable place inside himself, a way to reenter normal life, he didn't want to poison anyone else.

He looked down at Nell, his companion and aide, and once again saw his life with stark clarity. All these years, with one mission coming after another, with the time he wasn't in the field mostly used for training and planning, he'd never felt like a fish out of water. The member of a tightly knit fellowship, surrounded by comrades with the same job, the same worldview—he'd belonged.

Now he was a man who couldn't walk and who depended on a dog to keep him from sliding into a past that he no longer lived.

Yeah, he had no business bringing anyone else into this mess, even peripherally, until he got his head sorted out.

But Ashley sure had tempted him.

Chapter 2

Ashley went to school in the morning with nearly
a bushel basket full of apples for her students. She'd
swiped some for the pie yesterday, but the basket was
still brimming. A great time of year for apples, and
she'd made a tradition of ordering a bushel each fall
for her students.

They all loved apples, and while she limited them
to one a day, they still disappeared fast. With a class
size of nineteen, four to five days would nearly empty
the basket. When they got down to the last few, a
spelling bee would determine who got the last of them.

Her students usually loved the treat, and she felt
good about being able to give it to them. Special orders were no problem at the grocery, and she'd been
doing it for so many years that the produce manager

always had a list of prices and quality for her. This year he'd recommended the Jonathans, a type of apple she loved herself.

The students began arriving, and when they saw the apples, excitement began to grow. They'd heard of her tradition. "Not until after lunch," she reminded them.

Then Mikey's mother rolled him in and pushed him up to the table the school had provided specially so he could get his wheelchair under it comfortably. It was also wider than usual so his mother could sit beside him throughout the day and help with his assignments. She turned the pages in the books for him to read, and when worksheets had to be filled out, she asked him which answers he chose.

Today Mikey appeared to be in a fairly good mood. Ashley had the greatest admiration for his mother, Marian Landau, whose patience never seemed to flag. It couldn't be easy for her to drive him in every day and then sit beside him throughout the school day. She could have chosen homeschooling, but she had told Ashley that she wanted him to have social interactions.

"They might not all be good ones," Marian had said. "I know how cruel kids can be. But I also know how nice they can be, and I don't want him raised in isolation. Sooner or later he'll have to deal with the rest of the world."

So far this year, not a single student had been cruel to Mikey. Some hung back, as if uncomfortable, but a few routinely made an effort to speak to him, or to ask him to join their groups when they split into them.

A fund-raiser was being planned to get Mikey a better wheelchair, an electric one he'd be able to control with puffs on a straw. Dang, those things were expensive, Ashley thought as she called her excited and slightly rowdy group to order. But then so were service dogs, and Cadell Marcus was already trying to solve that problem. She spent a moment's hope that Zane would actually call Cadell and offer some advice.

"Okay," she said when everyone was settled and looking at her, "there's an apple rule. The rule is simple. If we get all of our morning's work done before lunch, everyone gets an apple. If you guys cut up and waste time…uh-oh."

Giggles ran through the room. She smiled and plunged into the morning's math lesson. The introduction to fractions always caused some confusion, but today she had apples and a small paring knife to help her. Given the times, she'd had to get permission to bring that knife, small as it was. She couldn't help remembering her own childhood, when every boy had carried a pocketknife. No more. The zero-tolerance policy that had begun sweeping the nation a couple of decades ago had finally reached this little town. Considering how many of her students lived on ranches, at home they very likely carried their pocketknives and used much more dangerous implements.

An awful lot of her students, girls and boys alike, would be going hunting this fall with their parents.

In fact, one of her lessons at this time of year was about hunting safety and laws. Sometimes she was able to get the game warden, Desi Jenks, to come in and give a talk.

But fractions required her whole attention, even with slicing an apple into halves, quarters and thirds. It was difficult for kids, for some reason, to see it for real and then transfer it to symbols on paper. That always took a while.

Eventually she had the pleasure of seeing understanding begin to dawn.

By the end of the day, however, despite recesses to let them run off energy, her kids were getting antsy. Their response to weariness was not to fall asleep, but to need something new to do. When she dismissed them, they tore out of the room like a stampeding herd.

But Mikey and his mom remained. They always did, to avoid the crush. Ashley pulled her chair over to chat with them a bit.

"How's it going, Mikey?" she asked. "Do you hate fractions, too?"

He smiled shyly. "They're easy."

"Well, glory be," Ashley said, clapping her hands together. "*Someone* gets it."

Mikey laughed.

Marian spoke. "Cadell is trying to get us a service dog. I think I mentioned that. Well, he's trying to train one for us."

"I can hardly wait," Mikey piped up.

"But..." Marian hesitated. "The dog *can* come to school with him?"

"Of course. Just let me know before you bring him so I can lay the ground rules." She looked at Mikey. "You are going to make so many kids jealous, being able to bring your dog to school."

As soon as she said it, she wished she could take the words back. She was sure Marian didn't find anything about Mikey's situation enviable. She was relieved that Mikey didn't take it wrong. He laughed. "Yup. I'm special."

"You sure are." Ashley looked at Marian and saw the shadows in the woman's eyes, the unguarded moment when her entire face sagged. Their eyes met, understanding passed, then Marian put on her cheerful face again.

"Time to go, Mikey."

Ashley walked them to the front door and waved them goodbye before returning to her classroom to gather up her own items. Lesson planner, papers to grade and some books she used for planning.

A teacher's day was never done, but she didn't mind it in the least. Nothing could compare with watching a child conquer a difficult subject or idea. Nothing could compare with the child's moment of triumph when understanding dawned.

The fractions, however, were going to take a little longer. She laughed to herself and headed out with her jacket and backpack.

As she was leaving, she ran into the seriously pregnant Julie Archer, the kindergarten teacher. "Coffee this weekend?" Julie asked. "Connie and Marisa have already said yes."

"You sure we won't be meeting in the waiting room at the hospital?"

"I wish!" Julie smiled. "Nobody told me the last month would be the longest. Nobody."

"Why scare you?" Ashley asked. "Besides, since I've never been pregnant, I couldn't possibly have told you."

"The other girls could have," Julie retorted. "Lucky Marisa, she was early. So, Saturday. Around two?"

"Unless something comes up, absolutely."

By the time she arrived home, Ashley was beginning to feel her own fatigue from the day. Those fourth graders kept her on her toes. They were bright and inquisitive, and heaven help her if she ever misspoke or inadvertently contradicted herself. Which, she reminded herself, meant they were paying attention.

But it wasn't a job that gave her a chance to let her guard down and relax, and today she'd had lunchroom duty as well.

She glanced toward Zane's house. His van was still in the driveway, but otherwise the place looked unoccupied. Well, he wanted to be left alone, and she guessed he was getting what he wanted.

Inside she started a small pot of coffee for herself, hoping to find a little energy for the work ahead. Her students had done a lot of math problems for homework last night, plus today's worksheets, and she needed to grade them all. The quicker the response, the better the students learned.

Then there was dinner. She looked in her pantry,

then in her fridge and nearly groaned. There was food, but not one thing looked appealing to her. Besides, for some reason she didn't feel like cooking. What she wanted to do was pull a box or can off the shelf, or a dinner tray from the freezer, and be done with it.

Her fault for not following her program of cooking on weekends and freezing meals for herself. She'd let it slide, and now she was going to pay. Even a search to the very back of her freezer didn't yield a container of stew or lasagna.

She finally poured a cup of coffee for herself and sat at her kitchen table, drumming her fingers on the wood, thinking. She was more efficient than this. Usually. But lately she seemed to have been letting things slide, like her meals.

And when you let things slide, as she told her students, you got yourself into the last-minute woes. Now, tired or not, she needed to cook.

Mentally throwing her hands up, wondering what had been getting into her lately, she went back to the pantry and started rooting for ingredients. She prided herself on efficiency, so what was going on?

She found some yellow rice and remembered the thick slices of ham she'd bought to cook for breakfast. Some of that cut into the rice would make a meal along with veggies. Saved.

She was just pulling her rice cooker out from under the counter when she heard a knock at her door. It didn't sound like the usual *tap-tap*. The raps were spaced farther apart. Curious, she went to open the door.

Nell, Zane's golden retriever, was standing there, wagging her tail with a rawhide bone in her mouth. She must have used that to knock on the door. Wow.

Then she looked past Nell and saw Zane in his wheelchair at the end of her sidewalk.

"Check her saddlebag," Zane said. "Your pie plate is in there."

"Oh, thank you! You could have just called me to come and get it." But she looked down at the dog and smiled. "However, I do like your errand girl." Bending, she dared to give Nell a quick pat before lifting the flap on the saddlebag and pulling out the glass dish.

She straightened. "So she knocks on doors, too?"

"Yup. The pie is great. I still have nearly half of it in my fridge, but I'm not sure it will survive until morning. Thank you."

"Glad you enjoyed it." Then awkwardness hit her. Ordinarily she would have invited him in for a cup of coffee. But there was no way he could get up the three steps to her porch. Her house was as inaccessible to him as a fortress. Discomfort commingled with sadness washed through her. This was awful.

He gave a whistle, and Nell turned and trotted back to him.

Ashley decided to just be frank about her awkwardness. "I'm sorry I can't invite you in for coffee, but I don't know how you could get up here."

He smiled faintly. "That's what I have arms for. Anyway, I only wanted to bring back the pie plate. My mother guarded hers like a dragon with a hoard of gold. If a neighbor didn't bring one back soon enough, she'd go over to hunt for it."

Ashley had to laugh. "I'm not quite that attached." He started to wheel away when impulse took her by surprise and she said, "I was just about to start making my dinner. Yellow rice with ham, broccoli on the side. Would you like some?"

He froze. She watched it happen. He didn't even look at her, but he was no longer moving. Oh, God, he'd warned her he wanted to be alone, and now she'd ignored him. After this, he might never want to talk to her again, and she would have only herself to blame for that.

Or he could just bite her head off right now and leave her in a quivering mess. God, what was wrong with her? He'd been perfectly clear, and she'd just been perfectly stupid.

Then he astonished her. He turned his head and looked at her. She braced for the scolding. Instead, he said, "I'd like that, if you don't mind."

Then he rolled away along the sidewalk and up his ramp.

She didn't move for a minute or so while he entered his house, with Nell's assistance for the door, and disappeared.

She *had* heard that right, hadn't she? He'd *like* her to bring over dinner?

Back inside, she changed out of her wool skirt and sweater into jeans and a blue flannel shirt. Okay, then. If she was going to cook for two, she was going to do it over there. If that was too big a trespass, she wanted to know it now.

She had never been into playing mind games. While she felt bad for all Zane had been through, that didn't mean she was going to let him run hot and cold like a kitchen tap. Either he wanted *real* company, or he didn't. If he expected her to just bring over a plate of food, she wasn't about to do that. She was part of the package.

She jammed most of what she needed into her rice maker and a paper bag to carry the rest of it next door, then looked at the fresh pot of coffee she'd just made. Dang, she wanted another cup of coffee. There'd been none since this morning.

Well, she seemed to remember he had a coffee-maker on his counter. If not, she'd come back for hers. For now, she switched it off.

She had the odd feeling she was about to enter a boxing ring. Well, time would tell.

Zane wondered what had possessed him. Asking her to bring dinner over? The next thing he knew, she'd probably be delivering food to him and try-ing to help him in ways he didn't want to be helped.

Independence mattered to him. Yeah, he needed some assistance, like the bar over the bed that helped him transfer to and from his wheelchair. The shower seat and security bars. The dog, his wonderful Nell.

But most of that meant he could still look after himself in ways that mattered. He could cook on a counter that was at chest height, although it wasn't the easiest thing. He could do most everything one way or another with a little adaptation.

But he really *did* have a problem with PTSD. Why it had all blown up on him after he lost the use of his legs, he didn't know. He'd survived a lot of years going in and out of danger and war with few apparent problems. Then, *wham!* It was almost like once the focus was broken *he* became broken.

Unfortunately, when the shift had occurred in him, he'd found triggers everywhere, things that could throw him back in time. Sounds, smells, even some voices. And sometimes he couldn't figure out any reason for it to hit him. Those instances were the worst of all, because he had no idea what to avoid. Sometimes he didn't even have a flashback, just a surging, almost uncontrollable rage.

So he'd come here to wrestle with it by himself. He knew there was a group here he could join, but he wasn't yet ready to do that again. It would be good for him, but the move had disturbed him in strange ways and he felt a need to settle in first.

Wondering at himself, he wheeled to the kitchen and began the complicated process of making coffee. He had to lock his chair in place and pull himself up on his elbows to fill the pot and put the grounds in the basket. Practice had made it easier, but it was a crazy dance all the same. Still, he'd have had to live without coffee and a lot of other things if he hadn't learned to pull himself up.

Once the pot was turned on, he settled back into his chair. Then came the knock at the door. He unlocked his chair and rolled out to greet Ashley, thinking that he needed to get new knobs for the door. Nell could operate the lever kind, but the round knobs just picked up a lot of tooth marks.

But for now, he turned the knob himself and allowed Nell to do the rest of the work as he backed away to make space for Ashley to enter. She had her arms full.

"What's that?" he asked.

"Dinner," she said cheerfully. "I'm cooking it here, because I am not running back and forth with plates of food. I mean, really."

Nell closed the door, then the two of them followed Ashley into the kitchen.

"Oh, good, coffee," Ashley said. "I've been jonesing for a cup all day. Can I pour you one when it's ready?"

He could do it for himself, but for once he bit the irritable retort back. "Sure. Thanks. I didn't mean for you to go to all this trouble, Ashley."

"Maybe not," she answered as she unpacked her bag and the rice maker. "I seem to remember asking you. My idea. Not a problem."

She hunted around to find what was available. Kitchen utensils had been left there since his parents' time, and he was reasonably certain that Carol had included them in her cleaning.

Out came a wood cutting board, a chef's knife, some small bowls, a measuring cup and a microwave dish.

"I am so grateful for microwaves," she said as she

bustled about. "I'd starve to death if I couldn't thaw and cook in one. That'll do for the broccoli. But first the yellow rice." She lifted a yellow bag. "Personal recipe."

He had to chuckle a little in spite of himself. "I think I've had that recipe before."

"Probably. Someone stole it from me and put it on supermarket shelves everywhere."

She dumped the contents into the round rice cooker, then began to dice a thick slab of ham. "Meals in minutes, that's me," she remarked.

Soon she swept the ham into the cooker with the edge of the knife, added the water, plugged it in and pushed a button. "Maybe twenty minutes on that," she announced.

Then she headed for his refrigerator. "I hope you have butter."

"I do."

"Good, I like it on my broccoli."

After putting the frozen broccoli in the microwave dish and dotting it with butter, she pulled a spice container out of her brown bag and sprinkled it on the veggies.

"What's that?" he asked.

"Mustard powder. It makes the taste milder, and anyway, it's good."

He backed away until he was beside the table, watching her whirl around his kitchen with practiced ease. It had been a long while since he'd enjoyed the sight of a woman cooking, and she seemed to like it. She shortly proved him right.

"It's always better to cook for someone else," she said. "Cooking for one is so boring. I make a lasagna, put most of it in my freezer in meal-size containers and then eat it forever. I also do that with other foods that freeze as well to try to give myself some variety. But... I slipped up the last few weeks, so tonight I cook. Nothing fancy, but if I'm going to do it, it's nicer to share."

He was sitting there like a lump, he realized. At least he could try to make conversation. "So you don't like to cook?"

"Not for just me. Sometimes I cook for my friends, which is fun. A bunch of us gals get together regularly and take turns. Not doing that this weekend, though. I guess we're meeting for coffee."

It almost sounded like an alien world to him. Meeting friends for coffee. How many times had making coffee meant freeze-dried crystals and water warmed over canned heat? When he had the crystals and dared to make even a small flame.

Finally she brought two mugs of coffee to the table. "Black?" she asked.

"Nothing else." After all these years, he wouldn't know what to make of any other kind.

She handed him a mug then took the seat across from him. "I'll clean up after."

"I can do that," he said quickly.

"Sure, if you want. It means I get to hang around longer waiting for my rice cooker."

His eyes popped to her face, and he realized she was teasing him. *Teasing* him. The fact that he hadn't recognized it immediately, the fact that it had been so long since anyone had teased him when it had been a routine part of his life in uniform…well, he really *had* put himself in a long, dark tunnel. And maybe not all of it was necessary.

But until he could trust his reactions, be sure some little thing wouldn't just cause him to blow, he felt it was safest to protect others.

But who was he protecting, really?

Shaking his head a little, he remained silent while Ashley served dinner, giving him a plate heaped with yellow rice and a good-size portion of broccoli.

"Thank you," he managed to say. Did one ever get tired of always having to thank others? He sure did. He was used to taking care of everything himself, and his new status in life often irritated him.

Yet, he reminded himself, this woman was guilty of nothing except kindness. He could have turned down her offer of dinner. He could have kept his fortress walls in place. But he hadn't, so the least he owed her this evening was courtesy.

The problem was finding something to talk about. God, he'd been so self-absorbed for so long he had only one subject—his own problems. Disgraceful.

"How was your day?" he asked. That seemed ordinary and safe.

"Pretty good," she answered. "I used apples to teach fractions, which are always a pain to kids, but hey, they got to eat the results of the work."

He drew up one corner of his mouth. "How many kids in your class?"

"I'm lucky. Nineteen. A pretty good size at that age. Not so many that we can't do class projects. And Mikey seemed to be in a great mood today."

He nodded, eating some more rice. "This is great."

"I love it, too," she agreed.

"So, Mikey. How does that work when he's quadriplegic?"

She sighed, and her face shadowed. "His mom has to come with him every day. Bless her, she never seems to mind. But someone has to be able to turn pages for him and write his answers on worksheets. There are a whole lot of people working on a fundraiser to get him a motorized chair he can control with puffs of air, and someone's looking into mounting an ebook reader on one for him. I mean…well, you'd know. Independence isn't easy to find. This world is not designed for the disabled."

"No, it's not," he agreed. Although he was pretty sure it was getting easier in some ways. But still. He thought of a fourth grader consigned to a future of quadriplegia and it pained him. Talk about the unfairness of life. At least what had happened to him had been a known risk of his job. All that kid had been doing was going for a fun horseback ride.

"Anyway," Ashley continued, "he's adapting remarkably well. Very resilient. He impresses me."

Unlike him, Zane thought sourly. Although paraplegia wasn't his biggest problem; his mind was. If he ever managed to whip that into shape, life would probably be better.

However, a sudden change in perspective gave him

a view of himself as others might see him, and he didn't like it. Oh, well. He knew the rages that could bubble up unexpectedly inside him. He never wanted anyone else to suffer from that. Who cared what anyone on the outside thought? All they'd ever see was the guy in a wheelchair.

"Do you know anyone around here?" Ashley asked.

"After all these years? I doubt it. Doesn't matter, anyway."

"No, I guess not."

Well, he had told her he wanted to be left alone. Then the first asinine thing he did was let her bring him dinner. "I told you I'm antisocial."

She nodded, then studied him with those startling blue eyes. "It can't have always been that way. In the military you were part of a team, right?"

"I'm not in the military anymore."

"No kidding," she said a bit tartly. "However, we have a few guys in this county who might get where you're coming from. They've walked in your shoes, and some of them have had to struggle with being home."

"So?"

He guessed that was it for her. She rose, leaving the remains of her dinner on the table. She grabbed her jacket and slipped it on, then picked up the rice cooker and the bottle of mustard powder. "You said you could clean up. Have at it."

Then, without another word, she walked out. He heard the front door close behind her.

A whimper drew his attention to Nell, who was sitting beside him.

"Damn it, dog, I don't need your opinion, too."

She gave a little moan then settled beside him with her head on the floor between her paws.

Yeah, he was a jackass. He knew it. He nurtured it. Better to be alone with his demons than inflicting them on innocent people. That had become his mantra.

At that moment he wondered if it wasn't also his excuse.

Ashley sighed as she stood in her kitchen cleaning the rice cooker at her sink and wondering where that burst of temper had come from. That man seemed to bring out the worst in her. Yesterday she'd gotten acidic with him, and today she'd walked out on him—rather rudely, if she were to be honest about it.

And why the heck had he accepted her offer of dinner? He'd obviously been uncomfortable, and finally he'd felt it necessary to make it clear yet again that he wanted to be left alone. He didn't even want to talk with other vets.

When she summed up the total of conversation that had passed between them, she figured it wouldn't fill one typed page.

God, she didn't want to be a snippy, sarcastic person. A good reason to grant his wish for solitude. It would be easy enough to pretend he wasn't even there.

Her life was full enough anyway, what with school and helping with the project to get Mikey a better wheelchair. In fact, there was the fund-raiser at the church on Saturday evening that she still needed to do a few things for.

But she couldn't help feeling bad for a man so alone, even if it was by choice. She spent a lot of time as a teacher making sure that no child was left out or ostracized, because a sense of belonging was so important to human beings.

Well, Zane was a grown man. None of her business, no matter how she felt about it. Plus, he'd kind of warned her that he was still a bit unstable mentally. PTSD. Awful. Certainly not something she could help him with.

She dried her hands, then pulled out her folio to start correcting papers. Except for taking dinner over to Zane, she'd have started a while ago. Time to catch up. Immediate feedback was important to learning. Nothing the kids had done today would matter to them in a week.

The phone rang just as she was spreading her work on the table. She picked up the cordless handset to hear her friend Julie on the line.

"Hey, word has it you were seen visiting Zane McLaren. How is he?"

"Very much antisocial and very much wanting to be left alone. Straight from his lips."

"Oh." Julie sighed. "That's sad. Any number of people have mentioned him to me, wondering how he's doing."

"And he said he'd very much appreciate not having a parade of well-wishers at his door, so pass it along."

"Well, dang. I thought we'd have something new to talk about."

Ashley laughed. "Hurry up and have your baby. Then you'll be too busy for gossip."

Julie's answering laugh poured through the phone. "I'm sure Trace would agree with you. I can't figure out if he shares my impatience or if he just wishes I'd settle down."

"Maybe a bit of both. Listen, I've got a bunch of papers to correct. Saturday, right?"

"Oh, that's why I called. The weather's going to be beautiful Saturday. A couple of the girls suggested we meet at your place and have our coffee on the porch. You have a big enough porch and enough chairs."

And she lived next door to the mystery man, Ashley thought wryly. "Sure, that's fine. Who's bringing the coffee cake?"

"Marisa said she would. She's looking forward to turning the youngster over to Ryker for a few hours."

"I can imagine. Okay, Saturday. Here."

"Done."

Ashley hung up, shaking her head. She wondered if she ought to give Zane a warning, then decided she was being ridiculous. He didn't have to poke his head outside. He could just tough it out indoors.

Chapter 3

Saturday afternoon turned into the last taste of summer. Autumn leaves still blew gently around on the breeze, but the weather was warm enough that light clothing allowed the women to sit outside on Ashley's porch.

Julie Archer had been Ashley's friend forever, and now that they taught at the same school, the friendship had only deepened. They could discuss various student problems with a deep understanding. Julie's auburn hair and green eyes had always made her a striking woman. She also rarely withheld her thoughts.

Connie Parish was older than the rest by a little over a decade, but she had fit seamlessly with them. The mother of three as well as a sheriff's deputy, she had her hands full and she swore the Saturday get-togethers were a lifeline.

Marisa Tremaine had been widowed a few years ago, and now was married to her late husband's best friend, who also happened to be a good friend of Julie's husband.

Ashley sat as the lone spinster among them and she was quite happy with her lot, thank you very much. She honestly couldn't imagine how she would handle the addition of a family to her already busy life.

"So Nora and Hope couldn't make it?" Ashley asked about two of their other kaffeeklatsch regulars.

"Getting ready for the fund-raiser tonight. Hope must be out of her mind. She promised ten dozen cookies. And Nora is bringing five pies."

"Wow." Ashley blinked. She felt like a skinflint with her offering of a few dozen rum balls.

"We're getting there," Julie said. "With the bake sale tonight and the donations, I bet we come close to our mark for that wheelchair."

"I hope so," Connie remarked. "I was blown away by the price of those things. It's not like you're buying some toy for your amusement. It's essential."

Ashley answered, "And it has to be able to do more, like change his position so he doesn't get sores and lift him so his mother can help him get into bed. It's not your basic model."

The women sat silent for a moment, and Ashley guessed those with children were imagining themselves in the shoes of Mikey's mom.

Then Julie visibly shook herself. "We're close. And Trace's friend Ken is working on a tablet to attach so Mikey can do a lot of things simply by using his chin on a push plate. I have half a mind to wrap that chair in aluminum foil and put NASA stickers down its side. It's going to be halfway to a spaceship."

That leavened the moment. Soon laughter returned and stories about everyone's kids began to be shared. Ashley never ceased to be amazed by the inventive hijinks kids could get up to. She didn't see a lot of that in the classroom, where they were usually on their best behavior...or what passed for it.

She went inside to get a fresh pot of coffee and warm up her friends' mugs. When she stepped outside, Nell was standing there, wearing her saddlebag.

"So you have a secret admirer," Julie joked. "Whose dog?"

"Zane's. I guess he sent something over. Nell is a service dog."

"Oh, wow, wouldn't Mikey like that," said Connie.

"I'm trying to persuade Zane to work with Cadell on the kinds of things Mikey might need. Or at least I mentioned it."

Curious, she passed the coffeepot to Marisa and let her pour for everyone. Opening the saddlebag was easy enough; it wasn't snapped closed. Inside she found an envelope addressed to her.

A message from Zane? Surprised, she dropped onto her chair and opened the flap of the envelope. Inside a brief note was wrapped around a check: "For the wheelchair."

Not even signed, but when she looked at the check, she gasped and her heart slammed. "Good heavens!"

"What?" the other women demanded.

She looked up. "Zane just sent a check for five hundred dollars for Mikey's chair."

A chorus of exclamations greeted that news. In a moment everyone was talking at once. This brought them a long way toward their goal and doubled what they had expected to make from the bake sale at the church.

The check was made out to Ashley, probably because Zane didn't know the name for the fund-raising group, but as she held it, her resistance to Zane and his attitude melted away. It was a generous act, very generous, and a trusting one. He clearly had no doubt she would put the money where it was intended to go.

Wow.

But Nell still sat in front of her, looking up as if her mission wasn't complete. Ashley jumped up, saying, "Stay, Nell," and went inside. She tucked the check in her wallet, then pulled open the drawer where she kept writing materials for rare occasions when a handwritten note was needed.

On a notecard that said *Thank You* on the front, she wrote, "We are all so very grateful for your generosity, Zane. This will go a huge way to getting Mikey his chair. We can't thank you enough."

She signed her name and the name of the group, then stuffed it in an envelope with his name on the front.

Outside, Nell still waited patiently. Ashley lifted the flap of the saddlebag and tucked the note into it. She gave Nell a scratch behind her ears, then said, "Take it to Zane, Nell."

Tail wagging, the dog was off like a flash.

All heads turned to follow the dog as she dashed

across the yard, leaped onto the ramp and disappeared inside.

"Wow," said Julie.

"Wow," agreed Connie.

"We've got to get Mikey a dog like that," Marisa said.

"Next step," said Connie. "I think trained service dogs are nearly as expensive as the wheelchair."

"It doesn't matter," Ashley said. "I was talking to Dory and Cadell last week. He's working on training a dog already, and Dory said she'd meet any expenses on that."

Marisa nodded. "And she made a large contribution to the wheelchair fund. She's serious about helping."

Marisa stood up. "This has been fun, gals, but Ryker is probably desperate for some relief. Jonni's going through a difficult stage. I think *no* is the only word she doesn't understand."

"And I need to get my daily walk in," said Julie.

Soon everyone had said their goodbyes and left, and the porch was empty of everyone except Ashley. The afternoon was beginning to cool a bit, and she thought idly about getting her jacket or just going inside. She had time before the bake sale tonight.

She closed her eyes, enjoying the fresh air, full now of the scents of autumn. Then something bumped her knee.

Her eyes flew open, and she saw Nell sitting in front of her. No saddlebag this time.

"What are you doing here?" she asked the dog.

Her answer was a doggie grin and a tail wag.

Then she heard Zane call, "Dang it, Nell, what are you doing?"

She looked over to the house next door and saw Zane sitting on his porch. "You didn't send her?"

"I absolutely did not, and she's never supposed to leave me unless I tell her to go. Now look at her."

"Are you blaming me?" Because that's what it sounded like.

"Hell, no. But that dog thinks for herself, and I can't imagine what she's thinking now. Nell, come."

Nell started to rise then sat down again.

"Nell," Ashley tried, "you need to go to Zane."

Nell looked over at Zane.

"Go on," Ashley urged.

"Nell, come," Zane repeated.

With something that sounded very much like a sigh, Nell rose and trotted back over to Zane.

"That was weird," he said. "She's never done that before."

"Well, I swear I'm not encouraging it. I didn't even give her a treat of any kind."

"I'm sure you did nothing wrong," he answered. "She just took a notion. If this happens again, she may need a training refresher."

"Maybe curiosity overcame her. Or maybe since you sent her once, she thought it would be okay to come again."

"I wonder." Then he astonished her with a laugh. "She's far from an automaton. That's why I said she thinks for herself. And she's bright. Maybe she's getting bored over here. As soon as I get my trike together, I'll get her some more exercise."

"Trike?"

"An extra wheel attached so the front of my wheelchair so if I hit an obstacle while moving fast my chair can't tip and throw me into a face-plant."

She nodded, picturing it. "Need any help putting it together?"

A long silence greeted her offer. She had just about decided to go inside when he answered. "If you can spare an hour or so sometime, it would be helpful."

Ah, a crack in the armor. Well, every step was a good one. And after that donation he'd made, she'd have gladly done a whole lot to help him out. "To-morrow afternoon?" she asked. "About two, maybe?"

"That would be great." Then he turned and disappeared inside with his dog.

Well, well, well, she thought, deciding to head indoors as the chill began to get to her. Time to get ready for the bake sale tonight, anyway. She had a shift from seven to nine. Anything left over would be sold tomorrow after services, but she hadn't signed up for that. There were plenty of willing hands when it came to Mikey.

And very few when it came to Zane, but he wanted that way. At least he could accept help when it was offered. She supposed that was a big step for a pro-fessed hermit.

The next day when she came home from church, Ashley was practically walking on air. Not only had the bake sale gone well, but upon seeing how close they were getting to the goal for the wheelchair, quite a few checkbooks had come out to add larger amounts.

Then, this morning, the pastor had announced that they'd received the grant they'd applied for. They could now order Mikey's wheelchair, "with racing stripes if he wants them," the pastor had joked, causing the entire congregation to rise and applaud.

The standard coffee and doughnuts afterward had been a happier-than-usual affair, with a lot of smiles and laughter. Everyone was feeling pretty good, and the pastor was going to make the trip out to the Landau ranch to tell Mikey and his parents the good news.

For her part, Ashley was looking forward to sharing the news with Zane. His check had been a huge help in putting them over the top, as had the grant. Now they had a little elbow room to get the child exactly what he needed.

She was still surprised that Zane had sent so much money, though. After announcing he was a practicing curmudgeon, apparently Mikey's plight had touched him.

She knew so little about being paralyzed. She supposed she ought to frankly ask Zane what other things they might be able to help Mikey with. So much that the family had had come from disability aid, the bare minimum, and she couldn't even begin to imagine the lacks the family might still be experiencing. Right now either parent could lift Mikey into bed or onto a couch to sit, but what would happen as he grew? How many other needs must be met?

Zane would probably have a good idea, if he was willing to share.

Zane cussed himself for being a stubborn mule. At some point, he was going to have to admit that he couldn't always be completely independent, and he was looking at a case of it right now.

The toolbox had a handle. He'd been able to lean over the side of his chair, heft it and carry it into the kitchen. The box of parts for his extra wheel was a different matter. It sat on the floor in the small extra downstairs room defying him, and he had no way to reach it or move it.

Nell watched him, tilting her head quizzically from side to side, unable to do a damn thing about it. He was glad he'd swallowed his pride enough to ask for Ashley's help, even though it galled him, because otherwise…well, he'd have had to hire someone, he guessed. Not impossible, but he didn't know where to begin in this town, and anyway, he didn't feel comfortable about it. Maybe it was some leftover machismo, but for some reason he didn't want to hire someone to put his wheel on. He wanted to do as much of it himself as he could.

Stubborn cuss, that was him. Unfortunately, stubbornness could lead to stupidity, and he was coming dangerously close. Instead of just hiring help, now he was imposing on a neighbor. Didn't that make a lot of sense, he asked himself with a snort of disgust.

Nell apparently heard Ashley's arrival before he did. She dashed away to the front door and waited for the knock or the bell. Trusting Nell's instincts, Zane wasn't far behind.

He opened the door to see that beautiful strawberry blonde dressed for work in jeans and a flannel shirt. She'd even caught her hair into a ponytail, which was cute. And she was smiling.

"Ready to start?" she asked.

He hesitated even as he began to roll back from the door to give her entry. "I should have just hired someone. I can't keep imposing on you."

"I didn't have to say yes, and I don't feel imposed upon." She looked down at Nell. "Okay to pet her?"

"You might as well. She seems determined to become part of your life, too."

Ashley laughed, then squatted, giving Nell a good rub and scratch around her neck. Then she rose and stepped past, allowing the dog to close the door. "So what do we need to do?"

"Assemble the parts to attach the wheel to this chair. Once it's all together, I can put it on or take it off with some locks. Naturally, because it wouldn't work indoors, but..." He shrugged. "Thing is, I like to get a good speed going when I'm out with Nell. She wants to run, and the workout feels good to me, too. So...this is all about stability."

As he spoke, he was wheeling his way back to the spare room. Nell's steps followed him.

"Will Mikey need something like this?"

"I doubt a motorized chair will allow him to go fast enough to worry about it. How's the fund-raising, by the way?"

"Fantastic," she answered enthusiastically. "Between your check—which was awfully generous—the bake sale last night and a small grant we finally received, Mikey's new wheelchair will be ordered soon."

He summoned a smile. "I'm glad to hear that."

She touched the box on the floor with her toe. "Parts in here?"

"All of them."

She nodded, as if grasping why he couldn't get to it himself. "Do you want to assemble it here?"

"In the kitchen. I'm going to need a place to sit while we do it, because I need to get out of this chair."

"Got it." She squatted and began to pull packing tape away. "Anyhow, if you have any suggestions for things Mikey might need, let me know. We've got a small list of things, but who knows what we over-looked."

"He lives on a ranch?"

"Yeah."

"Well, if he wants to get outside, he's going to need good, wide wheels. Like these," he said, patting his own. "Like you'd find on a mountain bike."

She peered up at him. "I'm quite certain none of us thought of that. Any other ideas, let me know. As the pastor said this morning, we now have enough to give him racing stripes if he wants them."

Once again Zane felt an unusual smile on his face. "Flames. I suggest flames."

Ashley laughed. "Yeah, he'd probably love that."

As she pulled out parts, she carried one piece after another into the kitchen.

"I can carry some of that," he protested. "I just couldn't reach the floor."

Her head snapped up. "Oh. Yeah. Sorry."

He felt like a jerk, but he wasn't going to let her do all the lifting and carrying. He wouldn't ask that of anyone.

She piled some of the stuff on his lap and he wheeled himself out to the kitchen, where he was able to place the smaller stuff on the table. Of course, some of it had to go on the floor again, which was kind of like moving his problem from one room to the next. He could have rolled his eyes at himself.

But the light was better in the kitchen, and they were going to need it for an assortment of screws, which naturally weren't all the same size and were all black.

Once everything had been moved, he levered himself with practiced ease from his wheelchair to a kitchen chair. It bothered him to have her see him move his legs with his hands, but there was no way to avoid it if he didn't want them draped every which way.

At least she didn't appear bothered.

"I really should have just found someone to hire," he said again.

She eyed him. "Yeah? Well, if I can't help you get this together, you can do that. I'm not sure who deals with this stuff, though. A bike shop?"

He hadn't really thought about that himself. Back in Virginia, he'd gotten everything he needed provided by the VA and some of his old buddies. And once his chair was all put together, occasional tightening with a wrench kept it that way.

"I never thought about a wheelchair tipping," she remarked as she handed him a piece he asked for from the floor. "I've seen those extra wheels, but I never knew what they were for."

"Well, this is what *I* need it for. I can't speak for everyone else. Anyway, you see those small wheels on the back of the chair? Everyone has them because the likeliest way for us to tip is backward. My front rig is more for speed. I want to go fast. It helps prevents a disaster from a crack in the sidewalk."

"I bet Nell loves racing."

"The faster, the better."

The next hour went smoothly enough. They paused once to make some coffee, but otherwise Ashley was kind of quiet and focused on following directions when she needed to. And as usual, he managed to do most of it himself and then, too late, wondered if he was making her feel useless.

"I couldn't have done this without you," he said as he tested the fittings.

"Sure." She smiled faintly.

He turned to look straight at her and wondered if he'd managed to offend her somehow. It was entirely possible. His social skills had gone to hell some time ago. Well, if he had, maybe it was all to the good. She was entirely too attractive to have around much, especially since he didn't want to drag any woman into his world.

"Wanna take it out for a spin?" she asked.

One way to get through what now felt like an awkward moment. His fault, as usual. "Sure. Nell would love that."

He shifted from the kitchen chair back to the wheelchair.

"You amaze me by how easy you make that look," she remarked. "I bet it took some practice."

"Everything takes practice." He lifted his feet onto the footrests, then backed the chair up enough to turn it and head for the foyer.

Ashley opened the door for him, since the extra wheel put it beyond his reach. "I've got to get some lever door handles," he remarked. "I keep thinking about it and forgetting it. Nell could manage those."

"Good idea."

She was withdrawing from him. He could feel it. Good. The more distance, the better—for both of them. Nell pranced alongside him. She recognized the signs of an impending run.

Before he started down the ramp, he paused to look at Ashley. "Thanks so much for your help. Nell thanks you, too. She's needed a good outing for some time."

"Sure." She smiled, a smile that would have dazzled him if it had reached her eyes. He left with Nell, wondering what the hell he'd done wrong. And doubting that he'd ever know.

Ashley went home after watching man and dog depart at a pretty good clip down the sidewalk. She really hadn't been all that much help, except for picking up things from a floor he couldn't easily reach.

She probably couldn't imagine half the challenges he must routinely face.

But she shouldn't really care. He'd warned her off at the very beginning, and she was still surprised he'd asked for her help. She suspected he hadn't liked having to do it. There was something about his determination to put the whole contraption together himself.

She could understand his desire to be as independent as possible. Things she and most other people took for granted were denied to him now. He'd probably piled up a whole lot of dings to his ego since he became paralyzed. Self-sufficiency was his goal, and she was quite sure that ordinarily he managed it.

But then there'd been his remarks that had led her to believe he suffered from PTSD. Maybe for him that was an even bigger problem than being able to get around. The psychic wound could be far worse than the physical, and probably was. Worse yet if he couldn't predict what would set it off or when it approached.

Yeah, if she suffered from something like that, she might want to hide out, too.

Sighing, she pulled out her schoolwork and made herself a cup of cocoa, deciding to finish her grading at the kitchen table rather than in the office she'd made for herself in the spare room. It was a nice, cozy office, but she preferred it on cold, gray winter days when it felt warm and snuggly. On a day like today with brilliant light pouring through the kitchen windows, the office would have felt more like a cave.

Today she had a lot of chicken-scratch problems

with fractions. Number-two pencils didn't always erase well, and while the darker lead was easier on her eyes, black smudges covered everything. She had to smile. Most of these kids tried so hard, and judging by the smeared erasures they'd tried extra hard with this.

She wouldn't be surprised if they needed to spend a few more days with fractions. These assignments would certainly tell her.

But her thoughts kept wandering to Zane. A complicated man—surely an understatement. His gift to the fund-raiser for Mikey had been more than generous. His desire to be left alone had been belied by his acceptance of dinner with her and then his request for help.

But after he'd asked for that help, he'd made her feel all but useless. He hadn't been rude or anything. It was almost like he needed to prove something. Yes, she'd been able to help, but only a little, mostly with picking up things he couldn't reach.

She supposed that was help. What had she expected when she went over there? That he needed her to assemble the whole piece?

Not likely. She'd done what he needed and no more, and now she should examine her own reasons for being disturbed by that. After all, she routinely told her students to complete tasks on their own, giving help only when their efforts seemed doomed.

Was Zane so different? He was following the advice she would have given to her students. Do it yourself…if you possibly can.

So what was eating her? The absence of a lengthy, in-depth conversation?

She closed her eyes and leaned back a bit, thinking about him. Dang, he was attractive, especially when he managed a smile. Those rare smiles leavened his whole face and drew her to him. But he didn't want her to be drawn, and maybe that was her entire problem.

All her life men had been interested in her. While she wasn't one to stare into a mirror, she knew she'd been blessed with reasonably attractive looks and hair that caught men's eyes. She'd never gone begging for a date unless she didn't want one. Usually she didn't. The attraction wasn't often a two-way street, and less so as she grew older. Most of the time when she dated, she got turned off to the guy relatively quickly. One longer relationship had left her feeling as if he were trying to shoehorn her into a Donna Reed–style box. That was not for her.

Now she was on the other end of that equation for the first time—a guy who wasn't interested. Maybe that was all that bothered her.

She laughed out loud at that and decided she'd gone round the bend when it came to Zane. She was happy with her life, felt nothing was lacking. Was she going to let the hermit next door throw her off balance?

Nope, she decided. She had her work and her friends, and she really didn't need a romance to muck it up.

Which brought to mind her first boyfriend, all the way back in high school. When they had broken up after a month or so, she'd been giddy with relief. With him out of the picture, she could get back to her *real* life, with her friends, pursuing her own interests.

She should have learned from that, but she hadn't. No, she'd tried a few times more…and felt every bit as giddy when it was over.

Then a thought struck her, causing her cheeks to flame. What if Zane couldn't have sex? That seemed highly likely given his injury.

Which meant being attracted to him, if he recognized it, might only make him feel worse.

She stared straight at the probability, work forgotten, and realized she needed to tread very carefully with him. Keep it friendly or stay away.

Because the last thing she wanted to do was make him feel worse.

Chapter 4

The following Friday when Ashley pulled into her driveway after school, she glanced toward Zane's house. All week it had looked as if nothing over there had moved or changed. She hadn't even seen Nell out in the yard.

Oh, well, none of her business. She'd been working, and since her class was prepping for tests next week, she'd had a lot to do after school and at home. She held regular tutoring sessions after classes were over for the day, and attendance increased right before tests.

No kaffeeklatsch this weekend. Everyone was busy. She'd miss it, but it happened from time to time. Halloween was right around the corner, and as soon as the tests were over, she was going to have a whole bunch of kids making paper pumpkins with weird faces. She also needed to dig out some of her decorations from the attic to add to the festivities.

The kids were already getting excited, barely restraining themselves in their eagerness, but the tests put a layer of sobriety over them. Fun would have to wait.

In the meantime, it gave her a kick to drape fake spiderwebs around her shrubs and hang a ghost and a skeleton from the limbs of her trees. She hadn't quite gotten to the point of going for orange outdoor lights, but the best part for her was seeing all the little kids in their costumes.

Once inside, her grocery bags and backpack on her table, she thought again of Zane. No sight or sound of him? No evidence he'd been out? Not even the sight of Nell running around the front yard to do her business?

It may have been coincidental, but it niggled at her, anyway. What if something had happened?

She finally decided to head over and find out if he was okay. She could withstand getting chewed out, but she'd never forgive herself if he were in trouble and she'd ignored him.

She rushed to put her cold and frozen items away. The rest could wait. Jacket zipped against the deepening October chill, she hurried out her front door and next door to Zane's. The autumn evening was starting to darken, and she supposed it was a good thing that she could see lights inside the house.

When she reached the front door and knocked, she heard nothing for a minute, then the sound of scratching, as if Nell were on the other side trying to open the door.

Then with a click, the knob turned, and Nell pulled the door open for her.

All was quiet. No sign of Zane. Her heart sped up, and she stepped inside. Nell closed the door behind her then headed toward the kitchen. Ashley followed.

Zane sat with his head on the table and six or seven beer bottles in front of him. He didn't stir even when Nell nosed him. The place smelled like a brewery.

She could tell he was breathing, however, so she guessed he was sleeping it off. She just wondered if he might need some medical attention. Alcohol could be so toxic.

Tentatively, she called his name. "Zane? Zane, wake up."

He groaned faintly but stirred, which she guessed was a good sign. Then he pushed himself upright and looked at her from half-closed eyes.

"What are you doing here?"

"Nell let me in. I'm being a nosy neighbor. I was worried about you."

"No need." His speech didn't sound slurred, and gradually his eyes grew clearer. "I've been having trouble sleeping," he said when he saw her glance at the beer bottles. "They helped. I'm fine."

"Okay." Much as she hated to leave him like this, he wasn't asking her to do anything else. "Surely you can find something better than alcohol to knock you out. It's lousy for sleep and it's a depressant." With that she turned to leave.

"Hey," he said, his voice challenging, "who made you the expert?"

She faced him. "My aunt. She died of cirrhosis when she was forty-seven. You'd left by then."

Now he was fully awake, his gaze sharp. "I'm sorry," he said. "I'm so very sorry."

"Nobody made her drink herself to death," she replied frankly. "Certainly a lot of people, me included, tried to prevent it, but…" She shrugged. "Anyway, it's a lousy sleeping pill."

"I know," he said quietly. "And I didn't drink that all today. I've been feeling so tired I've let things go."

It was an apology of sorts. Without asking for permission, she grabbed the bottles and carried them to the sink, where she rinsed them. Then she opened the window over the sink to let in some fresh air.

"Recycling?" she asked.

"Don't have any yet."

She supposed it might be a problem for him to get all his bottles, cans and whatever to the transfer station. She imagined him trying to carry large bags to his van. Even if he could manage that, would the guys at the station be willing to unload them? "Want me to take it for you? That is, if you're not opposed to recycling."

For a second it looked like a dark cloud was lowering on his face, but then it blew away and he simply looked weary. "Or Carol could do it."

Ashley let it go for now. Carol was his hired housekeeper. Maybe it made him feel better to pay for a service than to accept a favor. She set the rinsed bottles on the counter.

"I can clean up after myself," he groused.

Lovely mood, she thought as she dried her hands on a kitchen towel. "I'm sure you can. I'll be on my way." Turning, she closed the window, because there was absolutely no way he could reach it, then started toward the door. Nothing required her to put up with his lousy moods or even intervene in any way if she happened to wonder if he was still alive. Zane could go dig himself a hole and stay there as far as she was concerned.

But as she stepped toward the door, Nell moved in front of her. She eased to the side, and Nell blocked her again.

"Come on, Nell," she said.

Zane snorted behind her. "I guess she doesn't think I should be alone."

Ashley pivoted. "Do *you*?"

For a few seconds, he didn't move. It was as if everything had stilled in the room, in the air. Then slowly, almost jerkily, he shook his head.

Was that an invitation? Well, she'd dealt with enough kids in bad moods and with problems to decide that it was, however reluctant.

Instead of just sitting, she started a pot of coffee, figuring it might help him with the last of the beer coursing through his system. He didn't say a word even when she placed a mug in front of him and sat with him at the table.

After downing half the mug of coffee, his gaze focused on her again. "You don't have to feel responsible for me."

"I don't," she answered, a half-truth. She'd feel some responsibility for any neighbor having a rough time.

"I told you I'm not fit to be around people yet."

"So it's been a rough week?"

"They happen. Trouble sleeping, more than anything. Nightmares. Agitation."

She drummed her fingertips against the side of her own coffee mug, then stopped. "Nothing can be done for it?"

"Yeah, there are pills. I hate the way they make me feel. Not myself."

"So beer is better?"

Amazement struck her as he suddenly half smiled. "Yeah, I make a lot of sense."

She smiled back helplessly.

"There was a time I could run off this kind of feeling," he remarked. "It's harder in a wheelchair. Oh, I can do it, but with all the stops at corners and so on, I'd probably have to spend most of the day working up a sweat."

"Maybe you need a gym. The hospital installed one a few years ago. Anyone can use it."

"I guess I should look into it." He shook his head a little, closed his eyes briefly, then drew a deep breath. "I remember being a pleasant person, once upon a time."

"You don't think you're pleasant now?"

"Hell, no."

A very sad self-evaluation. Ashley smothered a sigh and sought a way to make a real connection that had nothing to do with this man's troubles. The kind of connection she figured he needed a whole lot. The thought of him having no one to distract him in his life…well, she didn't know much about what he was going through, but she suspected being left alone to brood about it wasn't helping anything.

"You need to meet some people who get it," she finally said. "We've got any number around here who've come back from war. We *do* have an active veterans' group. Sitting here all alone… I know it's none of my business, but it doesn't seem like the best way to handle this. Too much time inside your own head."

"Which isn't a very pretty place," he remarked. "I don't know. Clearly the hermit thing isn't going to make it. A gym might help. And poor Nell gets so worried about me. Dang, I don't even know if I walked her since this morning."

"She opened the door for me," Ashley said a little wryly. "I think if she were desperate…"

"When I'm not myself, she knows she's not supposed to leave me." With that he called Nell and began rolling to the front of the house. The dog trotted happily beside him, tail high. "I've been neglecting you, girl," she heard Zane say.

Well, he didn't sound inebriated, Ashley decided. Maybe it was time for her to leave. She'd done enough of the nosy neighbor routine for one night. She followed them to the door. Zane rolled out onto the porch, and Nell took off like a flash, sniffing around the scrubby front yard as if it were full of wonderful secrets.

The dog's exuberance was beautiful to behold, and Ashley couldn't help pausing to watch Nell with a smile. "She sure loves life," she remarked, then froze as she wondered if she'd said exactly the wrong thing.

"Yeah," he answered. Then he surprised her. "Take a seat on the porch swing if you want."

She glanced at the swing on the far side of the porch, then at him. "You'll get cold if you stay out here."

"Nell can bring me my sweater or jacket if I ask her. Stay."

It didn't sound like a command but almost like a request, so, hesitantly, she crossed to the swing and sat on it. It creaked a bit and moved. She doubted there was any way he could get on it himself. At least not without help. He rolled his chair over to sit beside her.

"It's a quiet evening," he remarked.

"It won't be for long. Once Halloween hits, the kids are officially on the countdown toward Christmas. The excitement winds them up so they're running all over the place, and of course, their families will be shopping."

"The calm before the storm, huh?"

She laughed quietly. "Tests next week for most of the students. Once those are over, little reins in the excitement."

"Did you get excited when you were a kid?"

"Of course. Didn't you?"

"Always. Seems like a long time ago, in a land far away."

She twisted to see him a little better and pushed

the swing with one foot to sway gently. "Sometimes life hits us so hard that things that happened only recently seem like they were years ago."

She heard him draw a deep breath. "Yeah." Then he surprised her yet again. "Do you decorate for Halloween?"

"Just a bit. Some phony spiderwebs, a skeleton or two hanging from my tree. Why?"

"Just thinking about it. It's better than thinking about anything else at the moment." He turned his chair a bit so that he was looking right at her. Nell dashed up, apparently done with the yard, and settled right beside him.

She chewed her lip, a bad habit she'd picked up from her friend Julie, then asked, "You want to do something?"

"Maybe I should dress up like Frankenstein. Come on, Ashley, what kid is going to want to come up here to take candy from a stranger in a wheelchair?"

Bitterness laced his words. Her heart winced, but she kept the feeling from her face. "A lot, I'd think. Nell would help, too. She could probably hand out the candy."

To her relief he started to laugh. "She probably could." Leaning to one side, he reached down to pat the dog and stroke her ears. "Gotta do something about that doorknob, though."

"She *was* sure chewing on it."

"It's probably all scratched and covered with tooth marks then." Again he laughed. "Like I care. I don't know what I'd do without her."

"She's remarkable." Ashley decided to plunge in again. "Do you think you could talk to Cadell about what Mikey would need?"

His face shuttered for an instant, and she had the feeling he was holding some kind of internal conversation. "I'd need to meet Mikey," he said. "I'd need to know what he can still do and what he wants. And by the way, I'm no expert. I don't know how the dogs are trained."

"Do you know who trained Nell? Maybe Cadell could call him. He's said several times that he'd like help with training service dogs. His bailiwick is police dogs, search-and-rescue dogs, bomb-sniffing dogs…"

He interrupted her. "We need bomb-sniffing dogs *here*?"

She had to laugh. "No. Not really. But we did have a scare a couple of years ago, and the sheriff started pining for a dog. Which made me think… Have you met Jess McGregor?"

"I haven't really met anyone," he reminded her drily. "Who's this McGregor?"

"Jess is the guy who had the bomb scare. He's a physician's assistant at the hospital clinic. An amputee. He'd probably be the perfect guy to set you up at the gym. And from what his wife has mentioned, he's still struggling a bit, too, from the war."

Again that stony face returned. Ashley nearly kicked herself. They had been doing all right with casual conversation about Halloween, but she had been the one to bring it back around. The guy had enough to deal with. He absolutely didn't need additional pressure from her.

"I'm sorry," she said. "I shouldn't press you. If you need anything, send Nell over."

But before she could rise, his hand snapped out and gently gripped her forearm. "Stay. Please. I've lost my social skills. I fall silent at all the wrong times." He let go of her immediately.

"But I've been pushing things on you that you don't want. I shouldn't do that." Really, she shouldn't. She decided she spent too much time being a teacher. Did she want to order the lives of everyone around her? Oddly, though, she missed his touch on her arm.

"You're trying to give me stuff to do instead of brooding. You're transparent, Ashley."

She felt her cheeks color and was grateful that it was dark.

"It's okay. I need some pushing, I guess. This whole hermitage idea isn't helping me sleep, it's not getting rid of the anxiety and it doesn't prevent me from slipping in time."

"I'm sorry." She stared out into the night for a few minutes, then asked, "Do you ever regret your choices? Most people regret at least some."

"No." The single word was uncompromising. After a minute or so he continued speaking. "I don't regret volunteering, either for the navy or the SEALs. I still believe we were doing important work. I just hadn't counted on how it could mess up my head. That was an unexpected…dividend, I guess."

"Lousy dividend." God, this was sad. She remembered so vividly when he'd been the star athlete who seemed to have the world on a string. Now he was a haunted, tortured man who couldn't even go out for a real run. Life could be so cruel sometimes, like with Mikey. What had that kid ever done except mount a horse to go for a ride as he had many times before?

"What exactly happened with Mikey?" Zane asked. "I think you told me but I'm forgetful sometimes." He tapped his head.

"Thrown from a horse. Like most ranch kids, he was pretty experienced, did a lot of riding. But a snake scared the horse, the horse bucked Mikey off, and I guess we should be glad that both horse and Mikey survived."

"That sucks," Zane said flatly. "Stinking bad luck. In my case I was in a war zone. I was choosing to take the risks. But that kid…" He shook his head.

She had the worst urge to reach out and take his hand. To find some way to offer comfort even though she couldn't think of anything that would actually work. "So your paralysis isn't your biggest problem?"

"My paralysis is a challenge, that's all. No, it's the other stuff."

She thought about that for a few minutes. A challenge? The thing she thought might cast anyone into a hellish depression was just a challenge? "That's a remarkable attitude."

"I got bigger problems." He shrugged. "Lots of people have bigger problems. I'd like to meet this Mikey kid. Think it's possible?"

Ashley didn't hesitate. A man who felt his paralysis was simply a challenge would probably be very good medicine. "I'm sure he'd like to meet you," she answered. "Want me to set it up?"

"Yeah. With some leeway in case I have a bad day and I'm taking cover behind the furniture."

He said it lightly, but Ashley understood there was nothing light about it. This man inescapably relived things most people would never know. "You'd like Jess," she said. "We've got some other former SEALs and special-ops types around here, too. If you ever want to see a face other than mine, let me know."

"Your face is nice to look at."

The compliment amazed her. She looked quickly at him and saw he was smiling. "Okay," he said. "Meet Jess. Check. Bring him over some time."

She rose reluctantly. "I have a lot of schoolwork to do yet. I'm sorry, I have to go."

"I hope you mean that. You'd be the first person in a long time." But he nodded, gave her again that half smile that didn't quite reach his eyes.

Ashley walked away, feeling as if she had interrupted something by going over there. One of his episodes of PTSD? Maybe. She just hoped it didn't pick up where it had left off.

Zane watched her walk away before he realized he was getting chilled. Once inside with Nell, he helped himself to some of the remaining coffee while she settled nearby with her bone. The rinsed beer bottles sat on the counter like accusing fingers.

"Couldn't wake me up, huh, Nell?" He received

her quizzical look. He must have gotten too drunk to
respond and she'd given up, even when he'd started
to sober up. Not that it was part of her job description
to wake him up from an alcoholic stupor.

The alcohol had silenced the screams in his head, but
Ashley had been right—that wasn't a good way to go.

Sitting alone in his kitchen as the night continued
to deepen, and with a background sound track that
wouldn't quit—the noises of war kept playing—he
faced himself.

The SEALs had demanded more of him mentally,
physically and emotionally than he ever would have
believed possible. He'd met every challenge, passed
every test and performed every mission and duty they
had given him.

So what had happened to that guy? Lack of legs?
A challenge, as he'd said. No, something had pried
his brain open and let stuff out of the can that he'd
never expected to see again.

But why? That was the thing no one could explain
to him. Why? It was a natural reaction to trauma, last-
ing longer when the trauma had endured longer. But
why? Because the brain couldn't absorb it all in one
big chunk? Or was there something else going on?

He wished he knew, because it would be another
tool to use. Damn it, he needed some tools. Drugs
took the edge off, but they didn't get rid of it. Nell
did a lot for him, pulling him back from the edge repeatedly.

But time and again, sometimes for reasons he
couldn't begin to detect, he headed back to that edge.

Vets and counselors both had told him it usually eased up with time. It might never go away totally, but it would ease.

He just sometimes wondered if he could hang on long enough.

But his thoughts soon drifted back to Ashley. The woman had kind of barged into his life, but he didn't mind it. Not at all. Very much the teacher, though, pushing him to meet other people. He wasn't sure about meeting the amputee, Jess McGregor. It sounded as if he'd found the keys to the kingdom already.

But that Mikey kid. That one grabbed him. Bad enough to be paraplegic and approaching forty. Quadriplegic at nine or ten? Unthinkable. Rolling out of the kitchen, he went to get his laptop computer and bring it back to set on the table. Nell kept happily gnawing away, apparently not sensing that she was needed just now.

At least he'd managed to get Wi-Fi in this town. The new thing, the installer had told him. He could plug into the router if he wanted to, but the capacity to go wireless everywhere in the house was good. Made his life easier, although he didn't spend a whole lot of time doing it.

It didn't take him long to find Cadell Marcus and his rather sketchy page about dog obedience training, with a brief mention of his work with police dogs. The guy didn't seem into tooting his own horn. Or maybe around here, he didn't need to. Zane hadn't been gone so long that he didn't remember that everyone knew everyone else around here. They must be telling some interesting stories about him now.

He picked up his phone and dialed Marcus. He expected to get voice mail, given the guy's webpage said he was also a sheriff's deputy, so he was surprised when the man himself answered.

"Hi, Deputy, this is Zane McLaren. Do you know Ashley Granger?"

"Sure thing. A friend of my wife's. At least so far as any woman who keeps her head buried in a computer can have friends, which is the story of life with my wife. And I know who you are. What's up?"

"Ashley said you were looking for help to train a service dog for Mikey... I'm sorry, I don't know his last name."

"There's only one Mikey I'd be thinking about. Mikey Landau. Yeah, I'd like to help him with a dog, but I'm kinda limited in my knowledge. I mean, I can practically train a dog to stand on his head and whistle 'Dixie,' but I need to know what's useful. You have a service dog?"

"Definitely."

"Well, I'd love to see it in action. Do you want to come out here? Ashley can show you the way and it would give me more of an idea right now than watching your dog in the house."

"I can do that," Zane answered. "I'm hoping to meet Mikey soon, too, because it would be good to talk to him about what he wants and needs."

"Tell you what," Cadell Marcus said. "Get Ashley to set it up and we can all meet with Mikey and you and your dog. Seeing your dog in action might help Mikey make his wish list."

Well, that sounded like a real freaking party, Zane thought as he hung up. Hadn't he vowed not to do this again?

But then he thought of that little boy and told himself to man up. He might be able to help a kid.

Chapter 5

Early on Sunday morning, with Zane at the wheel of his van, Ashley guided him toward Cadell Marcus's ranch. Other than a few brief words in passing, they hadn't spoken since Friday except when Ashley finally managed to pull everything together with Mikey Landau and his mother, Marian.

Ashley was a little disturbed by how often she thought of Zane, by how often she felt an urge to run next door. Well, maybe today would satisfy the urge and it would leave her alone. He certainly hadn't reached out to her in any way.

"I hope I can talk to this kid," he said as they turned onto a rough county road. "I told you my social skills aren't what they used to be. You've experienced it."

She looked toward him. "I think you'll find Mikey easy to talk to. You have a little bit in common to begin with, and he's just a kid. He'll probably bubble with questions and all you'll have to do is answer them."

"So he can still breathe on his own?"

"Yes, thank God."

"That's good."

Silence fell again. Nell had ceded her front bucket seat to Ashley without any hesitation. Now she stuck her head forward and sniffed. Instinctively, Ashley started to reach up to pet her, then caught herself. Not without permission.

But almost at once, Zane pulled over onto the dirt shoulder and turned off the car. "Sorry," he said.

Nell had pushed forward between the seats, and Zane gripped her fur while she sniffed him then licked his face.

Ashley wondered if she should get out of the car to give Nell more room to do whatever it was she did for Zane, but the dog didn't seem needlessly worried. She licked Zane's face several times, and then a shuddering sigh escaped him.

"It's okay," he said.

All of sudden, Ashley was very glad she hadn't tried to get out of the van. She would have hated for Zane to think she was afraid. "Stress?" she finally asked.

"Maybe. I think I told you, I don't always know the triggers. But this wasn't bad. It barely started before it was over." He rubbed Nell a few more times then started the van again. "It's all gotten a lot better because of Nell. She catches me as soon as it starts. I don't know what this kid is experiencing, but it would be great if he could have a dog like Nell."

Ashley had no doubt of that. Her hands knotted a bit in her lap. Zane was getting to her. His loneliness, the problems he had to live with. She wished with all her might that she knew how to make life better for him. A man with just a dog didn't seem like a whole lot for anyone.

"You know," he said suddenly, "this was exactly the kind of thing I intended to avoid when I came here."

Her stomach fluttered uncomfortably. "Meaning?" She hoped he wasn't referring to her.

"Getting involved. I'm not good for people."

"I wish you wouldn't say that." Anger sparked in her. "You need to give other people a chance to decide that for themselves. Anyway, it's kind of you to agree to help Mikey if you can, and after that you can go home and pull the door in after you."

He didn't respond immediately, but finally he gave a quiet laugh. "Firebrand."

Well, she *had* been a little out of line, but she wasn't prepared to take it back. The man clearly had some very generous impulses, to judge first by his check for the wheelchair and now by this. Yeah, he was having a rough time, but that didn't mean he was *bad* in any way.

"Think I'm drowning in self-pity?" he asked abruptly.

"I don't know. I don't see enough of you to know. I gather you're dealing with some heavy emotional baggage—hardly surprising given your past—but you're also the same guy who dismissed his paralysis as a challenge. That doesn't sound like self-pity. But really, I don't know what made you think you couldn't have a friend or two."

Another silence ensued. They were nearing the turn onto Cadell's drive when he spoke again.

"My neighbors."

"What about your neighbors?"

"They got me evicted. I was crazy. I had rages. I annoyed them and frightened them when I wasn't quiet. I scared them when I emerged from a bad spell and went out to the store looking like a mountain man. And that was just part of the list. They were scared I could get violent. Harm them."

"Did you ever?"

"No."

"Never threatened?"

He glanced at her. "No. Not until I realized I had a week to get out unless I wanted police help to do it. Then I was tempted to say something. Instead I spent most of the week packing while being yanked back from the edge by Nell."

Shock filled her, followed by an anger so strong she barely recognized it as her own emotion. She'd been angry about a lot of things in her life, but few things made her this mad: child abuse when she caught it was the only thing that sent her over the top. Then she felt her heart start to break.

Now this. "What did you do after?" she asked quietly, pointing him to the left turn. The sign by the road made it pretty clear they had arrived. He braked and turned carefully onto the gravel.

"Got a motel room by the week and decided to move back here as soon as I could get the place ready enough. If I upset folks around here, they might be able to get me committed, but they can't evict me."

"No one here is going to do that to you."

"How can you guarantee it?"

"Because I know a lot of vets who'd come racing to your side."

He shook his head a little. "Where I was before? I was near the VA hospital. My support group. By the time they showed up, it was too late."

It was her turn to shake her head as they bumped down the drive toward the house. God, this was almost too awful to think about. "I bet you didn't call any of them, either."

He surprised her with a dry response. "Now what could have given you that idea?"

She might have laughed at his self-deprecating humor, except she was still too mad. She couldn't believe his neighbors had treated him that way. Surely, they must have known his situation? Everything inside her roiled as she thought of that ugliness, all of it directed at a man who had suffered in the service of his country.

"They had kids," he said as he parked next to Cadell's official vehicle. "Of course they didn't want me there."

He'd said sad things to her before, but this one made her chest tighten and her eyes burn. It was amazing that after that he'd even be willing to meet Mikey. That he cared enough to try to help someone else's kid.

She shot him a sidelong look as he began to unbuckle himself and decided that Zane McLaren was one heck of a stand-up guy. Better than he even knew himself.

She wished there was some way she could get him to see that.

All of a sudden he froze. "Are those *ostriches*?"

All the tension fled from the van, and at last Ashley felt it was safe to laugh. "Yes. For real. Cadell inherited them. He was thinking about getting rid of them, but his new bride won't let him. They love her."

"Someday I want to hear that story."

"Well, he kind of had a love-hate relationship with them at first. They can be nasty, I guess."

Then she saw Cadell come around the side of the house from his backyard kennels. "There's Cadell," she said and climbed out to give Zane enough room to pivot his seat and get into his wheelchair.

Cadell greeted her warmly with a one-armed hug, then turned his attention to Zane, who was by now lowering himself to the ground with his lift. Nell hopped out beside him, and when he'd rolled onto the ground, she hit a switch and everything folded and closed back up.

"Now that's a well-trained dog," Cadell remarked, watching Nell trot alongside Zane as he wheeled toward them.

"Very," Zane said, extending his hand. "Zane McLaren."

"Cadell Marcus. Is the ground too rough for you to come around back?"

"No problem. I'll enjoy the workout."

Cadell smiled. "I want to hear all about this dog of yours."

"Nell."

"Hi, Nell," Cadell said. The dog's tail wagged in acknowledgment. "Mikey and his mom should be here in half an hour. That'll give me some time to pick your brain."

"Just so long as you understand I didn't train her. I'm enjoying the fruits of it, but it owes to other people."

Cadell nodded. "That's okay. Once I see what she can do, I can get another smart dog to do it. And maybe add on some things that Mikey will need."

The two men were making their way around the side of the house now. Ashley followed, listening, sensing the birth of a bond between them.

"He'll need more and different things than me," Zane said. "I've still got useful arms."

"Yeah," Cadell answered. "I get it. And I'll tell you a secret."

Zane tipped his head upward as they reached the edge of the kennels and a fenced and wired corral. "What's that?"

"Today, if you'll let me, I'm going to ask Nell to teach a few things to another dog."

Zane stopped wheeling. "Nell? Teach?"

"Trust me, she can. And she'll be proud of it. Plus,

Mikey will enjoy seeing it. If you'd ever worked on a ranch with a bunch of herding dogs, you'd know how well they can teach each other."

"I'm looking forward to seeing this," Zane replied. "I know how smart Nell is, but I never thought of her as a teacher. Or maybe she's been teaching *me*." He glanced around to Ashley. "No offense to you, Teach."

Ashley laughed. "None taken."

Cadell guided them to a bench beside the corral where Ashley could sit. Nell perched immediately between her and Zane.

Cadell spoke. "In my work with police dogs, we tend to stick to German shepherds and Belgian Malinois, but in my readings it seems Labs often make the best service dogs. You know anything about that?"

"Not exactly. Most of the ones I've seen have been retrievers or Labs like Nell here, but I've seen a few other kinds, smaller dogs. I guess it depends on what they're needed for. Big dogs are good for doing a lot of tasks that a short dog couldn't manage. For example, I met a woman whose dog warns her she's about to have a seizure. She had a small dog, a mixed breed, but he was perfect for her. That's all he had to do. Alert her."

"But Nell does a lot more, obviously."

Zane stroked her head. "A lot more. When I drop something, she picks it up for me. She can bring me items from the cupboards or pantry, at least from the lower levels. She lets people in the house and closes the door after them. I've had her bring me the phone a few times. The list goes on. The thing is, Cadell, I try to do as much as I can for myself. It would be awfully easy to become lazy and let the dog do it all, but it wouldn't be fair to either of us. Mikey's going to need a lot more than I do."

"Obviously." Cadell was looking thoughtful.

"If I wanted," Zane continued, "she could bring me clothes from my dresser. She's brought me beverages from the fridge. Cleaned up after me. But most of all I need her to help me keep stable."

Cadell nodded. "Well, we'll just have to see what Mikey needs when he gets here. I'm sure his mom will have some ideas. Is it all right if I take Nell into the corral with another dog?"

"Sure. Nell, go with the man."

Ashley watched in amazement as Nell glanced at Zane then walked away with Cadell. Soon she was in the corral, and another dog was joining her. A short-coated golden Lab ran around playfully while Nell sat and watched as if indulging a young child.

"Nell runs around, doesn't she?" Cadell called.

"When I tell her it's okay."

"All right then. Let's see if I can get her to make Joey here sit."

To Ashley that looked like an almost impossible thing at the moment. Joey was on a personal romp.

But then Cadell spoke. "Nell, sit. Joey, sit."

Nell sat; Joey kept running. "Joey, sit," Cadell said.

There had to be a better way, Ashley thought. Didn't most trainers use treats? She thought she remembered watching someone teach their dog to sit by repeating the word and raising a treat before the dog's nose so that the dog sat down automatically to get it.

But not Cadell. Once again, "Joey, sit."

Apparently that sent some kind of message to Nell. She took off after the miscreant. Bit by bit she rounded him up until he was in the middle of the corral and looking a bit confused. Then Nell sat and woofed.

Joey looked at her and started to move away. Nell lowered her head and woofed again. Then, to Ashley's absolute amazement, Joey imitated Nell and sat.

"And there it is," called Cadell.

"What just happened?" Ashley asked. "I don't get it."

"Dogs have their own language," Cadell said. "Nell let Joey know she was the boss when she chased him, then she cemented it. Joey will now, within reason, do what Nell shows him how to do."

With that Cadell approached the fence and looked at Zane. "Can you come out here from time to time to help?"

Zane visibly hesitated. "Just with Joey?"

"Man, I've got a dozen people who need service dogs. But if that's all you got time for, I'd be happy with it. Nell can teach the basics fast, then I take over and the dog will start accepting the commands from me. Dogs train quickly, but they learn faster from each other. So, whenever you can."

"I'll help," Zane said. "Some, anyway."

"Great. I'll give Nell back to you now." He opened the gate, and when Zane called, Nell came dashing to his side, leaving a slightly confused Joey behind.

When Joey stood up, Cadell said, "Joey, sit." Amazingly, the dog did. Cadell grinned. "Way to go." Then he walked over and patted the dog. "Okay, guy, you can run now."

Joey looked up quizzically, but with a little push from Cadell, he started bounding around again, working off puppyish energy.

Cadell closed the gate and rejoined them. "Now, maybe we've got a little something to show Mikey when he gets here."

Which seemed to be now, Ashley thought, hearing what sounded like a car door slamming.

"You guys wait here," Cadell said, trotting out to the front.

Zane looked at Ashley. "I wouldn't have believed that if I hadn't seen it."

"I wouldn't, either," Ashley admitted.

Zane surprised her, reaching across Nell to take her hand. "Thanks for talking me into this." This time the smile reached his eyes.

"I didn't talk all that hard. This was *your* decision." But his hand holding hers felt so good. His touch was warm and strong without being uncomfortable. She turned her hand over and tightened her grip on him, just a little, to let him know his touch was welcome, but she was nearly overcome by the worst urge to just lean into him and find out what he smelled like, what he felt like, how his arms around her would make her feel.

How awful it would be to do that to him. That man was paraplegic. It would be the worst tease of all time to let him know about her steadily growing sexual interest in him. She dismayed herself. But she didn't let go of his hand.

Soon she heard Mikey's excited voice. "Ostriches! Real live ostriches! I heard about them but I didn't believe in them!"

A smile stretched Ashley's cheeks, and when she glanced at Zane she saw he was smiling, too. The boy's excitement was contagious.

"I want to see more," he said.

"After the dogs," Cadell answered. "But you still can't get close. They might peck you."

Twisting on the bench, Ashley saw Cadell pushing Mikey's wheelchair over the rugged ground while Marian walked beside them. She looked delighted at the outing, almost as delighted as her son.

"I have to admit," she said, "I never imagined they'd be so big."

"Dinosaurs," Cadell said lightly. Then he pushed Mikey's wheelchair to a position near Zane. Mikey's smile faded into a serious expression as he looked at the man.

"You can use your arms?" Mikey asked.

"Yeah," Zane answered. "That makes me lucky. And my dog, Nell, helps a lot. Nell, say hello." He pointed to Mikey.

Nell rose and walked over to the boy in the wheelchair. First she sat and looked at him. Then, as if realizing he couldn't reach out to touch her, she inched forward and rested her head in his lap.

Ashley glanced at Marian and saw the sheen of tears in her eyes as Joey murmured, "Wow." Then the boy's head popped up. "I want one, too," he told Cadell.

"That's what we're here for. See Joey out in the corral? We're going to train him for you. It'll take a little time and you're going to have to talk to me a lot along the way so I know what you want and need. You okay with that?"

Mikey's entire face brightened. "Oh, yeah!"

Before long, Mikey was out in the corral with both Nell and Joey, Nell helping Cadell make some basic points.

As much fun as it was to watch, a half hour later Ashley heard Zane sigh faintly. She immediately turned her attention to him. "Are you okay?"

"Yeah. Tired. Stress."

She hadn't thought about that. He'd come here to be a hermit, and now he'd spent a great deal of time with a bunch of strangers. He wasn't used to that, and it must be exhausting. At once she stood up. "Cadell? We need Nell back. Zane's getting tired."

"Mikey probably is, too," said Marian, speaking for the first time. She'd obviously been enthralled watching her son feel excited about a new world opening up.

She came to stand in front of Zane. "I can't thank you enough." She offered her hand.

He shook it briefly. "Thank Cadell and my dog. I'll see you and Mikey again, I'm sure."

"I hope so. Mikey's been feeling like the odd man out. I think you helped with that whether you know it or not."

Zane seemed lost in his own thoughts as he rolled

himself back to his van, Nell at his side. Ashley didn't say anything, figuring he'd pushed himself about as far as he wanted to go for one day. It had been amazingly generous of him.

The silence continued on the drive back to town. Ashley wanted to tell him what a kind thing he'd done today, but somehow she didn't feel he'd appreciate it. He struck her as a man who did what he chose for his own reasons, and complimenting his generosity would probably feel like a patronizing pat on the head.

Anyway, the hermit had probably already had as much human interaction as he wanted for one day. When they got home, she was going to thank him and go back to her place.

Then she remembered his story of how his neighbors had treated him, and the ache returned. She got that people could be difficult to live with, but surely they must have known he was a vet. For crying out loud, he was a man in a wheelchair! But he'd made excuses for them, saying they had children to worry about.

She sighed quietly, wondering about the whole story. Maybe when he went over the edge it could be loud and frightening. Maybe he yelled things that people didn't want their kids to hear. About war. About death. She could grasp that, but to evict him?

Not the kind of neighbors she wanted.

As they neared town, he broke the silence. "Is Maude's still as good as it used to be?" He referred to the City Diner, which everyone called by its owner's name. Maude was an unforgettable gorgon, and she remained in business only because of her fabulous cooking and scrumptious pies.

"Yes, it is."

"Wanna stop and get something?"

Her brows lifted. Once again he was taking her by surprise. "I thought you'd had enough of people for one day."

"I can also recover, you know. I don't want my own cooking today. So...should I stop? I'd like your company."

Maybe that would make it easier for him? Because he'd never really expressed a desire to spend time with her before. But Maude's was often loud, and those plates and cups banging on the table could sound like gunshots.

"You remember she slams down the cups and plates?"

He nodded. "I appreciate you wanting to spare me, but there are some things I need to get past. Going into the diner is at the top of my list. I've thought about those steak sandwiches of hers for years. And the pecan pie."

"Okay, then." She was game if he was. And Nell would be there if he started to have a problem.

There was a van-accessible handicapped parking place not too far down from the diner. He slid into it and turned off the ignition before facing Ashley. "I can't make any guarantees," he said. "I could go off the edge."

"I didn't ask for a guarantee. If you want to try, I'm game."

* * *

One hell of a woman, Zane thought as he went through all the steps of getting himself out of the van and his wheelchair onto the sidewalk. Nell, still wearing her vest, realized something unusual was about to happen. He didn't put it on her for hanging around the house.

He looked at Ashley and once again thought how beautiful and appealing she was. His groin gave a throb of desire, and he gave a moment of thanks that his injury hadn't deprived him of his sexual abilities. Partial spinal cord injury. One advantage in that, not that he'd taken much advantage of it.

But it made him feel almost like a whole man, being able to look at a stunning woman and feel his body respond. It made him feel so good that he didn't mind that he couldn't do a damn thing about it. At least not now. It *did* put a smile on his face.

The diner didn't have a ramp, but the lintel wasn't too high for him to manage. He sensed Ashley's desire to help—she had this way of fluttering quietly, something she probably did often as a teacher—so he reassured her. "I can do this. I'll ask you to open the door, though. Nell might damage the knob."

"All right." Smiling, apparently glad to be able to do *something*, she pulled the door open. With practiced expertise, Zane tipped his chair back a little, got his front wheels over the lintel, and entered the diner.

It didn't surprise him when the place quickly quieted down and every eye fixed on him. He'd known it would happen. He just hoped he didn't have a lot of people who wanted to come over and recall his high school exploits. He wasn't that kid any longer. Not in the least.

Ashley quickly pulled a chair out of the way so he could roll up to the table. Nell parked right beside him, at the ready. Ashley sat across from him.

Then, bit by bit, the diner's normal noises resumed. And little by little he allowed himself to relax. Nell thrust her head under his hand, asking for a pat now that she could relax as well.

Maude, looking as if she hadn't changed one bit in all the intervening years, stomped over with two menus. "Good to see you back, Zane. Coffee?"

"Yes, thanks. Ashley?"

"Ashley likes them latte things I make."

"Indeed, I do." Ashley smiled. "Thanks, Maude."

"I guess some things do change," Zane remarked as Maude went to get the coffee. "Lattes here? Never would have dreamed."

"I'm still wishing for a Mexican restaurant. And a Chinese one, too. We *did* get a chain pizza place on the edge of town, though. Popular hangout."

"Mostly with young folks," he guessed. "Man, what I'd have given for that when I was…" He stopped. He didn't want anyone else taking him down that particular avenue of memory, so why do it himself?

"It came too late for me, too," Ashley remarked, easing a moment in which tension had started to grow in him again.

Nell poked his arm with her nose and he looked down. "I'm okay, girl."

High school was so far in the past, and so much had happened to him since, that it felt almost like someone else's memory, or like a book he'd once read. He couldn't even connect with that young man who'd had such a sunny future and had been blessed with so much athletic talent and so many friends. That guy had used his gifts in the SEALs, forever putting a wall up between him and his youth.

He looked across the table at Ashley, who was studying her menu as if she didn't already have it memorized. When he looked at his own, he saw that it hadn't changed a whole lot. Maude's famous steak sandwich was still there, and his mouth watered a bit in anticipation. Ashley chose a chef's salad for herself. Women and their salads, he thought with amusement. Men and their steaks... He almost laughed.

While they waited for Maude to serve them, a tall, powerfully built man with streaks of gray in his dark hair came over. Zane felt tension creep along his nerves. He recognized the expression in the guy's eyes.

"Hey, Ashley," he said pleasantly. "Introduce me?"

Ashley bit her lip for a second before looking at Zane. Not knowing what else to do, Zane offered his hand. "Zane McLaren."

"Seth Hardin. I must be one of the few guys who didn't grow up around here, so I never met you before. I'm the old sheriff's son. Nate Tate's kid."

Well, that explained the resemblance, but not the expression in the eyes. Seth pulled out the chair beside Ashley. "I won't interrupt your dinner. I just wanted to introduce myself to a fellow traveler."

Tension began to wind in Zane again. "SEALs?"

"Yeah. Retired a few years ago. Team 2."

"Team 3."

Seth nodded. "There are a few of us around, spec-ops types. Ashley knows my number if you ever want to hang out with any of us. We usually get together on Thursdays once a month to chew the fat together. There's my wife, too. Former combat search-and-rescue pilot." Then Seth stood. "Nice meeting you." With a smile and a nod, he walked out.

Zane's lunch plate clattered onto the table in front of him. Ashley's followed. For a brief while Zane didn't even smell the delightful aromas.

Then Nell nudged him back to awareness, and he saw Ashley eyeing him with concern.

"I'm fine," he said. "Fine. Let's eat."

"That was nice of Seth," Ashley offered as she speared some of her salad.

Was it? Zane supposed it was. After all, he'd exposed himself by coming in here, and if the worst that happened was meeting a fellow SEAL, he'd be doing well. He knew he'd taken a risk facing the noise and Maude's famous slamming of plates and cups on the tables, but he'd only had the slightest slip, almost undetectable to him but picked up by Nell, who had yanked him right back.

"I wonder if Maude would kill me if I gave Nell some steak."

"I don't know." Ashley grinned and looked around

until her gaze landed on Maude. The large woman, frowning as usual, stomped over to them.

"Something wrong?" she demanded.

Ashley spoke before Zane could. "Zane wants to give his service dog a little of his steak. Do you mind?"

Because Maude's feelings had to be treated more carefully than she treated her customers. Zane had been amused by that in the past. He decided to be amused now.

"Don't give that dog none of your supper," Maude groused. "You need to eat."

She walked away, leaving Zane and Ashley to look at each other.

"Guess not," Ashley said, her lips quivering.

"Guess not," Zane agreed. Not that Nell was supposed to eat when she was on duty. Nell knew that, but he could almost feel her salivating. It wasn't like she had a chance at steak every day. But she remained calmly beside him, attentive to him, not to his plate.

He was on his second mouthful of that piece of heaven known as a steak sandwich when Maude slammed yet another plate on the table, one that held a decent-size steak all cut up. "Give the animal that. Just make sure you put the plate on the floor. Don't need no health inspectors on my back."

Before Zane could thank her, she had moved away, talking to other customers in her gruff way.

"Um, wow?" Ashley said.

"Yeah. Wow."

"Need help getting the plate to the floor?"

"Thanks, but I think I can do it. If I can't, I'll let you know." Twisting, he managed to bend far enough to get the plate to the floor without dropping it. Nell eyed him. "Eat, girl. It's okay."

Nell didn't need a second invitation. It also didn't take her very long to empty the plate, but as she licked her chops, she looked completely content.

He bit into his own sandwich while Ashley said, "Dogs eat so fast. I always wonder how they can enjoy it."

"I think they're wired differently when it comes to food. Imagine a wolf pack lazing around sharing an elk."

She laughed. "Good point, Zane."

The sandwich was every bit as good as memory had claimed, and before he left with Ashley, he ordered a second to take home with him. Ashley had finished only half her salad and scooped it into a takeout box while he waited.

Little by little, now that he was done eating, departing diners and newcomers passed his table. Many said quietly, "Welcome home, Zane." They didn't pause, didn't stop to try to converse, just made those quiet statements.

The wheelchair, he figured. It made people uncomfortable. They probably didn't *want* to have a conversation, because they just didn't know what they could say.

Great conversation killer, he thought as he pushed himself back from the table. "I got it," he said to Ashley as she started to pull out her wallet. "Please."

She nodded, smiling faintly. With his boxed dinner on his lap, he wheeled up to the cash register and pulled his wallet out of his breast pocket.

Maude came around and stared at him over the counter. "No charge."

"But…"

"I said no charge. Don't be arguing with me. Trust me, it won't happen again, and I better be seeing a lot of you around here."

Zane hardly knew how to react. On the one hand, she was being generous, which he didn't need and which kind of embarrassed him, and on the other, it sounded as if she were scolding him. Well, he remembered there was no arguing with Maude. "Thank you," he said. Funny how hard it was to say those words sometimes.

"Thank *you*," she answered. "Now get outta here. Weather's turning bitter and that jacket ain't enough. Hope you got a better one."

Chapter 6

Maude was right about the weather. The drop in temperature just during the time they'd been inside was startling. When he was securely buttoned into the driver's seat, he looked over at Ashley. "I didn't expect any of that."

"If you want friends in this town, you seldom have to look hard."

He leaned forward, turning on the ignition, pulling them back onto the street. "I don't remember the old sheriff having a son."

"I'm not surprised. He didn't know about it, either. Apparently his wife, to whom he wasn't married at the time, got pregnant with Seth while Nate was in Vietnam. Her dad made her give the baby up, and what with her father's interference, I guess, Nate never heard about Seth until Seth showed up on his doorstep, a grown man in his late twenties. The whole county buzzed about that one."

"I can just imagine," Zane answered drily. "Gossip enough for months."

"Almost ended the Tate marriage, too, from what I remember. Anyway, everything's all patched up and fine for years now."

"And his wife? A CSAR pilot?"

"She was. Afghanistan, mostly. Anyway, she's piloting our medical and rescue helicopters now."

Things had certainly changed around here, he thought as he drove back to his house. Even Maude, who had once seemed as unchangeable as the mountains, had softened up a bit.

A veterans' group meeting. He didn't remember if there'd been one when he was in high school, but he supposed he wouldn't have been interested. His thoughts turned back to those years, and he realized he had some assessing to do.

"Come in?" he asked Ashley as they parked in his driveway.

She didn't hesitate, which relieved him, which meant he hadn't done something to disturb her today. Yet. "Sure," she said and climbed out.

His own exit took a little longer, and Ashley was waiting for him on the porch by the time he rolled up the ramp.

Nell took a quick dash in the yard, then followed eagerly into the house. The dog was good at fitting in her business when she had the chance.

"Stay for a while," he asked Ashley. "I can offer you a soft drink if you'd like."

She held up her latte cup. "Still plenty here."

He rolled into the kitchen and up to the table, where he placed the box holding his extra meal. He didn't go into the living room much. Getting on and off the sofa was a pain, hardly worth the effort most of the time. He supposed he could hang a bar in there like he had over his bed so he could pull himself up and over, but he hadn't felt particularly motivated yet.

But then, almost before he knew what he was doing, he tugged on Ashley's hand until she slid into his lap.

"If I'm outta line, tell me," he said gruffly. "No social skills, like I said."

He watched one corner of her mouth curve upward. "I don't usually like to be manhandled. However, this time I think I'll make an exception. What brought this on?"

"You have any idea how long it's been since I had an attractive woman in my lap?" With those words he felt almost as if he had stripped his psyche bare. Had he gone over some new kind of cliff?

Ashley didn't know what to make of this. His words had been an apology of sorts, but he'd still pulled her onto his lap. She twisted her head, trying to read his face, knowing he'd been honest in his way, but seeing doubt begin to creep into his eyes.

It was true she didn't like being manhandled, even in small ways, but this felt different to her. As if actions had needed for once to replace words, even with her. But the doubt troubled her. She didn't want him to think he'd offended her or done something wrong. It had taken a long time to get this close to him, to get him to go out to Cadell's place, to see him willing to enter the diner and share a meal with her in front of other people. The last thing she wanted was for him to crawl back into his hole.

Taking a huge risk, she lifted her hand and pressed his cheek until his head turned toward her. Then she stole a kiss right from his lips. She couldn't be any clearer. She just hoped he wouldn't think she was a tease, given his paralysis.

Instead he wound his other arm around her and pulled her in for another kiss, his mouth warm and firm on hers, his tongue entering her mouth as if he hoped to find her soul within.

Glorious desire ran through her like a hot river. She'd thought a lot about Zane, but she had never allowed herself to think very much about how sexually attractive he was. He was in a wheelchair. She didn't want to make him feel bad in any way. But now…now…

He tore his mouth from hers and pressed her ear so close to his chest she could hear his heartbeat. It seemed to be racing as fast as hers. She just wished she could melt into him.

He cleared his throat. "I'm going to let go of you."

Of course he was, she thought as disappointment caused her stomach to drop and her mood to sink. What else could he do?

Without a word, she slid off his lap. She thought about leaving but decided that might be a bad thing to do so soon. Hard to believe that late-afternoon sunlight still poured into the kitchen, that everything slammed back into place as if an earthquake hadn't just happened.

She struggled to find her voice. "I think I'd like a beer." *Go for the normal, as if nothing had happened. Don't make him feel worse.*

"In a sec," he answered, his voice still rough. "You need to know something."

"What?"

"That being in this wheelchair doesn't make me harmless."

She blinked, not sure what he meant. Not harmless? She'd never thought of him as being harmless, legs or no legs. He looked as if he could be a threat with just his upper body. "I never thought—"

"That's not what I mean. I don't mean I might hurt you, although I guess I could. No, damn it. I meant… I can still have sex. I didn't lose that. So… I—I shouldn't be pulling you into my lap. I have no right, and I don't want to upset you."

"Upset me?" Her head was whirling now. He'd just given her some wonderful news—for him, at least—and he was worried about upsetting her? "I think that's great, Zane. Really great. It makes me so happy to hear."

"Yeah." He looked away. "Thanks. But I got a whole bunch of problems you don't want to deal with, so…"

He was confusing her more by the minute, bouncing around, trying to say something he couldn't quite get to, she guessed. Was he trying to say that nobody would want a paralyzed guy? Hardly. That no one would be willing to deal with the emotional toll war had taken on him? Some might not be, but she knew some spouses who did and never complained.

His isolation struck her anew, and she wished she knew how to ease it. "That beer?" she said again. Give him time to figure out what he wanted to say. Give her time to try to figure out why he'd said it.

Without a word, he rolled to the fridge, maneuvered the door open and brought two beers to the table.

"Thanks," he said as he popped the caps off the longnecks.

"For what?"

"For pushing me to help Mikey. Kid's a real pistol. I think he had a good time."

"I'm sure he did. Did you?"

"Yeah, actually. Even enjoyed myself at Maude's."

She smiled, holding the icy beer. "So I guess you don't have to be a hermit all day, every day."

"Maybe not." He took a pull on his beer. "Being in Maude's, though…"

She waited, trying to get a handle on her own roiling feelings. She wasn't sure what had just happened or what might happen next. Or if anything was going to happen. But her stomach felt full of butterflies, her entire body still ached with need from being in his arms and she had a strong suspicion he'd probably find a way to keep away from her. Maybe that was best. She still didn't know him that well. She'd seen plenty in him that she liked, and plenty that ought to be worrisome.

"Something about being at Maude's," he said, starting again. "I don't think much about my days before the navy. Especially now. That person seems like such a stranger."

"You said something about that, didn't you? Like a book you'd read?"

"Did I say that out loud?" He arched his brow. "Anyway, yeah. A character out of a movie. Doesn't feel real to me anymore. But I was thinking back to it and realized I was a bit of a knucklehead."

She hadn't heard that expression in forever. "How so?"

"I told myself I was joining the navy so I could go to college. Considering how fast I leaped on the chance to become a SEAL, I don't think so anymore."

Again she was hesitant to speak for fear of saying the wrong thing. This man had warned her he could be a minefield with his PTSD, and she sure didn't have any idea what might trigger it.

A sound drew her attention, and she saw Nell contentedly chewing on a bone nearby. Apparently, the dog thought everything was okay.

"So, I've been kind of wondering at what really happened. What I was really thinking. Was it that I couldn't give up being an athlete, a big fish in that little pond? That I still had something to prove to myself? God, I can hardly remember that kid. All I know is I volunteered for the toughest, dirtiest job in the service."

She nodded silently.

"Something made me take a sharp turn within a few months of enlisting. But maybe it wasn't a sharp turn at all."

"Maybe not," she said cautiously. "If you don't regret it..."

"I don't, which probably sounds fairly crazy coming from a guy in a wheelchair who sometimes loses his marbles and needs a dog to keep him in the here and now, but I don't regret it. I don't like some of the memories. Hell, no. But I did an essential job. Nothing will take that awareness from me. Wait a sec."

He pulled back from the table and left the kitchen. She heard his chair rolling down the hall, then a little while later rolling back again. Nell never left her bone, and Ashley considered the dog to be the best barometer around.

When he pulled up to the table again, he put a wooden box on it. "My medals." He opened the lid and pulled out the presentation cases, opening them and laying them out before her. The only one she recognized was the Purple Heart, and it had a cluster. Did that mean he'd been wounded more than once? She'd ask later, not now. Let him get through all this.

He pointed. "Silver Stars, Bronze Stars, the Navy Cross...all those say I was a hero. But you know what? I don't feel like a hero. I did a job. An important job. And there wasn't one of my comrades who didn't deserve those medals at least as much."

He sighed and stared at the cases. "No hero. But I don't regret it."

"But you're troubled?" she asked tentatively.

"Only by wondering why I jumped into it when that wasn't my conscious plan. It's like something knocking on the door in my head and I can't let it in."

She stared at the medals, thinking they were poor symbols at best of what he'd been through. Impressive, but nowhere near like the doing of all that.

"I used to talk about throwing these away," he said, closing the cases and putting them back in the box one by one.

"You didn't think you deserved them?"

"I didn't think I deserved them any more than anyone else. Plus, they were like a reminder, which at times I didn't want."

"But you kept them."

"Yeah, a Vietnam vet talked me into it. Told me that someday someone who knew me would want them. Or that I'd get around to wanting them, because they were the only damn reward I was ever going to get."

Ashley drew a sharp breath as her heart squeezed. The only reward he would get? A pile of medals?

But in her heart she knew he was right. People thanking him for his service didn't begin to touch on all he'd done for his country. How could it? They didn't know; they hadn't been through it. Maybe it was a nice but nearly meaningless gesture from his point of view.

"So," she said, "you ever get annoyed by people thanking you for your service?"

He surprised her by laughing. "Sometimes. The first few times it feels good. Then it begins to sound rote. When I ditched the uniform, I was glad not to hear it anymore."

"I can imagine. Then you get treated like crap by your neighbors."

He shrugged, his laughter vanishing. "We all had our problems. They had theirs. Mine were adding to them."

"Are you really that forgiving?"

"Who am I to judge?"

Good Lord, what an amazing man. He might be gruff and sometimes prickly, and want little to do with people, but he'd just said he couldn't judge the neighbors who'd kicked him to the curb like so much trash.

She suspected he judged himself a whole lot and far more harshly. "Zane?"

He looked up from the beer he was turning slowly in his hands. "Yeah?"

"Apply a little of that forgiveness to yourself."

His brow lowered, and she wouldn't be able to blame him if he grew angry with her. She had no right to tell him anything, and certainly nothing so personal.

Then his brow smoothed. "You got it in one, Teach. I'm my own judge, jury and executioner."

"Executioner?" The word made her heart stop. Was he suicidal?

"Figure of speech. I'm not going to do anything that crazy. Too much karma to work out." Then he smiled faintly. "Sometimes you see right through me. When I got some therapy, they told me the same thing. Quit blaming myself. I did my job. I'd have something to apologize for if I'd deserted. Give myself the same breaks I'd give the next guy. Good advice, hard to do."

"Advice is usually hard to act on," she said drily. "If I'd followed all the good advice I'd been given, I'd be a nominee for sainthood."

That drew another laugh out of him, and almost helplessly, she joined it. He was a bit mercurial, but she was so glad he could still find laughter in himself. Not only glad, but relieved.

But the laughter faded, the quiet settled in again, and he seemed lost in thought. Nell was still content, apparently unconcerned, so he must be all right.

Taking a chance, she asked, "Didn't you have Nell when you were in your apartment? Before those people…well, they were horrid. What could you possibly have done?"

"No Nell then. As for what I did, I don't remember most of it. You see, when it hits, I'm somewhere else. Back over there. On a mission. Being shot at, seeing my buddies get hit… I'm really not aware of what I'm doing here sometimes. So I guess I was noisy, angry and did a lot of cussing in front of children, and I scared some people. At least that's what they told me. About a week after I moved into that motel, my buddies brought me Nell. It's because of her I didn't get evicted again, I'm sure."

She just shook her head, hurting for him.

"It's better now, obviously," he continued. "Nell. It's been a year. Mostly I've learned to avoid triggers. She's good at sensing when something is disturbing me, and she distracts me. And she never lets me get too far away mentally. I gather that's a big improvement. Well, I know it is. I'm here more often than not now. A year ago I wouldn't have dared to go out to Cadell's ranch for fear something would happen. I wouldn't have wanted to meet a kid, because I might lose touch and say things no kid should ever hear."

Impulsively, she reached out and took his hand. He didn't pull away, but he glanced at her before returning his gaze to the wooden box in front of him and the beer bottle beside it.

"You have a really bad case," she said.

"I did, I guess. Not unheard of. Better now. So I'm grateful. Especially grateful for Nell."

"I'm sure." She squeezed his hand gently, then let go. "We don't do enough to care for our vets. One of our high school teachers was widowed by the war. A year or so later, his best buddy came to visit her, to keep a promise. He'd suffered brain trauma and was kind of wandering, wondering what he could do. It turned out he was pretty good at helping around her farm, and they married eventually."

"Meaning?"

"Meaning I don't think he got very good care, at least not until he met my friend. They discharged him with all kinds of problems, and except for the way things fell out, he'd probably be living under a bridge." She tried to tamp down her anger, but it had already sparked. "No, we don't take good care of our vets. Not in some ways."

"There's no cure for PTSD," he pointed out.

"Well, maybe they need to get to work on it. It's not just vets who have it. All kinds of people who've been traumatized have it. Some can talk it out. Sometimes it never goes away. For some it just eases eventually. I have a college friend who became a journalist. She has PTSD from covering the scenes of accidents, fires, murders, plane crashes… She had to quit finally. A decade later it doesn't bother her as much. And talk therapy didn't help her deal with those pictures burned into her brain."

"It wouldn't," he agreed. "It can't. But with time… I hear they're not as strong and don't pop up as often. Nell's helped to give me some time." He paused. "Does Mikey have a problem?"

"Not that anyone's aware of. Not yet, anyway. He doesn't remember his accident at all. He woke up four days later in a hospital bed with no memory of it."

"Maybe that's a blessing."

"He sure has enough to deal with as it is. I just hope the memory doesn't come back. The darn kid still wants to ride a horse."

"Really?" Zane smile faintly. "Guts and gumption."

"Maybe. Somebody's talking about building him a special saddle, but his mom won't hear of it. Not yet, anyway."

"I can kinda understand her viewpoint."

"So can I." Ashley leaned back in her chair. "Listen, am I overstaying my welcome? You're an avowed hermit, remember?"

Again she drew a laugh from him. Something about today had made him feel very good. Getting out? Meeting people?

"I may be getting over being a hermit little by little. But in all seriousness, don't be surprised if I pull back into my shell occasionally. Sometimes it's best just to leave me alone."

"I can deal, as long as you understand that if I start to worry about you, I'm going to be knocking on your front door. And unless you lock it, I suspect Nell will let me in."

He chuckled. "Yeah, she probably will. Walk in any time, Ashley. You give me hope."

Hope? Her heart slammed. "Me?" She almost squeaked.

"Here I am hanging out with you. You've put up with me for hours now. I never thought that would happen again."

Wow. Just wow. She was complimented and stunned all at once. "I don't feel like I'm putting up with anything," she said truthfully. "You're okay to be with."

"Just okay?" The words sounded as if he were teasing, then he said, "Want to join me and Nell on a walk around the block? I need to get a bit of a workout, and I'm sure she needs to stretch her legs."

Nell's ears had perked the instant she heard

"walk," and now she was looking hopefully at Zane. Ashley smiled. "I'd like that, but I need to run next door to get a warmer jacket. It was getting cold out there. Be right back."

"I'll meet you out front."

The air had turned bitterly cold, making the autumn sunlight feel warmer by comparison. The early twilight was setting in as the sun sank behind the mountains, especially with the days shortening. Very soon it would be dark. Definitely time for a winter jacket.

Hers was hanging in her small hall closet, and her gloves were still tucked in the pockets. All ready to go. Her ears felt nipped just from the brief time outdoors, so she pulled up her hood before stepping outside.

Zane and Nell were waiting for her. Nell was dancing a bit at the end of her leash. Zane wore what appeared to be a down-filled black jacket, which added to his bulk. He'd turned his head over to a stocking cap that sheltered his ears, and he gripped the push rims with hands clad in leather gloves.

"Nell's certainly ready," he said as she skipped down her steps to the sidewalk.

"This has got to be cold even for her," Ashley remarked. "Holding still is probably painful."

"Do you jog at all?"

"When I can. Why?"

"I like to keep up a good clip. It won't be an easy walking pace, so let me know if I'm getting ahead of you or wearing you out. I mean it."

"No problem." She really didn't expect one. She did jog several times a week unless something intervened, and she couldn't imagine that he could go *that* fast in his chair.

She was shortly proved wrong. He wasn't kidding about keeping up a good pace. He pushed those rims over and over as hard as he could. Nell was trotting quickly at his side. She was probably the only one of the three of them who could have gone any faster, and not for long.

"Not fair," she said a bit breathlessly to Zane as they hurried down the sidewalk. "That dog has *four* legs."

He laughed. "I'll slow down soon, unless you want me to right now."

"Full steam ahead. I'm doing fine."

The air wasn't quite cold enough to make her chest ache, but it wasn't far from it. She loved cross-country skiing as a hobby, but rarely did she go fast enough to cause her bronchioles to want to spasm. Today was no threat, and it felt good to be stretching her body this way.

He was right, though, about having to stop at every corner to check for traffic.

"You know, there's a track at the junior college you could probably use if you want to keep a steady, fast pace."

"Maybe I'll check it out sometime," he said. "What kind of surface does it have?"

"I don't know exactly." She hadn't thought about what he might need for his wheels. "The high school is a cinder track. You probably couldn't use that, but the college has a fairly new track with a different surface."

"That might work."

Dang, he didn't sound the least breathless. She was beginning to feel out of shape.

But then he slowed down. "Close to a mile," he announced.

She thought about it. "I've never measured distances in town. How do you know?"

"Practice. It was actually 1.6 klicks. Over a kilometer and a half. Everywhere I've been in the world, the metric system has been more useful."

She strolled beside him at his more sedate pace. The twilight was arriving, the streetlights popping on. Nell occasionally wanted to sniff something, so he paused and let her.

Ashley watched, amused. "Did you tell her she's off-duty?"

"I always give her a chance to be a dog when I slow down like this. She needs it. I enjoy it. And trust me, she never loses her awareness of me."

They passed a few people, but given the time of day and the chilling weather, Ashley supposed most were inside preparing dinner and keeping warm. Those they did pass simply waved and called out a hello. No one tried to stop them for a conversation.

Her cell phone rang, and she struggled to get beneath her jacket and pull it out. It was Connie.

Connie's voice filled her ear. "Julie's gone to the hospital in labor. Trace is quietly freaking. You coming?"

"I will shortly. Thanks for letting me know, Connie."

She stuffed her phone into her jacket pocket. "After we get home, I need to go to the hospital. My friend Julie is in labor. I gather her husband could use some moral support."

"Don't wait on me. Go ahead."

She looked down at him in the dimming light, then noticed that Nell had lost all interest in trees and grass but was poised beside him. Focused intently on him. Something was happening.

"After we get you home," she said firmly. "Right, Nell?"

Nell gave a small whimper and nudged at Zane's arm.

Zane muttered, "Oh, for the love of…"

Nell rose and laid both her front legs on his arm.

"Listen to your dog, Zane," Ashley said firmly. "If you don't she'll lick your cheek and you'll grow icicles."

The humor didn't work. Nell's touch didn't work.

Just like that, Zane had gone away.

Ashley looked at Nell. "Let's get him home." She moved to the back of the wheelchair and Nell dropped to all fours, understanding. Something inside Ashley had quieted until all feeling fled. A self-protective emotional crouch. All she could think of was the fact that as big a man as Zane was, the wheelchair was surprisingly easy to push.

A most excellent wheelchair.

For a man who seemingly had just dropped off a ledge into the pit of hell.

* * *

Zane was astonished when he realized Ashley was pushing him toward the ramp to his house. "What the heck?"

"You zoned out. Nell was worried. I wasn't going to leave you sitting in the middle of a sidewalk. You don't remember?"

"Not a thing," he admitted. Well, not exactly true. He'd been remembering another place and time. Not for the life of him could he imagine what had cast him back there. A quiet street, his dog, his new friend, streetlights coming on…he'd never had an assignment that included streetlights. But something had kicked him over.

"I can get up the ramp," he said somewhat forcefully. He grabbed the push rims, taking over. He knew the instant Ashley let go.

"You had somewhere to go," he said.

"It can wait."

"It doesn't have to. I'll be fine."

"Zane…"

"I need to think about what just happened. I don't know why I cut out. Go worry about your friend and her husband. You'll be more useful."

"Fine." Her tone took on an edge.

He started pushing himself up the ramp, but he paused once to watch her walk away and into her house. Bad enough he'd zoned out, but did he have to talk to her that way? She hadn't done anything wrong.

But it was best for her if she stayed away. Best for

him. Never mind that he'd been enjoying her company. No one deserved having to deal with him.

"Come on, Nell," he said unnecessarily as he reached the porch and leaned forward to fling to the door open.

Just him and the dog. It was safest. No one got hurt. Because he seemed to have a built-in capacity for doling out pain.

Chapter 7

Ashley battled irritation as she entered her house and began to strip for a shower. What the heck had she done? She'd brought him home when he zoned out. Was that a crime?

Standing under the hot shower spray, washing her hair, she decided that she might be overreacting. The guy had evidently had an episode. He didn't seem to have any idea of why, and he'd been surprised to find himself back at home. That must be hell to deal with. Plus, he probably hadn't come back entirely from wherever he'd gone. So, yes, he'd been short, had wanted to get away from everyone. For all she knew he was both worried and exhausted. He might have been battling demons while he went away. Bad memories. They would hardly put him in a good mood.

By the time she'd finished blow-drying her hair enough that she wouldn't freeze by the time she got to the hospital, she was feeling a whole lot more charitable toward Zane. He couldn't help it. She knew that. What did she expect? That he'd come back from a bad episode and be all cheerful and sunny?

Of course not.

She pulled on a warm blue jogging suit and her other pair of running shoes, grabbed her wallet so she'd have money to ferry coffee and food to Trace if he needed it, then bundled up and headed for the hospital.

A glance at Zane's place showed that lights were on, so he wasn't sitting in the dark. That much was good, she supposed.

But what an odd day. First the visit to Cadell's ranch, where Zane had seemed to unwind and make a connection with Mikey. Then the utterly unexpected invitation to join him for lunch at Maude's, followed by asking her to walk with him.

Maybe he'd overloaded. He probably wasn't used to that much company anymore. It was as if he'd been reaching out for the first time in what must have been a very long time for him, given what he had told her, and then something had snapped inside him, isolating him once more.

She guessed she could understand that. She could certainly forgive it. Whether she'd expose herself to more of it remained to be seen. Attractive as he was, he might be more of a complication than she was truly willing to deal with.

At the hospital she went to the maternity waiting room and found Connie there with Trace Archer, Julie's husband. A tall, lean man, he couldn't be a stranger to tough times. As she understood it, he'd been shot in his right hand and to this day suffered an awful lot of pain from it. Julie had once confided his only relief from it would be amputation. So far he hadn't wanted to use that escape hatch.

She gave Trace a quick hug. "So where are we?"

"Likely going to be an all-nighter," Connie answered. "Marisa wanted to come, but Jonni's down with some kind of stomach bug and while she could have left him with Ryker, she didn't think the bug would be welcome here."

Ashley shook her head, smiling. "I'm sure it wouldn't be. Can I get anyone coffee or something to eat from the cafeteria?" She knew Trace swallowed coffee as if it were the staff of life.

"I'd love some coffee," he said. "But please, not from the machine in the hall."

Ashley grinned. "I read you. Connie?"

"Nothing for me unless you see a reasonably fresh-looking turkey sandwich. I haven't eaten since breakfast."

As Ashley walked through the halls toward the cafeteria, she remembered the half a salad she'd left behind. Oh, well. Besides, she wanted something a little more substantial now, anyway. Hunger had started gnawing at her stomach during the walk with Zane.

Nearly everyone she passed recognized her and knew that Julie was in labor. It was the kind of good news no one felt the need to keep a secret. She paused briefly a few times for short, general conversations, then entered the cafeteria. They were still serving dinner, and there were some good sandwiches to choose from. She got Connie her turkey and also picked up a roast beef for Trace. He might not feel like eating, but if this went on all night, he'd need the energy. Nerves probably had his candle burning at both ends. It wasn't as if he'd been through this before.

When she got back to the waiting room with her tray, Trace had begun pacing and Connie was skimming a magazine. Connie must be a calming influence, Ashley thought. She'd done this more than once. Yet Trace was pacing.

"Here's your coffee," she said to Trace. "And a roast beef sandwich. You'd better eat. You need to keep your energy up."

"Maybe in a bit," he answered, taking the large coffee. "Thanks."

Connie looked up, a smile dancing in her eyes. "Men suffer more than we do, I sometimes think."

"Well," said Trace, "I was supposed to be with her. How calm can I be when I'm stuck out here?"

Ashley exchanged looks with Connie, then asked, "Trace, you're supposed to be her coach?"

"We took classes together."

Connie rose, tossing the magazine aside. "Ashley, you stay with Trace. I'll find out what's going on."

"Absolutely." She bit her lip in worry as she wondered what had gone wrong. If Trace was supposed to be his wife's coach, shouldn't he be with her?

Trace perched on a chair, coffee in his good hand, his banged-up one in a leather glove and cradled close to his body as if he didn't want it to bump anything.

"Connie will find out," Ashley said as reassuringly good. "All that practice as a cop? She gets answers."

He offered her a mirthless smile. "I just want to know what's going on. Is something bad happening? God, Ashley, I love that woman."

"I know you do." She wished she had comforting words, but she seemed to be out of them. In fact, when she thought about it, she'd been unable to offer any real comfort to anyone in a while. None for Zane, certainly, and now none for Trace. When had life gone so cockeyed?

But now she, too, was worried about Julie. They'd grown up together. She didn't want anything bad to happen to her friend. Nothing. She desperately wanted Julie to come through this with a healthy baby.

Impulsively, she reached out and laid her hand on Trace's thigh. "It'll be okay."

Empty words, but he nodded. He gave her the faintest, palest of smiles.

It had better be okay. If something went wrong, she wasn't sure she'd be able to handle it any better than Trace.

Then Connie popped into the room. "I just spoke to her, Trace. She's fine. Somewhere something glitched, and they didn't have a record that you were to be her coach. So you can go in now. You, too, Ashley, but briefly. Julie asked for you."

As Ashley walked down the corridor with Trace,

she said, "I can't believe they'd keep the husband out, paper or no paper."

Trace had begun to feel better. He smiled. "Maybe we have a tendency to faint."

That drew a relieved laugh from Ashley. "Somehow I don't think you will."

"Sure. Like I've ever heard my wife scream before. That could be very different."

Ashley hadn't thought about that. "Julie doesn't strike me as a screamer," she answered. "She strikes me as a cusser. If it gets rough, she may divorce you before morning."

Trace laughed, his whole demeanor changing. "Yeah, she could do that. You never have to wonder what that woman thinks about anything."

When they entered the labor room, it was surprisingly quiet. A fetal monitor beeped, but Julie was sitting with the head of her bed up, her knees a bit bent and a smile on her face, quickly banished by a grimace as a contraction came.

Her brow looked a little damp with perspiration. She reached out the hand that wasn't attached to the IV to Trace, and he took it. "Everything's fine," she said. "Everything. I kept asking where you were, and nobody seemed to get it. I decided you must not have arrived yet."

"I've been sitting in the waiting room wondering why they wouldn't let me see you."

"That's what Connie said. Somebody fell asleep at the wheel. It doesn't matter now. Hey, Ash, how you doing?"

"I'm doing fine. It's you we're all thinking about."

"Considering billions of women before me have done this, I wouldn't waste a whole lot of concern." She winced and began panting. At once training kicked in and Trace started coaching her.

Looking around, Ashley found a chair and pushed it over so Trace could sit beside his wife. When Julie relaxed again, Ashley said, "I got Trace a roast beef sandwich." She held it up. "Think you can get him to eat?"

"Put it on the table," Julie said. "It's going to be a long night. I'll get him to eat it. But he probably wants more coffee."

"She got me some," Trace objected.

"Ha. I've never seen anyone drink coffee the way you do."

"I'll get some more," Ashley said quickly. Whether Trace wanted the coffee or not, she felt these were moments he'd like to share privately with his wife. He was certainly entitled to them.

A nurse buzzed in to check on things just as she was leaving. She apologized to Trace for not bringing him in sooner. "Honestly, we don't try to lock out fathers. I really can't imagine how this happened."

Ashley slipped out and trekked toward the cafeteria again. She wondered if she ought to stay the night to shuttle coffee back and forth.

Connie caught up with her near the cafeteria. "I'm thinking about going home. Julie said the nurses are predicting she won't deliver before morning. First babies take a while."

"Until they don't," Ashley remarked, causing Connie to grin. "Listen, I can sleep in tomorrow. Are you on duty?"

As a sheriff's deputy, Connie's hours could be irregular. "Nope, I'm off, and I'm honestly glad Ethan can babysit. Sometimes I need a break from that, too."

"Three little kids? I'm not surprised. The oldest is probably more help, though."

"She helps when her life doesn't get in the way. But you spend all day with youngsters."

Ashley laughed. "And I get to send them home at the end of the school day."

"I forgot that lucky part."

A couple of hours later, however, Julie didn't seem to want much company other than Trace's, so Connie and Ashley both left, promising to return early in the morning.

"Big event," Connie said as she climbed into her cruiser. "The first one is the best."

"Maybe someday I'll know." Not that she'd ever been in a rush. Content with her life as it was, she wasn't looking to change it drastically anytime soon.

Trace called with the news, waking Ashley at seven in the morning. "Healthy baby boy, Julie's resting, and no, we haven't decided on a name yet, because I don't want my son to be called Trace." There was tired humor in his voice, though, and happiness. "Julie wants to see you, Connie and Marisa, but not until much later. No offense, Ashley, but she's pooped."

"None taken. I'm just thrilled for both of you."

Happiness for Julie suffused her morning. She'd watched her friends go through this and had some idea of the magic of bringing a child into the world. She also had some idea of the work and fatigue involved. Time to go grocery shopping and start cooking a lot of refrigerator and freezer meals so Julie and Trace could focus on their new baby. She almost whistled a tune in delight.

A quick check of the weather warned her that the day had remained as chilly as the night. She dressed in a fresh green fleece top and pants, stuffed her feet into boots rather than running shoes, and was just pulling on her jacket when she heard a scratching at the door.

Startled, she held still and listened to be sure she'd heard something. The scratching came again, quiet, as if whatever was doing it didn't want to create damage.

She opened the door and looked down into Nell's brown eyes. The dog didn't look happy and whimpered a bit, shifting from leg to leg.

Ashley didn't need any more invitation than that. Quickly zipping her jacket, she stepped out into the cold morning and watched her breath create clouds. Nell hurried her across the yard to the ramp. The front door of Zane's house was open a crack.

Even though the dog pushed the door wide-open, she hesitated on the threshold. "Zane?"

She was answered by a heartfelt curse.

Nell whimpered and took a few steps toward the living room, then looked back.

Ashley took the hint, closed the door against the

cold and hurried into the living room. Dismay and
concern immediately filled her as she saw Zane lying
on his side on the floor, the tipped wheelchair not
far away.

"What happened?" she asked, hurrying to him.

He cussed again, and using his arms, pulled himself a few inches toward the old sofa.

"For Pete's sake, Zane, what happened? And let
me help. Stop cussing."

He didn't exactly follow that last order. "I'm too
heavy," he growled. "You can't help. No legs. Just
deadweight."

A pang speared Ashley, but she refused to let sympathy for him get in the way of doing something prac-
tical. "Cut it out. Either let me figure out how to help
or I'm calling the EMTs."

"Hell, no."

She didn't ask him what he was objecting to and
didn't give him a chance to explain it. She had a bit
of temper, too, and it was rising again. Stubborn cuss,
she thought. How long did he plan on lying there?
Nell obviously couldn't lift him.

Thoughts of making sure he had a way to call for
help ran through her head as she squatted beside him.
"Okay," she said. "Listen to me. I can see how strong
your arms are. I doubt you need me to pull on you
to get you to the sofa. What about if I help lift you at
waist level? Or just your legs?"

Mercifully he fell silent and motionless, reflecting
on the problem. "Deadweight," he said. "I can pull it,

but I'm dragging on the rug. I need to get rid of this damn rug. Too much friction."

"Rug, later. You, now. Where should I lift, Zane?" Never mind the question of what he had planned to do about the tipped wheelchair once he reached the couch. They could discuss his planning later. And they were going to, she decided. Absolutely.

"Let me try lifting your legs. Would you be better on your back or on your front?"

Again he was silent for a few seconds. "On my back," he decided. "For now at least." As he spoke, he used one arm to turn himself over.

Now he would no longer be dragging himself, but using his arms to lift and walk backward. She could see the advantages in that immediately.

Kneeling, she got between his legs, slipped one arm under each of his thighs and said, "Tell me when to lift."

He nodded, his expression steely. "Now."

He was no lightweight, and whatever he was doing in physical therapy had clearly kept his legs strong. She could feel the heft, feel the muscles even though they were flaccid. Still, lifting them was not impossible.

He pushed up with his arms and walked back on them while she held his legs. The couch was coming closer. He stopped once, not seeming to be out of breath, so she suspected he was halting for her sake. Since her arms had begun to ache a little, she wasn't about to object.

They didn't talk at all during that break. She wondered if he was feeling awful about needing her help. Well, probably. He was over here trying to be self-sufficient, a self-proclaimed hermit, and now this.

They crabbed their way closer to the sofa until he was sitting upright against it. Ashley shook out her cramping arms. "You know, Zane, you shouldn't be afraid to call for help sometimes."

"Why? Because Nell came for you?"

She sparked. "You ought to be damn glad she did. I have no idea how to get you off the floor, so you better start thinking. As for Nell, except for her you wouldn't be relaxing now."

Nell, who had lain down to watch the process, perked her ears at the sound of her name.

Zane sighed. "You're right. She wasn't supposed to leave me, but I guess she had a better plan."

"Well, since she can't dial the phone…" Ashley crossed her legs, still sitting on the floor, and spread her hands. "Don't you keep your cell with you all the time?"

"I left it on the table. Even I get forgetful at times. Besides, I didn't need to call anyone."

"Of course not. You could have just cussed your way to the couch over the next several hours."

To her surprise he smiled faintly. "Guess so. Thanks, Ashley. You were a great help."

"Was? You still aren't back in your chair, and I have no idea how we're going to manage that from here."

"I can do it. It's not easy. Of course, it helps if the chair is upright and locked."

She looked at it doubtfully. Or maybe amazed. "Really, you can get from the floor into it?"

"Sure. If I couldn't I doubt I'd be able to live alone. I have a seat in my shower. I have a bed with a rod over it to lift myself. I have lots of useful things around here. But some things I still gotta do by sheer strength."

She nodded slowly, wondering at the dimensions of the problems he faced. She suspected she didn't know the tenth of them.

"If you wouldn't mind, turn the chair upright and bring it over here. I'll show you."

So she turned the chair over, brought it to him and watched as he set the locks. "Hang on to the push bars, if you don't mind. Just for some extra stability, but I've done this when I'm all alone, so don't get uneasy."

Then, with a strength and ease she could scarcely believe, he lifted himself on to the couch and turned himself partially over while holding onto the wheelchair seat and pressing on the couch seat. Then, with a great thrust of his arms, he lifted himself from the couch until he was sitting sideways in the chair. Another twist and he was seated properly.

"I can't believe you just did that!"

"There was a time I wouldn't have believed I could do it, either. It's one of the reasons it's so important to keep my upper body in shape." Leaning forward, he lifted his legs and settled his feet on the footrests. "All done."

She was impressed. Totally impressed. She bet

he could have done it without the couch if the chair hadn't tipped. He probably wanted to get to the couch just to get off the floor and decide what he needed to do next.

"So what exactly happened?" she asked, studying the rug. "How did you tip?"

"Honestly? I don't remember. I came back to myself cussing a blue streak with Nell licking my face, and I was on the floor. I must have zoned again. I don't think it lasted very long, though, because my face wasn't totally covered in dog slobber."

"What a description!" Since he was making light of it, she decided to do the same. To a point.

He rolled toward the kitchen, and because he hadn't indicated in any way that she should leave, she followed to make sure there weren't any aftereffects. And to discuss some important arrangements, whether he liked it or not.

She watched him stretch and reach to make coffee and remarked, "I bet the shop class at the high school would love a project of making your kitchen more useful to you. And I happen to know the shop teacher."

He glanced over his shoulder. "I'm managing."

"I can see that. Of course you are. But wouldn't it be nice to have things at a comfortable level? You could do even more then if you wanted to."

He switched on the coffeepot and turned his chair so he was facing her. "Have a seat, Teach. How much are you going to press me about this?"

"I don't know. I just don't see why your life should

have to be harder because you're more stubborn than an army mule."

For an instant she feared she had gone too far. His face reflected no expression. Then a loud laugh burst out of him. "Touché, Teach. Touché."

Relieved, she pulled out the one chair at the table and sat. "We need to talk about some other things. Like you being able to call for help when you need it. I get that you're an independent person. I think you're absolutely amazing. But if something bad happens you have to be able to reach out. So carry your cell with you all the time. Please. Nell knows to come get me, but what if I'm not home?"

His smile faded. She suspected he didn't like to be faced with his limitations, but that was too bad. Now she had to worry about him because he'd refused to let her call for the EMTs for help… She hesitated. "Do you know how often the fire department gets calls for a lift assist? Very often. And they don't mind doing it. If you want, I'll introduce you to the chief and let him explain that they don't mind. You're not the only person in this county who has a problem getting up once they've fallen. Every year someone from the department comes to talk to my class, and every year they talk about how much they like being able to help people."

"I thought they'd prefer a fire."

She couldn't stifle a laugh. "I'm sure they do. Smoke eaters, every one."

But the tension she'd felt growing in him eased. After a few seconds he nodded. "You're right. I'm too stubborn. But I need to be stubborn. There are a lot of things I can do now only because I didn't give up."

She nodded, believing he was right but also hurting for him. He'd once been a SEAL. A powerful man. Someone capable of feats that no amount of training could make possible for just anyone. He'd lost more than his legs. He'd lost his purpose, his identity. He'd had to carve out a huge chunk of himself.

She couldn't imagine what it must be like for him. And she desperately wished there was some way to make it better. So often in life, she wished she could make things better for someone, usually when there wasn't a damn thing she could do.

"I'm sorry," she said finally. "I have no business lecturing you. I'm just worried about you."

"Why in the hell should you worry about me?"

"Because I like you a whole lot."

At that instant, every bit of air in the room seemed to vanish. Their eyes locked, and she wondered if she'd ever breathe again. Her insides turned to hot syrup.

"How much do you like me?" he asked baldly.

She swallowed and managed to drag in some air. Why the heck had she said that? It wasn't necessary, and it opened the door to all kinds of complications she was sure they both wanted to avoid. "Let's not go there," she said, her voice sounding rusty. "You don't want it. You've made that clear. And I'm happy with my life the way it is. Just leave it."

She looked away a moment, deciding to change the topic *fast*. "Julie had her baby, a boy. Trace called to tell me this morning. No name yet. He says that's because he doesn't want his son to be called Trace."

Several seconds of silence followed, then Zane chuckled. "I guess that means Julie does. Most dads would leap at that."

"Would they?" Feeling calmer internally, she was able to look at him again. Why had she danced so close to a possible flame? She decided she'd better think about that later. "So how did you tip your chair?"

"I was probably diving for cover."

That bald statement painted an image so clear in her that it was inescapable. No more intellectual acknowledgment that this guy's psyche had been wounded. No more vague thinking about the PTSD he was dealing with. Somehow those words, when combined with finding him on the floor, made it vivid, extremely vivid. Real. Something she finally had to face head-on. She closed her eyes, absorbing the blow, truly anguished for him.

Where did people ever get the idea that they could send soldiers off to war and get them back completely unchanged, completely unscarred? That they should be able to live that kind of horror and then just forget about it? Because it made the people at home so uncomfortable?

At every catastrophe, counselors were brought in to help people deal with death, destruction and loss. And those were usually instantaneous, or relatively short-term. There was nothing short-term about going back to war time and again. To go on the kinds of missions she suspected SEALs went on. Seth Hardin had mentioned something about six months on and six months off. Like that could erase the six months on mission?

"What are you thinking?" Zane asked. "You're not looking very happy."

"I don't look happy all the time." Then she relented. For once he was reaching out to her, and she didn't want to shove him away. "I just suddenly got hit by reality. The reality you're experiencing. It's one thing to think about in the abstract—it's another to get punched with it."

He frowned and his hands clenched. "You feel punched?"

"By what you're enduring. No intellectual exercise."

"Sorry. I didn't want to do that to you."

"I know. You didn't try. It was just when you said you'd probably been diving for cover...well, I guess some little protective shell I've been wearing just went away. It's okay. I think I needed to lose it."

But he swore, anyway. The next thing she knew, he'd wheeled up next to her and reached out, lifting her right out of her chair and onto his lap.

"Don't wiggle," he muttered. "I don't want to tip again."

She held perfectly still until he held her firmly on his lap, and wondered what she was doing there. She certainly hadn't said anything to make him feel like he needed to hug her, but that's what he was doing. Or maybe he needed the hug.

She felt as if part of her had just been run through a shredder and the results weren't pretty. Just like him, now she was going to have to put herself back together in a new configuration.

She leaned into him, sensing his strength—and not only his obvious physical strength. This man had fought in wars, and now he'd come home with the war on his back and was still fighting. She began to truly comprehend the huge suicide rates among veterans.

"Ashley?"

"Yeah?" Breathing wasn't getting much easier. He could probably hear it in her voice.

"I want you."

Well, that did it. She couldn't breathe at all now, her eyes closed and she softened throughout her entire body as a heavy beating began at her center. "And?" she whispered.

"I shouldn't. I can't be good for anyone right now. You saw why. But I still feel it…"

She was still wearing her jacket, but he pulled down the zipper and slipped his hand inside, cupping her breast through fleece. His thumb stroked over her engorging nipple, somehow extremely sensitive even through fabric. "God, you feel good. Tell me to stop. Please. I don't know how to handle this…"

Something in his tone called her back from the precipice. He wanted her, but he was worried about it. Either he feared the coupling for some reason or he feared the outcome. She managed to pull in a long, shaky breath.

She opened her eyes, reached for his cheek and

turned his head toward her until she could brush a kiss on his lips. Hoping her legs would hold her, she slid carefully off his lap.

She looked at him, sitting there with his face tight, his hands clenched.

"Sorry," he said. "I should have more self-control."

"Don't expect the impossible," she said as she gathered herself and recentered. "I want you, too. But promise me something?"

"If I can."

"Don't tease me like that again until you're ready to go through with it." She zipped up her jacket and settled her knit hat more firmly on her head. "I was going to the store. I want to cook some food to put in Trace and Julie's freezer so they can concentrate on their new son. I'll see you later."

Then she turned and walked out of the house, feeling as if she was leaving part of herself behind. A connection had just been made. She felt as if some cord stretched between them now, and she had no idea whether that was good or bad.

She'd find out, though. She was sure of that.

Chapter 8

Julie came home with the baby a day later. The girls had all gotten together, and the freezer on Julie and Trace's mud porch was full of easy-to-reheat meals. The layette had been taken care of weeks ago, so there was little to do.

Knowing that Julie would be tired and just want some quiet with her family, Ashley didn't hang around for long. Just long enough to add some more oohs and ahs to the ones they'd provided late yesterday and to remind Julie and Trace that they were there if the new parents needed any help at all.

But Trace would be there, Ashley thought with a smile as she headed back to school, her lunch hour over. He'd apparently had some kind of dangerous hush-hush job before but had retired on disability because of his hand. He was looking around for ways to occupy himself, and Ashley thought one had just landed in his lap. Julie wanted to continue teaching kindergarten. House husband, anyone?

Mikey had bubbled during the morning, telling everyone about the service dog Deputy Marcus was going to train for him, and about Zane's Nell. By the time she got back from lunch, the kids had decided to beg her to get Zane to bring Nell to the classroom.

Oh, Lord, how was she supposed to manage that? She could just imagine Zane's reaction. She quieted the excitement as best she could, promising to ask but reminding them that Mr. McLaren wasn't perfectly well yet and might not feel up to it.

Some disappointment tempered their eagerness, and they settled down. Ashley continued with her lesson plan, preceding tomorrow's testing. Then Halloween would take over. Dang, she hoped they forgot their desire for Zane to visit them. She'd been surprised that he'd been willing to meet Mikey, self-professed hermit and all, but he'd done well with the boy, maybe because they had something in common with their disabilities. But a whole classroom of nineteen kids? She wasn't seeing it. Let the approach of Halloween drive everything else from their minds, please. Well, except their schoolwork.

On the way home she bought a large pumpkin to put on her porch, although she wouldn't carve it until the day before. She vividly remembered the year she'd been early and the fruit flies had found her pumpkin. Ugh. Never again.

For the classroom, she had some plastic pumpkins that lit up and a simple skeleton to hang in one corner. After the tests. She also stopped at the bakery to order a couple dozen decorated cupcakes for her students. Bad, she knew, but she compromised by having them made with pumpkin bread and skipping the icing in favor of some plastic pumpkin faces to be pressed into them. After all, part of her job was supposed to be teaching nutrition. Kids would eat cupcakes and candy regardless, but she could err a little on the side of "not too bad."

She used the side door of the house after her shopping, entering from her driveway through the mudroom. Nice that these older homes still had them. She couldn't imagine how difficult it would be without one. Even as just one person, she tracked in plenty when it was rainy or snowy. Nice to confine it to one place and leave her boots there. Easy to clean when it dried.

She unloaded groceries and the pumpkin, checked her messages, and then decided to give Julie and Trace a quick call just to see if they needed anything. Trace answered, sounding a bit tired. "Not much sleep. All's quiet now, Julie is snoozing and I'm next in line. I thought babies slept a lot."

Ashley suppressed a laugh. "They do. Usually. Sometimes, though…"

"Yeah, Julie thinks the baby's aware of the big change from the hospital to here. Maybe it's draftier or colder. I don't know. Are babies that aware?"

"Probably more than we want to think. No cussing, Trace."

It was his turn to chuckle quietly as he hung up.

Then Ashley realized she had surprisingly little to do. Review sheets had been the work in class today, and they'd all been corrected on the spot, to help prepare for tests.

She could evade herself no longer. Plopping down in her living room, she thought of Zane again. Of being on his lap, of his bold move that had left her weak with desire, followed by his declaration that she should stop him because he was no good for anyone.

It bothered her that he felt that way, but he might be right to the extent that he wouldn't be good for *her*. She was also aware of her own tendency to develop a strong emotional attachment with any man she had sex with. She'd figured that one out a long time ago and reordered her priorities accordingly. Relationship before sex.

So what was happening to her now? She didn't need all the problems with this spelled out for her. Definitely not. He wasn't well because of his PTSD. His paralysis…well, she felt that wouldn't necessarily be a problem for her. It hadn't bothered her yet except for what it meant to him.

But falling out of his wheelchair because he was diving for cover? A whole different ball of wax. That would be part of any relationship with him. Before she took a single step toward that, she had to check herself, to be sure she wouldn't hurt him by being unable to live with his disability.

That was hard to know. At best right now it would be a guess, but the only way to be sure would be to live with him. Ha! Talk about a recipe for disaster.

Anyway, he'd said he wanted her, not that he wanted a relationship with her. Big difference. If he wanted a one-night stand, he was going to have to look elsewhere, because it wasn't going to be her. Some women might be built that way, but she knew for sure she wasn't.

Sighing, she got up, changed into more casual clothes for cooking and decided to make herself a small casserole out of smoked turkey, boxed stuffing, green beans and leftover mashed potatoes. Thanksgiving in a bowl. With some turkey gravy from a jar, it was scrumptious and easy.

Which got her to wondering what she was doing for Thanksgiving this year. One of the gals always invited her to join their families, and usually she accepted, bringing all the pies and a relish tray. Connie had three kids, so the spread was always big, especially if the rest of the Parish family was eating at her place. But sometimes they went to Micah Parish's ranch for the dinner, and then she wasn't invited. Nothing was meant by that. It was a huge family gathering, and there were so many members of the Parish family she often felt out of place even at Connie's house.

Maybe she should think about making the dinner herself. Marisa and Ryker had no one else except their baby. Julie wouldn't have time or energy even to think about it. Yeah, she could do it here. She started thinking about how many of her friends to invite and how many she could fit in her snug little house. Man, they'd be shoulder to shoulder. It might be fun.

She'd just finished layering her casserole and sprinkling some fried onion rings on the top when she heard a familiar noise at her front door. Nell.

Wiping her hands on a towel, she hurried toward it, grabbing her jacket along the way.

Yup, it was Nell, looking impatient yet strangely happy. Almost grinning. Surely she was misreading the dog.

"What happened now, girl?"

But there was only one way to find out. She followed the dog at a trot and entered the open door of Zane's house.

"Zane?" she called out.

"In the kitchen."

She headed in there and found him to be perfectly all right. In fact, he looked about ready to start cooking. "You're okay?"

"I'm fine. Why?" Then he looked at Nell. "You didn't," he said to the dog.

"She did," Ashley confirmed.

"She's not supposed to do that, dang it. She's never supposed to leave me unless I need medical help. What's gotten into her?"

"Beats me." Ashley had a suspicion, though. Not that she'd say it out loud. She looked down at the dog, who was now sitting, grinning and swishing her tail hopefully. "Have you made dinner yet?" she asked.

"Just starting."

"Well, stop. I made a casserole big enough for four, and I was about to pop it in the oven. Let me just bring it over and bake it here. Meanwhile, you can try to figure out why Nell is interfering with your life."

"Humph," he grumped. "Maybe she thinks I need to change it."

"Don't ask me," Ashley said lightly. "Be right back." And there she went, forgetting all her good resolutions about involvement and relationships. Sheesh. Maybe she needed a head doctor.

Zane stared in perplexity at Nell. She'd never gone off like this before. He guessed she liked Ashley, which made the dog a great judge of character, but he didn't want her messing up Ashley's life by running over to get her every time she felt bored.

"Are you bored?" he asked the dog. As if she would answer. Well, he couldn't blame Nell if she occasionally wanted a different face in this house. He wasn't the greatest company. Or maybe he just needed to get her out for more walks. It would probably do both of them some good. He'd been confining his walks to the dark hours so he wouldn't run into a lot of people. It was safer than facing the questions or concern and sympathy. Safer than listening to people recall the athlete he'd been so long ago.

Considering he still hadn't figured out all his triggers, the less he had to do with people, the better. He didn't know if they still rode people out of town on a rail, but he'd sure as hell been evicted from his apartment.

He didn't want to make a scene in the street, upset people, maybe scare kids. He also didn't want to become the dangerous hermit that kids crossed the street to avoid and eventually built horror stories around.

He sighed, thinking he was going to have to parse things out before too much longer. And maybe that's all Nell was trying to tell him. *Figure it out, jerk. There are answers.* Maybe he'd just given up looking for them. That eviction had hit him in the gut in ways that still surprised him.

Ashley returned, bearing a medium-size glass casserole dish, covered in aluminum foil. "Nell," she said. "Close the door."

Nell took the order like the champ she was. Ashley turned on his oven to preheat it. "I call this Thanksgiving in a bowl," she said. "Some of my favorite holiday foods in it, including smoked turkey."

"Sounds great." He hesitated, aware that he needed to be sociable. It got even harder when he was beginning to crave the woman with all of his body that was still capable of feeling anything. "You know, Ashley, I never heard about your parents. Did they move away?"

She sat facing him and shook her head. "The weirdest thing. They went to the Texas coast for a vacation. Mom got caught in a riptide and Dad went to rescue her and... The riptide had just started, they were beginning to put up the warning flags, but too late for my folks."

She looked away, and he hated himself for asking. "I'm sorry. Truly sorry. And sorry that I stirred it up."

"You didn't. It's been hard, I still miss them, but it was eight years ago, Zane. I've learned to live with it."

"It's hard when it's so unexpected like that."

"Maybe not as hard as watching your parents suffer from terminal illness," she answered, thinking of his parents, both of whom had been claimed by different kinds of cancer just a year apart. "I don't know," she added. "I can't compare. Maybe there is no comparison."

The oven beeped that it had preheated, and she went to put the casserole in. "Timer?"

"On the counter, probably in the vicinity of the wine bottles. I haven't used either of them."

She found and set the timer, then said, "Why so much wine? Especially if you don't drink it?"

"Mom loved to cook with it." He smiled. "There was one period when I was young that I got awfully sick of every meal tasting like burgundy. I don't know what got her started on that kick, but apparently she stuck with it after I left, because there are a few unopened bottles there."

"The others could be vinegar by now," she remarked as she returned to the table.

"It's possible. I haven't felt an urge to find out." He shook his head a bit. "When did you buy the house next door? You decided not to keep the ranch?"

"Wasn't much of a ranch anymore," she said. "Mom and Dad sold it maybe ten or so years ago to a neighbor. No son to leave it to—I wanted to teach—not ranch, and they started wanting to do a bit of traveling. So they bought that house."

He nodded slowly. "I hope they got more trips in than the one to Texas."

She smiled and he was relieved to see it. "Yeah, they did. Europe for three weeks, a cruise that Mom swore was the most relaxing experience of her entire life, Mexico…they stuffed in quite a bit once they were free to do it and had some extra money."

He smiled back at her. She actually sounded happy that her parents had done those things, even if the last trip had resulted in their deaths.

"I suppose," she said slowly, "that you've seen a lot of the world."

"Not the kinds of places you'd take a vacation." Far from it. There were pockets of hell on earth. Places he'd never wish any human being to be caught in. Unfortunately, people were there. He yanked himself back from the edge. He didn't want to flip out again, not in front of Ashley. She'd seen the results once, and he knew he'd disturbed her.

He needed to stop thinking about her, anyway. Yeah, he wanted her. But he had nothing to offer anyone except a broken body and a broken mind. He should keep reminding himself of that before he hurt someone. However, there was no escaping the fact that being a hermit was going to be a little difficult.

Nell had brought Ashley over here on purpose. Zane had absolutely no doubt of that. Then there was the Mikey kid, and his need for a service dog. Meeting that boy had pierced him. Imagine being that young and facing life with quadriplegia. He reckoned he was damn lucky himself.

"Zane?"

"Hmm?"

"You were frowning. Is something wrong? Do you want me to leave?"

"God, no!" His reply was vehement.

Her brows had knit. "Did I do something wrong when I mentioned that you must have seen a lot of the world?"

He shook his head. "Not you. It's okay. I just started thinking about things I shouldn't think about, so I put it away, thought a little about you, then about Mikey. I'm fine."

She smiled, evidently willing to move on. "Mikey's something else, isn't he?"

"I know he's awfully positive, or at least he was at Cadell's place. And he made me feel that I was truly lucky."

Her face shadowed a bit as she nodded. "I can see that. Every time I try to have a pity party over some ridiculous thing, it doesn't take long for some thought to pop into my mind to remind me how lucky I really am." She smiled at him. "I have a Pollyanna brain."

He laughed at her description, and the laughter felt good, easing the windup he'd felt growing and had been stepping down on. *As long as you can laugh...* He couldn't remember where he'd first heard that, but he suspected it was true. And he'd seen people laugh in the most god-awful circumstances imaginable. "So what do you have pity parties about?" he asked.

To his surprise, she blushed faintly. "Well, that's the thing. When I get that way from time to time, it's usually because a lot of small stuff has gone wrong and I feel like the universe is piling up on me. Now you take each item individually, and it feels really stupid. But if Murphy's been hanging around for a few weeks, making every blessed thing go wrong..." She shrugged. "I especially love the periods where I seem to be all thumbs and keep dropping things. Or the ones where I mess up every recipe I try to cook. I know I'm just distracted and not paying attention..."

"Why do you get distracted?"

She tilted her head to one side, just a bit. "I have students. Some of them don't always do well. Some of them struggle. Some of them are living with abuse. Now that last one, the instant I get proof, I can do something. But the others? I worry."

"You have a gentle heart." It was true, he thought. She had a bit of temper, which he'd seen on a couple of occasions, but mostly she was good-hearted. Gentle.

He remembered her gorgeous hair from when they were in school ages ago, but the years between them had made it impossible to know her. Besides, he'd been busy with his own life, full of sports and a girlfriend, and she lived on a ranch, which kept her away from many school activities. Not that he'd have been much interested in someone so much younger. Years were a great separator at that age.

But those years no longer mattered, and as far as he could tell she had grown up to be an exemplary woman.

As he sat there with her, however, her presence

kind of pushed him back in time to high school, to his life before.

"You know, I've mentioned this before," he said abruptly, "but I can hardly remember the kid I was before I left."

"I'm not surprised. That was a while ago. I don't remember much of high school, either."

"I'm not thinking so much in terms of things that happened. Some events stand out in my mind, of course, but it's more who I thought I was. What was going on inside my head."

"And how it took you to the SEALs?"

"Bingo." He shook his head a little. "That wasn't my conscious intent, as I told you. Nope. I was offered a slick scholarship after I completed my training. Looking back, I sometimes wonder if that promise would have panned out regardless. Anyway, I guess it's impossible to reenter my head all those years ago."

His change in course had been troubling him lately, mostly since coming back to Conard City. He remembered that when he'd passed all the testing and had been admitted to training—which had been an extreme test itself—he'd written home about it. The answer from his mother had said more than words. She'd congratulated him then added, "I hope you made the right choice." That could have meant a lot of things, so he'd just assured her he had and then had lost himself in one of the world's toughest training programs.

By the time he emerged, he'd been cemented to his comrades and the SEALs as if they had been welded into one. Which they had been. The bonding had run deep. Being invalided out had left him feeling as if his skin had been ripped off.

All those years, all those faces, all those voices—a brotherhood. Which was not to say some of the guys couldn't be jackasses, but…they were still welded together. It had felt unbreakable. Then, *bam*! It had been broken.

"I think," he announced suddenly, "that I may never figure out why I changed my mind about what I was going to do in the navy, but I know what it cost me to have to leave."

"I can't imagine."

He looked at her sweet face surrounded by those copper curls and said, "What if you couldn't teach anymore? Suddenly. Without warning. No adjustment time."

He watched her face change, suffusing with horror or loss, he couldn't tell which.

"You *do* understand," he said quietly. "It would just about kill you, wouldn't it? Well, I'm dealing with that, too. It's gotten a lot easier, but I'm still dealing with it. I guess that's why I keep trying to figure out why I did it in the first place. Like that will answer anything."

Then she said something that reached his walled-off heart. "You know, I don't think it would hurt me as much to have to give up teaching as it hurt you to leave the SEALs."

An ache he usually suppressed blossomed in him. "Why?"

"Because I'd still have all my friends and other activities. You lost it all, Zane. All of it. That's worse than I can imagine."

Mercifully, the oven timer dinged and Ashley rose, turned it off and hunted for hot pads or oven mitts. She found the mitts, a very pretty pair, in a drawer near the oven.

Where was this conversation going, she wondered. She was beginning to get uneasy. He was looking for an answer she wasn't sure he'd ever find, but at the same time he was reaching out to her in a way that almost hurt. As if in some way his loss was becoming hers.

She decided to change the subject quickly. "Halloween this coming week. Do you want to hand out candy?"

"I think the kids would be scared to come to my porch. I'm a stranger in a wheelchair."

"With a dog," she reminded him, then remembered her class. "Oh, God."

"What?"

His expression was curious, no darkness there. Well, what if her question totally changed that? She almost didn't ask, then realized she'd just about promised her kids she would.

"You can say no," she began. "But my class listened to Mikey this morning and they were begging me to ask you to come talk to them and tell them about Nell. Actually, to bring Nell to school."

To her amazement, his face didn't turn to stone. In

fact, he didn't even frown. "So I have Mikey to thank for Nell's sudden popularity with the fourth grade?"

Ashley laughed as she pulled the casserole out of the oven. "I guess so. But like I said, you can say no."

"Well, I can hardly send Nell alone. We're joined at the hip."

She placed the casserole on the counter. "It needs to set for a few minutes. Are you volunteering to come meet nineteen rambunctious nine-and-ten-year-olds?"

"Not yet, but I'll think about it. I enjoyed meeting Mikey." His eyes settled on her. "Kids are different, Ashley."

"How so?"

"So innocent. So blunt. So curious. Even though I was deemed a problem for kids at the apartment house, I never held anything against the kids. Never."

"They probably weren't behind the attempt to evict you," she said forthrightly. "I know people just a bit. Adults create more serious problems than most kids ever will."

She started hunting for a serving spoon and plates. She could have asked him, but she needed a moment to collect herself. He'd shared some very personal stuff with her, and now he was actually thinking about coming to visit her class? The avowed hermit?

Nah, he wouldn't do it. He wanted to be left alone, and the stimulation of a classroom full of kids might not be good for him. She hated to think how he might feel if he had an episode at the school. Heck, she'd

feel awful herself if something triggered him because
of her request.

Well, she'd kept her promise to her kids. She'd
wait a few days and then ask him what he'd decided.

She put the plates on the table, moved the casserole to the center and began scooping some onto his
plate. "Say when. Turkey, green beans, gravy, mashed
potatoes, stuffing."

"Sounds fabulous and I'm starved."

So she gave him several large scoops before giving herself a much smaller portion. For a beverage,
she gave them each a glass of ice water. "Don't burn
your mouth."

He laughed a little. "Do you know how long I went
wishing I had something hot enough to eat that it
could burn my mouth?"

Then he surprised her by reaching for her hand.
"I think I need to be thankful. Can you say grace,
please?"

Bowing her head, trying to ignore a totally inap-
propriate response to his touch, she complied with a
prayer she had learned in childhood. When she looked
up, his eyes were still closed.

"Thank you," he said. "I keep forgetting I have
blessings to count."

Tears burned in her eyes, but she refused to let
them fall. She didn't want to make him uncomfortable, but he was reaching deep inside her, touching
her in ways she realized she had never been touched
before. He was winning a place in her heart. Well,

her friends and her students had a place there—why shouldn't Zane?

Turning her attention to her meal, she assured herself it would be all right. Just friends. He'd let her know he wanted her, but both times he'd backed away, so he could be trusted not to try to take it further.

In the meantime, better to think of other things. "So, Halloween?"

"I need to get some candy."

She smiled, glad he was going to meet the area kids. "Just don't wear a scary costume."

"What?" He widened his eyes humorously. "You don't think I'm scary enough just as I am?"

She had to laugh. "Actually, you're not scary at all. I imagine you could be if you wanted to, but you're not scaring me."

"Good," he said and let it drop.

"Then there's Thanksgiving," she continued. "I've pretty much decided I'm going to have a few friends at my place, rather than wait for them to invite me, which they usually do. Connie will be tied up with her big family, but there's Marisa and Julie and their husbands and babies. Amber and Wyatt probably can't come, because he's a judge and he always has a big bash at his place..." She realized she was rattling on and looked up. Zane was smiling faintly at her. "Sorry."

"No need. The casserole is fabulous. It's like most of a Thanksgiving meal."

"That's the idea. Anyway, Zane, you're on the invitation list if you decide you want to come. Up to you.

I don't think it's going to be a whole lot of people, but I'll keep you posted so you can decide if you'd feel... uncomfortable."

"Thank you." Then he laughed again. "You and Nell. You're trying to change my life."

"Sorry."

He shook his head. "No need to be sorry. Since I got here, I've been feeling a whole lot less like I just need to lick my wounds."

Her heart leaped. "You're feeling better?"

"I don't know. I just know for a long time, especially after the eviction, I felt caved in on myself. Maybe I'm past it." He looked to the side. "What do you think, Nell?"

The dog woofed.

"I thought so, since you keep running over to bring Ashley here."

"Or maybe she could smell what I was cooking," Ashley joked. "Is she allowed people food?"

"Not usually. Okay, I cheat once in a while," he admitted.

"I think that's part of having a dog. I'll give her just a bit of this, if that's okay?"

"Let's skip it. Onions and garlic, in sufficient quantity, could make her sick."

She bit her lip, thinking. "I don't want to trespass with Nell. She's already doing something she shouldn't, like coming to get me when you didn't need help. I guess I shouldn't even feed her a dog biscuit."

Only then did it occur to her what she'd done. She'd invited Zane to Thanksgiving at her house, a friendly gesture but poorly thought out. He hadn't answered, and while she hadn't expected an immediate answer, for the first time she realized what he was probably thinking about: How the heck was he going to get into her house? No ramp. Which would mean asking for help, and she'd already seen how little he liked to do that.

"Oh, man," she said quietly, forgetting her meal.

"What?"

"I just thought… My house isn't very accessible. I didn't mean to put you on the spot, Zane." She lifted her gaze to him and found him still smiling faintly, almost gently.

"You are the most thoughtful person," he said.

"Clearly not. I put my foot in it."

He just shook his head. "Nope. Let me think about it, okay?"

"Absolutely." But now she felt miserable. She'd practically thrown his disability in his face with an invitation she shouldn't have made impulsively. Dealing with her kids, she had to be more forward thinking than this.

He surprised her by reaching for her hand again. "Stop it."

"Stop what?"

"Feeling bad for inviting me. You know what you just did?"

"Yeah." With no way to take it back. No way to truly apologize for reminding him he could no longer just go anywhere he wanted, that he sometimes needed help. She ought to staple her lips together.

"No, not what you're thinking," he said quietly. "You just treated me as if I didn't have any disability at all. Like you were sitting with a normal friend at this table."

Mild shock rippled through her. What a remarkable way to respond to her ham-handedness. She turned her hand over to clasp his fingers. "You're amazing."

"Hardly that. But thanks for letting me know you don't constantly see that I'm crippled." He squeezed her hand and let go, picking up his fork again.

Ashley sighed, feeling relieved and hoping he wasn't just being nice. "I hate that word. *Crippled.*"

"Well, it's true."

"I still don't like it."

He arched a brow at her. "Why dance around it?"

"I'm not dancing around anything. I just don't like that word. It always strikes me as somehow cruel. You can use it if you want. I don't like it."

"I've been living in a very different world these last eighteen years. Very little nicety."

"Then I must sound like a prude." That also didn't make her feel very good. Was she becoming the stereotypical schoolmarm?

"Not at all. I was just explaining. I told you I'm rough around the edges. Most of my social skills were practiced among a group of men. Gotta tell you, it's a different world."

She believed him. At last she let go of her concerns and decided to just enjoy the meal. For a guy who hadn't wanted to be bothered at first, he was being extraordinarily friendly to her. Just enjoy it.

"Did you ever marry?" he asked her as he continued eating.

"Nope."

"Surprising."

"Why? I swore off men a long time ago. Not worth the effort. Relationships break up and it's painful. Then there was the time I learned I was the other woman just a bit too late."

"Man," he said. "That stinks."

"It sure did." She managed a laugh. "Best to avoid those complications. So what about you?"

"A few casual relationships. I wasn't the type to rush into anything, and I was seldom home long enough to take it slow. By the time I shipped home, whoever she was had usually found someone else. Can't say I blamed them."

"Why not?"

"Because waiting for me was like waiting for bad news."

Chapter 9

Waiting for me was like waiting for bad news.

Zane's words followed Ashley through the next few days. Through the tests, through the grading, through the building Halloween excitement as her class helped her decorate the room and special arrangements were made for Mikey to supervise some of it because he couldn't physically help.

In the streets outside, Halloween erupted into the world on nearly every front porch and front yard. While no one yet went all-out on the holiday—nothing like Christmas—nearly everyone found at least a small way to make the already special day more special for the trick-or-treaters.

In the early twilight, electric pumpkins leered their crazy smiles at passersby. Ghosts made of sheets with straw heads stuffed inside hung from tree limbs. An occasional house sported orange lights. One house in particular had a yard full of cutout black cats in all sizes made by the home owner.

And keeping the lid on her kids was getting more difficult. Their excitement was contagious. Her spirits lifted with theirs.

Then there was Zane. She hadn't seen him or heard from him since the night she'd brought the casserole over. Now it was the weekend again, with Halloween on Monday evening. Like every other teacher, she warned her kids not to stay out too late. The next day was a school day.

Some of the stores downtown set up to hand out candy as well. The hospital would x-ray the candy and apples for free.

So everything was right in the world. Except she hadn't heard from Zane. Nell hadn't come over, so she had to assume he was okay. She still wanted to set eyes on him.

She carried a bag of groceries and another bag full of candy for the kids into the house and decided she needed to carve her pumpkin at last.

But even as she put everything away and brought the pumpkin inside for carving, she couldn't get her mind off Zane.

She scolded herself for her foolishness. She had no claim on him and no business worrying unless there was a reason. As she put the pumpkin on her kitchen counter, however, she realized what was really bothering her. They'd had a very frank discussion over that casserole, and part of it had been about her making a mistake by inviting him to Thanksgiving and him calling himself a cripple.

While she didn't ordinarily obsess about things, she was obsessing now. No amount of telling herself to think about something else was really helping. Zane danced around in the back of her mind all the time. If she had half a brain, she'd just stay away until the fascination passed.

The weekend coffee with her friends evaporated. Connie was on duty all weekend. Julie was preoccupied with her new son—who had apparently been named after his father, over Trace's objections—and Marisa said she and Jonni had a cold and Ryker was taking care of them.

It was one of the few times Ashley regretted being single. The feeling didn't last long, however. All she had to do was remember her past mistakes. They stood in her mind like large yellow warning signs on a road.

All things considered, she'd gotten off easy. No divorce, no kids from a broken home. Yeah, it was okay.

But as she looked at the pumpkin and thought about hanging out the decorations she'd pulled down from the attic and placed in the living room, she decided she didn't like the faint anxiety that was nagging at her because of Zane. She was worried. What if something had happened and Nell hadn't come to get her? Or she'd been at school and…

"Oh, cut it out," she said to her empty house. She grabbed her jacket, picked up the pumpkin and went next door. She'd say hi, ask if he wanted to carve this pumpkin because she could get another one, and then maybe she could settle down.

She spared only a moment to recognize that she might be getting herself into some heavy emotional ground here but assured herself she'd get past it. She'd gotten past stronger emotions than this strange, unfulfilled attraction.

It would certainly help to learn he was doing just fine without her company. Yeah. That was what she needed to discover.

Zane opened the door to her, Nell at his side and wagging her tail.

"I came to visit the dog," she said, "and I wondered if you might like to carve a pumpkin. If you don't already have one."

Zane looked down at Nell. "You have a fan club," he told her, then smiled at Ashley. "Come on in. Isn't that the pumpkin I saw on your porch?"

"Yeah, but I can always get another one. How have you been?"

He let Nell close the door behind her, and she stole a moment to fill her eyes with him. Every time she saw him, he seemed to have grown more attractive and the pull she felt toward him was even stronger. Maybe this visit hadn't been such a great idea.

"I was just making some coffee, if you'd like some."

"I'd love some." She let him lead the way to his kitchen.

"Just put the pumpkin on the table. I was going out to get candy and maybe a pumpkin this evening."

So he was doing fine and hadn't needed anyone. She almost blushed in private embarrassment, glad that he couldn't guess she'd been obsessing about him all week.

"I've been okay," he said. "I accepted an invitation to the vets' group. I'll go next week."

And he was putting his life back together. What did he need her for now?

"Your friend Seth is pretty persuasive," he continued as he ferried cups of coffee to the table. "Other than that I've been doing a lot of thinking."

"Good thinking?"

"Necessary thinking. It's been a week since I had an episode. That's made it easier. Time to try to find a way to make a life, I guess."

Her heart leaped with furtive hope. Maybe he was finding something good in himself. She took the chair and watched him roll over to the table. "So…what's changed?"

"Since I got shipped home, it's been like…well, I don't know how to explain it. It was tough, sure. A lot to deal with. The PTSD especially unnerved me. Even when I was okay, I was worrying about the next bout. So I guess I hunkered down. Tried to build a bunker, not that it could keep anything out. Then the eviction. I decided I was through. Finished. Done."

She nodded, understanding what he was saying. "Very hard."

"Ah, it was just cowardice."

She gasped. It pained her to hear him talk about

himself that way. "No, not really. Not after all you'd gone through."

"Cowardice," he repeated. "Hiding from the world? Hiding from my problems? If there's one thing I should have learned as a SEAL, it's that life isn't fair, that turning your back on the mission is desertion and…" He shrugged. "Not to say I won't backslide, but I've got a new mission. Take this mess and make something useful out of it."

The smile that filled her face also filled her heart. "Oh, Zane, that's wonderful!"

"Remains to be seen," he said gruffly. "But I'm beginning to believe I had my head screwed on backward for a long time."

He'd had an awful lot to deal with, she thought. Of course he'd had trouble sorting himself out. She remembered how impressed she had been when he'd said he saw his paralysis as a challenge. Apparently, he'd decided to take on everything else the same way.

"Unfortunately," he said, "I can't batter my PTSD into submission. But I think if I find a way to keep busy doing something productive, away from obvious triggers, I might have less trouble with it."

"I don't know enough about it to judge, but it sounds good to me." When he offered his hand, she took it and tried not to think about how badly she wanted to settle herself on his lap and feel his arms around her again. His hand on her breast. His mouth on hers.

Whoa! This guy was living next door to her. No getting away. She'd better be careful.

But deep inside she'd begun to have feelings she hadn't had in many years. Excitement. Anticipation. Unspoken hope that something would happen. Like a teen in the throes of a crush.

It had better wear off, she warned herself. Zane had his mission to work on, and she didn't want any problems for either of them.

"So your kids want me to bring Nell to school?"

Surprised, she felt her jaw drop a little. Really? But what if he changed his mind? He could in an instant if he started to have problems. But that was true in any case. Pleased that he'd offered, cautious that he might not be able to do it, she expressed appreciation but was careful not to nail him down. "Would you? They'd love it. But there'll be a lot of racket…"

"I think I told you I like kids." His smile was crooked. "Just no fireworks."

She got his meaning. "No fireworks," she promised, trying to sound casual.

Then he leaned forward in his chair, bringing their faces closer together. "Do you have any idea how easy it is to talk to you? It's been a long time since I shared so much with anyone. Somehow with you it seems natural."

Warmth suffused her. "What a compliment." But she wasn't thinking about that. She was *feeling* his nearness, something very different indeed.

"With you," he said slowly, "things just spill out of me. And it's good, because when I hear myself saying them, it's as if stuff falls into line."

"Well, I've often found that saying something out loud makes me realize how stupid it is."

He cracked a surprised laugh. "That, too. But you're special, Ashley."

Now she blushed, something she hadn't done in a long time. "Not me," she said.

He shrugged. "You don't have to believe me, but it's not like I haven't met women since this happened. Do many women want to indulge in noble self-sacrifice?"

She drew a sharp breath, horror stealing through her. Could he really believe...? She felt as if he had just stabbed her. Wounded her. Her stomach turned over, but then anger arrived. "That's not me," she said sharply, pushing back from the table. "Sacrifice yourself!" Which was a terrible thing to say when she considered how much he had sacrificed for his country, but damned if she was going to wither. If he felt that way...

"Not you," he nearly snapped. "Sit down, damn it. And I guess you're not always easy to talk to after all."

Ouch. She winced and tried to let go of the anger as she slowly settled into her seat again, reluctantly willing to give him a chance to explain.

"Are you always so defensive?"

Oh, man, she wanted to sink. She didn't see herself that way, she didn't think she was, but she had just nearly erupted because of a general remark that didn't apply to her at all. At least not directly. She hadn't thought of herself as someone to see a slight in everything, but now she wondered. Worse, she knew from experience that a defensive person could be almost impossible to deal with.

It took her a moment to answer. "I never thought I was before." The ground under her feet seemed to be shifting. Could it be true?

"So it's just with me?"

That was nearly as unsettling as the idea that she might always be defensive. "I don't know. I'm sorry. I've always had a bit of a temper, but not over just anything."

"Temper is fine," he answered. "I have my share. What I was trying to get at was when I was in rehab, then later when I had my own place before everything went south, a number of women seemed interested in me. Crazy, considering I was a mess."

"I don't think that's crazy," she said quietly.

His gaze snapped to her face, but instead of responding to her comment, he continued. "Anyway, one of them, a volunteer at rehab, seemed to take a real shine to me. It was nice for a while. I was getting pretty good with the chair, so they started giving me passes, and we went out for lunch, occasionally for dinner. But after about two months, I discovered something, and there was no way I could argue myself out of it."

"What was that?" Her mouth was still dry from the horror and brief flare of anger, her heart still squeezed with pain—whether for him or herself. With one remark he'd caused her self-perception to teeter. She reached for the coffee mug to drink, to wet her mouth again. Man, this guy drew feelings out of her far too easily. Being around him seemed to put her on an emotional roller coaster.

"I discovered that I was the cross she wanted to nail herself to."

She stopped breathing. Shock froze her insides. Had he just said…? "How?" she whispered.

"I overheard her almost bragging to her friends about the sacrifices she made for me, about how glad she was to make them, and none of it was about me, but all of it was about her. Her self-created halo was almost blinding."

Ashley looked down. She couldn't even speak. It was awful, just awful, to consider how that must have affected him.

He astonished her, slamming his hand down on the table. "Sorry," he said when she jumped. "But I don't want to be an object of pity, and I don't want to be someone's path to sainthood. So I guess I'd better get it together."

She gathered herself, ignoring the ache he'd made her feel, the ache for all he was dealing with, the ache because there was really nothing she could do, short of finding a magic wand. In just a few minutes she'd ridden a whole host of strong reactions, and now her hands trembled a little, her fingers felt cold, her mouth as dry as sand. What was going on here? She felt out of her depth, as if she might drown at any moment. Matters were shifting rapidly, and she was no psychologist to offer help or even judge what was happening here.

Slowly, she raised her head. "When you got here, all you wanted was to be left alone."

"True," he acknowledged.

"What changed?"

"You think I'm blowing smoke?"

She shook her head quickly. She was certain he was telling the truth as he saw it right now. But it seemed so sudden! "Not at all. It's just such a big change in such a short time."

"It's the guy I used to be stepping forward again." He drummed his fingers briefly. "Enough of this crap. Feeling sorry for myself, hiding out, fearing another episode. I wasn't built to live in fear. I wasn't built to avoid challenges. I never used to. The only thing that's changed is inside me, and I don't like it."

That might be simplification, but she didn't want him to suspect she didn't believe what he was saying. It would be so easy to offer a casual response that might leave him wondering if she doubted him. *Careful choice of words*, she reminded herself. *Very careful.*

"Give yourself some slack," she said eventually. "Good heavens, Zane, you've been through a terrible amount of trauma. The war, your paralysis, your PTSD. How could you not want to hunker down for a while? How could you not *need* to? You're not Superman, and even he had his Fortress of Solitude. I think your reaction was probably very normal."

"Maybe." His gaze grew distant. Ashley immediately looked down at Nell, but she seemed calm and unworried. For a while, nobody spoke. Ashley felt as if an emotional whirlwind had just blown through her. The change in him seemed startling and sudden to her, but she had no idea how long he'd been approaching this moment.

Just because he'd claimed to want to be a hermit when he first arrived didn't mean he hadn't been thinking about all of this for a while. Not the man he used to be? Of course he wasn't. He'd been through hell. She suspected the can-do SEAL was rising in him, though.

He'd said this was like a mission. He'd never turned his back on a mission, and some of them must have been terribly difficult. If seeing it in that light helped, then he should go for it.

Maybe it *was* a mission. She put her chin in her hand and closed her eyes, considering it. He was still young, with a lot of years ahead of him. If seeing himself as soldiering through—as he had so often in the past—helped him, good for him. It might actually be the most positive way for him to deal with everything.

She had to give him points for determination. She'd been quite impressed with his attitude toward his paralysis, and now he was stretching that to cover the rest of his life. A challenge.

She opened her eyes and found that he didn't appear quite so far away. Okay, the guy had been a hero and had evidently become one the very hard way more than once. He had the grit and determination to pull this off, if anyone did.

"I like the way you think," she offered.

His eyes trailed back to her. "I was just remembering times when I did things that initially seemed more impossible than this. I mean, what's this except living? Everyone has to do this, and for some it's harder. I'll see where it goes." Then he smiled faintly. "Does everyone in the world dump on you this way?"

"I don't feel dumped on. I feel honored." True, she did. He'd been incredibly frank, offering a trust that struck her as breathtaking. He'd practically opened his soul to her.

"Anyway," he said. "Pumpkin. Class to meet Nell. Cadell called this afternoon and asked if I could bring her out to his place for some additional work with Mikey's dog."

She almost gaped and felt a small bubble of laughter in the pit of her stomach. "You did get dragged into it."

"Into the world. I hope I didn't kick and scream too much." But he smiled faintly. "Anyway, want to come with me to see Mikey's dog tomorrow?"

She didn't hesitate. "Sure. I love Cadell's dogs. If he was just handing them out, I'd take one. Maybe his wife, Dory, will be there. She's new in town, too, but nobody sees much of her. She's a computer geek who works odd hours, I understand. I'm told she insisted on Cadell keeping the ostriches."

"You mentioned that." His brows lifted. "I still think it's weird that he has them."

"So does everyone else. Join the crowd. Pumpkin?"

He glanced at the digital clock on the microwave.

"It's dinnertime. How about we take care of that then decide about pumpkins and candy tomorrow?"

Just like that, he'd cemented them together that evening and the next day. A long way from being a hermit. She wished she felt as confident in this extraordinary change.

Being a SEAL had made Zane hypersensitive to some things. The tone of a voice. The faint microexpressions that continually crossed a face. It had been necessary to his survival and worked often even when he couldn't understand the language. Reading his fellow SEALs had become second nature.

So he'd read Ashley and had no doubt that she was uneasy right then. She'd met a grumpy man who said he just wanted to be a hermit, and now here she was, a couple short weeks later, with a man who was busting out of his hermitage.

Of course she wondered if something was wrong with him, if the change was only temporary. Outwardly she'd handled it well, but inwardly she was struggling, probably wondering when he'd next withdraw or grouse at her over nothing.

But the truth was, the self-declared hermit had been the temporary him. A reaction to being evicted. A conscious decision to make sure something like that never happened again. He'd had enough. Life was difficult enough these days without accusatory neighbors. So he'd gone into an emotional crouch, and he rather despised himself for it.

No, he didn't want to be scaring people with his

PTSD. Losing it wasn't good for anyone, himself included. But it happened, and it would continue to happen for the rest of his life, although with less frequency, he hoped.

When he looked at Ashley, he saw a woman who had accepted him as he was. She'd come over when Nell went to fetch her. She'd helped him get up off the floor and scolded him for refusing to ask for help. She'd had to guts to ask him to help with Mikey's dog, and then the guts to ask him to visit her classroom.

He was just glad she hadn't seen him in one of his total wipeouts, cussing and swearing and trying to dodge bullets that weren't there. He suspected she'd handle it as well as the rest, though. She'd certainly handled finding him lying on the floor because he'd been trying to dive for safety.

Remarkable woman. Sexy woman. Still, he was too messed up and didn't want to mess her up as well. Although she *had* invited herself over because she hadn't seen him all week. Worried about him. She didn't need that, either.

Dinner. He'd mentioned that, hadn't he? The question was what to do about it. He certainly didn't want her to think he expected her to cook for him. "You said there was a pizza place somewhere?"

She nodded. "Just east of the city limits. A popular teen hangout." She screwed up her face a little. "I may have taught most of those kids and I'm sure they wouldn't appreciate me showing up there. But the shop *does* deliver."

He liked that idea. He didn't want to disrupt enjoyment for a bunch of teens, either, and him showing up in a wheelchair might dampen their fun. "What do you like on your pizza?" he asked.

"Anything except pineapple and anchovies."

"Ah, no pineapple pizzas for you."

She laughed, and he was delighted to see it reached her eyes. "I might like it with another name," she admitted. "But that's not at all what I think of when I think of pizza."

"Me neither," he admitted. "Is this pizza good?"

"Good enough. It might disappoint someone from New York or Chicago, but at least the crust rises. None of that cracker-type crust."

"I suppose the pepperoni is good everywhere. What about veggies?"

Zane enjoyed chatting with her about something so innocuous. Comparing the relative merits of different vegetables on a pizza seemed like the safest and most comfortable place he'd been in a while. When they finally agreed on what they both wanted, she pulled out her cell phone.

"Observe," she said lightly. "I teach nutrition as part of my syllabus, and yet I have the pizza place on speed dial."

He laughed. "Pizza's probably not as bad for anyone as some other things."

"Like soda pop full of sugar," she answered drily.

"Or the candy we're about to hand out by the ton on Monday."

He watched her laugh, the sound easy and full. Dang, he liked everything about this woman. He liked the way temper sparked in her blue eyes when he annoyed her. He liked the way she kept acting as if he were perfectly normal even though he was quite sure he was not. And he liked the way she seemed to have completely moved past his disability.

He was paralyzed, obviously. He knew that it usually disturbed people, made them uncomfortable. But from the very start, she hadn't seemed at all uncomfortable. Just concerned. Her concern wasn't a terrible thing, certainly nothing he minded, especially since she didn't overdo it.

But she was drawing him out of his self-preoccupation, too. Because of her he had other things to think about, even some things he could conceivably look forward to. He was nervous about meeting her class, because he didn't want to have an episode in front of them. They might be scared. But there was Nell, he reminded himself, kneading the dog's neck. She'd alert him before he completely slipped away. He'd probably have time to leave the classroom.

Of course, if he pulled himself out of his self-imposed pit, he'd have to figure how he could be productive for the rest of his days. He'd always been productive, at least until his wounding, and he couldn't stand the idea that he might spend the rest of his days in this wheelchair, in this house, and not do one useful thing for someone else.

Ashley finished ordering the pizza. He'd pushed his credit card over to her, but she'd ignored it and used her own. Man, he could probably afford this pizza better than she could on a teacher's salary.

"Got any super career ideas for a paralyzed vet?" The question popped out of him. He expected her to kind of shrug and say she'd have to think about it. She surprised him.

"Sure," she said. "A temporary one, anyway."

"What's that?"

"Let my friend's shop class come over and turn your kitchen into a project. They'd learn a lot, and you're not the only person in this county who could use the kind of modifications you'd need. You could even show them, so they wouldn't be guessing."

"Why would they want to do that? It's a big project."

"Alex—that's the teacher—has been bemoaning the fact he doesn't have any really big projects for them. The auto shop? Sure, there's always a car that needs working on. But cabinetry and things like that? He says he's too limited, the things they can do are too small. And these are students who want a future working with things like this." She hesitated. "You'd probably have to pay for the materials, though."

"That wouldn't be a problem," he admitted. He'd saved most of his pay over the years and had a steady disability income, much of which he hadn't needed to spend during his time in the hospital and rehab.

"So, tell you what. I'll bring Alex over some time and you two can hash out the possibility."

Zane felt himself smiling faintly. This woman didn't let the moss grow. She moved immediately. He liked that. "Still, that's hardly a career," he reminded her.

"Stopgap," she admitted. "But I'm sure there are plenty of other things. Alex might have some ideas. You need to meet Jess McGregor. He was a medic in Afghanistan and lost his leg. Now he's a physician's assistant running the minor emergency clinic at the hospital. He'd probably have some good ideas, too."

His smile grew. "You're going to save me in spite of myself."

She flushed. "Sorry. You asked about careers, and my mind and mouth took off."

"It's okay." For some reason it was more than okay. She felt like an ally, which he liked, and not like a taskmaster pushing him, which he'd resent. "Maybe you just helped me get it all in focus when you asked me to help with Mikey's dog. I like you, Ashley. It's not just my dog that has a crush on you."

He watched her eyes widen, heard her indrawn breath, and he enjoyed it. But the doorbell rang. "Pizza," he said, letting the sudden sexual tension slip away.

Best for both of them, because he might never be good for anyone. But for a few seconds there it had felt great.

Chapter 10

The next morning Ashley awoke with an unusual sense of anticipation. Last night after they finished the pizza, they'd agreed to meet again this morning, first to go to see Cadell and the dogs, then to go to the market for candy, a pumpkin and whatever else they needed.

So a routine chore, grocery shopping, felt like a genuine outing to her, and she was definitely looking forward to seeing Mikey and the dogs. But mostly she was looking forward to the time with Zane. When he'd first arrived here, she'd never expected anything like this. Never thought he'd want to be out and about and certainly never dreamed that he'd want to spend time like this with her.

A niggle of concern troubled her as she showered,

dried her hair and dressed. The man she had talked to might be ephemeral. She didn't know him well enough to know if he had major mood swings, ones that could change him suddenly. She wasn't worrying about his PTSD. That was something to be dealt with when it happened. No, she was wondering if he might be an emotional chameleon. The change still seemed fast to her.

But he'd said he'd been thinking about it for some time. Maybe getting out to Cadell's place and meeting Mikey had simply brought to fruition a change he'd been wanting to make for some time. Maybe it had finished the process of deciding he could still be a useful member of society.

Boy, feeling that he was useful had to have taken a ding, dealing with the problems he had. There must have been times when he'd felt caught in a nightmare, paralyzed, haunted by the war in ways he couldn't control.

But he'd said last night that the man he used to be was talking. That actually made sense to her. He'd taken some terrible blows, but he was still, somewhere deep inside, the guy who had been a determined athlete and an even more determined SEAL.

She decided that when she went over there, she would suggest he put his medals on display so he could remember the guy who'd done all those daring deeds. Maybe that would help him reclaim himself.

Then she stopped. No, she was not a psychologist. Those medals might cause him more pain. He'd already told her that he'd wanted to throw them away and had kept them only because an older vet had told him he might want them someday, and that they were the only reward he was going to get.

Which was pretty pathetic, when she thought about it. How could a box full of medals make up for losing your legs and part of your mind? Honestly, nothing could make up for that.

Glancing at her phone, she saw it was time to grab her parka and go to Zane's. Maybe it was time to keep her mouth shut and let him lead the way. He was the only one, after all, who had any idea where he wanted to go from here.

As she climbed the ramp, Zane's front door opened. She saw a happy Nell first, her tail wagging, then Zane as the door opened wider. He smiled, too.

Autumn had truly begun to move in, whispering of winter. The wind gusted just before she reached the front door, blowing fallen leaves around.

"Hurry in," Zane said. "Ice cube season is on the way."

"It feels like it," she agreed as she stepped into the warmth of his house. "I hope it doesn't snow and interfere with Halloween."

"Don't you keep up with the weather?"

"Only when I'm concerned." The door closed behind her, sealing her in warmth.

"I'm compulsive about it. Years of experience and training, I guess. So I can proudly tell you there's no snow in the forecast and we might see a slight warming on Monday. In the meantime, button up. Coffee?"

She hesitated. "Isn't Cadell expecting you?"

He shook his head. "Mikey has a cold. His mom's worried and doesn't want to bring him out, so no practice today for his dog. Add to that, Cadell said he'd been called in early to cover for another deputy, so there's no point in us going out there at all. I'm sure Nell would have loved running around in the paddock and I wouldn't mind a closer look at those ostriches."

She laughed, tossing back her hood and unzipping her parka. "Not too close."

"Well, I'm not sure I'd want those huge beaks too close," he agreed. "So, coffee? Did you have breakfast? I baked some cinnamon rolls from freezer dough."

"The roll sounds wonderful. I had an egg and toast, but I'm not too full to eat one of those."

"Then the store," he said as he wheeled into the kitchen. Today he wore loose jeans and a light gray sweatshirt. For the first time she wondered how he managed his clothes, but she didn't ask because it seemed intrusive.

She reminded herself of the jujitsu this man had performed to get himself up off the floor onto the couch and then into his chair. He probably had as many moves as a cat by now, or he simply wouldn't be able to live alone.

Once again he ferried the coffee to the table for them, remarking that caffeine was a good antidote to the cold. "I ought to know. I relied on it in quite a few cold places."

The rolls were already on a plate in the center of the table, and a moment later he set out two smaller

plates. "Feel free to eat with your fingers. Do you
like to butter yours?"

"I like them just as they are," she said, helping herself to one roll. At least they weren't gigantic. Sinful,
but not gigantic.

Nell settled on the floor between them, gnawing
contentedly on a rawhide bone.

"When does Carol come to clean for you?" she
asked, to make conversation that would keep her from
voicing errant thoughts, such as that he looked more
delicious than the rolls. In fact, she wished she had
the nerve to just sit on his lap and see what happened next.

Bad idea, she scolded herself. Entanglements too
often produced pain. Besides, he'd already made it
plain that he had good reason to doubt a woman's interest in him. It must have made him feel just awful
that a woman he'd been dating had only wanted to
offer herself as a sacrifice. Lord! He deserved so
much more than that. For example, a woman who
didn't think living with him was a painful or difficult task.

So far she herself hadn't seen a single reason to
feel that way. He had some tough problems to deal
with, all right, but they were tough for *him*. Someone
who cared about him would share his pain, not seek
praise for putting up with it.

She stifled a sigh, for fear he would question her
about it. Simple truth was, she honestly liked this man
a whole lot. She wanted to get to know him better.
She wanted to spend more time with him. Then there

was the sexual attraction that stayed with her even when she was elsewhere. Zane just kept popping into her head, occupying her thoughts and making unexpected appearances even when she was focused on something else, like teaching or grading or planning her lessons. If she wasn't careful, she was apt to let thinking about him take over her life.

Maybe, she thought as she licked her fingers delicately, she ought to just have sex with him and settle that issue. Maybe when the heated fog of desire wasn't winding its way around every cell in her body, she could break free of the fascination.

"You're smiling," he said.

"A silly thought, one I'd rather not share." She wiped her fingers on a napkin and reached for her coffee. "What kind of shopping do you need to do today?"

"Only a little. Carol does that for me. You asked, so... She comes for the big cleaning on Mondays, then drops in a couple of mornings a week to take care of odds and ends and see if I need anything for the larder." He gestured to a magnetic pad on the refrigerator. "She saves me a lot of trouble, because unless I get a basket for my chair, I can't carry much, and even with a basket I wouldn't be able to carry much more. Sometimes I think I need a little wagon as a trailer."

The way he said it, the image it created, made her laugh. "That would be a sight. A little red wagon."

He smiled. "It would work, though. I've tried pushing a cart. I can, if I'm careful. But then there's the problem of putting items in it. Not everything can be tossed like a baseball."

That made her laugh again. "You're remarkable," she said honestly. "You really *do* take that chair as a challenge."

"No other way to look at it," he said firmly. "It's the rest of it that I've let overwhelm me. That has to stop."

She didn't know how he was going to stop it, but she figured he was probably determined enough to do just about anything he put his mind to.

A short while later they left for the store. He parked in a handicapped space near the front doors, one with the hash marks on the correct side of the van for his lift. She stood there waiting for him and Nell and looked at the car parked in the next slot. No handicapped plate. No handicapped hang tag.

She suddenly felt embarrassed that she'd never paid attention to that before, but at the same time realized she wanted to have some words with whoever was parked there. Really?

When Zane reached the ground and closed up his van, he wheeled toward her, Nell at his side. "What are you so fascinated by?"

She pointed. "Do you see a hang tag? Or a handicapped plate?"

He lifted a brow. "It's probably on the dash."

So she marched to the front of the car and looked. "Nope," she announced. "You go on inside. I want to talk to this person."

He tilted his head, studying her. "Ashley, you don't have to."

"No, maybe not. But there are plenty of people

around here who need these spaces. I admit I never really paid attention before, except not to park in them. Now...well, I'm offended."

"Firebrand," he remarked. "Look, you don't know who it is. The person might give you trouble. It could be someone nasty."

"Oh, I'm sure it's someone nasty," she said, putting her hands on her hips and ignoring the way the chilly breeze nipped at her cheeks. "If they're not entitled to this parking space, they're nasty."

"Or just thoughtless, or in a hurry, or trying to avoid freezing. Let it go, Ash."

She faced him. "Why? What would you have done if you hadn't been able to find a space? Parked out at the end of the lot where you could get two spaces together? And what happens if you come back and someone's filled the space where you need to use your lift? You'd be stuck."

He seemed not to have an argument for that. She felt a small bit of satisfaction that she'd made her point. "Look, I'm not out to embarrass this person if they just forgot to put up their tag, but if they couldn't park two slots farther away because they're lazy? Yeah, I want to embarrass them."

Then she saw that he was pressing his lips together while his eyes danced. "You think I'm funny?"

"I think you're an avenging angel."

She frowned. "I'm no angel. Like I said, this is something I'd never really thought about before. But now that I have...well, I'm going to do something. You and Nell go inside before you get cold."

"I'm not going anywhere without you," he retorted. "And I'm sure Nell feels the same. We'll turn into icicles together while we wait."

She huffed a bit, her annoyance refusing to abate. "Doesn't it ever make you mad when you see this? Doesn't it bother you?"

"It used to bother me a whole lot more. These days…well, I try not to think about it."

"But it's so wrong! Yeah, I'm angry."

"Righteous anger," he remarked, pivoting his chair and rolling toward the door of the store. "Let's go." Nell trotted at his side, leashed. Ashley realized that she didn't often see Nell on a leash. She was almost certain the dog didn't need it, either.

"Why did you want me to let it go?" she asked curiously as they hurried toward the store.

"Because you didn't have any idea what kind of person you'd be dealing with, which is dangerous, and because I learned a long time ago to pick my fights. Besides, it was probably just thoughtless. A lot of people don't get it. Then there's the possibility that it's some young mother with a small child, who saw two empty spaces were together and she thought it couldn't hurt to take one to avoid the cold. Or what about someone temporarily on crutches who wouldn't get a hang tag?"

Ashley flushed faintly. "So I overreacted?"

"I wouldn't say that. It's just that I've been dealing with this longer than you have. There were times when I was embarrassed when I gave someone a hard time over it. You could say I learned the hard way."

"I wasn't being very charitable," she admitted, a hot sliver of shame striking her. She always tried to be charitable, but there she'd been, criticizing someone she didn't know who might not deserve it. Who might have special circumstances of their own.

"You got angry on my behalf. Far be it from me to criticize you for it. It's just that I've been dealing with this a lot longer, and while some people are simply jerks, most people are innocent of any intention to create a problem. They're only going to be a minute, or it's raining cats and dogs, or..." He shrugged as the automated doors opened before them. "Lots of reasons it's hard to get really angry about."

She could see his point of view, of course. She'd never been an unreasonable person, but being out there with him, thinking of Mikey also facing such problems...well, it had frosted her, obviously.

Time to ease up and enjoy the company, and it wasn't difficult to do. Zane seemed in reasonably good spirits, as if announcing his intention to change his life around had made him feel good. Nell added to the enjoyment, drawing a lot of attention. She seemed to know it and was almost prancing beside Zane.

A number of people welcomed him home but didn't try to delay him. A few kids wanted to rush Nell and had to be held back by their parents with the advice, "Never run up to a strange dog, and never bother a working dog."

Which led to some interesting conversations started by Zane. He *did* like children, it seemed, and he had no problem with halting and chatting, backing up their parents' warnings, explaining why service dogs shouldn't be distracted. "If she's paying attention to you, she's not taking care of me, and I could get sick."

That explanation worked like a charm with the kids, who immediately settled down. A couple of times, Zane called Nell to order, telling her to "sit and mind." If she'd been growing distracted, it ended there. Instantly her gaze fixed on him.

It wasn't a major shopping trip, which was good, because by the time he'd had a few conversations with the kids, Nell's attention to him was changing, and she butted his arm carefully.

"Time for me to go," he said.

Looking into his eyes, Ashley didn't question it. He had what she had heard called *the thousand-yard stare*. "Can you make it to the van?"

"Yeah. Yeah."

"Go. I'll check out. I won't be long."

She watched him start rolling toward the door, Nell at his side. The dog was no longer prancing proudly. Now she barely took her nose off his arm.

Time to hurry, Ashley thought. Not that there was much. Big bags of mixed candies to pass out, a jug of cider and pumpkin pie that Zane had wanted, and some Polish sausage that Ashley had wanted. The butcher here made his own, and it was mouthwatering. On impulse, she grabbed some hoagie buns deciding to make sausage dogs for dinner for both of them.

As long as Zane felt better.

* * *

Zane struggled to hang on to the present while the past kept trying to push its way out of the graveyard where it never seemed to stay buried for long. Nell helped, nudging him, whining at him, forcing him to focus on getting back into his van and closing the door. He didn't move to the driver's seat, though. Not yet. He had to be sure he wouldn't start the engine when Ashley climbed in the car and suddenly be driving down some mental road where every oncoming car posed the threat of a bomb or gunfire.

In his brain, images overlaid each other, not quite like double vision because the images were different, but more like two films one on top of the other. His ears seemed to be hearing sounds that didn't exist—explosions, gunfire, screaming.

Nell's whimpering and even a few barks reminded him of the world that was actually around him, keeping him from slipping completely over into the past.

Anxiety rode him like a devouring monster. He gripped the arms of his chair until his fingers ached. *Stop it*, he yelled inwardly. *Stop it. That's gone. Done. No more.*

Then Nell jumped up into his lap and began to lick his face with her rough tongue. That reality began to trump the old ones that were trying to take over.

"God, girl, you're going to leave me raw!"

Nell woofed just as the passenger door opened and Ashley slid groceries onto her seat and looked in.

"How are you?" she asked, twisting to look at him.

"Coming back," he answered cautiously. He hadn't

really slipped in time, but he'd come close, and he wasn't absolutely certain he was steady yet.

"Let me put these groceries in the back. We can sit here as long as you need."

It was a good thing that he couldn't feel Nell's weight on his lap. She was by no means a small dog, and it still amazed him that she could manage to balance this way on his thighs. Now she was sniffing him like an anxious mother dog, checking him out. She must be able to smell the changes in him. He could think of no other way she could be so on top of his moods.

Releasing the arms of his chair at last, he wrapped his arms around his dog, buried his face in her neck for a moment and gave thanks for Nell.

And for Ashley, who didn't hover over him, never once tried to deprive him of his own agency. He'd had people try to do everything for him, like a certain ex-girlfriend, and he'd hated the smothering. Ashley didn't offer to do a damn thing, not since the very beginning, but he also knew from experience that she would help when needed.

He hated needing help. Sometimes there was no escaping it. Trying to be independent could reach a level of foolishness if he wasn't careful. Like that rug in the living room. There was no way he could remove it himself; he'd have to get someone in to do it, so that if he ever tipped again for some reason he could slide across the floor. That rug was rough enough to make it difficult.

That was when he knew the difficulty had passed.

Ashley was climbing in the front passenger seat. When he let go of Nell, she dropped to the floor of the van and didn't try to poke him or lick him again.

It was over. As his episodes went, it hadn't been that bad. He'd never completely lost touch. As for the trigger...maybe all the people in the store? Maybe he'd become stressed by the attention, by talking to the kids? If so, that was something else he needed to get over. He guessed he'd learn a lot about his limits when he spoke to Ashley's class.

He was able to drive them home. Ashley brought his groceries to him and placed them on his lap, except for the cider jug. "I should carry this in," she said. "If it slips Nell could cut her paws."

"Or try to drink it," he said lightly. "You going to stay for a while?"

"I still need to decorate my place. I've got my pumpkin hollowed out, but it needs a face."

He took that as a friendly farewell and figured he deserved it. "Let me know what I owe you for the groceries."

She waved her hand, dismissing it. Then she smiled, that beautiful smile that warmed his heart. "Do you like roasted pumpkin seeds?"

"Love 'em."

"Then I'll bring some over later if you want. I toasted them last night. And I have stuff to make us dinner if you like Polish sausage."

Inside, she put the jug of cider on his table, then took her own candy out of the bag and left with a friendly "See you later."

The house was once again empty of everything except him and Nell. For the first time since his injury, the solitude felt lonely.

He looked down at Nell. "She just left. How can I already miss her?"

Nell had no answer except a sweep of her tail.

A couple of hours later, Zane decided he couldn't stand it anymore. He needed activity, exercise. The trip to the store hadn't been enough. He needed a change of scenery, too.

The instant he started to pull on his jacket and gloves, Nell quivered with excitement, her tail waving so quickly it almost blurred.

"Yeah, you need it, too, don't you, girl?" Zane hardly needed her response.

As soon as they stepped out the front door and he closed it behind them, he received a surprise. Ashley was hanging a Halloween flag from a branch on the tree in his front yard, a black one with a grinning skeleton printed on it.

She heard them and peered over her shoulder. Since she was standing on a ladder, he called out, "Be careful!"

"I am," she answered. "I hope you don't mind, but I figured I didn't need it all in my yard."

He didn't mind. He was kind of pleased. "How much of that do you have?"

"Just a few more things. Want some cobwebs?"

"If it's not too much trouble."

"I'm going to hang them, anyway."

Zane looked down at Nell. "Amazingly enough, I'm looking forward to Halloween."

Apparently feeling his happiness, she swept her tail over the porch boards.

Once the flag was hanging and tossing in the chilly breeze, Ashley climbed down and looked at it. "Good enough," she said, eyeing it. Then she turned toward Zane. "The skeleton glows in the dark. Much better at night. Be right back."

He watched her dash across to her house. Her own yard was evidently complete, with a ghost hanging from one of her trees and rippling very nicely. Cobwebs draped from her porch rails, not overdone, just a bit here and there. And her pumpkin, endowed with a smiling face, now sat on the top step, ready to be lit.

A few minutes later she came back carrying a clear plastic bag full of white stuff. "Where would you like it?"

"The same as what you did at your place. It looks good on the railing."

She smiled. "Also easier to clean up. Some of our neighbors here will put it everywhere, and I swear some of it winds up serving as snow at Christmas because it gets so tangled on things. Not that we need fake snow then. At least not usually."

She climbed the ramp, joining him and Nell on the porch, and studied the task before her.

"I can help," he said quietly.

Her head whipped around. "Of course you can! I'm just so used to doing this by myself."

She handed him the bag after pulling out a handful for herself. "I think it's got another year left in it. See what you think."

She went to the far end of the porch so he headed for the other. Of course he could do this. It might not look that good because he lacked practice, but he'd get it good enough.

When he pulled a ball of it out and tried to tug it apart, it spread into a filmy netting. Not exactly spiderwebby. More like a cobweb, but clever. He hung it in patches over his end of the railing, and at the bottom of the bag found a huge rubbery spider. He held it up.

"Where's this live?" he called to Ashley.

"Anywhere you like, but not too close to your steps. Some little kids get really frightened."

So he tucked it into some of the webby stuff and wheeled back to take a look. "What do you think, Nell?"

Nell cocked her head, giving him that "Are you out of your mind?" look she sometimes achieved. He laughed.

Ashley joined them a minute later, scooping the remains into her plastic bag. "All done," she said brightly. "You must be getting cold. I'm feeling it myself."

"I was just getting ready to exercise with Nell. Around the block a few times, as fast as I can safely go."

She leaned back against the porch railing. "There's a special wheelchair for racing, right? It would let you go faster?"

"In the road, and yes, there are special chairs. For now I'm content with the sidewalks, although I've begun to wonder if I might be able to use the track at the high school or college."

"I have no doubt. But go for the college. They have that new material, whatever it is. The high school has cinders, remember. Give 'em a call. I'm sure they'll say yes. I see people out there jogging all the time, and they're not students. It's probably okay unless a team is training."

"Thanks." He began to roll toward the ramp. "Wanna come with?"

He was glad when she smiled and said yes. Maybe too glad. He'd better watch himself with this woman. All he could do was blight her life.

Ashley enjoyed the brisk walk with Zane and Nell. Zane kept up a reasonably good speed, one that qualified as exercise for her. Cars drove past, people waved, but except for a few kids outside playing they didn't meet anyone on foot.

"I guess it's too cold," Ashley remarked.

"Doesn't it get a lot colder here? I seem to remember…"

"Then you probably remember how few people take a stroll come winter." She laughed. "Shoveling snow was it. Car the rest of the time."

He smiled as she jogged his memory. The track events he had participated in happened mostly in the spring and mud, but come late October even the football team was getting ready to wind down its season.

Hot drinks, warming capes, helmets over knit caps, and some days even ski masks. Yeah, he remembered.

They crossed a few streets and rounded a different area of town before they turned to come back. It was definitely growing colder, and Zane noticed that Ashley coughed a few times.

"Are you okay?" he asked.

"Dry, cold air. No biggie. When I get back inside, my nose will start running. I hate that."

He laughed and pushed up the pace a little bit. Nell was enjoying every minute of being outside. She kept turning her head his way, as if checking that he was okay, then she'd continue prancing at his side, a brisk pace that she carried off with amazing grace. He wondered if even in his salad days he'd run as gracefully as the dog.

"So," he said to Ashley, "got any big dreams for your future?"

"Dreams?" It seemed to him that her step hitched just a bit. "Not really. I'm saving for a big vacation eventually, but mostly I'm pretty happy with my life. I'll probably be teaching fourth grade until they force me out the door."

He laughed quietly. "So nothing short-term?"

She didn't answer. But then, slowly, she turned her head and looked at him. Their eyes locked, and it was his turn to hitch as he rolled forward. Nell looked back, astonished at the sudden slowing.

But he couldn't help it. He'd been attracted to this woman since the instant he set eyes on her, and the attraction hadn't quieted one bit. Now, as their gazes met, he felt an electric zap that ran through every cell in his body, at least the ones that could still feel. He felt himself hardening in response and had a hazy thought that it was good his jacket covered the evidence.

But then he noticed that she had stopped as well and that her breathing had become more rapid. She felt it, too. Felt the electricity between them, the heightening desire, the need to venture into uncharted waters to find the waiting treasure.

Oh, God, he thought, dragging his gaze away. Trouble. Bad for both of them. What woman would want to take on his problems? And he wouldn't ever want to treat her in any but the most respectful and caring of ways. No one-night stands with this woman. His regard for her was too high. Plus, he had a little self-respect of his own.

They moved again toward his house and reached it with only a little more light conversation. But he still didn't want to say goodbye.

This woman had made it possible for him to connect again. Admittedly, it was only one connection, but it was a great experience in that it didn't involve another vet like himself. Those connections were easier to make, having a shared experience. Ashley was so very different, and her difference seemed to lighten him.

A regular woman liked him and treated him like he was capable. Worth a celebration, he thought. Plus he suddenly couldn't bear to see her walk away. "Come in for some cocoa?" he asked.

Chapter 11

"Sure," she said without hesitation. "Cocoa sounds great. Listen, I bought some Polish sausage and buns at the market. Want to join me for dinner?"

He paused as he let Nell push the door open for him. "I assume you mean here."

"Well, unless I could levitate one of your ramps over to my place, I guess so."

She said it lightly, as if the fact that he needed ramps, lifts and wheelchairs was a negligible matter.

He made instant cocoa from individual packets. As he boiled water in the microwave, then added a dollop of cream to each mug to make it richer, he thought about the thousands of times he'd cooked his meals over small cans that burned with a tiny flame, everything coming out of a packet, most of it needing only a little water. And the coffee crystals he seldom wasted the time to heat.

"Man," he said suddenly. "Too much time in the field. I need to remember how to cook normally again."

"I use this cocoa, too. No apology necessary."

She'd doffed her jacket by the time he turned his chair and brought her mug to the table. Then he got his own and joined her.

"So," she asked, "have you thought about modifying your kitchen? I mentioned it to Alex, and he was ready to jump on it. Great experience for his students."

He half smiled. "You know, when I first came here I'd made only the absolutely essential changes."

"Why?" Her brow creased.

"I thought I'd told you. Because I didn't know if I'd decide to stay. Bathroom, check. Bedroom, check. Front-loading washer, check. But kitchen? Big expense unless I was going to stay. Plus, doing it up for me would make the house unattractive if I decided to sell."

Her smile faded. "I didn't realize that, Zane. I'm sorry if I've been pushing you. I just assumed…" She trailed off and looked almost sad.

"You assumed I'd come home for good. Why wouldn't you? I never told you otherwise."

"I see." She averted her face and drew a long breath.

She felt bad, he realized with astonishment. She didn't want him to leave. Seriously? He cast his mind back, wondering what he might have done to make her give a damn what he did, whether he came or went. Little enough, he decided.

"I didn't say I'm leaving," he said. "I haven't thought much about it since I met you. I'm not thinking about it now. You did something special, Ashley."

She turned her head. "Me?"

"You. You made me feel like I really have come home. I see that I haven't gotten out and made a whole lot of friends or anything, but...you've still made me feel like I'm home. And welcome. So...no, I'm not leaving."

Her expression lightened. "I'm glad to hear that. And you have reached out, you know. Look what you're doing for Mikey. You've decided to join the veterans' discussion group and come to my class and talk to students. Those are big steps for you, aren't they?"

He held out his hand, palm up, an invitation, and felt her smaller one as she laid it there almost trustingly. Her fingers felt a bit chilled as he squeezed them and let go. "Drink that cocoa and warm yourself up. And yeah, they're big steps, but it annoys me because they shouldn't be."

He liked the way her eyes softened. "Zane, I told you before, cut yourself some slack. You're doing all that now."

"Cutting myself slack was something I never did in the SEALs and I shouldn't do it now. I'm only thirty-seven. A lot of years ahead. I can't let them be pointless ones."

"But it takes time to set a whole new course in life."

He laughed without any mirth. "It didn't take much time to change my entire life."

She pressed her lips together and looked down at her mug. "You're right. It didn't. But maybe this is a little different."

"Only in that I have the luxury of picking and choosing and moving at a snail's pace if I choose. Look, Ashley, I didn't mean to sound like I was dismissing you. I've still got problems to deal with and I know it. Look at the way I had to leave the store this morning."

She lifted her head. "Was it too noisy?"

"That wasn't it. I was thinking about it before we took our walk. I think it was the chaos."

"Chaos?" She frowned.

This time his laugh was more genuine. "Chaos," he repeated. "I'm sure it doesn't look like that to you, but when I get into new situations I naturally grow more alert."

"I think most of us do."

He shook his head a bit. "But not high alert, life-threatening alert. That in itself isn't bad. It's a trained response—it's saved my life and the lives of others. But when I get in that mode, I'm trying to keep my eye on everything. Threat ready. No threats in that grocery store. Logically, I knew that. But being hyperalert and trying to keep my eye on all the moving people... I guess it started to overwhelm me."

He let her absorb that while he considered making more cocoa. Maybe coffee. Certainly something warm, because this house felt drafty today. Maybe he ought to check the heat, but just as he had the thought he heard the rumble of it turning on, then a little while later warm air blew through the vent. Okay, heat was fine.

And Ashley was still silent. He was beginning to worry that he'd said something wrong. Maybe told her too much. He shouldn't be talking to her about these things, anyway. She was a civilian. There was an unspoken rule among vets that some things should never be discussed with those who had never walked in their shoes. The world's innocents would never understand some things.

Finally she looked up. "Thanks for the explanation, Zane. I think I understand better now. I couldn't imagine what had troubled you. Now I know."

"And next time there'll probably be a different explanation. You know, you'd think after all this time I'd know where my triggers are. Guess not."

"It doesn't matter, does it?"

Surprise rippled through him. "Of course it matters."

"Why? I mean, some obvious things can be important to avoid, but you've tried avoiding damn near everything, haven't you? How are you going to avoid the grocery? I just mean…" She trailed off, biting her lower lip. "Sorry, I'm talking out of turn."

But she wasn't. He reached out, seizing her hand this time and holding it tightly. She'd opened a new way of thinking about all of this, and he was turning it around, absorbing it, trying to decide exactly what it meant.

"You might be right," he said after a few minutes. "I'm going to think about it. For example, I had to leave the store, but Nell was enough to keep me grounded. Next time maybe my reaction won't be so strong."

She nodded, listening.

"I can't avoid everything…" But he trailed off. Her blue eyes met his again, and that electricity zapped between them once more. In that instant a switch flipped and he forgot nearly everything else. He wanted to resist, for her sake, but when he saw her chest rising and falling with quickened breaths, read his own hunger reflected in her face as if her whole being was leaning toward him… What if he was imagining it?

But the words slipped past his guard. "Ashley… I want you."

"I want you, too," she breathed. "So very much. I've been arguing with myself, but it won't go away."

He nodded, swallowing hard. "Are you sure you want to deal with this?" He patted his useless leg. "There's nothing graceful, nothing…"

She squeezed his hand hard until he stopped speaking. "I'm sure if you could you'd want to just close the door behind us and leave everything to the imagination."

Surprised, he almost laughed.

"However," she went on, clearing her throat a little as her voice grew rusty, "I'd rather not close the door. I'm not asking for grace. I'm asking for you. Do you trust me enough?"

Nobody had ever put it to him that way before. Did *he* trust *her*? The tables were turned.

He knew how awkward this could be. With his saintly girlfriend, he'd had to go alone and get undressed and into bed before she wanted to have sex. She didn't want to see his disability laid out before her in all the complications it created with a simple thing like dressing or undressing.

For her he'd been fine in his wheelchair. Then she could smother him. But at points in between…

Hell, why was he thinking of that woman now when here was Ashley telling him she didn't care about all that? She wanted him the way he was. Well, he was damn well going to find out right now.

He backed out from the table and around to her side. "Sit on my lap?" he asked.

She didn't hesitate, rising from her chair and sliding into his embrace. Her arms wound around his neck.

"I can feel you," he murmured, closing his eyes, savoring the sensations, treasuring them. "In important places, I feel you."

"I feel you, too," she whispered. "I love it. I've been thinking about this for so long…"

It felt like forever, though it hadn't been. It was as if this moment was destined and he'd just been waiting. "Hang on," he said gruffly. Then he started rolling them toward his bedroom. That wasn't graceful, either. He hadn't widened halls or doors, but he'd gotten pretty good at three-point turns. As they bumped around, Ashley gave a little laugh but never loosened her hold on him.

"I like this," she said.

"Clumsy."

"No, more space needed, that's all." Then she set him afire with a kiss to his cheek that trailed to his lips. For a few moments the wheelchair stopped in the hallway, and as impatient as he was, he didn't care.

Her tongue sought his, tasting of chocolate, warm and enticing, promising greater wonders to come.

"Slow down," he said as he pulled his mouth away at last. "Or we'll be done before I get us to the bedroom."

"Then we'll just have to do it again," she answered. Her voice had grown husky with desire, a sound that pumped his passion even higher. *Do it again?* Oh, yeah.

The bedroom was a revelation to Ashley. A steel contraption rose from the floor and reached over the bed. Her first thought was *monkey bars*, but that wasn't it at all. As she surveyed it, she realized they were bars to help him get into and out of bed, to lift himself up and move around a little. Probably he used them to help him dress and undress.

Movement would be important, she thought. Until Mikey she'd never understood, but his mother had confided one of the reasons they wanted a better wheelchair was because of pressure sores. Mikey couldn't stay in one position too long.

It must be the same for Zane. He needed to get out of his chair, to get into a position that didn't put all his weight on his buttocks and legs. If he got a pressure sore, he'd probably never feel it. Later she'd ask him how often he needed to move.

"Ashley?"

She stopped staring at the apparatus and turned her head to kiss his cheek again. More important matters to think about right now, and desire that had quieted for a minute now began to hammer at her again. Screw the bars, screw everything—she wanted this man with every cell in her body.

"This will be awkward," he murmured.

"Stop worrying about it. Want help undressing? I wouldn't mind that at all." A quiet little giggle escaped her at her frankness.

He laughed briefly. "I like hearing that, but…" He paused. "If I'm going to dash cold water on this, I want to know now. So let me do it. You can see it all, the way it is for me now, okay?"

She understood his point. If she was going to have any problems with his reality, it was better not to even get started. She didn't think she would, but there was only one way to prove it.

So she slid off his lap. Her legs felt a little rubbery, and part of her just wanted to brazenly strip and fall into his arms. But he had to be ready, and he was determined to let her see it all for herself.

Her breaths became shallow as anticipation filled her. She couldn't imagine that anything was going to make him less desirable to her. Not one thing.

He wheeled over until he was sideways beside the bed, then reached up to grab an overhead bar. Then, with powerful arms, he hand walked himself until he was fully on the bed.

"I couldn't do that in a million years," she remarked.

"I've always been able to do it. This is one of the few things I didn't have to learn. Upper-body strength was always part of my training."

But then he didn't seem to want to talk anymore, and she heartily agreed. Watching him held her attention, and watching him was making her entire body feel like warm syrup. She gripped a handy bar to steady herself.

He pulled his legs around, leaving them slightly splayed as if for balance. Then, sitting upright, he tugged his shirt over his head…and revealed the reason he could sit like that without propping himself: his abdominal muscles rippled and flexed, a perfect six-pack. She'd never seen one before in real life and felt her cheeks warming. Dang, he was gorgeous.

But then came the difficult part. He reached for the snap on his jeans then fell backward so he could unzip them. Man, she wanted to go help, to pull that packaging away and see the entire gift of him naked. But she stayed herself, licking her suddenly dry lips. Oh, man, had she ever felt a hunger this strong? What was it about this man?

"Now's the fun part," he muttered. He gripped the overhead bar with one hand and pulled himself up until his hips left the bed. Then with his free hand, he pulled his pants down below his hips on one side. Then he switched hands and repeated for the other side.

Ashley grew aware of only one thing. His erection

was now fully revealed. Her heart hit top speed like a racehorse, and her knees nearly gave way. Her center began to throb in an ancient rhythm. She couldn't wait. But she had to. Must.

She closed her eyes briefly, then snapped them open, unwilling to miss even a second of filling her eyes, mind and heart with him.

He repeated the process several times until he'd pulled his jeans and shorts down below his knees. Then, in the most amazing way, he jackknifed his body until his hands reached his ankles, and tugged strongly until the last of his clothing came off.

"Told you it wasn't pretty," he said, looking at her at last, almost as if he expected to see rejection.

Ashley shook her head stiffly. "I've never seen anything more amazing in my life. I couldn't do that if I tried. I'm stunned that you don't just give up and wear loose jogging pants."

He smiled. "The more I give up, the more I lose. Come here."

That was easy enough to do. She was already weak with desire, and she fell onto the bed effortlessly. Maybe because she couldn't stand another moment. She kicked off her shoes before moving her legs to the bed.

Zane twisted, propping himself on his elbow, smiling down at her. "Now you," he said.

She reached for the hem of her sweatshirt, ready to pull it over her head, but he surprised her by helping. When he at last tossed it aside and looked at her, she felt the touch of his gaze like tongues of fire.

"Oh, Zane," she murmured, then gasped as he ran his palm down her side and across her midriff. He lowered his head, kissing her deeply, as if he wanted to reach her very soul. She felt herself beginning to float on the hot tide of passion, leaving the rest of the world behind.

Then his hand cupped her breast through her bra, and she arched into his touch, a small cry escaping. A spike of need drove through her.

He lifted his head at once. "You okay?"

"No," she said flatly. She pushed him a little so she could sit up, then she dispensed with her clothes swiftly. "You can advertise your disrobing skills some other time. I. Can't. Wait."

He laughed, but somehow it didn't dispel the rising heat that built between them, a blaze about to ignite into a firestorm. He tried to run his hand all over her, along her moist petals, but she hadn't been kidding about not being able to wait. Somehow he had brought her to the very peak of passion, and she didn't want to risk anything shattering the moment. She clung to his head as he sucked at her nipples, first one then the other, and soon she was out of her mind. She pushed him back while simultaneously gripping his shoulder.

"Now," she gasped. "Now."

As far as she was concerned, they could try the whole Kama Sutra. Later. Right now she wanted only to feel him deep inside her, answering the empty ache he had planted between her legs.

"I can't move my hips, so…" His voice was husky, rough. She didn't need him to finish.

Pushing him onto his back, she mounted him from above, her hair hanging around her face, her eyes feeling heavy. "Take me," she whispered.

Nothing in her life, no other lover, had ever made her feel the way Zane did. He reached down and he took her. Filling her with a satisfaction so deep it permeated her. She needed him deep inside. She ached for it.

His hands clamped on her hips, guiding her movements as she threw her head back and gave herself up to the miracle of being human.

He took her, all right. To the stars and back. She felt him jet hotly inside her, and then she shattered into a million glorious pieces.

Zane...

She lay curled against him, her head on his shoulder, his arm around her. The scents of lovemaking filled the room, but so did scents of Ashley. He fingered her beautiful hair gently and stared at the ceiling, giving thanks that war had seen fit not to take moments like these from him.

There'd been that girlfriend, the one who had been practicing for sainthood by smothering him, but sex with her hadn't struck him the same way sex with Ashley had affected him.

Maybe because it hadn't been just sex? He shied away from the thought, not wanting to head into those places. He looked at himself and often thought only a Mother Teresa wannabe could be happy with him.

But he'd escaped the one who had, and now he'd

wound up holding a woman who didn't try to give him one ounce of help he didn't ask for. She made him feel competent, capable. She even made him think he could do useful things, like helping Mikey with a service dog, like talking to her class. Like looking into other things where his chair wouldn't be a problem.

Which left his PTSD. That worried him, because he knew how bad it could get. Once it had gotten him evicted. What if he went over the edge like that again?

But Nell... Nell had so often called him back that he was beginning to wonder if she could prevent him from falling off the cliff. Even if he did...

Well, Ashley had so far not seemed disturbed when he went away, only concerned that he was all right. She'd sat through several episodes already, and said very little about it, leaving it to him to decide if he wanted to talk.

She was, in short, amazing. And she did it so easily. Maybe it came from dealing with kids for so long. Maybe she was used to seeing them struggle with something and used to not stepping in unless they absolutely couldn't get it.

She was certainly hands-off with him. She treated him as if he were just any other guy.

Which, he supposed, he was. Just any other guy. Sure, he couldn't walk. Sure, he had moments when he slipped in time, but everyone had problems, right?

He sighed quietly, wondering what he was trying to do here. Rationalize it all? Absolve himself in advance if he somehow hurt Ashley? Because it seemed to him that he was bound to do that. He didn't trust himself not to, not after all that had happened.

But in a very short time she had opened him up in ways he had thought he'd never feel again. He liked having her around, even though he'd decided he never wanted anyone around him again. He'd told her things that he'd never shared. He'd even told her how he felt about his medals, which except for one conversation was something he'd kept strictly to himself. In fact, she was the first person he'd ever shown them to.

And, in her wonderful way, she didn't try to argue him out of his feelings about them. She probably qualified as the most accepting person he'd ever met.

Sure, she'd ridden him about being able to call for help if he fell, but that wasn't out of bounds. She'd gently suggested he might be able to help Mikey if he got over himself a bit. She'd *asked* him if he wanted to participate in Halloween. And her suggestions about a kitchen remodel hadn't been pushy. She'd dropped it as soon as he said he might not be staying.

Then there was Nell. He suspected if he gave Nell free rein, she'd be knocking at Ashley's door all the time. The dog knew she wasn't supposed to leave him, but, well… Nell had a mind of her own. And sometimes she let him know what she thought of his isolation.

Nell, his personal live-in psychiatrist, apparently thought he needed his own pack. Heck, she'd probably like to see a few other dogs from time to time herself.

Maybe that was the key. Neither dog nor man was designed to live alone.

Ashley stirred. Her arm moved on his chest, rubbing gently. "You are the most beautiful man I've ever known."

"Beautiful?" The word stunned him. He saw himself as all busted up and broken in every way. Not beautiful.

"Beautiful," she repeated. "Physically beautiful, and mentally beautiful. Your heart is bigger than you give yourself credit for."

"Oh, really…" His mind began to rebel.

"Hush and just listen. You wanted to help Mikey. Much as you said you needed to avoid people, you helped that child. First with a big check to help get him the wheelchair he really needs, and then by going out to Cadell's to help with the dog. You can try to convince the world, Zane, but you're no Scrooge. Not in any respect. You're innately generous. You've just been dealing with too much baggage to realize it."

"Ashley…" But he wasn't really protesting. She'd planted a kernel of warmth in his heart, a place that had felt cold and empty for too long.

"Anyway," she said, "you don't have to believe me. I'm cold and hungry, so can we make love again later, after we eat?"

That surprised a laugh out of him. "Absolutely."

"You don't need me to help you dress, right?"

"I do it every day." Even though he might have taken great delight in her assistance this once. Passion was renewing its flow through him. But still…

She kissed his shoulder. "I thought so." Then before he could stop her, she kissed his shoulder again and popped out of bed. As she pulled on her clothes, she said, "I'm going to run next door and get those sausages and buns. Make us some coffee when you get to it."

Then she darted out.

She left him smiling. He had his orders: get dressed and make coffee. Just like a normal guy. God, he loved the way she treated him.

Chapter 12

The entire weekend passed in a haze of lovemaking and mostly idle conversation. Ashley felt as if they were hunkered together in a private world, and she was perfectly willing to forget everything else. All of it.

Being with Zane was a constant delight and surprise. Occasionally they got serious, and she talked a bit about her past and her failed relationships.

"It was always easy to get a date," she admitted.

"I believe it," he answered, stroking her bare arm with his fingertips as they lay face-to-face in bed. "You're a stunner."

"Maybe. All I know is I never lacked for a date…if I wanted one. Which doesn't mean anything worked out. My mother once said dating is like trying on clothes. You look and say no, no, no until finally everything is right and you say yes. I came close to saying yes only once, and it wasn't the time I found out I was the other woman. That wouldn't have turned me off to relationships."

"What happened?"

She smiled faintly. "I woke up. I don't know how else to phrase it. It happened nearly overnight. I decided that I didn't really like the guy enough to spend the rest of my life with him. I'm sure he was okay and that he made someone else happy, but he wasn't for me. You know how you like your independence."

He spoke with a little humor. "I rather insist on it, don't I?"

"I do, too. His ideas about women…well, they clashed with mine. Not terribly, but enough to jar me. I like working. I love teaching. I wasn't going to give it up so he could be the breadwinner. I realize that was part of his self-image as a man, but as a woman…"

"What?" he prodded.

"I don't ever want to be economically dependent on a man. A million things could happen that would leave me needing to support myself and maybe a child or two. So, while he never made a big issue of it, never brought it to a head and a big fight, he was constantly nudging me into a more traditional role. I'm not built that way."

"No, you're not," he agreed.

"After that I pretty much stopped dating."

"Why? Just because of him?"

She shook her head. "No. Because I realized that

had been the problem one way or another with every guy I dated. The one I hated most of all was the guy who insisted on ordering for me in restaurants. By the third date we were done."

He gave a short laugh. "I can sure as hell see why. Damn. Ordering for you? That's insulting."

"Maybe not in his world, but definitely in mine." She looked into his eyes. "So, Mr. Independent SEAL, I hear you guys are the ultimate in machismo. Do you want the little woman staying at home?"

He laughed, a full-throated sound of humor. "We're all about toughness. But I'll tell you something. Most of us, having to be away so much, vastly prefer to leave behind a woman who can take care of herself and everything else that comes up. Now, I'm not going to say we don't have any male chauvinists in the crowd, because I'm sure we do. But…many of us would rather not be worrying about the home front when we can't be there. We'd like to come home to a happy family, not a miserable one. Besides, as one of my buddies said, if you leave a woman at home alone with nothing to do but wait, she might find other ways to entertain herself. So…" He shrugged. "I can't speak for everyone, but I never had a thing for traditional roles."

She smiled. "Maybe because you were secure enough in your manhood you didn't have anything to prove."

He fell quiet, staring into space, but Nell, who'd taken up station behind him on the bed, didn't seem disturbed. "Funny you should say that," he replied presently. "My CO remarked on that once. He said you can tell the guys who've been on an active mission. They don't have anything to prove to anyone." Then he shook his head a bit. "But machismo? I don't like that word. It has so many negative connotations now. So I'll just leave it at toughness."

That was fine by her. She burrowed into his shoulder just as his hand found her breast and began teasing her toward the pinnacle of desire once again. She spared a moment to wonder wryly if she was going to be able to walk when she went back to work, then gave herself over to the wonder of Zane, the wonder of being free to touch him anywhere, everywhere, the freedom of enjoying his every caress anywhere on her body.

She felt as if she'd cast off shackles she hadn't even been aware were binding her. Fiery starbursts began to explode in her head and she straddled him once again, leaning forward so that her hands were on his shoulders, watching his face as she rode him, feeling him slipping in and out of her.

His eyes never closed. He stared right into hers even as his face began to relax, then to tense again as passion wound ever tighter in both of them.

Please, she thought as culmination overtook her at last in a blinding explosion, *don't ever let this end*.

Sunday night she had to go home to prepare for school the next day. She hated to do it but figured the space might be good for both of them.

She certainly knew she needed time to think. She

knew she was growing deeply involved with Zane. She'd warned herself about her predilection to fall for guys when she made love with them, but she didn't think it was just that.

So she was worried. She'd given a lot to him, emotionally, and received a lot from him, and she didn't want it to end. But she also feared it would. He hadn't even really committed to staying in this town. What if he decided he needed a cabin on an isolated mountainside to be comfortable with himself? What if he just decided this little town was too small and any plans he had of making a future for himself would just wither and die here?

As she well knew, far too many young people left here as soon as they could, looking for brighter opportunities and brighter lights in general. It was a problem for all small rural towns, and she had no idea what could be done about it.

The community college had helped, but most of the students who went there left for four-year schools or jobs elsewhere. Before the semiconductor plant had closed, it had promised a future for young people, but it hadn't remained.

The proposed ski resort on the mountain, which somehow never seemed to come to pass, though attempts had been made repeatedly…well, what kind of jobs would it provide for the most part? Not that it mattered, since the landslide had put construction on hold indefinitely while more surveys were done. So far all Conard City had gotten from it were brick-paved sidewalks in the downtown, fancy new streetlights in the main areas around the town and some fresh paint in a few places.

So what the heck was a guy like Zane supposed to be able to do here? Bleak prospects indeed.

Her phone rang several times, disturbing her work. She'd turned off her cell as soon as things heated up with Zane, and now as her friends touched base she simply said she'd been visiting someone and refused to say any more. Each of them in turn giggled, suspecting something romantic, but she blessed them for not pressing.

She and Zane didn't need to be an item. They *weren't* an item. They'd had a weekend fling.

Like she believed that's all it was.

Shoving her disturbed thoughts aside, she bent her attention to her work. She couldn't afford to let that slip, not for any reason. Soul-searching would have to wait.

So would remembering the weekend. Her mind kept summoning memories that made her shiver with delight and longing. She never wanted to forget a single detail.

But math papers stared back at her, and she gave herself a hard mental shake. Later. She'd deal with everything else *after* she finished her work.

Just as she was sliding the papers and lesson book into her backpack, there was a rap at the front door. Glancing at the clock, she saw it was nearly eleven.

Good grief. She jumped up immediately and wasn't at all surprised to see Nell standing there with a bone in her mouth, her own self-improvised knocker.

"I'm coming," she said immediately and yanked her jacket off the hook. Her heart raced as worry and fear consumed her. What was wrong? Was Zane hurt?

She closed her own door, not worried about locking it, and raced after the dog. As she approached the ramp, she noticed the light from inside seemed dim. Flickering.

Flickering? Oh, God, fire?

Scared half to death, she raced up the ramp, patting her pocket for her phone, realizing she'd left it at home. Her stride broke just a little, but she decided it was more important to get inside and check on Zane. If she needed to call for help she could do it then.

Nell pushed the door open and Ashley raced inside.

And found herself standing in a candlelit wonderland.

Sitting in his wheelchair at the foot of stairs he would never climb, Zane watched Ashley with a faint smile as she froze just inside the door and looked around, her mouth dropping open. Candles flickered on every flat surface in the small foyer, in the living room and kitchen. He'd wanted to do his bedroom as well, but common sense took over. Candles posed a danger and he didn't want them burning where he couldn't keep an eye on them.

"Hi," he said, watching her look around.

"Zane… What…?"

"For you," he explained simply. "Beauty for you."

She looked at him, wonder on her face. "This is so special, but how…?" She just shook her head.

"Freitag's was open. I ventured out and bought every candle they had. Because…you."

Vaguely she heard Nell close the door behind her. Then her terror of just moments ago hit her hard. "Do you realize how scared I got? It looked like there was a fire in here, and Nell showing up so late…" She almost hated herself, given what he'd done for her, but the adrenaline hadn't settled yet.

His smile faded. "Damn. Didn't you see the note in her side pocket?"

She turned and looked at the dog. Indeed, the corner of a piece of paper stuck out from a slit in the dog's service vest. The last of the adrenaline began to seep away.

"I'm sorry," she said, turning to him again. "I jumped to a conclusion."

"Clearly."

Had she ruined this for him? For an instant she almost hated herself. "I'm sorry," she said again, beginning to feel miserable. "This is so beautiful! It's like a wonderland."

"I hoped you'd think so." It was his turn to pause. "Will you ever be able to believe that Nell has come for you for some reason other than that I'm in trouble?"

The question hung on the air, seeming weighted with significance. Something important was happening here.

She struggled for the right way to answer, not wanting to give him the wrong impression. "Zane, when my phone rings at this time of night, I answer expecting bad news. Nobody makes a friendly call at that hour."

His face relaxed. "I didn't think of that. So Nell was like a too-late phone call?"

She nodded, saying not another word.

He swore quietly. "Not the effect I planned at all. The note asked if you could come over for a surprise."

"It's a fantastic surprise," she assured him, looking around again. "The instant I saw it, my first thought was that I'd stepped into wonderland."

His smile began to return. "That was what I wanted. I guess you were full of adrenaline when you got here."

She nodded. "I didn't mean to ruin it for you."

"You couldn't possibly ruin it for me." His face, which often looked hard when he was lost in thought, which spoke of a hard-lived life and past tragedies, was suddenly so gentle her throat tightened up in response.

"Could you come a little closer?" he asked.

She stepped toward him until she stood right in front of him. He patted his lap, so she shed her jacket, throwing it to the side. She hardly noticed that Nell grabbed it and dragged it out of the way as she settled onto Zane's lap.

Wrapping an arm around his shoulders, she kissed him warmly, then leaned back to look around at all the candles. They cast a dancing glow over everything that was almost otherworldly.

"I know it's late," he said. "I was sitting here after you left and realized I was missing the hell out of you. I knew you had to work, so I amped myself up to go out, and as I was driving by I saw that Freitag's was open."

"It's the time of year," she answered. "Usually the sidewalks are rolled up at around six or seven. Well, except for Maude's diner."

"I remember. Anyway, I was just killing time. They have a nice ramp in their doorway, so I went in to wander around. Very nice ladies in there. They even pushed a few tables of clothing to the side so I could navigate. I picked up a few items of cold-weather gear and then...then I saw the candles. I was surprised they had so many. Must be the approach of Christmas."

"Maybe," she said, watching his every expression, drinking him in as if the hours without him had parched her deep inside.

"Anyway, I saw those candles and thought of you." He gave a quiet laugh. "I bought so many those dear women had to help me carry them out. But they were laughing and teasing me, demanding to know if I was buying them for a special lady."

She felt her own smile grow and her heart swell. "Thank you, Zane. Nobody's ever done something so...so...amazing for me before. It's like the biggest-ever fiery bouquet."

"I hoped you'd like it." His arm closed around her waist and snuggled her even closer. "Ashley?"

"Hmm?" She rested her head on his shoulder, inhaling his wonderful scent: man, soap and now candle wax.

"You haven't known me very long. I mean, it's only been a few weeks."

"I know." She nearly sighed, trying to square this explosion of candles with the feeling that he was about to break off their relationship. He'd wanted to be a hermit, after all, and she'd kind of spoiled that. But she didn't want to give him up.

"But I don't think falling in love requires time."

Her heart stopped. She couldn't draw a breath. What was he saying? She managed to push out his name with the last air in her lungs. "Zane?"

"I'm probably crazy," he said. "In fact, I know I am. But I've never felt about anybody in my life the way I feel about you, Ashley. I'm mad about you. I don't want to be without you. I want a future with you."

At last she could draw a breath. She tilted her head, trying to see his face, feeling his other arm wrap around her in a bear hug.

"I won't blame you if you tell me no. I've got a lot of problems, and you might not want to deal with them. I'm not sure why anyone would. So I'm not asking for any kind of answer unless you want to walk away right now."

Finally some strength seemed to be returning to her. Her heart felt swollen with hope. She ached with it.

"It kinda just happened. I'm not going to ask you to marry me, even though I want to, but that wouldn't be fair. What I *am* going to ask is that you'll try life with me for six months or so. To see if you can stand it, if you want me and all my mess."

Six months? He wanted a six-month trial when she

realized in an amazing blast of self-understanding that she wanted it all, and she wanted it all right now.

"Zane…"

He lifted one hand and put a finger to her lips. "I love you, Ashley. You eased your way into my heart before I even knew it was happening. You warm me. You take away the chill. And you treat me like an ordinary man. I can't begin to tell you how much that all means. So if you'll give me six months to try to win you…"

Win her? She wiggled until he let go of her. She slid off his lap and faced him. Now he looked as if he expected bad news.

"I love you, too," she said baldly. "The whole time I was next door trying to work, it kept hammering at me. I love you. But I was afraid you didn't want me or anyone else… You wanted to be a *hermit*!"

His expression lightened. "Not anymore. And certainly not when it comes to you. So I get my six months?"

"Only if you insist. I'd marry you tomorrow."

His smile was so wide and bright that it was like dawn. "Six months," he repeated. "You deserve that. Then I'll ask you to marry me."

"Oh, ask me now, darn it." She dropped into his lap again. "Ask me now and I'll settle for a long engagement as long as I can move in with you."

He threw back his head and laughed, the freest, happiest sound she had ever heard from him. Then he turned his face to her as laughter died. "Marry me, Ashley."

"Absolutely," she answered as her heart began to sing. "But I don't want a wedding on Valentine's Day."

He blinked. "Why not?"

"So cliché. The day after. But not one day more."

Then she wrapped her own arms around him and twisted to kiss him until they were both breathless.

Behind her Nell gave a happy bark.

A while later, surrounded by the flickering candles and the warm scent of wax, he said, "Thank you for coming over to welcome me home."

"I feel like I came home, too," she answered. A place she thought she'd already had until Zane. He'd given her a different kind of home, one she hadn't known she was missing. A home in his arms.

* * * * *

Melissa Senate has written many novels for
Harlequin and other publishers, including her debut,
See Jane Date, which was made into a TV movie.
She also wrote seven books for Harlequin's Special
Edition line under the pen name Meg Maxwell. Her
novels have been published in over twenty-five
countries. Melissa lives on the coast of Maine with
her teenage son; their rescue shepherd mix, Flash;
and a lap cat named Cleo. For more information,
please visit her website, melissasenate.com.

Visit the Author Profile page
at Harlequin.com for more titles.

A NEW LEASH ON LOVE

Melissa Senate

Dedicated with appreciation to animal shelters
and rescue organizations worldwide.
Thank you for all you do.

Chapter 1

The gray-muzzled, three-legged Lab mix gnawing on a chew toy in his kennel at the Furever Paws Animal Rescue sure reminded Matt Fielding of himself. The dog was big, and so was Matt, at six foot one, with muscles honed by the United States Army. Matt wasn't missing a leg, but he'd come scarily close, an IED injuring him to the point that he'd been medically retired three months ago, spending that time—until yesterday—in base rehab. He had only a slight limp now, but kneeling down in front of the old dog's kennel had taken a good fifteen seconds.

I'd take you home in a heartbeat, Hank, he thought, his gaze on the dog's chart. The ten-year-old was an "owner surrender." Among the sadder words, for sure. His heart went out to the old guy stuck in this limbo between homes—like Matt was. But his sister would kill him if he walked through the door of her pristine house with a huge senior dog. And getting on her bad side right now wasn't a good idea.

The former army corporal had his order—and it was to find his sister's eight-year-old daughter, Matt's adored niece, Ellie, a suitable puppy. Suitable, of course, was a relative term. Old Hank might have spoken to Matt's soul, but he wasn't here to find himself a dog. Pets required commitment and a solid home, not a guy who had no idea where he'd be a week or two from now. Thirty-six and his life up in the air. If anyone had told Matt, so focused from the time he joined the army at eighteen, that one day he'd be at a loss for what came next, he wouldn't have believed it. Until three months ago, he *was* the US Army. Now, he was a civilian. With a slight limp.

It's barely noticeable and is symbolic of your service, so don't let it get you down, his sister had said yesterday when he'd arrived back in his hometown of Spring Forest, North Carolina, for the first time in five years. Little Ellie had saluted him, and he'd swept her up in a hug. But living in his sister's guest room, despite his adorable niece telling him knock-knock jokes that made no sense but still made him laugh, wasn't ideal. He needed to figure out what came next.

Right now, though, he needed to focus on his mission. *One thing at a time, one moment at a time*, his doc and the nurses at the rehab had said over and over.

So, back to suitable pups.

"Hank is one of my favorites," a woman said, and Matt almost jumped.

He knew that voice. He turned to the left and looked up, and standing not ten feet away was Claire Asher.

Claire.

From the look on her beautiful face, it was obvious she hadn't realized it was him. For a moment he couldn't find his voice. All he could do was take in the sight of her, his chest tight and his throat closed. He'd spent so many nights over the past eighteen years thinking about her, wondering how she was, where she was, if she was happy, his memories getting him through some iffy times. And now she stood almost within reach, pale brown eyes wide, mouth dropped open.

She had a leash in her hand and a big cinnamon-colored dog in a purple polka-dotted harness beside her. *A boxer, maybe?* Matt wondered, finding it easier to focus on the dog than the woman—who was staring at him with the same shock that had to be on his face.

"Matt?" she said, wonder in her voice.

The dog next to her tilted her head, his dark-brown ears flopping to the right.

He nodded and stood up, which took the same fifteen seconds getting down had. "I'm here to find a dog for my niece." Going through his mind was, *You look amazing. How are you? I've thought about you constantly. What are you doing here? I've missed you.* Thank God none of that had come rushing out of his mouth.

"Ellie," she said, surprising him. "I've run into your sister a few times over the years."

He nodded, his gaze going to her left hand. No ring. Hadn't he heard she'd gotten married a while back?

"You look great, Claire." She really did. Tall and as slender as she'd been back in high school, she was the Claire Asher he remembered—would never forget. Her silky, wavy, light blond hair was shoulder-length instead of halfway down her back, and the faintest of crinkles at the corners of those green eyes spoke of the passage of years. The last time he'd seen Claire she was seventeen. Now, she was thirty-five.

"Are you on leave?" she asked.

He shook his head. "I'm a civilian now. Just got back in town yesterday. I'm staying with my sister for a bit. In fact, my sister is why I'm here. She and her husband promised Ellie a puppy for her birthday next month, so I told Laura I'd scout it out. I heard great things about Furever Paws just from asking about pet shelters at the coffee shop."

Claire beamed. "It's a very special place. I volunteer here." She gave the dog beside her a pat. "This is Dempsey. I'm fostering her until she finds a forever home."

"A *furever* home," he said, pointing at the rectangular wooden sign on the wall with the message in silver script: *Where furbabies find their furever homes.*

She smiled—that beautiful Claire Asher smile that used to drive him wild.

"If only you'd come in yesterday or this morning," she said. "Every Saturday and Sunday we hold adoption events here at the shelter. Four puppies found forever—*furever*—homes, plus five adult dogs and five cats."

"So these dogs in the kennels weren't chosen?" he asked, eyeing Hank, who was still chewing on his toy bone.

"Not this weekend. But we get a crowd every Saturday and Sunday, and sometimes it takes a while to find an ideal match. That's the most important part of the process—that the match be just right, for the pet and the adoptive family."

He nodded. "Is there a match for an eight-year-old girl whose requirements are 'super cute, snuggly and won't destroy a prized stuffed animal collection'?"

Claire laughed. "Follow me. I think I know just the pup." She led him down the row of kennels to the end. A puppy was spinning circles in the kennel, chasing her tail and letting out loud yips.

"My ears," Matt said with a smile. The puppy sure ticked off the "adorable" requirement. A springer spaniel mix, according to the chart, five months old, she was chestnut-brown and white with long, ruffled, floppy ears. Ellie would go nuts over her.

"Yeah, that's why she's still here. She yipped for twenty minutes straight at both adoption events. Including every time someone came near her kennel. She's only been here a few days, though. Another volunteer and I have been working with her a bit. She just needs some training. She's very sweet."

And loud, Matt thought. *And...active.* "Does she ever actually catch her tail and stop spinning?"

Claire laughed again. "Yes. Peanut butter treats get her to do anything."

"Would she be right for Ellie?" he asked. "My sister likes calm and orderly. I think she wants an old dog in a puppy's body."

"Well, it's important to match temperaments, and puppies can be trained, but puppies are puppies—little kids. They make noise, they're super active, they eat shoes."

"Ellie never ate a shoe, far as I know."

She laughed and touched his arm, the most casual gesture, but the feel of her fingers on his skin sent a lightning bolt through him. Standing here with her, her hand on him, it was as if they'd never broken up. Claire and Matt, high school sweethearts, married with four kids, four dogs, four cats—that's how many Claire had said she wanted of each. Plus a parrot and lovebirds. And a box turtle. He could go on.

Sometimes, over the years, late at night, Matt would berate himself for breaking up with Claire after graduation. He'd told her he needed to be focused on being the best soldier he could be, leaving it at that, and the pain on Claire's face had almost made him tell her the truth. That he wasn't and had never been and never would be good enough for her, that he'd hold her back, keep studious, bookish, intelligent Claire from fulfilling her big dreams of leaving Spring Forest for the big city. Matt wasn't a big city guy, and he'd planned to be career-army. Now, he didn't know what he was. Too many rough tours of duty, first as a soldier, then as a mechanic on dangerous missions, had left him…broken.

And here in Spring Forest, he didn't recognize himself or belong.

Focus on the mission, not yourself, he ordered himself. "I think my sister wants a temperament like Dempsey's," Matt said, gesturing at Claire's foster dog. The pooch was sitting, hadn't made a peep and didn't react in the slightest to the commotion around her.

"Dempsey is the best," Claire said. "A couple months ago, she was found chained outside an abandoned house. I don't think she ever had a home before I took her in, so I've worked hard at acclimating her to the good life—which means passing muster on housetraining, manners, obedience, the whole thing. Now she's ready for a home, but she keeps getting passed over."

She knelt down beside the boxer and gave her a double scratch on the sides of her neck, then a kiss on her brown snout. Claire shook her head and stood up, her gaze on the dog.

He might not know Claire anymore, but a stranger could tell how much she loved that dog.

"Can't you adopt her?" he asked.

"I always want to adopt every dog I foster, but that's not my calling here," she explained. "Fostering is about preparing dogs for adoption so they can find homes. If I adopted every dog I fostered, I'd have over twenty at this point. Plus, every time a dog I work with finds a home, I can foster a new pooch."

"Must be hard to let them go," he said. "Don't you get attached?"

"Definitely," she said. "But because we do such a good job of matching furbabies and adoptive parents, I know they're going to a great home. I do worry about how attached I am to Dempsey, though. I can't explain it, but we definitely have a special bond." She gave the boxer mix another scratch on the head, and the dog looked up at her with such trust in her eyes, even Matt's battered heart was touched. "Oftentimes, that bond is there right away."

"I had no idea about any of this," he said. "There's more involved in choosing a dog than I realized. Can you help me find the right puppy for Ellie?"

"Of course," she said. "There are a few other puppies here that Ellie might like, but they all need some training. Maybe you can bring Ellie back with you and we can see who she bonds with. Furever Paws is in the process of finding a new director, so I'm helping with just about everything, from meet and greets to training to fostering to cleaning out kennels."

He glanced around the kennel area of the shelter, which had a warm, welcoming vibe to it. "It's great of you to give your time," he said. "When should I bring my niece in tomorrow?"

"I'm done teaching at the middle school at three, so I usually arrive at three thirty."

So she *had* become a teacher. That had always been her dream. But back in high school she'd wanted to leave Spring Forest and see the world, teaching her way through it. Maybe she had, for all he knew. "Works for Ellie too," he said. "See you tomorrow, then."

For a second they just looked at each other, neither making a move to leave. He wished he could pull her into his arms and hug her, hold her tight, tell her how good it was to see her, to hear her voice, to talk to her. He'd missed her so much and hadn't even known it. Which was probably a good thing. He had nothing to offer her.

As he gave Dempsey a pat and turned to walk away, he couldn't quite figure out how he could be so relieved to be leaving and so looking forward to coming back.

He paused in front of Hank's kennel. *Life is complicated, huh, boy?*

Hank tilted his head, and Matt took that as a nod.

To catch her breath and decompress, Claire took Dempsey into the fenced yard, which was thankfully empty of other volunteers. She let Dempsey off leash and for a few moments watched the dog run around the grass, sniffing and wagging her tail.

Matt Fielding. Everyone always said you never forgot your first love, and that had been very true for Claire. She'd truly believed he would be the man she'd marry and spend the rest of her life with. And then boom—a few days after a magical prom night, he'd broken up with her.

Her first boyfriend in college had proposed, and maybe the promised security had had something to do with why she'd said yes when she hadn't loved him the way she'd loved Matt. To this day, she didn't know if that had contributed to her divorce, but five years into her marriage, she'd found out that her ex-husband was cheating and in love with someone else. Now, she was living in the house they'd built out in the Kingdom Creek development, without the husband or the kids they'd talked about or the dogs they were going to adopt.

The craziest thing was that, just last week, her sister had said that Claire's problem was that she'd never gotten over Matt, and to do so she'd need to find a guy who looked like him. Tall and muscular, with those blue eyes, Matt was so good-looking and so…hot that few men in town even came close to resembling him. But apparently her sister had found someone who fit the bill, and had arranged a double date for tonight.

Half of her wanted to cancel. The other half thought she'd better protect herself against Matt's being back by going out on this date, even if her heart wouldn't be in it. Claire wanted a relationship—she wanted love and to find the man she'd spend forever with. She wanted a child—children, hopefully—and at thirty-five, she wasn't exactly a spring chicken.

"How did everything get so topsy-turvy, Demps?" she asked the dog, who'd come over with a half-eaten tennis ball. "I know you know all about that," she added, throwing the ball. Dempsey, in all her fast, muscular glory, chased after it, leaping through the air like a deer.

There was nothing like watching dogs at play to

make Claire feel better and forget about her love life—the old, the nonexistent and the upcoming. She smiled as Dempsey dropped the ball at her feet. She threw it a few more times, then left the dog in the yard to play while she went to help clean the kennels that were now empty due to the lucky pups that had been adopted today.

As she reentered the shelter, she saw Birdie and Bunny Whitaker in their waterproof aprons, hard at work with the disinfectant and hose. Claire adored the sixtysomething sisters—no-nonsense Birdie and dreamer Bunny—who lived together in the lovely farmhouse on Whitaker Acres, the same property the shelter was on. Opening Furever Paws had been a longtime dream of the Whitaker sisters ever since people had begun abandoning animals on Whitaker land, a pocket of rural country in what had become urban sprawl. At first they'd started an animal refuge, but when it became too much for them to handle financially, they filed for nonprofit status and started the Furever Paws Animal Rescue almost twenty years ago. Aside from the shelter with dogs and cats, the sisters kept goats, pigs, geese and even a pair of llamas on the property. They opened up Whitaker Acres to the public a few times a year so that visitors could enjoy the land and animals. Kids loved the place.

As Claire cleaned Snowball's kennel—the white shepherd-Lab mix had been adopted this morning and immediately renamed Hermione—she was glad the shelter could take in more strays and drop-offs. Furever Paws had room for about a dozen each of dogs and cats, and twice that many were cared for in foster homes, like Dempsey.

"I'll miss that adorable Snowball," Birdie said, hosing down the kennel across the way. "For twenty years I've been telling myself not to get attached to our animals." She shook her head. "Old fool." Tall and strong, her short silver hair gleaming in the afternoon sunlight, Birdie grabbed the mop, dunked it in the cleaning solution and went at the floor of the kennel until it met her satisfaction.

"I already miss Annie Jo," Bunny said, taking out the bed, blanket and toys in the next kennel and stuffing them in the huge laundry bin. Bunny looked a lot like Birdie but was shorter and plumper, her silver curls soft against her sweet face. "I love what her family renamed her—Peaches. Back in the day, a beau called me that," she added, wiggling her hips.

Claire smiled. The shelter always named the strays and those left on the doorstep. Every now and then, adopters kept the shelter names—most recently a cat named Princess Leia, who'd been there for months. Birdie and Bunny loved naming the incoming animals, and whenever they couldn't come up with a name, they held a meeting with the staff—the full-time employees, such as the shelter director, foster director and vet technician—and the volunteers, like Claire.

"Who was that very handsome man here a little while ago?" Bunny asked with a sly smile as she started sweeping out the kennel, reaching over for a stray piece of kibble that Annie Jo—Peaches—had missed. "My, he was nice to look at."

"I'm surprised you didn't rush over to ask how you could help him," Birdie said to her starry-eyed sister, wringing out the mop in the big bucket.

"Well, I *would* have," Bunny said, "but I saw Claire come back in with Dempsey and decided to leave him for her. Trust me, if I were even *ten* years younger…"

Claire laughed as Birdie shook her head again, her trademark move. Neither Whitaker sister had ever married, though Claire did know that Bunny had been engaged in her early twenties until her fiancé had tragically died. Birdie never talked about her love life, and though Claire had tried a time or two to get Bunny to spill about Birdie's romantic life, the sisters were clearly loyal to each other's secrets. As they should be.

But no matter how much or how little experience the Whitaker sisters had in the romance department, they were both wise—Birdie in common sense and Bunny in keeping an open mind and heart. Talking to the two always set Claire straight, or at least made her feel better.

Which was why she was going to be honest right now.

"That was the guy who broke my heart into a million pieces after high school graduation," she said. "Matt Fielding. I cried for six months straight."

"And then married the first guy who asked you out," Birdie said with an *uh-huh* look on her face.

"Yup," Claire said, spraying disinfectant on the bars of the last kennel and wiping them down with a clean rag. "But there's hope for me. Guess who has a blind date tonight? My sister and her husband set me up."

"Ooh," Bunny said, her blue eyes twinkling. "How exciting. To me, blind dates are synonymous with 'you never know.' Could be the man of your dreams."

Birdie wrinkled up her face. "Blind dates are usually the pits." She glanced at Claire, instantly contrite, then threw her arms up in the air. "Oh, come on. They are."

Claire laughed. "Well, if the date takes my mind off the fact that my first love is back in town? Mission accomplished."

"Oh boy," Birdie said, pausing the mop. "Someone is still very hung up on her first love."

"Oh dear," Bunny agreed.

And before Claire could say that *of course* she was—*you did see him, after all*—that cute little springer spaniel she'd shown Matt started howling up a storm.

"Someone wants her dinner *now*," Bunny said with a laugh.

"I'm on feeding duty for the dogs," Claire said, putting the disinfectant back on the supplies shelf and the rag in Bunny's laundry basket. "If I don't see you two before I leave for the day, congrats on a great Sunday. Five adult dogs adopted plus the puppies and cats."

"It was a good day," Bunny said. "Good luck on that date tonight."

Claire smiled. "Who knows? Maybe he *will* be the man of my dreams."

She was putting on a brave front for the sisters—not that she needed to, since she could always be honest with them. But sometimes Claire reverted to that old need to save face, to not seem like she cared quite so much that she was single, when she wanted to be partnered, to find that special someone to share her life with, to build a life with. She loved Dempsey to pieces, but most nights, unless she had book club or a social event like someone else's engagement party or birthday, it was her and the boxer mix snuggled on the sofa in her living room, watching *Dancing with the Stars* or a Netflix movie, a rawhide chew for Dempsey and a single-serve bag of microwave popcorn for her.

There was room on that couch for a man.

But in any case, Matt Fielding was not the man of her dreams, whether she was "hung up or him" or not. Seventeen-year-old Claire had been madly in love. Now, she was a thirty-five-year-old divorced woman staring down her biological clock. "Man of her dreams" was silly nonsense. Hadn't the supposed man of her dreams dumped her almost two decades ago as if she'd meant nothing? Ha, like that was part of the dream?

Matt Fielding was not the man of her dreams.

If she said it enough, she might believe it.

And if there was no such thing, then what *was* she looking for in a partner?

She'd never put much stock in checklists, since she could rattle off a list of adjectives, like *kind*, and nonnegotiables, like *doesn't rip apart his exes or his mother on the date*, but everything came down to chemistry. How you felt with someone. How someone made you feel. If your head and heart were engaged. She'd never experienced chemistry the way she had with Matt Fielding. But her motto ever since she'd started volunteering for Furever Paws was: Everything is possible. The most timid dog, the hissiest cat, could become someone's dearest treasure. *Everything is possible*. Including Claire finding love again. At thirty-five.

She peeled off her waterproof gloves and tossed them in the used-gloves bin, then headed toward the door to start filling bowls with kibble and sneaking in medicines where needed.

"Oh, Claire," Birdie said. "Some advice. In the first five minutes, ask your date if he likes dogs. If he says no, you'll know he's not for you."

Bunny tilted her head. "Now, Birdie. Not everyone loves animals like we do."

Apparently, the entire Whitaker family loved animals to the point that all their nicknames were inspired by animals. Birdie's real name was Bernadette. Bunny's was Gwendolyn. There was a Moose—Doug—who'd sadly died long ago. And a Gator, aka Greg, who advised the sisters on financial matters.

"The man of Claire's dreams will love dogs," Birdie said. "That's nonnegotiable. If her blind date says dogs slobber and bark and are a pain in the neck, she can tune him out the rest of the night."

Claire smiled. As usual, Birdie Whitaker was right.

Chapter 2

Matt held his niece's hand as they entered the Main
Street Grille later that night, the smell of burgers and
fish and chips reminding him how hungry he was.
His sister, Laura, and her husband, Kurt, had insisted
on taking him out to dinner to celebrate his homecoming.

"His home*staying*!" Ellie had said, squeezing him
into one of her famous hugs.

He adored the eight-year-old. He barely knew
her— had rarely seen her since she'd been born because of his tours—but the moment he'd arrived yesterday, she'd latched on to him like he was the fun,
exciting uncle she'd missed out on, and of course, he
couldn't let her down. He'd played soccer with her.
He'd read her two bedtime stories last night, then

she'd read him one, and he'd almost fallen asleep right there in her pink-and-purple room. This morning, he'd played Hiker Barbie with her in the backyard, his Barbie falling into a ravine, and her Barbie saving her with her search-and-rescue skills and the help of Barbie's golden retriever, Tanner. She'd spent a good hour talking to Matt about dogs, after she'd instructed Tanner to grab his Barbie's jeans cuff and pull her up to safety. The girl was dog-crazy. And he was Ellie-crazy. He was determined to help her find just the right pooch to love.

With Claire Asher's help. Amazing.

"We love this restaurant," Laura said as the hostess led them through the dimly lit space to a table for four near a window. "During the day, it's more of a diner, but at night it transforms into a pub. Apparently, it's quite the nostalgic place to get engaged."

Matt glanced around the restaurant. There were quite a few obvious dates.

And, oh hell, was that *Claire*?

On an obvious date.

He turned away so that his staring wouldn't draw her attention. Then, as he sat down, he took another glance. Dammit. Yes, it was. Four tables away, diagonally. She was sitting with her own sister, Della, and two men were across from them. The one across from Claire looked slick. He had gelled hair and trendy eyeglasses and was holding court, making Claire laugh.

Crud. He used to make Claire Asher laugh.

At least she's happy, he told himself.

"What are you having, Uncle Matt?" Ellie asked.

"I'm getting the mac and cheese. No, the cowabunga burger. No, the mac and cheese. Or should I have the spaghetti and meatballs?"

He focused his attention on his niece. The poor thing had an incredibly crooked strawberry-blond braid with weird tufts sticking out. Ellie had asked him to do the honors for tonight's "special dinner," and Laura had given the tutorial as he went. When he was done, his sister had had to leave the room to keep herself from bursting into laughter. But Ellie, checking out his handiwork with a hand mirror and her back to the hall mirror, declared her braid *just perfect!*

"Well, I know your favorite is mac and cheese," he said, "and since this is a special night, I think you should get your favorite." Matt forced himself to look at the menu and not Claire.

But she looked so damned pretty. The candle on the table just slightly illuminated her. She'd dolled up a bit since her shift at the shelter. Her pink-red lips were glossy, and her light blond hair was sleek to her shoulders. She wore an off-white V-neck sweater, and a delicate gold chain around her neck.

"That's right," his sister said, smiling at Ellie. "This is a special night—celebrating Uncle Matt's long-awaited homecoming."

"Homestaying!" Ellie said with a grin.

That got his attention. Because *was* this something to celebrate? Thirty-six and living in his sister's guest room? No clue where he was headed, what he'd do. Visiting his family while he figured things out made sense, he reminded himself. He had ideas, of course.

And skills. But he felt wrong in his skin, suddenly adrift in this different life.

You're an American hero and don't you forget it, his sister had said when he'd mentioned that earlier. *You'll adapt and build a new life—hopefully here in town.*

With Claire Asher to run into everywhere he went? No, sir. He was two for two on his first full day in Spring Forest. He couldn't do that to himself on a daily basis. But until he decided where to go and what to do, Spring Forest, it was.

He took one more look at Claire out the side of his menu. *Oh please.* Her date was offering her a bite of something. As Claire smiled and leaned forward to accept the fork—with her hand, thank God, and not with those luscious lips—Matt felt his gut tighten and his appetite disappear.

He'd help Ellie find her dog. Which meant seeing Claire one more time tomorrow. And then maybe he'd leave town. There was no way he could figure out what the hell he was going to do with his life if he was going to constantly run into her—and be unable to stop thinking about her.

Dammit.

Now she was laughing at something Slick had said. Great. Tonight was a *real* celebration.

Claire's date liked dogs. Loved them, in fact. He—Andrew, thirty-five, divorced, two children of whom he shared joint custody—even had a dog, a yellow Lab named Sully.

And Andrew was very attractive. Her sister hadn't been kidding about him looking like Matt, to a degree. They had the same coloring, the dark hair—though Matt's was more military-short—the blue eyes, the strong nose and square jawline, both men managing to look both refined and rugged at the same time. Andrew was in a suit and tie, but Claire had seen Matt Fielding in a suit only once— on prom night, the black tuxedo he'd paired with a skinny white silk tie and black Converse high-tops. That night, she'd thought there was nothing sexier on the planet than her boyfriend.

Her date for tonight was charming and kind and attentive, asking all kinds of questions about her job as a teacher. He showed her photos of his kids and beamed with pride about them, which Claire found sweet and touching. Over the past few years, when she'd started worrying that she wouldn't find Mr. Right-Part-Two, she'd thought about marrying a man with kids and becoming a great stepmother. And there was adoption, of course. Her single friend Sally had adopted a little girl from foster care, and though there were challenges, she'd never seen her friend so happy, so fulfilled.

Another of Claire's mottoes over the past few years had been: If you want to find your life partner, if you want to have a child, however that child may come into your life, you have to keep your mind and heart open.

And now here was seemingly perfect Andrew. Even clear-eyed, hard-nosed Birdie Whitaker would be impressed by him and the prospects of a second date. She could just hear romantic Bunny running down how things would go: *And then a third date at that revolving restaurant on the zillionth floor in the fancy hotel in Raleigh. Then amazing sex in your suite for the night. Then exclusivity. Then a proposal on your six-month-iversary. You'll be married to a wonderful man and have stepchildren to dote on and love by summer—you could be a June bride if you're only engaged four months!* Oh God, sometimes Claire thought it would be wonderful to be Bunny.

Problem was, though, that despite how wonderful Andrew seemed, Claire felt zero chemistry. Zero pull. The thought of getting to know him better didn't really interest her. The idea of kissing him left her cold.

No fair! And she knew exactly why this man who loved dogs, who'd even showed her a slew of photos of handsome Sully on his phone, wasn't having any effect on any part of her at all.

Because for the past few hours, as she'd been getting ready for the date, Matt had been on her mind. How could he not be? She hadn't seen him in almost twenty years and then, whammo, there he was today, at her sanctuary, the place where she always felt at home, at peace. Matt Fielding suddenly kneeling in front of a dog's kennel at Furever Paws. Unbelievable.

She'd started out the evening thinking she would not let being all verklempt at seeing her first love derail this date. And so she'd put a little more effort than she otherwise might have into her hair and makeup and outfit, as if trying to force herself to give the date a real shot instead of knowing her heart just wouldn't be in it.

And now, as Andrew signaled their waiter for their check, which he insisted on paying for the table, all she wanted was to be back home, sipping this excellent chardonnay in a hot bath to soothe her muscles after the long day at the shelter. And to deal with being flooded by memories of Matt. The first time they'd met. Kissed. When he'd opened up about his older brother, who hadn't come home from Afghanistan. His parents' pride and worry that Matt had enlisted in his brother's honor. That they may lose another son. Matt had promised his mother he'd email every night to say good-night, to let her know he was okay. And he had for years; his sister, Laura, had shared that with her when they'd run into each other a few years back.

Matt had ended up outliving his parents, and when Laura had let Claire know when they'd run into each other another time, she'd said that Matt got through it only because he wouldn't have to worry about shattering their hearts a second time, after all.

All these memories had come rushing back while she'd been applying mascara and stepping into a gentle spray of Chanel N° 19. Her date with Andrew Haverman, attorney-at-law, never stood a chance.

Claire shook her head at herself.

"So, I hope we can go for a drink," Andrew said as he signed the credit card slip. He slid a hopeful, very-interested smile at Claire.

Claire's sister stood up, prompting her husband to

do the same. "We have to get up pretty early tomorrow. You two go, though," she added with her own hopeful smile, glancing from Claire to Andrew and back to Claire.

Don't you dare mess this up! Claire could hear Della shouting telepathically to her. *Get Matt Fielding out of your head this instant! I know you! GET. HIM. OUT! Andrew has a dog named Sully!*

Despite the dog, despite everything, she couldn't get Matt out of her head. As her date was pocketing his shiny gold credit card and receipt, she glanced around the restaurant, trying to think of an excuse. She didn't want to go for a drink, extend the date. She didn't want to see this man again, despite, despite, despite. Avoiding her sister's narrowed stare, Claire kept looking around the restaurant, sending a smile to a former student at a table with her parents, another smile to a couple who'd adopted two kittens from Furever Paws a few weeks ago—and then her smile froze.

Claire felt her eyes widen as her gaze was caught on a very crooked strawberry-blond braid halfway down a little girl's back. She'd seen a similarly hued braid— though a very tidy one—on Matt's niece when she'd run into his sister and the girl a couple of months ago in the supermarket.

Oh God. Don't let me look next to her and see Matt.

But there he was. Now staring at her. Glaring at her, actually.

Whoa there, guy.

But suddenly her date was standing up too, and so

she had to. Her group would walk right past Matt's table. There was no way she couldn't say hello, if not to Matt, then to his sister.

Awk-ward.

"You've *got* to be kidding me," Claire's sister hiss-whispered in her ear as they headed toward the door—toward Matt's table. "No wonder you've been so distracted!"

"Actually, I just noticed him a few seconds ago," Claire admitted. If she'd known he was there this whole time, she would have excused herself to the restroom to hyperventilate.

"Claire!" Matt's sister said with a surprised smile as they were about to pass.

Oh hell. Claire paused as her group moved on to the waiting area, collecting their coats from the racks. Her sister was furiously gesturing her over by tipping her head to the side, her mouth in a comical grimace.

"I hear I owe you a big thank-you, Claire!" Laura was saying. She sat across from Matt and next to her husband. "Matt mentioned he ran into you at Furever Paws and that you're going to help Ellie choose a puppy tomorrow."

Claire glanced at Matt, who was now sitting with a total lack of expression on his handsome face. Better than the glare? Not really.

"I'm so excited, I'm going to explode," Ellie said, her hazel eyes shining. "Thank you for helping me! I can't wait to see the puppies!"

Aww. Ellie was adorable and sweet. "My pleasure," Claire said.

"Just remember the rules, Matt and Ellie," Laura said, raising an eyebrow between the two. "House-trained is a must. And the puppy must know basic commands before he walks into our home. Oh—and no bigger than medium-sized when fully grown."

Uh-oh, Claire thought. She'd have her work cut out for her there. Did any of the puppies fit the bill? Certainly not the springer spaniel, who'd peed right on Claire's foot this morning while she'd been fluffing her blanket. Though she *was* expected to be medium-sized. And the three other contenders were house-trained, but two would be huge, and a consistent "sit" was still beyond all of them, in spite of lots of training with high-value treats.

"Your date is waiting for you," Matt practically growled, gesturing toward the door.

Her sister was still furiously head-gesturing for Claire to get the hell away from Matt Fielding and join the present and possible future—not be stuck in the past.

Awk-ward, she thought again as she smiled at everyone and dashed toward her group.

But as her date held the door open for her, she dared a glance back at Matt.

And he was looking right at her, his expression more readable now. He was angry-jealous!

He'd dumped her, remember? To live his own life on his terms.

"So, that nightcap?" her date asked, helping her into her coat.

Do not look over at Matt, she ordered herself, aware that he had to be watching right then.

"To be honest, I just saw a ghost," she said, surprising herself with her candor. "I think I'd like to just call it a night."

Her sister rolled her eyes and shook her head so imperceptibly that likely only Claire caught it.

Her date looked confused.

"An ex," her brother-in-law explained to Andrew.

"Ah. I get it," Andrew said. "Happened to me just last night while on another blind date, and crazy as it was, I ended up with the ex for the rest of the night." A salacious expression lit his face. "One-time thing," he rushed to say, seeming to realize he'd said too much.

At least Claire wouldn't have to feel too bad about ditching him.

As they headed to her sister's SUV, she could still see Matt's face so clearly in her mind. How could she not be over him? How? Eighteen years later?

He was coming to the shelter tomorrow. She'd see him again. He had a purpose and so did she, and then he'd leave and that would be that.

Yeah, right.

Corporal McCabbers was telling Matt about his girlfriend back home; Penny was her name, with long red hair and green eyes. He and McCabbers sat in the back of the vehicle, headed for a broken-down US Army truck that they had to get running pronto.

Ten more days and I'm home, McCabbers was

saying, and Matt envied his buddy's ability to lose
himself in his memories and hopes for the future—
because his woman was still his woman. Matt had a
string of hookups and failed off-base, short-term re-
lationships. There'd been women over the years, but
Claire Asher's face was always the one he saw in his
dreams, his fantasies.

And home? There'd been no home for almost two
decades. Home was wherever Matt was.

"There's the truck," he heard the driver call.

He and McCabbers waited for their vehicle to stop,
for the all-clear from the driver to duck out toward
the truck under cover of night.

No sooner had their boots hit the dry, dusty ground
than a burst of flame erupted before Matt's eyes, the
explosion throwing him back hard.

The pain in his left leg was unlike anything he'd
felt before. "Fielding!" he heard McCabbers shout-
ing. "Fielding!" And then he'd felt nothing at all.

Matt bolted up, a trickle of sweat running down his
chest, his breath ragged and coming hard. He glanced
around, and then closed his eyes.

He was home. His sister's house.

Letting out a breath, he dropped back down on the
soft sheets and pulled the comforter up to his chest.

He didn't have the nightmares as often as he used
to. In rehab, where he'd woken up after being uncon-
scious for two days, he'd had the dreams every time
he'd fallen asleep. But as his wounds healed and his
leg strengthened, the nightmares had lessened. The
memories remained though.

He could still picture dragging himself over to Mc-Cabbers and tying his shirt around the wound in his buddy's leg, which had looked a hell of a lot worse than Matt's own. The driver of their vehicle had been able to get back to them, dragging him and McCabbers into the truck and booking it out of there, saving their lives. McCabbers had gone on to marry his girlfriend six months later in Las Vegas, on one crutch but otherwise alive and well.

Matt had a hell of a lot to be grateful for. And Claire Asher deserved to be happy. Wasn't that why he'd broken up with her all those years ago? So she could have a better life than the one he'd be able to share with her?

Still, he couldn't stop speculating about how Claire's evening had progressed. If it had progressed. If she'd invited Slick home. If he was still there.

None of your business, he reminded himself. Help your niece find the perfect puppy, then pack up and find a place where you belong.

Chapter 3

"That very good-looking man and a little girl are out front," Bunny whispered with a smile as Claire came in the back door of Furever Paws on Monday afternoon. Claire returned Sunshine to her kennel and secured the door, noting the time of the walk on the big whiteboard on the wall. The year-old rottie mix had been at the kennel for two days, and was slowly warming up to walking on a leash. "Says he's here to see Claire Asher about adopting a puppy." Bunny smiled slyly.

Claire shook her head at Bunny's expression. "Well, he is."

"I can't wait to hear about your date," Bunny said, her blue eyes twinkling. "Find me later and tell me everything."

Do I want to be reminded of any of it? No. "There's nothing really to tell. No chemistry, even if he was great on paper."

Bunny nodded. "I get it. A blind date, no matter if he's Pierce Brosnan, can't compete with a first love on the brain."

Especially when that first love is in the same restaurant.

Claire glanced at the clock. It was exactly three thirty. She'd practically raced here after finishing up at school, grateful that her last period of the day was monitoring a study hall. She'd wanted to get to the shelter with some time to spare before Matt arrived so that she wouldn't be flustered. So, she'd taken Sunshine out, grounded herself on her turf and was ready by the time she got back inside.

Claire left the dog kennels and headed to the main lobby. She almost sucked in her breath at the sight of Matt, looking as good as Bunny had noted. He wore a navy-blue Henley, a black leather jacket and dark jeans.

She gave him a fast smile, then turned her focus on Ellie, who was practically jumping in place.

"Hi, Miss Claire!" Ellie said with a huge grin on her adorable face. "I can't wait to see the puppies! Can you believe my mom finally said okay to me having a dog? I've been waiting years!"

"Well, you *are* only eight," Matt pointed out, giving her still-crooked braid a playful pull.

"I've wanted a dog since I was two," Ellie said.

"But I had to show my mom I could take care of a dog. And I can! And I will!"

Her handsome uncle smiled. "I know it."

"Well, to the kennels, then," Claire said, leading the way. This was good. They were both ignoring running into each other last night. "We have four puppies and three dogs between a year and a half and two—they've got a lot of puppy in them too. Let's start with the puppies and see who you like."

She glanced at Matt, who was quiet.

"Just one rule," Claire added to the girl. "No putting your fingers in the kennels. Some dogs might nip because they're a little nervous or need more training time."

At Ellie's serious nod, Claire stopped in front of a six-month-old shepherd mix, Tabitha, whose amber eyes darted over at them. She stood and barked up a storm, sending the other dogs into a commotion, and ambled over to the bars of the kennel. She sniffed the air for a treat and when one wasn't forthcoming, she padded back over to her bed and began chewing on her rope toy. Tabitha had an ear infection that required medication for the next week, and the irritation might have been making her act out a bit.

"She's really cute," Ellie said with a bit of a frown. She knelt down in front of the cage. "Hi, puppy. I'm Ellie."

The puppy barked like crazy again and came over and sniffed the air again, then went back to her bed.

Ellie tilted her head and bit her lip. Claire could

immediately tell the girl didn't feel a connection with Tabitha.

"And next we have a five-month-old springer spaniel puppy," Claire said, moving to the spinning pooch in the next kennel. In true form, Belle began spinning in circles, trying to chase her tail.

Ellie gasped. She dropped down on her knees in front of the kennel, watching the puppy with delight on her face. "Hi, there! Hi, puppy!"

The puppy stopped spinning and came closer to Ellie.

"Remember, sweetheart, don't put your fingers in the kennel," Matt said, and Claire nodded at him.

Belle barked, excitedly wagging her tail, jumping up at the kennel door and trying to sniff Ellie. She sat down and barked at Ellie, then made a play bow.

"She wants to play with me!" Ellie said. "You are so adorable!" she added. "You're exactly what I dreamed about!"

Belle began barking like crazy and spinning around, desperately trying to catch her tail in her mouth.

Claire widened her eyes and looked at Matt, who was grimacing.

Ellie laughed, her entire face lit up with happiness. "I see your name is Belle, and I know that means beautiful, and you are, but I think you look more like a Sparkle. That's what I'd name you, Sparkle." She bolted up. "This is the one! This is my puppy!"

Claire couldn't remember the last time she saw

someone so excited, and she saw excited kids a lot during the course of adoptions.

"Yup, you're the one, Sparkle!" Ellie said, dropping down to her knees again and smiling at the puppy.

Who squatted and peed right on the floor, the mess seeping into the corridor to the point that they all jumped back.

"Oops," Ellie said. Then she seemed to remember what her mom said about housetraining, and worry slid into her expression. Her shoulders slumped, and her face scrunched up for a moment. Claire could tell the girl was trying not to cry.

"Well, Sparkle is definitely not housetrained," Matt said gently, a hand on his niece's shoulder. "And she sure is noisy and busy. Why don't we—"

"I'll clean it up!" Ellie added, looking from her uncle to Claire, and back at the puppy, and then back at Claire. "Are there paper towels or something?"

Claire smiled and got the roll of heavy-duty brown paper towels. "I'll take care of it, honey." She quickly mopped up the mess.

"Your mom made her requirements very clear, sweets," Matt said. "So even though Sparkle is cute, she's a long way from being trained and she seems kind of hyper."

Ellie's little shoulders slumped again, and she sucked in a breath.

Aww. This was always a difficult thing, when someone fell for an animal that wasn't the right fit for the home. "Ellie," Claire said, "two kennels down is an adorable chiweenie named Tucker who's house-trained and knows basic commands. A chiweenie is a cross between a Chihuahua and a dachshund. He'll be small even when fully grown, so he's a great size for a kid."

Ellie followed Claire to Tucker's kennel, her head hung low. "I've never heard of a chiweenie before." But there was no excitement in her voice.

"Meet Tucker," Claire said, gesturing at the little dog, who was as calm as could be. He lay on his bed, gnawing on a rope toy. He was very cute, with floppy, cinnamon-colored ears and a long snout, and tended to look like he was smiling.

Ellie gave him something of a smile. "Hi, Tucker. You seem nice."

Tucker didn't even glance up.

"He can be slow to warm up to people," Claire explained.

But Ellie raced back to Sparkle's kennel and knelt in front of it. "I wish I could take you home, Sparkle." She sat there and watched the dog chasing her tail.

Claire looked at Matt, whose expression matched his niece's. This couldn't be easy, and she probably should have thought to warn him that something like this could happen. She'd been a little too shocked yesterday when she'd seen him at the shelter to even form an extra thought. And last night at the restaurant, all rational thought had *poofed* from her head.

"Well, let's look at the other pups," Matt said, reaching his hand toward Ellie. He glanced at Claire.

"I'll bet there's another puppy that Ellie will fall in love with."

"Definitely," Claire said. "Because guess who's next, Ellie? A super sweet year-old shepherd mix named Dumpling. I'll bet you'll like him. He's super snuggly." He was inconsistent on commands, but he did know *stay*. He was slated to be on the large side of medium, which might be stretching it. Sometimes it was impossible to really know how big a dog would get.

"I guess I can meet him." But Ellie didn't get up from where she sat in front of Belle's cage. And even from here, Claire could see the glistening of Ellie's eyes. The girl was trying hard not to cry.

"Honey, maybe we could come back next weekend for the adoption event," Matt said. "These puppies will have had an extra week of training, and you might just fall in love with a dog you barely noticed this time."

"Okay, Uncle Matt," Ellie said, but she still didn't stand up. "It's okay, Sparkle. You'll find someone to love you, and you'll be best friends. That's what my mom tells me when I'm sad about not having a best friend."

Claire held her breath and glanced at Matt, whose broad shoulders slumped.

"As long as I'm nice and friendly, I'm doing my best," Ellie said to the puppy. "Then one day I'll make a best friend. It can happen anytime, Mommy said."

Claire swallowed.

Ellie let out a little sigh. "You'd be a great best friend, Sparkle. But maybe another girl will come here today, and you'll get to go home with her. Just be nice and friendly, okay, Sparkle?"

Oh God.

Ellie stood, tears shimmering in her eyes. "Bye, Sparkle. I love you."

Claire looked at Matt. He looked like he might cry too. And she'd seen him cry. Just once, a long, long time ago when he lost his brother.

Matt cleared his throat. "Tucker might be just right for you, once he gets to know you," he said, kneeling down to be eye level with his niece. "Then you get to say *chiweenie* a lot. 'I'm taking my chiweenie out. Chiweenie, where are you?'"

"I guess," Ellie said. She started to follow Matt toward Tucker's kennel next door. "Uncle Matt?" she asked, stopping. "I know Sparkle isn't housetrained like Mommy wants, but I could housetrain her. I've read all about how."

Matt seemed to consider that. "Well, let me send your mom a picture of her." He took out his cell phone and snapped a photo. "Ooh, that's a good one. I'll let her know Sparkle doesn't exactly meet the requirements, but that we're both willing to work extra hard training her." He texted something and then waited.

Claire was hoping Laura would be unable to resist the puppy's adorableness.

His phone pinged. "'Not housetrained?'" he read aloud. "'Doesn't know a single command? I'm sorry, Matt. No.'" He turned to Ellie. "Sweetie, you'll be at school from the time you leave at seven thirty until you get home at three," Matt said gently. "That's all day. That would put everything to do with caring for Sparkle on your mom's shoulders."

"Yeah," Ellie whispered, and her face scrunched up again. Claire knew the girl was willing herself not to cry.

"Could we put a hold on Belle—Sparkle?" Matt asked. "Just until we can talk to my sister face-to-face? Maybe she'll compromise on a requirement."

"But not both," Ellie said, her face crumpling again. "Sparkle isn't housetrained. She doesn't know any commands."

Claire's heart was so heavy, her knees might not hold her up much longer. "I'll put a hold until tomorrow," she assured him.

Ellie looked both hopeful and not. "Thanks for showing me the puppies, Miss Claire. Bye, Sparkle. I love you."

The little brown-and-white pup gave a little bark and then continued chasing her tail.

"She said bye back!" Ellie said, a smile breaking through.

Matt smiled and took his niece's hand. "Why did I think this would be a snap?" he whispered to Claire.

"Few things ever are," Claire said.

He held her gaze for a moment. "I'll be in touch as soon as I can."

So much for keeping her distance, cutting contact, moving on. Claire bit her lip and nodded, watching the pair walk away, Matt's arm around the little girl's dejected shoulders.

Oh, am I in trouble, she thought.

* * *

"No and no," Laura whispered after Matt made another pitch to his sister for Sparkle. They stood at the kitchen island, Matt badly chopping peppers for a salad while Laura checked the chicken roasting in the oven. The house sure smelled good. "But look at this face," he said, picking up his phone and showing her the adorable pup again.

"You're getting pepper bits on your phone," Laura said, refusing to look at the photo. "And could you cut those a little thinner?"

"Uh-oh, you're mad at me."

"Of course I am!" she said. "I explicitly said the dog had to be housetrained and know basic commands. This Sparkle is neither! And now I'm the bad guy."

"I know, and I'm sorry. But she's incredibly cute," Matt said. "And Ellie fell for her hard."

Laura sighed and put on oven mitts to take out the baked potatoes. "I just had all the area rugs cleaned, and the bedroom carpets are brand-new. I work part-time, I volunteer at Ellie's school. I can't housetrain a puppy, Matt."

Wait a minute.

Yes.

Of course!

Why hadn't this occurred to him before? "*I'll* train the puppy," he said. "I'll read a book, watch some videos. I'm sure I'll figure it out."

Laura looked at him. "Matt, honey, I appreciate that, but no. I don't want accidents in the house for weeks on end. I don't want a dog that doesn't stop or stay when I need it to. Sorry, Matt, but I'm putting my foot down."

She had every right. "Ah hell, I really screwed this up," he said. "I shouldn't have taken Ellie to see puppies she wouldn't be able to adopt."

His sister put a hand on his arm. "I'm sure that just the right puppy will come along."

"I guess," he said, hating that he'd have to disappoint his niece—and Claire.

"Thanks for helping with the salad," she said, eyeing the bowl of misshapen lettuce and oddly shaped peppers and cucumbers. She laughed, then shrugged. "I'll call it Uncle Salad."

"I'd better go call Claire and let her know to release the hold on Sparkle," he said.

Laura nodded. "I am sorry it didn't work out with this particular dog. And I do appreciate you doing the heavy lifting with the search. It's not easy being the yes or no woman."

He smiled. "I know."

"Dinner in ten minutes," she said, which meant he'd better go tell Claire now, and then Ellie.

His sister had always been no-nonsense, though when you had kids you probably had to be, or you'd end up with four untrained puppies peeing on the area rugs.

He nodded and headed up to the guest room and closed the door. Phone in hand, he sat on the bed and fished out the card Claire had given him, the shelter's information on one side, her cell phone on the back.

He punched in her number. The sound of her voice saying *hello?* sent a little tremor through him. He'd probably never get used to just calling her up, hearing her voice, running into her.

"Hi, Claire, it's Matt. You can let the hold go, unfortunately."

"I'm sorry. Is Ellie okay?"

"No. My sister's mad at me for making her the bad guy, so my brother-in-law is probably getting an earful right now and will be pissed at me too."

"Oh no," Claire said.

"I even offered to train Sparkle myself, but my sister won't go for it. I get it, but I wish this could have worked out."

"You'd be willing to train the puppy?" Claire asked.

"Sure. I mean, I know I don't have experience, but I'd do my research. It's not like I'm focused on anything else right now."

She was silent for a second, then said, "Matt, I have a crazy idea."

"I'm all ears."

"I live in the Kingdom Creek development—a house with a big fenced yard. There's a small one-bedroom apartment over the garage. Maybe you could move in temporarily to foster and train Sparkle, and when she's ready, she can be adopted by Ellie. Your niece can even help you train her."

Huh. Win-win for everyone, especially him in the short-term. He'd have his own place, even if it was connected to Claire's house. He'd have some space to figure out his future. And Claire had used the word *temporarily,* so she was making it clear he'd go when the puppy was trained.

Best of all, he had an immediate mission: to train a cute puppy for his beloved niece.

"I'll move in tomorrow," he said.

There was silence for a moment, then she rattled off the address and some information about the place. The apartment came with basic furnishings, so he'd just have to move his big duffel bag.

"Thanks, Claire," he said. "I know I'm probably not your first choice of tenant."

"At least I know you. Or did," she said. "The last couple I rented to was a disaster."

Or did. The words hit him like a left hook in the gut. "See you tomorrow," he said, needing to get off the phone, to break the connection with her.

But despite her saying goodbye and the click in his ear, an image of Claire Asher in a long, pale pink dress came storming into his mind. Prom night, so many years ago. They'd long planned to lose their virginity to each other that night as a tribute to their past and a promise for their future, but as the night went on, Matt knew he wouldn't touch her. She'd known he was going to enlist, like his brother had before him, but she kept talking about when he came home, saying that she'd wait for him, reminding him she'd be semi-local in Chapel Hill for college but that she could transfer depending on where he got stationed. But on prom night, with Claire looking like a movie star in that beautiful pink gown, the whole world open to her, all Matt could think about was smart, interesting Claire putting her life on hold when she deserved so much more.

Except she'd stayed in Spring Forest. Had gone to the local college. Married a hometown guy. Why? Why hadn't she used the opportunity of being free to spread those glittering wings of hers? He didn't understand it.

He supposed he'd have a lot of chances to ask her now that he'd be living in her house.

Chapter 4

"You *what*?" Claire's sister, Della, said as she handed Claire her sesame chicken from the Taste of China delivery bag. Della had come over to catch up on the blind date, running into Matt at the restaurant, and what-is-this-about-helping-him-and-his-niece-pick-out-a-puppy? By the time Claire got to the part about Matt moving into the "in-law apartment" to train the dog, Della was shaking her head with older sister wisdom. "You're going to be living together!"

"Hardly," Claire said, opening up the container of sesame chicken. Nothing, not even her nerves, could spoil her appetite for this deliciousness. "The apartment is completely separate with its own entrance. I'll rarely see him." She pulled apart her chopsticks and dug in.

Della narrowed her gaze and picked up a succulent bite of beef in garlic sauce and a broccoli spear. "Except the entrance is up those deck stairs." She pointed with her chopsticks toward the sliding glass door to the backyard, where Dempsey lay in her memory foam dog bed. "You'll see him every time you're sitting here. And considering we're in your living room and your kitchen is directly in front of us, you'll be seeing him constantly."

"He *is* nice to look at," Claire said. "So that's a plus."

Della put down her chopsticks. "Honey. There isn't even a word for how badly he hurt you. You can't go through that again. *I* can't!"

Yup, Claire remembered. All her plans for herself had gone up in smoke. Maybe another girl would have rallied and gone off to the University of North Carolina in Chapel Hill, as planned. Planned—ha! Back then "the plan" had been for Matt to be in basic training, then stationed somewhere stateside or overseas, and they'd see each other when he could come home for precious and rare breaks. She'd graduate, he'd come home for good and then they'd plan what was next. Except instead, he'd broken up with her with barely an explanation, and she'd been so heartbroken and confused that the pain had messed with her head. She'd been unable to think straight, to think of anything except how her life had been derailed.

Her poor sister had tried to get her to see that it was also an opportunity, to go to school and start her new life far away. But Claire hadn't been able to pull herself up and out of her heartache. She hadn't gone away to school, hadn't gone to college at all that first semester. Instead, she'd cried constantly, unwilling to get out of bed, unwilling to imagine a future without the guy she loved—without Matt Fielding.

Her sister had come over every day, bringing her food she ate one bite of, brushing her hair, making her bed around her, and finally, after three weeks, dragging her out of bed for a sisters trip to the Bahamas, whether she wanted to go or not. Della had packed her suitcase and forced her on the plane. The white sand and turquoise water, the fruity drinks and warm, breezy air had helped restore her.

Back home, she'd finally enrolled in the local college, married her second boyfriend, a man she hadn't realized was all wrong for her. Luckily, by then, her passion for becoming a teacher, particularly of middle school kids in the throes of figuring out who they were, had gripped her. Claire had run with it, getting her master's and advising extracurricular groups. She loved teaching. By the time her marriage had fallen apart, Claire had had her own busy life, which included volunteering at Furever Paws. Or at least that was what she'd told herself to explain why her husband's betrayal hadn't steamrollered her the way it should have.

I don't believe you ever really loved me, her husband had said when he told her he'd fallen for someone else, really fallen, and that he was leaving Claire. But he was wrong; she had loved him, very much. *I think you rebounded with me after your high school sweetheart destroyed you.*

Destroyed. Heavy word. One her sister would apply, as well. But Claire hadn't been destroyed. People had to be resilient, had to move on. Still, no sense not being careful with yourself to avoid having your heart smashed to smithereens in the future.

Claire smiled and squeezed her sister's hand. "Eat up. And stop worrying. Matt Fielding and I aren't getting back together. I'm just bringing together a little girl and a puppy."

"Except Matt and said puppy are moving in upstairs."

Claire put down her bite of sesame chicken. She could lie to herself all she wanted, but she'd never been able to lie to Della, who saw through her. "Every time I see him, my heart races and my stomach flip-flops, and these little chills slide up my spine."

"Yeah, that's called not having gotten over your first boyfriend. Who broke your heart. Who's moving upstairs. Who you said has no plans—to stay or go."

Claire sobered up fast. She had to be careful about Matt.

"I'm just saying, Claire. You want what you want—a husband and child. A family. You've been saying yes to men who ask you out in the supermarket. You've been saying yes to blind dates—although, you derailed a perfectly good one, even though I suppose you might have dodged a bullet with that one too. You know what you want. So don't get sucked in by a handsome face and memories, Claire. He hurt you terribly."

It didn't mean he'd hurt her again, though. Nec-

essarily. Eighteen years was a long time. Maybe this
was meant to be their second chance. He'd been put
in her path. And now he was moving into her rental
apartment.

Oh God. Their second chance? Now she was con-
cocting a fantasy about him? Why did he have such
a hold on her after all this time?

What she needed to do was to focus on what she
wanted out of life: the right partner and a child. That
meant really getting out there, and so that was what
she would do. She'd kissed her share of frogs since
her divorce, but there was bound to be a "prince" out
there somewhere. She'd focus on finding him, and
then the hold Matt had on her heart, mind and soul
would be released.

Right? Yes, right.

"I'll be careful," she promised her sister. "And by
the way, I'm open to more blind dates."

"That's my girl," her sister said, stealing a hunk
of sesame chicken from her container.

Maybe she'd even join a dating service to speed
things up, vet the men via email "chats" before they
even met.

"But no matter what, I'm here if you need me," her
sister said. Knowingly.

Claire bit her lip. Even her wise sibling knew how
strong the Matt Fielding hold was.

Cripes.

"Guess what, Ellie-Belly?" Matt said, sitting down
on the round braided rug in his niece's bedroom. *Not*

bad, he told himself as he realized he got down on his bad leg in record time and without wincing.

Ellie was playing "dog tea," serving her huge stuffed dogs who were sitting around the rug in a semicircle. Half had fallen over, but she'd prop them back up when it was their time for tea.

"What?" she asked, pouring for the white poodle beside her.

"What do you think about me moving to my own place nearby and fostering Sparkle and training her so that you could adopt her in about a month's time?"

Ellie gasped so loud that his sister came running up the stairs.

"Everything okay?" Laura asked, looking from her daughter to her brother.

Ellie flew into Matt's arms. "Uncle Matt just told me he's going to train Sparkle for me so we can adopt her!"

Laura smiled. "He told me all about it. I'll miss having you around, though, Matt. You just got here."

"I'll be five minutes away," he said. "And, Ellie, you're welcome to come over whenever your mom says it's okay. You can help me train Sparkle."

"This is the best day of my life so far," Ellie said, throwing her arms around Matt for another hug. "Thank you."

"Anything for my favorite niece," Matt said.

"Aren't I your only niece?" Ellie asked.

"What about Sparkle? Isn't she my other niece?"

"I guess she is!" Ellie said. "But don't tell her I'm your favorite. She'll get jealous."

"I won't."

He glanced at Laura, who was smiling. He looked at Ellie, who was also smiling. Even the stuffed dogs were smiling.

But he wondered if Claire was even remotely happy about the situation. She saw a win-win for everyone and had made the offer. But he couldn't imagine she'd be happy having him on her property.

"Matt, could you help me with something downstairs?" his sister asked, gesturing her head toward the door.

He already knew what this was about. When he'd told his sister about Claire's offer, she'd said it sounded like big-time trouble—for Claire. He'd brushed Laura off and finally gotten her okay for Ellie's sake, and then sprinted upstairs to avoid Laura's questions.

Downstairs, she pulled him into the laundry room and shut the door. "Look, it's been almost two decades since you and Claire broke up. So maybe there's no unfinished business. But I'm telling you right now, brother, do not play with that woman's head. Don't start something you can't finish."

"Who says I'm starting anything?"

"Hmm, moving into your first love's house? She's divorced. You're single. Trust me, something is going to happen."

"And?" he asked. Why did he feel so defensive? Because deep down he wanted something to happen? "What if something does?"

"Men." She shook her head slowly. "You're figuring out what to do with your life. Claire Asher is living hers. She's clearly dating. You hurt her once, Matt. All I'm saying is, if you're not sure about her, don't even go there. Leave her be."

"I'm not sure about *anything*," he said.

"Which is why she deserves better than a three-week stand, or however long it takes you to train Sparkle."

He sighed inwardly because his sister was right. As usual.

The next afternoon, Claire waited for Matt in the gift shop area of the lobby, putting together a box of necessities for Sparkle. She'd included a cute purple collar with white stars, a silver, bone-shaped temporary name tag with Sparkle's name and Matt's cell phone number engraved on it, two different types of leashes, a water bowl, a food bowl, the kibble Sparkle had been eating, a few toys and a packet of information on training and caring for a puppy. Since Matt would be officially fostering the pup, the shelter would take care of Sparkle's vet appointments, and right now the dog was up-to-date on all shots. In about six weeks or so, Sparkle would be ready to be spayed, but right now, all Matt had to focus on was training the pup to live with his sister's family.

When Matt walked in, Claire gave up on pretending she wasn't hopelessly attracted to the man. First love aside, Matt was fostering Sparkle so that his little niece could have the dog she'd fallen in love with.

That was pure kindness, especially since Matt had never had a dog nor grown up with one.

"Everything you need for Sparkle is in here," she said quickly, willing herself not to stare at him. "Let's leave this for now, and we'll pick it up when we bring Sparkle through."

"Me, a dog trainer," he said with a smile. "Who knew?"

"What you're doing for your niece is really wonderful," she said as they headed to the kennels.

"I'm just glad I can."

As they entered the kennel area, Matt made a bee-line for Hank. "Poor guy," he said. Hank looked at him, staring woefully. The dog got up and walked to the edge of the kennel, and Matt slowly knelt down to say hi. "Hey, guy." Couldn't be so great to be cooped up in there. "Maybe I can take Hank for a walk before we get Sparkle," he said to Claire. "I feel for him."

She smiled. "He'd love it." She picked up a leash from the rack and told Hank to sit, which he did, then she entered the kennel and closed it behind her. She put the leash on, then led him out and latched the kennel again. "There's a path out that side door you can take. It's a quarter-mile loop. I'll go finalize Sparkle's papers, and then we'll be good to go by the time you come back with Hank."

Again, he knelt down beside the senior dog, and she noticed it took him a beat longer than expected. Injury, she figured.

He gave Hank a scratch, then stood up as slowly. "How is this dog still at Furever Paws? He seems like such a good dog—he's calm, he's an old soul and he's awesome looking."

All true, she thought, her heart squeezing for the man and the dog. "I know. But older dogs, especially big ones, tend to languish. We make sure he gets lots of love and TLC."

He nodded and looked at Hank. "See you in a few," he said to Claire.

As she watched him walk away with Hank, she knew she was sunk.

Twenty minutes later, the paperwork was complete and Matt was back, Hank looking quite happy.

"You can do as I did just before," Claire told him, "Lead him in on leash, latch the kennel behind you, unleash him, ask him to sit, then come out and relatch."

"Got it." He did as instructed, standing in front of the kennel as though he was having a hard time walking away.

"And how about a biscuit for being such a great dog?" Claire asked, handing Matt the bone-shaped treat.

Matt slipped it through the kennel bars, and Hank slowly ambled over and picked it up with his mouth, then took it to his bed and began nibbling.

"See you next time, big guy," Matt said.

A few kennels down, Claire had Matt do the same with Sparkle, grabbing her favorite pink-and-purple-striped blankie to put in the box of her things.

"Wow, you are crazy cute," Matt said, kneeling down again and giving Sparkle a pat. "No wonder Ellie went nuts over you."

Sparkle barked up a storm, jumping up on Matt's leg.

"No jump," Claire said firmly. Sparkle remained where she was. "No jump," she repeated, gently moving the dog off Matt. "She'll get the hang of it."

"We'll learn together," he told the puppy. "We're both beginners."

I can help you, she wanted to say. *I'll share everything I know.* But then she'd be with him more than would be healthy for her heart and peace of mind.

In the lobby, Claire grabbed the box of Sparkle's things. She took a final look through, making sure she hadn't forgotten anything.

"What do I owe you for that?" Matt asked, taking out his wallet.

"Oh, since you're fostering, it's on us," she said.

"As a donation then," he said.

That was nice. She named a figure and he walked up to the counter, where Birdie happened to be sitting, training a volunteer on front desk coverage. She could tell Birdie liked Matt's generosity.

"You're doing a wonderful thing by fostering this pup and training her for your niece," Birdie said, giving Matt a serious once-over with her assessing blue eyes. "If you need anything or have any questions, call the shelter anytime. And of course, you'll have one of our best resources steps away," she added, nodding at Claire.

Matt glanced at Claire and smiled, then turned back to Birdie. "Thanks. I appreciate that. And I'm sure I will have many, many questions."

The bell jangled over the front door to Furever

Paws, and a thirtyish blonde woman wearing sunglasses and high heels walked in.

"I'd like to adopt a dog," the woman said, despite the fact that Birdie was in midsentence with her trainee. "Small, under twenty pounds. A female. She can't bark. And I don't like dogs with bug eyes." She glanced at Sparkle. "Oh, this one's cute. Did you just adopt her?"

"Yes," Matt said, picking up Sparkle and holding her against his chest, one arm seemingly protecting the puppy from the woman's long pink nails. "She's taken."

Claire stared at the woman. *Bug eyes? I don't like dogs that bark? Exqueeze me?* "Cute indeed but she's a big barker."

The blonde shivered and pushed her big white sunglasses on top of her head. "Oh. Well, I said I wanted a nonbarking dog. I can't stand yippers."

Birdie cleared her throat, her blue eyes steely. "Dogs bark. It's what they do."

Sparkle let out a series of yips to prove Birdie's point.

"My ears," the blonde said, covering them with her hands.

Could she *be* more dramatic?

"We have some beautiful short-haired cats," Claire said to the woman. "Mirabelle is particularly stunning. Cats, of course, don't bark. And they're under twenty pounds."

The woman raised an eyebrow. "Mirabelle? I do like that name. Cats are very queenly. Yes, I'd like to see her."

Birdie smiled and stood. "I'll show you the way."

The woman followed, her heels clicking on the floor.

"Why come in saying you want a dog if you can't handle barking?" Matt asked as they headed for their cars.

"Some folks like the idea of a dog, but the reality is quite different than their fantasy," Claire explained. "And others ignore what they don't want in a pet because they can't resist how the animal looks." She shook her head. "Last week, someone brought back a dog because she didn't like the way it followed her from room to room."

"You're kidding."

She shook her head. "I wish I were. I truly do."

"I guess some people don't know what they're letting themselves in for," Matt said. "Like me."

Claire laughed. "But you're doing this for a good cause." She reached her car and put the box in the backseat. "We'll be at the house in no time—Kingdom Creek is just minutes away. I think you'll like the privacy of the development."

"Kingdom Creek. Sounds fancy."

She shrugged. "It was the house I lived in with my husband. Was supposed to be *our* forever home. For a family and two rescue dogs and four cats. Maybe some birds and rabbits too. Now it's just me. And Dempsey, of course. Thank God for Dempsey."

Oh God. Had she said all that? *Our forever home?* What was wrong with her? *Just stop talking, Claire.*

"How long have you been divorced?" he asked,

presumably setting Sparkle down in case she had to do her business. The puppy immediately set to sniffing around her, and Claire focused on that instead of meeting Matt's eyes.

"Three years. He started cheating on me the year prior to our breakup. But he married his affair so he thinks that makes it okay."

She felt her cheeks flush with heat. Hadn't she just told herself to stop talking? The man was making her nervous. That had to be it.

"Cheating is never okay," Matt said, holding her gaze for a second. "I'm sorry you went through all that."

"What's that saying? What doesn't kill you makes you stronger?" *I got through you, Matt Fielding—of course I got through my divorce.*

"Don't I know it," he said with a kind of wistful nod.

"Guess we've both been through a thing or two."

He nodded again. "We both had been through a thing or two when we were a couple, Claire. I'd lost my brother. You'd lost your dad. It's always friggen something."

"Yeah," she said. "It is. Thank God for cuddly dogs, huh?"

He smiled and scooped Sparkle up, giving her a nuzzle. "I'll be right behind you." He nodded at the car next to hers.

A lone duffel was in the backseat. Was that everything he had? She supposed he couldn't accumulate a life's worth of possessions while on multiple tours of duty.

Fifteen minutes. And then Matt Fielding would be moving into her house, their bedrooms separated only by drywall. It had to be the worst—and best— idea she ever had.

"And this is the bedroom," Claire said as Matt followed her into the large room of the second-floor apartment.

He liked the place. The apartment was a decent size, the living room spacious, with French doors leading to the small deck and stairs down to the back-yard. That was his entrance, so he wouldn't necessar-ily run into Claire unless she happened to be out with Dempsey in this part of the yard. The bathroom had a big tub and spa-type shower, which was a plus when you were six foot one. He barely noticed the kitchen since he didn't cook much, other than basic spaghetti with jarred marinara sauce and never-toasted-right toast. But he did notice the windows—lots of them. Matt could breathe here, relax here. Considering that the proximity of Claire Asher made those things dif-ficult from the get-go, it was a real testament to how comfortable he felt in the apartment.

He put his duffel bag on the queen-size bed. He and Claire had created a lot of memories in their two years as a teenage couple, but "the bedroom" hadn't been a part of them. He'd barely touched her, though he'd been dying to. Hands skimming over her shirts and sweaters, sometimes slipping underneath. That was as far as they'd gone in those days. They'd been lip-locked constantly, and he'd fantasized every night about sex and particularly sex with Claire Asher. Now, standing inches from a bed, her light perfume enveloping him, awareness of her driving him mad, he wanted to lie down and take her with him.

Instead, he leaned down to give Sparkle a pat for being a good dog and not barking or peeing on the rug, as she'd done on the tour of the kitchen. Claire hadn't blinked. She'd grabbed paper towels, followed up with a Swiffer and that had been that. "It's a nice place. Don't you agree, Sparkle? A good training center for you."

Sparkle barked twice, looking up at him. The bedroom carpet was soft, which had to be a plus for a little dog.

"I'll take that as a yes," Claire said with a smile. "Okay, back to the kitchen. I have a whole folder of info for you."

"Info?" he repeated, following her down the hall.

"For your new life as a foster dad who'll be training a five-month-old puppy."

As she turned to head out of the bedroom, he reached for her hand, and she whirled around.

"I'm not even sure if I said thank you. For this," he added, gesturing at the room. "You saved the day for my family. Now I have an excited niece, a not-pissed-off sister and a not-pissed-off brother-in-law."

She laughed. "Well, the apartment was empty and the situation presented itself, so…"

"So, here we are."

"Here we are," she repeated, then cleared her throat and turned to go again. This *had* to be kind of uncomfortable for her. It sure as hell was for him. But in equally good and bad ways.

Back in the small white kitchen, Claire picked up a folder and opened it. "Okay, straight to business. This contains everything you need to know about training lessons and basic puppy care."

The little brown-and-white dog began turning in circles, trying to catch her tail, which was her trademark move. "Hey, Sparkle," Matt said.

The dog ignored him.

"Sparkle," Matt said again.

Ignored by a twelve-pound spinning pooch.

"Page two," Claire said, pointing at the folder. She turned to the bags she'd brought from the shelter, and took out a pack of small training treats.

She held a treat in her hand, her fist closed over it, and waved it near the dog. "Sparkle."

The dog stopped and looked at her hand.

"Yup, she definitely smells the treat. She can't see it, but she can smell it." The dog sniffed around. "Sparkle!" Claire said again.

The dog looked at her.

"Good dog!" Claire said, and gave her the treat. "We're teaching Sparkle her name. Every time you say her name and she looks at you—actually makes eye contact—give her a tiny treat. After she associates the word Sparkle with a treat, she'll realize she gets a treat every time she acknowledges it. Then we'll move on to calling her from another room."

"Huh. I guess I always wondered how dogs learned their names."

"I do expect you to do your homework," she said, pointing at the folder.

"Yes, Teacher. I absolutely will."

She smiled, and it lit up her entire face. "Now for a housetraining lesson. The plan will be to take Sparkle out first thing in the morning, then every hour, immediately after she eats, after she wakes from a nap and before bed. She'll get used to the idea that doing her business is meant for outside, not inside."

"Did you say every hour?"

Claire laughed. "It'll take a few days, but then you can stop that and move to after meals and naps."

"Well, Sparkle," he said, and before he could continue, the little spinning creature looked right at him! "Hey, she looked at me!" He reached into the bag for a treat and gave it to her. Sparkle sure did like these treats.

"Perfect. It really happens fast. In a couple of days, she'll know it's her name, and we can work on more commands like *come* and *stay*."

"You're a good dog," he said to Sparkle. The puppy turned and looked at him, which earned her another treat.

Claire smiled. "So she's had a few treats, and she last went potty on the kitchen floor. We don't want her to associate eliminating with the kitchen, so let's take her out. If she pees or poops, she gets a treat."

"Will she gain a hundred pounds?" he asked.

Claire smiled. "These treats are tiny and temporary. Plus, Sparkle is so busy and will get so much exercise running around the fenced yard that she can have all the treats she deserves."

"Key word is deserves, I figure," he said.

"Absolutely. No treats for just being adorable."

He laughed. "I'm getting the hang of this."

She handed him the leash. "Let's take her outside."

He followed her through the French doors to the small deck, and then down the stairs to the fenced yard.

Sparkle did her business, which got her a "good dog" and a treat. This dog training business was going all right so far.

"Well, I have two classes of essays to grade," she said. "But text or call if you need me."

Wait. You're leaving? Suddenly Matt felt a little out of his element at the idea of being all alone with the puppy. Sparkle was sturdy enough, he supposed, but there was something fragile about her too. She was a baby. Maybe that was it. "What should I do with her?" he asked.

Claire laughed. "Well, you could play with her out here, just watch her explore the yard and sniff around. Then you can take her upstairs and let her get acclimated to the apartment, show her where her crate and bed are, her food bowls, that kind of thing."

"And then what?"

She tilted her head, looking at him as if he'd gone a little crazy. "And then you just be."

"Be?"

"You go about your life. Unpack. Make yourself a cup of coffee. Take a shower. Watch TV. She'll do her thing. You'll be sitting on the couch and might find her trying to jump up to curl up next to you."

"Is she allowed on the couch?" he asked.

"This is a very dog-centric house," she said. "So, yes."

Sparkle came back over and sniffed his shoe, then looked up at him expectantly. He had a feeling she wanted another treat.

"I guess I'll let her explore out here a bit more, and then take her up. I can do my homework while she explores her new digs. I have to read up on the crate training thing."

"Well, I'm here if you need me," she said, kneeling down to pet Sparkle. Then she stood back up and entered the house through the sliding glass door beyond her patio. Right under his deck.

The minute she was gone, he missed her.

"It's just you and me, Sparkle," he said. He threw one of the little balls he'd stuffed in his other pocket— the one that wasn't chock-full of treats—and Sparkle went flying after it. He laughed. "Fetch!" he called. She did not fetch. In fact, she ignored the ball in favor of a leaf being tossed around in the breeze. He laughed and watched the pup explore the yard, sniffing at every blade of grass, and, ten minutes later, he realized he felt something he hadn't in a long time.

Almost relaxed.

Chapter 5

The force of the explosion propelled him backward and he slammed against a tree, his leg twisted at a strange angle, warm, sticky blood running down his temple. McCubbers. He had to check on McCubbers... He could hear whimpering. Fear. Pain. The sound—that whimpering—was inside his head, all around him. McCubbers, I'm trying to get to you...

Matt bolted upright, his breath ragged. Again, the soft bedding confused him until he realized he wasn't in Afghanistan; he was in his new apartment at Claire's house. He took in the pale gray walls, slightly illuminated by the moon, and the dresser with the square mirror over it. He closed his eyes and took a deep, calming breath.

Damn nightmare. Always the same one.

Except he could still hear the whimpering.

McCubbers definitely never made a high-pitched sound like that. Where the hell was it coming from? He glanced around for the source of the sound.

His gaze landed on the kennel across from his bed. Sparkle stood by the door, whining and whimpering.

"Hey, there," he said, getting out of bed. "Someone has to go outside?" He glanced at the time on his phone. Only 3:13 a.m. Such was the life of a puppy trainer. He slid his feet into his sneakers, put on his leather jacket, then unlatched the kennel and took Sparkle outside and down the deck stairs, trying to be quiet so as not to wake Claire. He had no idea where her bedroom was in relation to his deck or this part of the yard.

He led Sparkle to the grass on the far side of the yard. "Go potty," he whispered to the pup, per what he'd read in the pile of training articles Claire had given him. Apparently, it was a good idea for a dog to have a "spot," so they'd do their business quickly—a good thing in the middle of the night and when it was freezing. Right now, it was both. He still had two treats in his pocket, and gave one to Sparkle with a "good dog."

Back upstairs, he took off his jacket and sneakers, gave the little dog a pat, then put her back in the kennel and got into bed. Man, these sheets were soft. And the down comforter and pillows were already lulling him to sleep.

Whimper. Whine. Whiiiine. Whimper.

He peeled open an eye. "How am I supposed to sleep with that racket?" he asked Sparkle.

More whimpering. More whining.

"I'm not supposed to reward that," he said, getting out of bed again. "Tell you what. If you stop making those annoying sounds, I'll let you out for a little while. You can understand a bargain, right, Sparkle?"

And don't tell my sister, he added silently as he walked to the kennel. Sparkle immediately piped down. She looked positively thrilled when Matt opened the door. He scooped her up and brought up to his bed, the little brown-and-white mutt curling up beside him. She leaned over and licked his arm, then got up, turned around in a circle three times and settled back down with a sigh.

Dogs sighed? Who knew?

Her little eyes closed.

"Hey, wait a minute, sneaky. You can't get comfortable. You have to sleep in your kennel."

Sparkle started snoring, another thing he didn't know dogs did. The sturdy little weight of her felt kind of comforting next to him, and honestly, Matt was too tired to put her back in the kennel. He'd confess to Claire in the morning and see how bad an infraction it was.

"I'm already in the doghouse with Claire just by virtue of being me," he whispered to Sparkle, who opened her eyes as if she really was listening. "So best behavior tomorrow, got it?"

Sparkle got up and came closer, licked his face and burrowed her way under the comforter, stretching out on her side against his rib cage. He smiled and shook his head, giving her exposed belly a gentle rub.

"Who's training who here?" he whispered as the dog's eyes closed.

* * *

As Claire was bringing Dempsey outside the next morning at 6:00 a.m., she saw Matt in the yard, tossing a ball for Sparkle. The puppy did not fetch. She tilted her head and went running in the opposite direction.

Claire laughed and reached into her pockets for her fleece gloves. It was pretty chilly this morning. "Well, we can work on fetch once she's got the basics down."

Matt whirled around as though surprised to see her. "I thought fetch was hardwired into dogs," he said with that killer smile.

How could he look this good at six in the morning, with hardly any sleep? At around 3:00 a.m., she'd heard him open the door to his deck and go outside. She'd forced herself to stay in bed and not tiptoe over to watch him. Of course, she'd lain awake for more than an hour, remembering, wondering, thinking. She must have kissed Matt Fielding three thousand times in the two years they'd been a couple. Being in his arms or holding his hand or having his arm slung around her shoulders had always felt so good, so comforting, so right.

He'd told her that he was a virgin too and that he wanted his first time to be with her, but he wouldn't pressure her—he wanted her to tell him when she was ready. She'd felt ready but afraid in a way she couldn't explain to herself, let alone him, so she'd started telling him she'd be ready on prom night. Far enough away that she could mentally and emotionally prepare herself. For what, she didn't know. Sex, particularly with the love of her life, had seemed huge, monumental—the biggest deal in the world.

And then instead of sneaking off to a motel at midnight after the prom in their high school gym, where she and Matt had slow danced and kissed through most of the songs, he'd broken up with her. In his car, in the high school parking lot. He'd said he was sorry, but it had to be over between them, it was for the best; she'd see. She'd been so speechless she couldn't even form words in her head beyond *What?* And then she'd gone running from his car, her high-heeled sandals in her hand, and because she lived three houses from the school, he'd let her go.

All that next day she'd forced herself not to call him, storm his house, demand to know what the hell he was doing to them. She'd lasted two hours. She'd pounded on the Fieldings' door, but his mother had told Claire that Matt wasn't home, that he'd started his own pre-boot-camp regimen and was probably at the high school field. She'd wanted to rush over there but hadn't, hoping, praying he'd come for her once some time, meaning hours, had passed. He hadn't. So she'd gone to his house again, his mother casting compassionate glances at her as Matt reiterated everything he'd said the night before. It was for the best, he was leaving in the morning, separate paths, separate ways. He'd been so resolute, no tears in his eyes, when Claire had been gushing tears and choking on her sobs to the point that his mother had come into the kitchen with tissues and then hurried out to give them privacy again.

That was the last time she'd seen Matt Fielding until the other day at Furever Paws.

Her sister had said it was a good thing she hadn't lost her virginity to Matt, but Claire had always wished she had. That way, she could have hated him for using her for sex, *then* dumping her. Instead, he'd kept his hands to himself. Ugh, the whole thing was so complicated. Good guy one way. Jerk another.

But still so freaking gorgeous. And sexy. All that sunlit thick, brown hair. The intense blue eyes framed by long, dark lashes. His shoulders in that black leather jacket. His long, muscular legs in those worn jeans. Matt was pure hotness. Always had been, but now the tall, lanky guy he'd been had been replaced with a man.

Stop staring, she ordered herself.

Oh gosh—what had he said? Something about fetch being hardwired into dogs. "Well, the springer spaniel side of Sparkle has the retrieving thing to a science, but whatever she's mixed with might not."

"Ah, makes sense. I still have a lot to learn," he said. "How bad is it that I let Sparkle sleep on my bed last night?"

He'd always been a softie. Except when it came to not dumping her, that was. "It can be irresistible to let a dog—especially a puppy—sleep with you. It's really up to you, well, your sister and what her future plans are. If she's going to let Sparkle sleep with Ellie, then it's fine. Otherwise, it's better to get her used to sleeping in the kennel for consistency."

"Got it. I'll have to ask Laura. She can be a real

marshmallow about some things. I can see her letting Sparkle sleep with Ellie. I know that's what Ellie will want, for sure."

Claire was about to respond when raised voices coming from the house next door stopped her.

"I'm not breaking up with her, and you can't make me!" a boy's voice hiss-whispered from the next yard.

"She's all wrong for you!" a woman's voice said. "She's trouble and she'll bring you down. Suddenly you're thinking of *not* going to college? Over my dead body!"

"Whatever!" the boy shouted. Then a door slammed.

Claire glanced at Matt and whispered, "Seventeen-year-old Justin next door. For the past few months I've never seen him without a long-haired blonde."

"Blondes are trouble for sure," he said, reaching out to move a strand of hair the wind had blown across her cheek.

Claire froze, his touch so unexpected and so undeniably welcome that she couldn't speak.

"Sorry. Overstepped," he said, moving backward a bit. "I—" He clamped down on whatever he'd been about to say.

"If anyone's trouble, it's first loves living on your property, making you remember the good ole days." *Oh God.* Had she really just said that? *Sure, Claire, open up that can o' worms. Are you crazy?*

"Tell me about it," he said. "I was up half the night remembering."

"What were you remembering?" she asked. Because she couldn't resist. And she had to know.

"How crazy about you I was," he said.

"I thought you were. In fact, I thought you were as crazy about me as I was for you. But you dumped me. Remember that?"

Oh God, again. Had she actually said *that*? What was the point of having this discussion almost two decades later? *Lame, Claire.*

But then again, they'd never had this discussion. He'd broken her heart and then he was gone. Until a few days ago. So why not have it out, right here, right now? Being around Matt made her feel like that seventeen-year-old girl—in love, the whole world in front of her, everything possible. Until it wasn't.

He turned away, his attention on Sparkle for a moment as the little dog sniffed a tree trunk a few feet away. "I 'dumped' you because I was trouble."

"Oh, right. The imminent soldier, about to go off to serve his country, enlisting in his fallen brother's memory. Oh yeah, you were big trouble."

"I mean that I would have held you back," he said, his gaze on her. "You wanted so much back then. You had so many dreams and plans. And I didn't have any of that in me."

"Funny how I managed to be so in love with you," she said, shaking her head.

"I honestly don't know why you were. I had nothing to offer to you. I have less to offer you now. If I wanted to, I mean. If you wanted to—Oh, earth, swallow me up," he said, shaking his head. "Forget everything I just said. I'm just saying I would have held you back."

"Why would you make that decision for me?" she asked.

"Because I loved you that much, Claire. That's why." He looked at her, then at the ground, as if coming to some kind of decision. "I have some calls to make. Sparkle, come on, girl."

The dog glanced at him. He pulled a treat from the pocket of his leather jacket and the dog came running over. "Good, Sparkle," he said, holding out his palm. She grabbed the treat and followed him as he started for the stairs.

Because I loved you that much... Claire was so choked up she couldn't speak. And what would she say anyway? All of that was so far in the past.

I have even less to offer you now.

If that was how he felt, then he surely wasn't going to be her husband and the father of her children.

Do. Not. Get. Sucked. Into. The. Past. This man just told you he's not going to be what you want or need. Believe him. Don't be a fool.

But people could change their minds. People's minds could be changed.

Now she was arguing with herself?

There was only one way to nip this in the ole bud—take charge of herself before Matt Fielding got under her skin.

"Hey, Matt," she called up to where he was on the deck landing.

He stopped and looked down at her—clearly bracing himself for what she was going to say. Because regardless of how much time had passed between then and now, she knew him. For a moment, she let herself take him in, the way the morning sunlight hit his hair.

"You're doing great with Sparkle," she said.

She could actually see his shoulders relax.

"Thanks," he said. "My teacher prepared some great material, and I read the homework assignments."

She smiled up at him and nodded. He went inside, closing the sliding glass door behind him.

Yup, that's right, Asher. Keep it focused on the dog. Lighthearted. All about the dog. Because you're getting Matt Fielding out of your system right now. That was the only way she'd survive sharing her home, her yard, her love of dogs with him. She had to create barriers and distance.

She had to find the man she was looking for. The man she'd share her life with. A husband. A father for the child she wanted. Matthew Fielding was not that man.

She went back inside and fired up her laptop, typing *dating sites* into the search engine. There were so many, some easy to nix because of their ridiculous names, like Hotties4U.com. Her gaze stopped on SecondChanceSweethearts.com. Now that was more Claire's style. And this was all about a second chance at love, right?

She clicked onto the Create A Profile page. Hmm, she needed a user name. She typed in *AlwaysLearning*. "What are the three qualities that best describe you in a nutshell?" How was she supposed to answer that? She grabbed her phone and texted her sister with the question.

Della responded right away. Are you taking a Cosmo quiz or filling out a dating profile? Hoping for the latter!

Latter. Help!

Kind. Responsible. Seeking. Sounds a little dry but hey, you want to weed out the sex fiends and idiots.

That's definitely true. Seeking? Seeking what?

That's for him to find out. Many hims!

Ah. Her sister was good at these things.

She wrote her paragraph about her interests, blah, blah, blah, how much she loved teaching, about helping young people light up about books and express themselves, that she loved old movies and superhero flicks, that she could eat pasta every night for the rest of her life and never get bored, that she was looking for a man who was ready to start a family. She deleted that last part, then re-added it. That *was* what she was looking for. A life partner. A husband. A father for her children. So it made no sense *not* to put it out there.

She uploaded a recent photo, one Della had taken at her husband's birthday dinner party two months ago. Not too close up, not too far away, head to toe.

She paid up her $14.95 for a one-month membership and hit Submit before she could chicken out.

Take that, Matt Fielding.

* * *

Not five minutes later, as Claire was about to check her SecondChanceSweethearts account to see if she had any messages from hordes of men "wanting to know her better," the doorbell rang. Dempsey shot up with a bark and hurried to the door, staring at it.

She finished filling up her mug with toffee-flavored coffee and set it down, then walked over to the door. "Hey, Dempsey, maybe the perfect man is at the door, sent by SecondChanceSweethearts." Now, granted, she always talked to Dempsey regardless of the boxer mix's ability to respond. But she still might be losing her mind if she expected her Mr. Right to be at the door.

Actually, it was Matt Fielding at the door.

"I thought I should formally ring the doorbell rather than just go down the deck steps to your side door," he explained.

The side door was completely private, opening to the fenced-in yard, with evergreens completely blocking the view to the next house. She rarely closed the curtains since no one could see her sitting in her living room, watching a romantic comedy with Dempsey and a big bowl of popcorn. But now, anytime Matt came down those steps, he would see her.

"Everything okay?" she asked.

He nodded, then gave Dempsey, who stood beside her, a scratch on the head. "Just thought you should know the stair railing on the left side heading upstairs is loose. I could easily take care of it. I'm a trained mechanic, so I'm generally pretty handy if anything needs to be fixed. You refused to take any rent while I'm living here, so I insist on offering my services in trade."

She thought of Matt in her living room, kitchen, bedroom…a tool belt slung low on his hips, fixing all manner of things as she watched his muscles ripple and his very sexy rear fill out the faded old jeans he wore. "A cabinet in the kitchen has a loose hinge, and I never get around to finding the power drill," she said. "And I've been wanting to bolt the bookcase in the living room to the wall. You're going to be sorry you asked. I can probably come up with a list of ten things I've been meaning to call someone about."

Wait a minute, dummy! Was she really finding stuff for Matt to do inside her home? What the heck was wrong with her?

You want to be around him. And not just to stare at him when you think he doesn't notice.

"I can take care of all that," he said. "I assume you're working today—I can come back at three thirty if that's good for you."

Tell him it's not. Tell him you'll fix all the stuff yourself, or that you forgot you already hired a handyman. Tell him anything, but don't let him inside your home! "That works," she heard herself say. "I'm not due at Furever Paws till five today to help close up for the night."

"See you then," he said with a nod to Dempsey, and then disappeared down the stairs.

Fool, she chastised herself as she closed the door. *Your knees can barely hold you up when you look at*

Matt. Now, he's going to be in your kitchen and living room on a regular basis.

She had no doubt she'd find some reason to get him in her bedroom. That was how ridiculously attracted to him she was. Had it just been too long since she'd been with a man? Did *since her divorce* count as too long?

Way too long, her sister had said, which was why she'd begun setting Claire up with anyone who was single.

Ding!

Claire went to her laptop on the desk in the living room. She had four messages from the dating website. *That was fast.*

And necessary. Because if Matt was going to be Mr. Fix It in her home, she'd need more than a distraction from him. She'd need to know she was taking steps to protect herself from getting wrapped up in the past, in hoping for something that couldn't be.

HOT4U, whose profile photos were all shirtless, loved "quiet nights at home with his special lady." *Yeah, no doubt. Next!* Except the next two weren't much better. Online dating might not be the way to go. Hadn't her friend and fellow teacher Sandy mentioned that she had a single cousin who might be "just right for you"? She should forget online dating and focus on fix-ups from trustworthy people.

Claire took a fast look at the fourth message. Hmm. BigReader had one photo, a side view of an attractive, dark-haired man on a boat of some kind.

He was thirty-seven, an accountant, loved historical biographies, and here was the big one: he loved dogs.

Claire hit reply.

Within twenty minutes, she had a date for dinner tomorrow night.

Matt spent the day working with Sparkle and showing the little pup around town. He'd run into some old friends and now had plans for barbecue— "feel free to bring a date"—and beers at the dive bar on the outskirts of town.

"Didn't take you for the kind of guy who'd have some fluffy puppy with a purple collar," his old rival on the baseball team had said. Before he could say a word, a buddy had added, "Matt has a thigh-to-shin gash in his leg from his service to our country, so shut up." The rival had stuck his hand out and Matt shook it, and just like that, he was one of the guys again. But did he really want to make friends, build any kind of life here when he'd run into Claire all the time? No. He'd train the puppy for Ellie, fix all the broken things in Claire's house and then ride into the unknown. At least that was a plan, even if there was no actual plan.

He'd have to leave town. He'd thought about Claire all day—from old memories to how she'd looked this morning. Claire owned a house. She had an important career. She was passionate about her volunteer work. She had everything. And Matt? At this point, all he had was a duffel bag of clothes and a twelve-pound puppy that he'd be handing over once she was trained. *So leave your fantasies about her in your head*, he reminded himself as, tool belt on and power drill in hand, he rang her doorbell at three thirty. *Don't think about kissing her, even though you want to. Don't imagine her naked, even though you can't help it. Don't picture the two of you in bed, despite being unable to shake the image.*

She opened the door, and he immediately thought about kissing her—dropping the power drill on the floor and telling her he'd been able to think of little else but her since he'd run into her at the shelter his first full day home. But Dempsey was standing guard next to her, as always, peering up at him with those soulful eyes, reminding him of his promise to himself—and secretly, to her. Not to get involved. Claire Asher had always deserved better than him, better than what he could offer.

She wore a blue velvet jacket and a black-and-white skirt. Her teacher clothes. She smelled fantastic, like spicy flowers. Her hair was in a low bun and man, did he want to feel those silky blond tresses running through his fingers.

"I just got home," she said, opening the door wider and gesturing for him to enter. "I'll go change and meet you back in the living room. You can check out the bookcase that I want anchored. I keep being afraid that a dog Dempsey's size could pull it down if she jumped up. Hasn't happened yet, but it worries me."

"I'll take care of it," he said. He went to kneel down, and for some reason today—maybe the threat of rain in the air—he winced and it took double the usual time to get down. But he was halfway there and it would hurt worse to stand back up, so he balanced himself on the edge of the couch and eased into the kneel. *Don't say anything. Don't ask*, he sent telepathically to Claire as she gave Dempsey a rigorous pat on her soft but bristly fur. Sparkle was like a down pillow compared to Dempsey.

"War injury?" she asked.

Crud. He hated when attention was called to it, even though the ole bad leg had given him a pass for carting around such a too-cute puppy in a striped purple collar this morning.

He nodded, focusing on Dempsey. "IED."

Now it was her turn to wince. "Does it hurt much?"

Crud again. He didn't want that look in her eyes. Concern. Worry. Claire was a runner, or at least she had been, and back when they were a couple she was even faster than him. Now, he wasn't even sure he could walk a half mile, let alone run a 5K.

"Sometimes," he admitted.

"Sorry," she said.

He pulled himself up, wincing again, and he saw her reach her arm out as if to steady him if he needed it. This was exactly what he wanted to avoid. Feeling like half a man. He mentally shook his head away from those "poor me" bullcrap thoughts; he was lucky as hell and he knew it. Two in his unit had come back with much worse injuries.

"I'll go check out the bookcase," he said, heading over to it without looking at her.

He could feel her lingering in the room, and knew

she was wondering if she should say something, do something. How could he know her so well after all this time? Maybe when it came to the important people in your life, those who got under your skin, those who helped make you who you were, that feeling of "knowing them" never went away.

Great.

The bookcase. *Focus on the damned bookcase*, he told himself. He heard the soft click of Dempsey's nails on the hardwood floor, which meant Claire was leaving the room and Dempsey was following. *Good.*

The bookcase was waist-high and full of interesting things, like the stained-glass jewelry box he knew she'd inherited from her great-grandmother when she was sixteen, a lopsided vase she'd made in pottery class back in high school, a lot of books and family photos. On the top of the bookshelf was an open photo album. *Whoa.* The page was full of photos of him and Claire as a couple and some of him solo. He put down the power drill and picked up the album.

Had he really ever been that young? From seventeen to a hundred.

He turned to the first page and looked at each photo, smiling at Claire as a toddler with birthday cake all over her face, Claire as a little girl on a two-wheeler, her beloved father holding on to the back of the seat, Claire as a sixteen-year-old, with a tall, skinny boy standing a respectful distance away for the photo. *God, look at me*, he thought, *madly in love, afraid to show it, barely able to believe she liked me back.*

"Oh, um, I—" Claire said.

He turned around, still holding the album. Claire's cheeks were red, as though she were embarrassed at having been caught reminiscing. Which was exactly what he was doing now. She'd changed into jeans and a yellow sweater, and reminded him of the girl he'd known, who used to drive him wild just by existing.

"I can't believe I was ever that young," he said, his gaze back on the photograph of the two of them. "Or that the most beautiful girl in the world was mine." Okay, that had come out of his mouth without his say-so. But he sure had been thinking it. Back then and now. He stared down at the book and flipped the page. He and Claire dancing at prom. Kissing.

She walked over to him and glanced at the page. She pointed at the top left photo, of the two of them arm in arm for the "professional" couple shot the principal had taken of all the attendees. "I sure had no idea then what was going to happen by the end of the night. I thought my boyfriend and I would be sneaking off to a motel. Instead, I was sobbing in my room with a pillow over my head."

Punch to the gut. He hated how much he'd hurt her back then. "If you had any idea how much I wanted you that night, Claire," he said, putting the album down. He took her hands, and she looked up at him. "I was madly in love with you."

"I don't want to talk about the past," she said. "What I want is for you to kiss me."

Me too, he thought, everything else fading away. Like reason and the real world. He stepped closer and put his hands on her beautiful face, then leaned in to kiss her, gently and sweetly in case she changed her mind midway.

But that didn't seem to happen because she deepened the kiss, snaking her hands through his hair. She kiss-walked him backward to the couch and straddled him, trailing kisses along his neck. He was going to explode.

And then she began unbuttoning his shirt, her hands cool on his hot skin. Five seconds later, he had her sweater off, one hand slipping down under the waistband of her soft, sexy jeans.

"Help me get you out of my system," she whispered in his ear. "This is what I need."

He pulled back, her words a splash of cold water on his head. "What?"

"You and me," she said. "It's not going to happen—in the long run, right? Just like last time. So let me get you out of my system once and for all." She ran her hands inside his shirt, over his chest.

It felt so good. But he didn't believe her. So he pulled away and stood up.

"You think sex will get me out of your system?" He shook his head. "I already think about you all damned day, Claire. Sex will make me unable to do anything else. Sparkle will be peeing all over the apartment."

"So once again you're not going to sleep with me for my own good?" She walked away and stopped by the sliding glass door, then turned to glare at him. "How about you let me make my own decisions for *myself*."

"I won't sleep with you when I know I'm leaving soon," he said. "If that's 'like last time,' then so be it. I'm wrong for you. Just like eighteen years ago."

"I think I hear Sparkle whimpering," she said through gritted teeth, crossing her arms over her chest.

"No, you don't," he said. He'd become attuned to every little noise the puppy made over the past couple of days. If Sparkle had made a single peep, he'd have heard it. Claire wanted him gone, but shouldn't they talk about this? Shouldn't they get it straight and right between them? She had to understand where he was coming from.

She lifted her chin. "I have to grade essays. So this isn't a good day for you to work in the house, after all."

This wasn't what he wanted either. This bad kind of tension between them. He hated the thought of leaving this way.

"Claire, if you only knew—"

She held up a hand. "Matt, you've said it all. You find me attractive, but can't—on all levels. Have I got that right?"

Oh hell.

Her phone rang and so he headed to the door. *Don't say you're sorry or she'll conk you over the head*, he told himself.

So, he didn't, but he wanted to. He *was* sorry. And wished things could be different. Wished *he* were different.

Chapter 6

Ridiculous. This morning, Claire had been sure the way to get Matt Fielding out of her system was to spend $14.95 on an online dating service. Suddenly, just several hours later, the way to get over him was to ravish his body in her bed? To finally have sex with him? Was she insane?

Thank God he'd put the kibosh on that. Right? She went back and forth, depending on the minute. Yes, it was a good thing. She'd be a mess if she finally slept with the man she couldn't get over after eighteen years. And she couldn't afford to be an emotional mess. She had hormonal, pimply faced, identity-seeking preteens depending on her to be the calm, rational one. She had a foster dog who needed to be fed, exercised and played with. And she needed to be present for the dogs at Furever Paws, not be all teary-eyed and unfocused.

So, yes, score one for Matt. But then she'd think that maybe sex with him really would do the job, that the mystery of him, of "it," would *poof!*—disappear. She'd know what sex with him was like, and she'd move on. Wasn't that a possibility?

Luckily, Claire really didn't have time to vacillate endlessly about sleeping with Matt or not. She was due at Furever Paws at five, and then she was meeting BigReader, aka Connor Hearon, at the Main Street Grille at seven for dinner. He'd said during their two message exchanges that it was unusual to make dinner plans before spending much time emailing back and forth and chatting on the phone, but he had "a feeling about her." Claire, unfortunately, had lost all feeling and interest in meeting Connor, but she was not going to let Matt derail another date with a potential beau who could be what she needed and wanted right now. To be safe, she'd texted her friend and fellow Furever Paws volunteer, Amanda Sylvester, manager and co-owner of the Main Street Grille, to let her know she was meeting an online date there at seven and to keep an eye out for anything strange. Not that Claire knew what that would constitute. It just seemed a good precaution. Then she texted her sister BigReader's details as a "just in case" too.

You're my hero, her sister texted. Very happy you're putting yourself out there. This time next year, rock-a-bye baby… :)

Getting a little ahead of yourself, there, sister dear,

Claire thought. But at least Della had made her smile. Because was putting herself out there supposed to feel this…unexciting? Once again, she blamed Matt Fielding.

That really was handy, sticking him with the blame for everything.

Matt wanted to pick up another pack of training treats for Sparkle, so he drove out to Furever Paws. He could probably find the same treats at the supermarket, but he liked the idea of spending his money at the shelter. And he'd run out of places to go to avoid going home—he still felt funny thinking of the apartment at Claire's as home, but it was for now. Since their argument, he'd vacuumed all the dog hair and errant treats around the apartment, gone grocery shopping, returned his "not him" rental car and bought himself a used black Mustang from a car dealer he'd heard good things about. Then he'd spent a couple of hours in the park with Sparkle and worn the puppy out. They'd practiced commands—*come* and *stay*—and Sparkle was getting the hang of it. A woman had come over, oohing and aahing over Sparkle's cuteness, and because it was such a small world, she turned out to be his niece Ellie's third-grade teacher. Mrs. Panetta, whom he'd heard Ellie rave about, gave Sparkle an A+ for cuteness and her *stay* command.

When he'd left the pup at home ten minutes ago, she was fast asleep in the kennel, curled up with her bounty of toys in her little bed.

Matt pulled into a spot in the small gravel parking lot at Furever Paws. Huge oak trees surrounded the sturdy, dark-gray, one-story building. He walked up the porch steps, the logo—a large image of a cat and dog silhouetted inside a heart—painted on the front greeting him. He pulled open the glass door and walked into the small lobby. He remembered tall, gray-haired Birdie, one of the owners, from the last time he was here.

"Afternoon, ma'am," he said. "I'm Ma—"

Birdie turned her sharp blue eyes from the computer screen to him. "You left here a few days ago with one of our not-ready-for-prime-time pups," she said, her stern expression softening into a smile. "I know exactly who you are. It's nice to see you again, Matt. And call me Birdie. I'm not the ma'am type. *Pleeeze.*"

He laughed. "Well, Birdie, I'm here to pick up some more training treats for Sparkle. We're going to work on the *lie down* command tomorrow."

"Our gift shop has plenty," she said, gesturing to the wall along the side of the lobby. Claire had mentioned that the supplies were mostly donated; sales benefited the shelter, and he was glad to help.

He heard barking coming from down a long hallway behind the lobby. He could see a couple of doors marked Staff Only, and one at the far end that said Veterinary Clinic. There were two additional rooms, one marked Cats and one marked Dogs. From his vantage point, he could see through the large glass window of the Dogs room; a couple was sitting down and petting Tucker, the little chiweenie who seemed

a lot more interested in them than he'd been in Matt
and Ellie the other day.

The woman in the room tried to pick up Tucker
and got barked at; Matt could hear the loud barks
from where he stood. Then another woman moved
into view—and Matt would know that blond hair
anywhere. Claire. How had he forgotten that she'd
said she'd be volunteering at five? "He will not do at
all!" the woman snapped as she opened the door and
huffed out, followed by her husband and an exasperated Claire, with little Tucker on a leash.

*Maybe he's nervous and doesn't want to be picked
up by a total stranger who's hovering over him*, he
wanted to shout. *Jeez.*

"Perhaps you could come to our adoption event his
weekend," Claire was saying. "Many of our adoptable dogs are with foster parents, but they'll all be
here this Saturday and Sunday."

"Well, if they're less ferocious than him," the man
said.

Matt almost burst out laughing. Tucker was what—
thirteen pounds soaking wet?

"Tucker isn't ferocious," Claire said, and Matt was
impressed by the warmth in her voice. "Just a com-
bination of timid and stressed."

"Well, you did tell us he could be skittish and barky,"
the woman said, her tone calmer. "My fault for insist-
ing on meeting him just because he sounded cute."

Huh. Now Matt could see why Claire's way—
being civil and kind and gently explaining—was

smarter than his, which would have been to tell the woman she didn't seem like a dog person.

And he was starting to become one himself. So he sort of knew.

"Tucker could use a dedicated foster parent, but right now, all our foster homes are full," Claire added.

The woman eyed Tucker with disdain. Humph.

"He's not the one," the man with her said. "We're looking for 'just right.' A dog with a certain personality."

Matt sighed. From everything he'd read, even the most "just right" rescue dog wouldn't show his true personality till he or she was settled and comfortable in a new home. Basic temperament, sure. But personality would take time to emerge.

"Well, we'll be back Saturday," the woman said, and the couple headed for the door.

He watched Birdie send Claire a look that told him this kind of thing was common. Expectations and reality meeting and clashing.

Finally, Claire turned and noticed Matt, and he saw her stiffen. "Oh, hi. I didn't realize you were here. Everything okay with Sparkle?"

He nodded. "I could use more training treats," he said, holding up the four pouches he'd picked up from the wall display.

She nodded. "I'd better get Tucker back to his kennel."

"Can I follow you? I'd like to say hi to ole Hank, maybe walk him if that's all right?"

Birdie smiled. "He'd love that."

Did Claire just shoot Birdie a look? One that said, *Oh thanks, I wanted to flee his presence*? Yeah, he was pretty sure of it.

He followed Claire down the hallway. She pushed through the door to the Dogs room, Tucker following on his little legs. The dog seemed instantly calmer. He must have gotten used to this area, to the twelve or so big kennels with gated access to the outside—a small fenced area with grass and gravel. This had become home for the pint-size mutt. Matt sure hoped it wouldn't be for too much longer.

Claire put Tucker back in his kennel, and he immediately went to his bed and settled down with his chew toy. Then she joined Matt at Hank's kennel. The big brown dog with the pointy ears was sitting at the front as if he knew Matt was here to take him out for a stroll.

"Hey, ole guy," Matt said, kneeling down, easier this time than yesterday. "How are ya?" He glanced up at Claire. "Can I slip him one of these?" he asked, pulling a treat from the pocket of his leather jacket.

She smiled. "He'd love it." She looked at Hank, her expression clouding up a bit. "A man came in to look at the dogs soon after I started my shift. The guy liked Hank's soulful eyes on his first walk-through of the area, so I brought Hank into the meeting room, hopeful he'd found a match. But he decided he couldn't deal with a three-legged dog. He also didn't like the way Hank's ears didn't flop." She shook her head. "I love Hank's ears."

Matt did too. Seriously, those huge pointy ears

almost made Hank look like he could fly by batting them. "Passed up again, huh, guy?" he said, his heart going out to the beautiful dog. "How long has he been here?"

"Almost a month."

"Cooped up here a month? And no one wants him because he's missing a leg and doesn't have floppy ears?" He shook his head. Hell, Hank didn't wince or take fifteen seconds to get up and down the way Matt did with two legs. Hank *ruled*. Hank was the best. Hank was…his? "You know what, Hank? If it's all right with you, I'd like to take you home."

Claire gasped. "Really? That would be amazing!"

Ten seconds ago, he'd had no idea that he wanted to adopt Hank, but he must have wanted to all along. The idea of it was so *right*. He was meant to bring this dog home. Matt wasn't sure of much these days, but he knew that. "Hank's so calm I'm sure he'd be gentle with Sparkle, right?"

"Oh, yes. Those two have played together in the yard a few times since Sparkle first came in. They're great together."

Man, it was nice to see that smile again, such pure joy on Claire's face. Earlier, he'd been responsible for taking it off. Now, he'd put it back.

"Well, if I'm approved to adopt Hank, I'd like to give him a forever home."

"You mean a *fur*ever home," she said with a grin. She wrapped her arms around him and squeezed, then stepped back, her smile fading. "Sorry about that. Just a little excited for one of my favorites. Oh, Matt, I just know you two are a pair."

He held her gaze, her green eyes sparkling. He loved making her so happy. Even if it was about a dog and not the two of them.

And just like that, Matt left with Sparkle's training treats and a whole bunch of other stuff for his new dog, Hank, including a spiffy navy-blue collar and leash, a huge memory foam dog bed, a soft quilt and the toys that Claire said he seemed to like best. A small fortune later, but worth every penny, Matt and Claire had everything in his car, including Hank, who rode shotgun in the front seat. Matt put the passenger-seat window all the way down so Hank could put his face out if he wanted, even in the February chill.

"Your days in a kennel are over, buddy," Matt said, giving Hank a rub along his soft back.

Hank glanced at him in appreciation, Matt could tell, and stuck his snout out the window. The ole guy was smiling. No doubt.

"I could cry, I'm so happy for him," Claire said as she stood in front of the driver's window. "And not only does Hank get a great home, I get to see him all the time!"

Matt gave her a more rueful smile than he'd intended. Seeing each other all the time probably wasn't a good idea. Living in Claire's house probably wasn't a good idea. Hadn't his smart sister said exactly that?

Right now, he was going to focus on getting his new dog settled. He'd think about what the hell he was going to do about Claire Asher later. Much later.

Because as much as he knew living on her property was a problem, he didn't want to leave.

BigReader, aka Connor Hearon, was as attractive as his photo had indicated. Tall and lanky, with a mop of light brown hair and warm brown eyes, he gave her hope that she could find another man besides Matt Fielding attractive and interesting. Of course, Matt was on her mind. Taking over her mind, actually. When Connor mentioned he was reading a certain biography, Claire's first thought was that Matt would love the book about a climb up Mt. Everest, since he'd loved reading adventure memoirs as a teenager. When Connor ordered the Main Street Grille's special pasta entrée, Claire thought about how Matt would have gone for that too.

What. Was. Wrong. With. Her?

She knew what. Matt Fielding had adopted Hank. A three-legged senior dog that no one else had wanted. Who'd been languishing at Furever Paws for a month. And he'd adopted him despite already fostering and training a puppy for his niece. So, no matter what Matt said, his actions spoke louder to her soul than his words did to her brain. Did that even make any sense? It did to her heart, unfortunately.

He told you! He's leaving town! He's got some crazy notion stuck in his head that he's not good enough for you, that he has nothing to offer you. That all he has in this world is a duffel bag. And now a dog.

She let herself remember him telling her all that.

She *made* herself remember how he'd stopped them from ending up in bed—twice.

And then she forced herself to pay more attention to Connor and push Matt from her consciousness. She focused on the outdoorsman crinkles on the sides of those kind, intelligent eyes.

You know who else has a dog? This guy. Big-Reader. A man whose profile had stated that he wanted a long-term relationship leading to marriage and children.

"So you're divorced?" Connor asked, twirling his fork in his pasta.

"It's been three years," she said, then bit into her black bean burger. "But I just entered the dating world about six months ago. Ready to get back out there and all."

He nodded. "I've been out there for the past six months too. Eye-opening, huh?"

She smiled. "Well, this is actually my first attempt at online dating. I've been saying yes to fix-ups, but I thought I'd start engineering my own future."

"Fix-ups have gone more my way," he said. "I've noticed a lot of women fib about this or that. Like weight." He puffed out his cheeks.

Uh, really? Did he just say that? *Do* that? "Well, I've heard men post ten-year-old photos of themselves when they had more hair."

BigReader had a head full of hair, so it wasn't as though she was insulting him. Their conversation had taken a bit of a sharp turn, so she wanted to direct it back to kinder, gentler territory.

He seemed to realize that he was being a jerk. "Sorry. I don't mean you. You could probably stand to gain a good five pounds," he added, eyeing her breasts.

Get. Me. Out. Of. Here.

"Oh God, I'm really blowing this, aren't I?" He chuckled, because apparently that was hilarious. "I guess I'm just a little gun-shy about relationships. My last girlfriend was two-timing me. And the girlfriend before that was in it because she thought I made a pot of money." He snorted.

Jeez, couldn't he talk about movies or waterways he'd boated down?

She'd finish her dinner and make an excuse to leave immediately. "Well, at least you have that gorgeous dog, right?" she said, swiping a fry through ketchup. She recalled his profile pic with the majestic golden retriever sitting beside him on the boat. "It's amazing how much joy dogs bring to people's lives. When you're feeling down or you're under the weather, a warm nose and furry body next to you can be so comforting."

He snorted again—this time with a bitter edge. "I lost the dog in the divorce. More like I had no problem letting the ex have Banjo so I could demand what I really wanted. Worked like a charm."

Jerk.

He slurped his pasta, and there was no way she could sit there another second. Just when she was thinking of how she could end this date before he even finished his meal, her friend Amanda came over to the table. "How is everything?"

Claire knew Amanda pretty well since they'd spent many hours together at Furever Paws, and she could see the slight raise of her eyebrow—the question was more directed at how Claire thought the *date* was going.

BigReader held up a finger and made a show of finishing chewing. "The pasta's great, but, honestly? I didn't love the dressing on my salad. I like my Italian a little more…something."

"I'm sorry to hear that," Amanda said, her blue eyes on Connor. "I hope a complimentary dessert will make you forget all about that salad dressing. We have some great offerings tonight—"

"Gotta watch my figure for the online dating thing," he said on a laugh.

Amanda offered Claire a rueful smile, clearly able to see for herself how this date was going, then headed to another table.

"So," Connor said. "Back to your place for a nightcap?"

"I don't think we're a match," Claire replied honestly.

He shrugged again. "No worries. It's a numbers game. You gotta be in it to win it, right?"

Claire just wanted to be out of there. "Being in it isn't easy. It's hard sitting across from someone you have little in common with and didn't know yesterday when there are so many expectations."

"Well, there's your problem, Claire. Expectations.

If you're attracted, great. A little making out, even sex. If you're not attracted, buh-bye. Next."

"Well, I guess it's *next* then."

"With that attitude, you'll be single for the rest of your life." He got up and put a twenty-dollar bill on the table, which would barely cover his entrée, his two beers and his share of the tip. "Good luck out there. You'll need it."

"You too," she said, shaking her head, as Big-Reader made his exit.

"Good riddance to bad date-ish," Amanda said, sliding a slice of chocolate cake in front of Claire. "Compliments of the Main Street Grille for putting up with that guy for an hour."

Claire laughed. And dug in. But now what? How many of these dates was she supposed to go on? If it really *was* a numbers game, she didn't have the energy to date that many frogs to find someone close to a prince. Maybe she should stop forcing it. Let it happen naturally, organically. She had met a few single men while volunteering at Furever Paws, but sharing a love of dogs didn't necessarily mean they'd have much else in common. There was always the upcoming regional teachers conference, which might be a source of potential Mr. Rights. The local parks were full of them too. Joggers. Dog walkers. Bench readers. So she wasn't completely a hopeless case. Except maybe when it came to one man.

The man who refused to be Mr. Right was probably in her own backyard right now with his two pooches. She wanted to be home more than anything else in the world. But since her plan to distract herself from Matt's magnetic pull was a big bust, how was she going to protect her heart against him?

Matt had already taken a thousand pictures of Sparkle being cute, texting them to his sister to share with his niece, but now he had the photo of all photos. Hank, his big body curled up in his memory foam bed, the little brown-and-white puppy nestled along-side his belly.

Laura sent back an aww! and said Ellie was dying to come over to meet Hank and work with Sparkle—how about tomorrow?—so he set that up. After a month in the shelter, Hank deserved getting special fuss treatment from an eight-year-old dog enthusiast.

He glanced at the time on his phone—eight forty-five. "Come on, lazybones," he said to the pooches. "Let's go outside, and then you can curl right back up."

All he had to do to communicate his intentions was pick up a leash. Hank ambled over, Sparkle trotting beside him and giving his one front leg a sniff. Matt put on his leather jacket, eager for the days when he wouldn't have to shiver outside at night, and brought the dogs out. Hands in his pockets, he stood at the far end of the yard, away from Claire's patio. The lights were off inside, and he wondered where she was. *Date?*

Don't think about it, he told himself. The dogs did their business, so he threw a ball for them, Hank fly-ing after it, Sparkle on his heels. Wow, Hank could run well on three legs. He was so much bigger and faster than Sparkle that he got the ball before her every time.

He heard a car pull into the driveway on the other side of the house. Claire. He listened for the front door opening and closing, then saw lights flick on inside. The sliding glass door to the yard opened, and she came out with Dempsey. He couldn't help noticing she was dressed up. And wearing makeup, similar to how she'd looked when he'd run into her on her date with Slick. Both "dog shelter Claire," with a fresh-scrubbed face, ponytail and old jeans, and "date Claire" were stunning.

"Date?" he asked before he could tell his brain not to spit it out.

"Actually, yes." She threw a ball for Dempsey, who was too busy sniffing—and being sniffed by— Hank. The three dogs were moving in a comical circle of sniffing noses, bellies and butts, then stopping to stare off at some unseen critter before resuming their nose work.

"Find Mr. Right?" he asked, his chest tightening. Why the hell was he even going there? He didn't want to have this conversation.

"He used the dog as a pawn in his divorce to get what he wanted from his ex. She could have the dog, which he said he didn't want anyway, so he could get *x*, *y*, *z*. God, I hate people."

"*Some* people," he said. "You have the right to hate me, Claire. But I hope you don't. You—" *Shut up*, he told himself, clamping his lips shut. He threw a ball for the dogs, and this time they all went for it, Dempsey winning.

"I what?" she asked with something of a wince. He hated that he made her brace herself.

"You once made me want to be a better person," he said. "Yeah, I enlisted in tribute to my brother and to serve my country, but I also knew the army would give me direction—turn me into a good man."

She shoved her hands in her pockets, and suddenly he was aware again of how cold it was. "You were a perfectly good young man in high school," she said.

He shook his head. "I wasn't. You had a thing for me, so you didn't really care that I was barely scraping by in my classes or got into fights with bullies who liked to pick on those who wouldn't or couldn't fight back. I might have been sticking up for kids, but I got sent to the principal and suspended to the point that one more suspension would have gotten me expelled."

"Not everyone is academically oriented," she said. "And how terrible that you stood up for the underdogs. What a terrible person you were, Matthew Fielding."

A rush of dread filled his lungs. She didn't get it. "I had nothing back then and I have nothing now, Claire."

"Then why do I like you so much?" she asked. "Then *and* now? Huh? Answer that."

"Because you're romanticizing old times. Because I seem like some kind of hero for taking in that spinning pup and calming her down, and for adopting

Hank, who's the coolest dog in the world. No medal deserved there."

"You're consistent," she said. "I'll give you that."

"The truth is the truth. I am exactly who I appear to be."

"I know," she said, shaking her head, but there was a hint of a smile on her pretty face. "So, it pays to know the owner of the Main Street Grille. Amanda, who also volunteers at Furever Paws, gave me an extra slice of chocolate layer cake in a doggie bag for my 'awesome new tenant who adopted Hank.' That's you."

"But it's a doggie bag, so shouldn't these guys have it?"

She did smile this time. "You know full well that chocolate is toxic for dogs, so it's all ours. I'll give them each a peanut butter treat for welcoming Hank so nicely."

He guessed that meant he was going inside her house, having that slice of cake, continuing this too-personal conversation. He could—and would—turn it back to dogs.

She called the dogs to follow her, and they all trooped inside, Matt glad to get Claire out of the cold. In the kitchen, Claire gave them all treats, and then Dempsey showed Hank around the house, Sparkle at their heels. All three dogs ended up sitting in front of the door to the deck, staring out at night critters no one could detect.

"This cake is really something," Claire said, setting the slice on a plate and placing it on the kitchen table. She took two beers out of the refrigerator and slid one beside the cake.

Matt took a bite. Mmm, chocolate heaven. "This was thoughtful of you."

She took a sip of beer. "Well, you did a very thoughtful thing."

He raised an eyebrow. "Ah, you mean adopting Hank."

"It's a big deal," she said. "We were really worried he'd never find a home, and then, whammo, the perfect owner and home presents itself."

"I'm hardly perfect. And I don't have a home, Claire. Again, again, again, you make me out to be something I'm not."

"Or you just don't see yourself the way I do. The way a lot of people do."

"Were you always this bossy and stubborn?" he asked, then took another forkful of cake. "Oh, wait, you were." He smiled.

She smiled back at him. "So enough about us, tell me about you. How did your first few hours with Hank go?"

"Great. He's so calm. And even though Sparkle has mellowed a lot from when I took her in, I think Hank is even more of a calming influence on her. Nothing throws him. A slammed door, a pot lid dropping. He's unflappable. And did you see the way he can chase a ball? He's amazing."

She scooched her chair close and kissed him on the cheek, then threw her arms around him.

And, oh hell, it felt so good that he wrapped his

arms around her and tilted up her chin. "I want to kiss you more than anything right now." He wasn't going to deny himself this. The pull was too strong. The need too great.

"Be my guest," she said, puckering up.

He laughed. "How am I supposed to kiss you when I'm laughing?"

"Like this," she said, covering his lips with hers, the softness making him melt into a puddle on the chair. Everything about her was soft and smelled like spicy flowers. He couldn't get close enough.

"Want the rest of the cake?" he asked.

"No. I just want more of you," she said.

"Good." He scooped her up, his leg only slightly bothering him, and followed her directions to her bedroom, laying her down on the bed.

In seconds, her dress was over her head and in a heap on the floor, along with his shirt and pants. She kissed a trail along his neck and collarbone, her hands all over his chest and pushing down at the waistband of his boxer briefs.

"You're sure?" he whispered. "Despite everything?"

"I'm sure," she whispered back. She pulled open the drawer of her bedside table and took out a box of condoms. "These might be a few years old."

He found the expiration date. "These are actually good until *tomorrow*."

Surprise lit her green eyes. "Meant to be, then."

He didn't know about that.

But he couldn't resist Claire. Not tonight. Not for

another moment. Being with her felt so good, made him feel good about himself, even if afterward…

She said she was sure. She wanted to be taken at her word, had told him to stop making decisions for her, so maybe he really could let himself have this. Tonight. With Claire. Hell, maybe she was right, and it would get him out of her system and she could move on. And he would leave Spring Forest, headed for who knew where, Hank beside him, to start fresh.

Her hands were all over his back, in his hair, and then the boxer briefs were being pushed down. He undid her lacy black bra, inhaling that light perfume in her lush cleavage, and then her hands moved lower, and he lost all ability to think. Finally, eighteen years after meeting Claire, Matt made love to the only woman he'd ever loved.

Chapter 7

He was gone before she woke up, and as a teacher, Claire woke up at the crack of dawn.

Which meant he'd sneaked away in the middle of the night, unable to deal with the aftermath.

Ah, there was a note on her bedside table, sticking out under her phone.

> *C—Have early plans, didn't want to wake you.*
> *Took the dogs out, Dempsey too. See you later.*
> *—M*

Who had plans at 6:00 a.m.? No one, that's who. Plans to get away, maybe.

That was fine. Listen when someone tells you who they are and how they're going to hurt you. Wasn't that one of her many mottoes? Matt Fielding had made his intentions clear. And so she couldn't fault him for not spooning her all night and then waking her up with kisses along her shoulder, whispering sweet everythings in her ear. There was no everything. There was no anything!

That's fine, she repeated, getting out bed, grateful, at least, that she didn't have to open the deck door to let Dempsey out in the winter chill. A dog walker came every weekday at noon to let Dempsey out and throw a ball for her, and Claire had thought about asking Matt if he'd do that when he took out Sparkle and Hank at midday, but it was probably better that he didn't have a key to her house.

Sigh. At least the sex was amazing, she thought as she went into the bathroom and turned on the shower. *Amazing*. Being with Matt was everything she'd always imagined and more.

But he was leaving town after he finished training Sparkle.

Just keep your heart out of it, and you'll be okay. He'd done the shelter two big favors by fostering one dog and adopting another. He'd done her body a big favor by making her feel like liquid. Granted, she was all hunched and tense now, but it was worth it.

Her head set on straight, Claire got ready for work, with her heart only slightly sunk. By the time she arrived at the middle school, her mind was on her students—a welcome distraction, as they demanded so much from her in so many ways. They were reading the novel *Wonder*, which had every one of them fully engaged, and the day was spent on projects related to the book's themes of inclusion, acceptance and the power of friendship.

After the dismissal bell rang for the end of the school day, Claire graded quizzes and killed some time tidying her up her desk to avoid going home before Divorce Club—which was the pet name for the "book" club she belonged to. Two teachers at the middle school had started it, but when they discovered that all four members were divorced, talk had quickly turned from the book they were supposed to read to their lives and marriage and divorce. They met at a different member's house every two weeks. The meeting didn't start till four thirty, but Claire didn't want to go home and run into Matt. She just wasn't ready to see him or listen to his excuses or however he'd awkwardly explain his disappearing act.

Ah. Finally time. Claire drove over to Danielle Peterwell's house, which was near the area where Claire had grown up. She took a detour of a few blocks to drive past the house she'd lived in with her parents and Della and various dogs over the years. Nostalgia gripped her, and she sat there in her car for a few minutes, until a woman came out of the house with a baby in a carrier and a little boy. The boy scampered across the lawn for a few seconds—like Sparkle, Claire thought with a half smile—then she watched the woman put the carrier into the car and help buckle the boy into his seat.

Huh. Maybe the universe was trying to tell her something by having her stop here. Being all hung up on Matt wasn't going to get her that baby and little boy and a partner to share her life with.

She lifted her chin and drove over to Danielle's, determined to keep her head on straight—and on what she wanted most of all: a family.

At Divorce Club, the members all said their hellos and attacked the very nice spread the hostess had set out: miniquiches, fruit and a light sangria.

"Now last time, I'm pretty sure Claire had a blind date set up by her sister?" Jen Garcia said. "Do tell," she added, taking a sip of sangria.

She'd almost forgotten all about that guy—Andrew something. The lawyer her sister had fixed her up with. Two dates ago. "It actually started out pretty well, but he basically told me at the end of the date that he'd hooked up with his ex the night before."

"He randomly told his blind date that?" Lara Willkowski asked. "Idiot."

"Well, I kind of saw an old boyfriend at the restaurant," Claire admitted, "and when the date asked if I wanted to go for a drink after dinner, I told the truth about being sort of distracted."

"Date fail," Danielle said with a grin.

"Hey, wait," Lara said. "Was the old boyfriend Matt Fielding? From high school?"

Claire nodded and slugged some sangria.

Lara plucked a miniquiche from the tray. "I thought I recognized him. I saw him in the park the other day with an adorable little puppy."

"He's fostering the pup for his sister while he trains her. Sparkle's a gift for his young niece."

"Wow, *that's* nice of him," Danielle said pointedly.

The group knew how passionate Claire was about Furever Paws. "And yesterday he adopted a ten-year-old, three-legged dog named Hank," Claire said. "I'm sunk."

She wasn't going to mention last night. She basically had to forget it herself.

"And...?" Jen prompted.

Claire shrugged. "We're kind of on different paths."

Luckily, Danielle started talking about how she and the first guy she dated after her divorce were on different paths too, to the point that he moved to Nepal to climb very tall mountains. Which led to a conversation change to outdoorsy men who liked to hike when Danielle just wanted to go out to lunch or dinner and wear cute shoes. Jen, who loved to hike, had had a date with a couch potato the other night, and they were both willing to give it another try.

But there was nothing to *try* when it came to Matt. Claire just had to accept that they were in two very different places in their lives and looking for different things. She had to let him go.

Even after that glorious sex. Even after feeling so close to him that while he was making love to her, she kept thinking: *this is what homecoming feels like.*

Keep it together, Claire, she ordered herself. *Don't get all emotional right now.* The Divorce Club crew was great and would rally around her, but she didn't want the focus to be on herself.

She thought about what her late mother had told her when she was struggling in the aftermath of her divorce. *You sit with how you feel, and you accept that you're heartbroken. You don't have to pretend to feel fine. Just let yourself feel what you feel and grieve. It's all part of the process.*

Now, she'd take that good advice again and let herself sit with her feelings about Matt, though her emotions were all over the place, her thoughts about the situation ping-ponging as if Dempsey and Hank had the rackets. She'd always loved Matt and always would.

And unfortunately, last night, she'd fallen deeper.

"So do you think there's a chance you and Matt could pick up where you left off?" Danielle asked as she set out the dessert tray; four slices of cherry cheesecake. Claire was going to eat every ounce of that cake, despite the chocolate cake she'd had last night. In fact, she would probably let herself have all the decadent desserts she wanted this entire week.

"Only in my fantasies," Claire said.

"You never know," Jen said, forking a piece of cheesecake. "That's become my new motto."

But Claire *did* know. Unless she wanted to break her own heart this time, she'd keep her emotional distance from Matt Fielding.

Using a high-backed chair for support, Matt did the exercises his new physical therapist had had him do this morning. Zeke Harper, an old buddy from town, whom he'd run into at the park a few weeks ago while teaching Sparkle the *come* command, had recommended him. Zeke knew the guy from volun-

teering at a veterans' center, and had mentioned that
Matt still had some stiffness from his IED injury. The
guy had offered to work with Matt free of charge, but
could only fit him in at 7:00 a.m. The workout had
hurt but had felt good. Just like now.

When he'd woken up in Claire's bed this morning,
he'd almost been amazed it hadn't been a dream. He'd
lain there, also aware that for the first time in months,
he hadn't had a nightmare about the day he'd been injured, the day that had sent him home. He'd opened
his eyes to find Hank sitting at the edge of the bed,
staring at him with those soulful, amber-colored eyes.
Sparkle and Dempsey, meanwhile, were curled in
Dempsey's dog bed on the other side of the bedroom.

And then there was Claire. His beautiful Claire,
whose face and voice and memory had seen him
through the worst of his recuperation, like an angel.
He'd never expected to run into her in Spring Forest;
he'd never imagined in a million years she'd still be
in their old hometown. And then he woke up in her
bed, naked, next to a naked Claire.

He shouldn't have touched her, but maybe she was
right about them getting each other out of their sys-
tems.

Not that that was working yet. He'd thought of
little else all day but how good last night was, how
comfortable and natural and right. He had to keep reminding himself to keep things on a physical level,
to keep emotions out of it.

Because he was leaving. Probably sometime in
mid-to late March, a few weeks, six at most, he fig-

ured. Sparkle was coming along so well in her training that she'd be good to go very soon. Ellie had come
over after school today as planned, and Matt had
taught her what he knew. If Ellie thought he walked
on water before, now she looked at him with wonder
and called him the Dog Prince.

That had made him laugh. Matt Fielding, anyone's
prince. Even a dog's.

"Right, Hank?" he asked, giving the old guy a
belly rub. Hank immediately stretched out his long
body so that Matt wouldn't stop. "Maybe I am the
Dog Prince. Or do I have that backward?" he asked,
giving Hank a vigorous rub. "You're the best, dude,"
he said.

Hank just stared at him, but Matt knew the dog
could understand him.

A car pulled into the driveway, which told him
Claire was home. He owed her an explanation for
leaving the way he did that morning. After the night
they'd shared. Despite the note, he had to say *something*.

He heard her deck door open, so he went down
the stairs to the yard. The weather had turned colder,
just above freezing, and she stood there, her arms
wrapped around her coat.

"Hey," he said as she reached the bottom landing.
He should have put on gloves. He shoved his hands
in the pockets of his leather jacket.

She glanced over at him. "Hi." She threw a ball
for Dempsey, who went flying after it.

"I just wanted to explain why I left so early," he said, looking everywhere but at her.

"No need. You've made yourself clear, Matt. You don't owe me explanations. And I don't regret last night. Not a single second of it. And that includes you leaving at the crack of dawn. Last night was a long time coming."

He tilted his head. "Yes, it was."

"Well, it's freezing out here, so I'm going to get Dempsey back inside."

He nodded, wishing he could go with her, wishing for a repeat of last night, wishing again that things were different, that he had a future to offer her.

As she opened the sliding glass door and Dempsey scooted through, he said, "Claire?"

She turned.

"Did it work? Did you get me out of your system?"

She looked at him for a moment. "No."

Neither did I, he thought as she disappeared inside. *Neither did I.*

Claire avoided Matt the following week, which was difficult since she always waited until he came back in with his dogs early in the morning before taking Dempsey out. She wished things weren't so strained between them. She missed Sparkle and Hank. And Matt's niece, Ellie, had been over twice after school when Claire had gotten home. She'd wanted more than anything to join them in the yard to watch Matt teach Ellie training tips. But she'd stayed inside.

Ugh. This wasn't what she wanted. But in a month,

he'd leave in that black Mustang and she'd be here, living the same old life, just like the one she'd had before he'd come back. Except she honestly didn't think she could do that. His return had changed something in the air, changed *her*, and when he was gone, there was no way in hell she was going on bad date after bad date to find her life partner and the father of the child she wanted so badly.

"I should just devote my life to dogs," she said to Dempsey, running her hand over the fur on the dog's back and sides. She got a lick on the hand for that. As usual, Dempsey seemed to know when she needed comfort and curled up beside her on the couch, her head on Claire's thigh. "Dogs are not confusing like certain tall, dark and very good-looking humans."

On Saturday morning, Claire woke up early to head over to Furever Paws for the weekend adoption event. She would be walking Dempsey around the shelter with an Adopt Me! banner draped over her back. These events brought a lot of visitors to the property, so the staff and volunteers typically walked a few dogs around that they wanted to highlight. The other dogs were kept in their kennels, because the large number of people, with their strange smells and grabbing hands, could be stressful for them.

"Hi, Claire," Bunny said, putting the banner over Cutie Pie, the shepherd mix she'd been fostering.

Claire smiled at Bunny. "Everything set for the event?"

Bunny nodded, surveying Cutie Pie and grabbing a red bandanna from the display wall. She tied it around the dog's neck. "There. Now you're ready for your close-up." She straightened and glanced around, then leaned close to Claire. "Isn't Matt with you?"

Claire raised an eyebrow. "Matt is most definitely not with me. Why would he be?"

Bunny headed over to the desk where two volunteers were stacking adoption applications, foster applications, and information packets. "He called last night and asked if we could use some extra help for the adoption event. I said of course."

Why was Matt so damn helpful except when it came to their relationship?

"We got some very promising applications online for four dogs and six cats," Birdie said as she came in from the back hallway. "I've approved three for the dogs and four for the cats. One of the rejected cat applicants thought her already thirteen black cats might like another now that they're bored of each other." She rolled her eyes. "And the other one has a dog who hates cats but would surely learn to love pretty, long-haired Glenda."

Claire shook her head. "Well, good for the ones who passed muster." She knew the dog adoption applications would require a home visit, but if everything checked out, those dogs would be going to their forever homes. "I guess Dempsey wasn't among them?"

"Sorry," Birdie said. "I don't know why she keeps being passed up." She bent down and petted Dempsey. "You're a beautiful, sweet dog and someone is going to snatch you up soon. Mark my words."

There was a knock at the door. The shelter wasn't open yet, so it had to be a volunteer without a key. Matt.

Yup, there he was. Looking gorgeous in his black leather jacket, jeans and work boots. He greeted Birdie and Bunny and nodded at Claire. She nodded back.

"How can I help?" he asked.

Birdie set him to work hanging Adoption Event banners on the upper walls. As more volunteers and foster parents came in with their dogs, Claire lost track of Matt. Then she spotted him standing near the door with Birdie, who'd handed him a stack of information packets so that he could greet each potential adopter with all the info they needed on the available dogs and cats.

The morning passed in a whirlwind of activity. So many people came through the doors. Seven cats found new homes, and the four preapproved applicants for the dogs had all confirmed they wanted the dogs they'd fallen for online now that they'd met them in person. Two volunteers would do home checks today, and then the adoptions would be made official.

"I keep seeing Dempsey's profile on your website and clicking on it," a woman said to Claire, bending to pet Dempsey, who sat beside her. "I just love her coloring. Like my hair," she added on a laugh.

"Like cinnamon," Claire agreed, though she didn't think it was much of a reason to be drawn to a dog. Or maybe it was. People fell in love for all kinds of reasons.

"She's awfully big, though," the woman added, giving Dempsey a pat. "Aren't you, you big thing," she singsonged in baby talk.

Dempsey eyed the woman as if she were above baby talk, but Claire knew Dempsey loved it. When it came to shelter animals, baby talk was a very welcome thing.

After answering the woman's many questions, Claire asked if she'd like to fill out an application.

"I don't know," the woman said. "I was thinking of a much smaller dog. A cuter dog, you know? Not that Dempsey isn't cute. She's just so…boxer-y."

Sigh. "Well, she is a boxer mix."

This woman sounded all wrong for Dempsey. Like she'd maybe take her and then return her two weeks later. "You know what? Dempsey is beautiful, and I always seem to come back to her. So, maybe I can take her for a walk outside and see how it goes?"

Claire set her up with a leash and led the woman to the fenced yard. She stood by the door while the woman walked Dempsey. At least the prospective adopter was affectionate, giving Dempsey lots of TLC.

"I'd like to put in an application," the woman said when she returned.

Claire expected to be elated, but instead her heart felt like it weighed two thousand pounds. Granted, Dempsey's potential new mom was a bit wishy-washy, but adopting a dog was a big decision. Better to talk it out than be impulsive.

"Great," Claire said, handing the woman an application. "Why don't you take a seat here and fill it out." She gestured at the rectangular table that Matt had set up in the lobby with chairs and a canister of pens. "Then I'll go over it and pass it to one of the owners for final approval."

"Could that happen today? I was planning to binge-watch season two of my favorite show on Netflix, and I'd hate to have to be interrupted to walk her, especially in the cold."

Oh brother. *You can watch your shows anytime. Bringing home a new dog is a special occasion.* Claire frowned and rubbed Dempsey's side. "Well, we'll see," was all she would and could say.

As the woman got busy filling out the application, Claire put Dempsey into one of the kennels with a chew toy. "I'll be back for you, I promise." A strange feeling was lodged in her stomach, something she couldn't quite identify.

"Crazy day," a familiar voice said.

Matt. She locked Dempsey's kennel and stood up. "Someone put in an application for Dempsey. I can't believe it. She might have a permanent home."

"Looking good?" he asked.

Claire shrugged. "Hard to tell. People sometimes say nutty things when they're in unfamiliar territory. She'd be a first-time dog owner. I guess I need to give her the benefit of the doubt until I read through her application."

"Miss?" called a high-pitched voice. "Miss?"

Claire glanced out the window and down the hallway, toward the voice. The woman who wanted to adopt Dempsey was standing and waving at her. "Guess her application is ready."

Matt gave her a gentle smile. "I'm not quite sure if you want Dempsey to be adopted or not."

"Of course I want her to be adopted," she snapped. "I've fostered twenty-one dogs since I started volunteering here. Giving them up to the right home is the point." Her voice was sharper than she'd intended, and she let out a breath. "Sorry. Didn't mean to take your head off. Dempsey is special. I just want her to be in the right home."

"Understood," he said, putting a hand on her shoulder, and it felt so good, so comforting that she wanted him to pull her against him and hold her tight.

She'd always known she'd have to say goodbye to Dempsey someday. Same with Matt. The two in the same time frame? That, she wasn't so sure she could bear.

But she sucked in a breath and left the Dogs room to go read over the application belonging to Dempsey's potential adopter, her legs like lead.

Chapter 8

Claire held Gwyneth Cardle's application for Dempsey and read each line carefully. The woman lived in a single-family home, but there was no fenced yard.

"Since you don't have a fenced yard, are you prepared to walk Dempsey at least three times a day, for taking care of business and exercise?"

"Three times?" Gwyneth said, her eyes popping. "I'm figuring on walking her right before I leave for work at eight thirtyish, and then when I get home at five thirty."

Claire stared at her. "You realize that's nine hours."

"She's a big dog, though. I read that big dogs can hold it longer."

Claire marked an X next to Residence Information.

"So, Dempsey will be alone for nine hours each

weekday?" Claire asked. "No contact with people or dogs and no potty break or exercise?"

"I work," the woman snapped. "So sue me."

"You could hire a dog walker to come at noon," Claire said. "I work and that's what I do."

"Not everyone can afford that," Gwyneth muttered. "She'll have to hold it in."

Claire marked an *X* next to Understands Dogs' Needs and went over the rest of her application, which was as dismal. Under the area that asked what provisions she would make for the dog if she went on vacation, Gwyneth had written: "I really don't know."

Next.

If there would be a next. *Looks like you're mine a bit longer, Dempsey*, she thought, a feeling she recognized all too well as relief washing over her.

"Thanks so much for filling out the application and for your interest in Dempsey," she said to Gwyneth. "I'll pass the application to one of the shelter owners, and we'll be in touch by the end of the day."

"Could you not call before five?" she asked, putting on her jacket. "I'm planning on watching five episodes of my show today, so…"

Claire mentally rolled her eyes. "Well, one of the Whitaker sisters will contact you via email. So, no worries."

As Claire watched the woman walk away and stick her finger in an adoptable kitten's kennel in the lobby, despite the big sign that read: Please Do Not Put Fingers in Kennels, she thought about how satisfying it would be to stamp the application with Not Recommended.

On her way to the desk to do just that, Claire's phone pinged with a text. Jasmine, one of her teacher friends from the middle school.

Help! Babysitter canceled and tonight's my brother-in-law's wedding. Can you take Tyler? Six to midnightish.

Ooh. Tyler was a precious, adorable, baby-shampoo-scented seven-month-old with huge brown eyes and a gummy smile.

She texted back, Of course! I'll come pick him up so you don't get baby spit-up on the gorgeous dress I'm sure you're wearing.

Thank you!!! I owe you BIG.

Clare smiled. *Au contraire.* She loved babysitting, especially babies.

And what better way to try to get Matt out of her system than to focus on what she wanted for herself: a child.

That night, as Matt took Sparkle and Hank into the yard, he could have sworn he saw Claire walking back and forth in her living room with a baby in her arms. Seeing things?

Nope. Because there she was again. Walking and patting the baby on the back.

He swallowed. How many nights had he thought about "what might have been?" if he and Claire had married. Had children. Sometimes he'd think of them with a baby, sometimes with six kids. And then the images would fade because *come on*. Matt Fielding, someone's father? A thirty-six-year-old man with a duffel bag and a three-legged dog to his name?

He could see Dempsey staring forlornly out the glass door, hoping to be let out to play with her friends. But Claire clearly had her hands full and looked a bit exasperated.

As she looked out and spotted him, he quickly held up a hand and came over to the door. She slid it open just a bit since she obviously didn't want to let the cold air inside to chill the baby.

"I'll take Dempsey if it's easier on you," he said.

"Oh, thank God," she sputtered. "I love Tyler to pieces, but he's been crying for half an hour. He was fine when I picked him up from my colleague's house."

"So you're babysitting for the night?" he asked.

She nodded, rocking the baby in her arms. "It's okay, little guy," she cooed to the baby. "Everything is okay."

A bell dinged, and Claire glanced toward the left. "Oh crud. That's my oven timer. Could you hold Tyler for just a minute while I get the cookies out of the oven?"

What? She wanted him to hold the baby? The squawking, red-faced baby?

"Matt?" she asked. "I don't want to just put him down in his bouncer while he's so miserable."

"Okay," he said, stepping inside the living room and closing the sliding glass door behind him. He held out his arms, clueless as to how to take a baby, let alone hold one. She handed the baby over, and maybe it was the change of scenery of his face versus Claire's, but the baby stopped crying. Matt took him under the arms and cradled him against his chest, finding that holding the tot was just sort of instinctive. "Name's Matt," he said to the baby.

Claire burst out laughing from the kitchen. She poked her head out of the kitchen doorway. "Oh God, I needed that. Thank you." She poked her head back in and continued laughing.

"Something funny about what I said?" he asked, eyes narrowed toward the kitchen, from where the smell of warm cookies emanated.

She came back inside the living room, grinning. "Yes, actually. 'Name's Matt,'" she said, making her voice deeper. She chuckled and reached out to caress the baby's face.

"Well, shouldn't I introduce myself?"

"You don't spend much time around babies, do you?" she asked.

"Nope. But look at me now? Baby whisperer." He rocked the baby a bit as he had seen Claire do earlier. Tyler laughed.

Matt's mouth dropped open. "He laughed! Babies laugh?"

"They sure do. And he sure seems to like you. You *are* the baby whisperer."

"Whodathunk," he said, moving to the couch to sit down. Tyler immediately grabbed his chin.

"The dogs are all right on their own?" he asked.

Claire went to the glass door and peered out. "Hank appears to be overseeing the other two as he gnaws on a rope toy. Sparkle is sniffing under the tree, and Dempsey is digging in the spot I made for her to do just that."

"So, since you're babysitting and not bringing Dempsey to her new home, I assume that woman's application didn't work out."

"She thought leaving a dog home alone for nine hours every weekday was no big deal," Claire said. "I mean, maybe some dogs can handle that but it's not ideal. Given that she didn't seem a good match for Dempsey in most ways, I didn't recommend her."

"Well, I'm sure the right person will come along. Just like me for Hank."

She stared at him, and he wondered if she was applying that statement to herself, as well.

Tyler gripped Matt's ear and pulled with a squeal of joy.

"Ow," Matt said on a laugh. "Quite an arm you got there." He tickled the baby's belly and made funny faces at him, sticking out his tongue.

Tyler laughed that big baby laugh that was almost impossible to imagine coming from such a bitty body.

"You really have a way with babies," Claire said. "Ever think about fatherhood?"

His smile faded. "Of course not."

"Of course not?" she repeated.

"Claire. If I have nothing to offer a woman, I have nothing to offer a baby. I wouldn't inflict myself on an innocent life."

"You really don't see yourself the way others do," she said.

"Key word there is *see*. I know who I am. Others *see* an honorably discharged soldier. They don't look past the uniform and what it represents."

"Because it means so much," she said. "It speaks for itself."

"I didn't say I'm a bad person. Just that I have nothing to offer a family. So I'm not going there."

"Matt, you've been home only a couple of weeks. You expect to have your new life figured out already? I certainly don't expect that of you."

Once again, she just didn't understand. Making a baby laugh didn't mean he was cut out for fatherhood. Training a puppy didn't mean he was cut out for man of the year.

"Claire, do yourself a favor and stop trying to make me into something I'm not. I don't want a wife. I don't want a baby. I'm on my own. Me and Hank."

She stared at him. "I'll never forget you telling me that when you had a son, you were going to name him Jesse, after your brother."

His chest seized up and the back of his eyes stung. He pictured his brother, older by four years, the best person Matt had ever known. And his hero.

"Did I say that?" he managed to choke out.

"Yes, you did," she said softly.

He closed his eyes and got up and put the baby in

the bouncer, latching the little harness. He pushed the On button and the bouncer gently swung side to side. He watched Tyler's eyes droop and droop some more until they closed.

"Magic," she said, moving closer behind him.

He turned around and pulled her into a hug. "I did say that," he whispered. A long time ago, but he'd said it.

"And his middle name would be Thomas, after my dad."

He closed his eyes again. He remembered saying that too. She'd lost her father when she was only nine, barely older than Ellie. Then her mother had died a few years ago; he'd heard the news through his sister. "I'm so sorry about your mom. I don't think I ever said that. When my sister mentioned it in a letter, I wanted to write you, but then I thought I should just leave well enough alone."

"I wish you had written," she said. "I wish a lot of things."

He put his hands on either side of her face, and she looked up at him. There was so damned much hovering between them. History and feeling. He lowered his face, and she tilted up even higher to kiss him.

"I'm leaving by the end of March," he said, taking a step back. "Sparkle will be ready for my sister's house. I need to be clear. There's not going to be any baby named Jesse."

She stepped back as if he'd slapped her.

A dog barked, then others chimed in. Matt went to the glass door and looked out, his chest tight, his heart racing. The dogs were standing under a tree, staring up at a fat squirrel racing across one of the branches. "I'd better get these guys out of the cold."

"We all need to be let out of the cold," she said. "The deep freeze."

He glanced at her, then walked over to Tyler. "Night, little guy," he whispered, and then fled outside.

On Sunday afternoon, Claire accompanied Bunny on a home check for a couple who had an approved application to adopt Pierre, a two-year-old black Lab mix they'd met at the adoption event earlier that day. The Changs had an adorable toddler named Mia and lived in a classic white Colonial with a red door. They had a fenced yard, and had already decked out the house with everything a dog could need—plush beds in a few rooms, food and water bowls, toys and two sets of leashes and harnesses, plus an assortment of poop bags. These people were prepared to bring a dog into their family.

"Mia's first word was dog," Camille Chang said, the little girl on her lap.

Bunny smiled. "Well, Mia, I'm happy to let you know that you'll now have a dog of your very own."

"So all is well with the home check?" Michael Chang asked.

"All is well. You can come pick up Pierre anytime." She added her card to Pierre's paperwork, which included the Chang's application. Claire watched her write *Approved to adopt Pierre—Bunny W.* across the back of the card. "Just show this at the desk and he's all yours."

They left the very happy Changs and headed out to Bunny's ancient car with the Furever Paws logo painted on the sides.

Claire got in and buckled up with a deep sigh. When she realized she actually sighed out loud, she winced.

"What's got you all wistful?" Bunny asked. "Spill it."

Claire smiled. "You know when you want something but the someone you want it with isn't interested in any of it, including you, but you want him, and so you're just spinning your wheels in what feels like gravel?"

"I assume you're talking about our handsome new volunteer?"

Claire nodded—and then found herself launching into every detail of her relationship, and lack thereof, with Matt Fielding.

"Ah, well, he's interested all right."

"He's told me flat out he's not. Attracted, yes," she added, thinking she probably should have left out the part about ending up in bed. But the Whitaker sisters were hardly shrinking violets, and she'd always felt she could get personal with them. "Interested in a future with me? A family one day? No."

Bunny turned the ignition. "My hard-won wisdom is this, Claire. He's interested. In fact, he probably just doesn't know how to get from here to there. You've just got to flip him."

Claire raised an eyebrow. "Flip him? What do you mean?"

"You've said he doesn't think he has what it takes to be a husband and a father because he has nothing to offer. But he's shown you time and again he most definitely is husband and daddy material."

"Right," Claire said. "But where does the flipping come in?"

"By spending time with him, not hiding or avoiding him. The more he sees for himself who he is, the closer you'll get to your dream."

Her dream. Husband, children. Dogs. "Am I that transparent?"

Bunny grabbed Claire's hand and squeezed. "Sorry, but yes. You love that man."

Claire bit her lip. She did.

"So are you going to give up like you had no choice when you were eighteen? Or are you going to make that man yours?"

Claire smiled. "You make it sound so easy."

Bunny backed out of the Changs' driveway and headed toward the shelter. "He adopted Hank, Claire. He's halfway there already. He just doesn't know it."

"Halfway could go either way. Backward or forward," Claire pointed out.

"If you're a pessimist like Birdie, maybe." Bunny chuckled, then added, "Don't tell my sister I said that. She calls herself a *realist*."

"I think I need a dash of you to believe this relationship has a chance, and a dash of Birdie to keep my head out of the clouds."

And she wasn't so sure that adopting Hank meant Matt was setting down roots. Making something his. Creating permanence. Dogs loved unconditionally and didn't talk or ask for much. They were easy to love. People were much harder.

But Bunny was right—Matt's adopting Hank was a major sign of his commitment to love, honor and cherish that living, breathing creature. *A* living, breathing creature. It was a start, and all she had at the moment, so she was going to run with Bunny's dreamer ways.

"Oh, and Claire?" Bunny said as she pulled into Furever Paws' gravel parking lot. "He named his some-day son. I'm not sure you need more *sign* than that."

"That was a long time ago, when he was a different person."

"Was he? According to the broken record of Matt Fielding, he had nothing to offer you then and has nothing to offer now. So for him, nothing is different. If he could imagine being a father then, he could imagine being one now." She smiled and shook her head. "Men."

Huh. Bunny was absolutely right.

Except he was leaving by the end of March. "He's out of here in four weeks, Bunny."

"Or not, dear."

He'd left once. For eighteen years. Claire had no doubt the most stubborn man she'd ever met would do it again.

Chapter 9

Was Matt really walking the dogs around the front of Claire's house to avoid running into her in the backyard with Dempsey? *Yes.* He sighed, hating that it had come to this. How could he want to be with someone so much and want to avoid her at the same time? What the hell was that?

The front door opened and Dempsey's snout, followed by the rest of her and then Claire, came outside. Guess Claire had the same idea.

Awk-ward.

"Oh, hi," she said.

"Hey."

Dempsey started pulling on her leash, something he didn't think he ever saw her do. Must be a particularly interesting squirrel nearby.

Sparkle started pulling too and barking up a storm. "Whoa there, pup," he said. The only dog not pulling was Hank, but he was staring at something across the road.

Matt glanced toward where they were staring. A small, gray, scruffy dog was half-hiding behind the wheel of a car parked across the street. "See that dog?" he asked Claire. "Sure looks skinny and bedraggled."

Claire gasped. "It's him! I saw him a few days ago and tried to lure him with treats, but he was scared and then a truck passed by and must have spooked him, because he took off running."

"I don't see a collar," Matt said. "Poor thing must be a stray from the looks of him."

"I think so too."

"Here, I'll take Dempsey. Maybe you can lure him over with treats now."

Claire handed over Dempsey and pulled a treat from her pocket. "Here, sweetie," she said, bending down a bit as she moved forward toward the curb. The mutt was still half-hiding, staring at the dogs more than her—or the treat.

"Ruff! Grr-ruff!" Sparkle barked.

"Shh, Sparkle," Matt said. "You might scare him away."

Claire stepped off the sidewalk and onto the street. But just then, a teenager on a moped came racing down the road, and the dog took off running.

Oh no.

Claire ran after him, treat in hand, but then she

stopped, throwing her hands up before she came back. "I lost him. Poor guy. It's so cold at night, especially. I called the animal warden when I saw him a couple of days ago, but she hasn't been able to find him."

"Well, we know he likes this road. So maybe he'll be back."

Claire bit her lip. "I hate the idea of that skinny, hungry little thing out there on his own."

"I know. But let's hope for the best. You'd bring him to the shelter?" he asked.

She nodded. "Our vet, Dr. Jackson—we call him Doc J—would check him out with a full exam, and we'd go from there. The little dog seemed to be in good enough shape."

"I'll keep an eye out," Matt said. "Maybe he'll be back later."

She nodded. "Me too. But little dogs are hard to catch. So many places to hide. I don't want you to be disappointed if we can't rescue him."

"I will be. I know what it's like to think you have nowhere to go." He froze. *What the hell?* He hadn't intended to say that.

"You'll always have somewhere to go, Matt. You have your sister, and no matter what, I'll always be your friend. Even if I'm really, really, really mad at you."

That actually made him smile. "Are you? Mad at me."

"Yeah, I am."

The snapping miniature poodle two doors down was storming down the sidewalk, pulling her owner, who kept saying "One day I'm going to hire a trainer."

"Dempsey's nemesis," Claire said. "I think I'll head back inside. Thanks for holding her."

"Anytime," he said.

The second the door closed behind them, he missed Claire. He really hoped they'd find and rescue that gray dog. Because somehow, in no time at all, Matt had become a dog person. And because he wanted to do something to make Claire happy.

With Dempsey at Doc J's main office for a dental cleaning, Claire's house sure was…lonely. She attempted to bake a pie, which came out lopsided and missing something vital, like sugar, maybe. Then she cleaned both bathrooms and vacuumed Dempsey's fur off all surfaces. She watched two episodes of a TV show, then tried to read a memoir about a woman who adopted a dog after divorce and it changed her life.

But she couldn't concentrate on anything. She kept lifting her eyes to the ceiling and toward the right, wondering what was going on in Matt's over-the-garage apartment. Part of her wanted to march up the deck stairs, knock on that that man's door and tell him straight-up how she felt, point out that he clearly felt something too, and that he was being ridiculous. And that he'd better fall in love with her *this minute*.

Well, maybe she'd just tell him how she felt. He was leaving soon. If his response was, *Sorry, I just don't feel the same way* or more of *I can't because of this-that*, at least she wouldn't be mortified around him for long. But there was a chance she could get through to him. Flip him, like Bunny had suggested.

She went upstairs to her bedroom and sat down at her dressing table, planning to doll herself up a bit, but frowned in the mirror instead. *Take me or leave me. This is who I am. A woman who teaches tweens all day and gets down and dirty with dogs all evening at the shelter. Accept me, dog hair and all.*

She got up, went to the kitchen for a bottle of red wine and a block of one of her favorite cheeses, put on her jacket, then went out the deck door and up the stairs to Matt's entrance. She knocked. *Please don't let me humiliate myself—again*, she thought.

He answered the door with a towel around his waist, damp from the shower and looking so incredibly sexy, she couldn't find words for a moment. Luckily, two sets of canine eyes were staring at her as Sparkle and Hank stood beside him, assessing the interloper. She cleared her throat and gave each a scratch under the chin.

He eyed the wine and cheese with interest in his blue eyes. "What are we celebrating?"

"A second chance for us." She held her breath.

He shook his head. "Claire, you dodged a bullet with me. Why can't you understand that? My life is completely up in the air right now."

"Really? Looks to me like your feet are solidly on the ground. You have a home, family nearby, a *dog*."

He tilted his head. "I *do* have a dog, don't I? Never saw that one coming."

She smiled. "Life is happening, Matt. You might be trying to stand still because being out of the military is a culture shock for you. But life is moving around you, and you're responding whether you mean to or not. Hence, Hank."

"Hence?" He laughed.

"I'm an English teacher. So *hence*. *Hence*, Matt Fielding, shut up and let what is going to happen happen instead of trying to fight it for reasons that aren't standing up to scrutiny."

He smiled and shook his head. "I guess I could use a glass of wine."

Thank you, universe! she shouted in her head. She went into his kitchen and took out two wineglasses from a cabinet and poured. They clinked. And that was when the towel dropped.

Oh my. She'd seen him naked not too long ago, but oh wow, oh wow, oh wow. Matt Fielding was magnificent. Tall and muscled and strong. She lifted up her face to kiss him.

He kissed her and kissed her and kissed her, and suddenly, he was walking her backward, his lips still on hers, toward the bedroom.

"I can't stop thinking about you," he whispered, his hands in her hair as they stood just inside the doorway. "Everywhere I look, there you are—my apartment, my dogs, my past. I spent an hour searching for that little gray dog mostly to see your smile when I found him."

She was speechless for a moment. She couldn't even process everything he'd just said, so she focused on the easy part. "Did you find him?"

"He slowed down a few blocks from here, and I thought I could stop my car and lure him over with little bits of a mozzarella cheese stick, but something spooked him and he took off. I couldn't find him after that."

"I appreciate that you tried, Matt." She led him by the hand to the bed and kissed him again, slowly sinking down to the edge of the mattress.

This is so right, she thought over and over. *Can't you feel it?* she silently asked him. *There's no way you can't feel this.*

"You know what I think is unfair?" he asked, one hand in her hair, the other undoing a button on her shirt.

"What?"

"That you're still dressed while I'm naked."

She grinned and got rid of her clothes, aware of him watching her remove every last piece of wool and cotton and lace from her body.

"You do, right?" she asked, running her hands over his glorious chest, all hard planes and muscles.

He trailed kisses up her neck, pausing briefly to ask, "Do what?"

"Feel this. What's between us." She could actually feel him freeze, his body just *stop*. "I want you to stay. And I don't mean just the night, Matt. There, I said it. No one's a mind reader, right? Now you know."

He sat up against the headboard, grabbing part of the top sheet to cover him from the waist down. "I can't stay, Claire. And I really don't want to talk about it."

She stood up and quickly dressed. "Let me tell you something, *bub*."

"Bub?" he repeated.

"Yes, *bub*."

"I'm listening," he said.

"What you might not realize is that you actually do have one thing to offer, Matt. And it happens to be the only thing I want from you."

He stared at her. "I can't possibly come up with anything you could be talking about."

"The one thing you have to offer is *yourself*, Matt Fielding."

He shook his head. "Matt Fielding is a shell, Claire."

Grrr! "A shell? Does a shell of a man adopt a senior three-legged dog and buy every treat and toy and dog bed for his comfort? Does a shell of a man foster a nutty puppy for his smitten niece? Does a shell of a man volunteer at an animal shelter and move furniture around the Whitaker sisters' house? You *love*, Matt. Whether you want to admit it or not. You're just choosing to avoid commitment."

"That's where you're wrong. It's not a choice. This thing in here," he said, slapping a hand over his chest, "is blocked by a brick wall. It's there all the time. The dogs, two sixtysomething sisters with nicknames, and an eight-year-old with a crooked braid don't threaten my equilibrium. I'm not looking for attachments beyond them."

She crossed her arms over her chest. "So you're just a lone wolf."

"Better than what you're doing with Dempsey. You're so attached to her, when you're just going to have to let her go. I saw the look on your face, the tension in your body language when she got that application the other day. Loving Dempsey means breaking your own heart."

"Bullcrap. Love is all there is in this crazy world. Everything you've been through has helped build that brick wall in that chest of yours, but I can help break it down if you'll let me. You have to let someone in, Matt. May as well be me."

Please don't say Sorry *and turn away. Stop pushing me out of your life.*

"I am really sorry, Claire. But I'm leaving in a few weeks as planned."

She could use that brick wall over her own heart right about now. Because it was breaking again, and she was powerless to protect herself. So she did the only thing she could. She left.

After rushing downstairs from Matt's last night, Claire had kept busy by grading quizzes and baking and cleaning some more. At least her house was spotless. She'd spent the night tossing and turning in her bed, vacillating between giving up on Matt as the lost cause he said he was and being on Team Bunny and working on the flip. Which apparently she was no good at.

There was a rap at the sliding glass door. Matt stood there with Sparkles's and Hank's leashes dangling from his neck.

"Hi," she said, barely able to look at him.

"Hi. I just realized I forgot to bring down poop bags. Got two extras?"

Sigh. He could have run up and gotten some from his apartment. She supposed it meant he was trying, that he wasn't avoiding her.

"Come in out of the cold," she said. "I have some in the kitchen."

Just as she rounded the kitchen, her phone dinged with a text. It was from Birdie.

GREAT application just came in for Dempsey! Forwarding to you.

Goose bumps broke out along Claire's spine and arms. And not in a good way, she realized.

She went to her laptop on the kitchen island and opened Birdie's email and the application. Her heart sunk with every line. A single, middle-aged writer, who worked at home, didn't have a fenced yard but lived near wooded trails and would walk Dempsey at least three times a day, who "lost my furbaby last year to cancer and am finally ready to love another dog." She fell in love with Dempsey at the adoption event last week but had wanted to sit with her feelings, and yes, she'd love to have "beautiful, majestic, lovely" Dempsey.

Claire burst into tears, her hands darting up to her face. Her shoulders shook and her knees started to buckle.

"Claire?" Matt said, rushing over to her. "Hey, what's wrong?"

"I just love Dempsey so much. But this applicant… she sounds so perfect and just right for Dempsey. I know this woman will appreciate her as much as I do. I can feel it just by having read the application." Fresh sobs racked her entire body.

Matt pulled her into his arms. "Oh, honey. It's hard to let go. I know."

He didn't know. He didn't.

"I don't want to give her up. I love that dog, dammit."

"I know you do. Could you keep her?"

She felt herself go limp against Matt, grateful he was holding her. But then she remembered where she was, who was keeping her upright, and she sucked in a breath and stepped back, swiping at her eyes. "I go through this with every dog. I love them so hard, and it's my job to prepare them for their furever home. It's what a foster parent signs up for. I know there are 'foster fails' out there, those who do keep their dogs, but I feel like that would be wrong. I'm meant to take in dogs who can't find homes and work with them until they're so ready, they're irresistible. And now Dempsey is."

"She is pretty irresistible," he said, going over to Dempsey and petting her.

"You knocked for dog bags and got a crying Claire. Sorry you asked, huh?" She walked back to the kitchen, pulled two poop bags from the doggie-drawer and handed them to him.

"Never," he said, stuffing the bags in his pocket. "I'm here for you. You can always talk to me."

"Till the end of March, anyway."

He winced slightly. "I guess the key is not to love

the dogs when you have to give them away. I mean, you know you're not keeping them. It's not a permanent arrangement. So why get attached?"

She gaped at him. "How could I not?" Was he seriously asking this?

"You just don't. You know what you're walking into, and you create boundaries. That easy."

"Oh, really?" she said. "Well, it's not that easy for most people. Just you. I don't know one foster parent who hasn't gotten choked up about bringing their dogs and cats to their forever homes. Not one. And you know what, Matt Fielding? I don't think you'll find it so easy to let Sparkle go."

"Trust me, I will."

"Having Hank won't protect you from having to say goodbye to that adorable fluffy little dog that you trained for weeks."

"Boundaries. It's all about boundaries."

"I guess you'd know!" she shouted and ran into her bedroom and closed the door.

She closed her eyes and shook her head, wondering what had happened to good ole levelheaded, even-keeled Claire Asher.

The hot dude in the living room happened.

Dempsey's application happened.

Boundaries were for toxic people in your life. Not for the good ones. Not for the furbabies, who saved you as much as you saved them. Even if you were just their temporary foster parent.

She heard the sliding glass door open and close, and she breathed a sigh of relief that he was gone.

She ran back out into the hallway, and there was her beloved Dempsey, staring forlornly at Matt's back as he went to get Sparkle and Hank from the yard.

"Oh, Dempsey," she said, lowering to the floor on her knees and giving the sweet boxer mix a hug. "Your new mama sounds wonderful. She even has trails behind her house that you can explore."

Dempsey licked her face. Good thing too, because the tears came crashing down.

"I love you, Demps," she said, placing her forehead on the dog's warm neck, her body shuddering with fresh sobs. "I'm going to cry my eyes out and recommend the application back to Birdie. Then when it's time to bring you to your new home, I'll cry some more and foster a new pooch, and the cycle will start all over again. Because that's what it's all about.

"I might be heartbroken to lose you, but at least I feel something."

Chapter 10

"Where should I put this, Birdie?" Matt asked, picking up the huge fifty-pound bag of dog food that someone had donated to the shelter.

After what had just happened with Claire, he'd needed to get out of the house and, at the same time, feel connected to her, to what she was going through. He hadn't wanted to think too deeply about why. So he'd grabbed his phone and called the shelter, and Birdie happened to answer. He'd asked if she could use an extra pair of hands at Furever Paws right now, and she'd said *always*, so he'd driven over.

"We have a storage closet in the back hallway," Birdie said. "I'll show you. How's our Hank doing?"

Matt smiled. "He's doing great. He keeps that little spitfire Sparkle in line, that's for sure."

Bunny came out of the cat adoption room and smiled at Matt. "I miss his sweet face. But I sure am glad he's with you now."

He pictured Sparkle and Hank, who were probably curled up in the huge memory foam dog bed, Sparkle in her preferred napping position, with her head tucked between her front paws. *Would* he have trouble giving Sparkle up? He had a feeling he would if didn't have Hank. And if he didn't have Hank, he'd have to go get himself a Hank. So why didn't Claire have a dog of her own? Suddenly, it struck him as strange. He'd have to ask her the next time he saw her—if she was speaking to him.

"Oh, Bunny," Birdie said, turning to her sister as she stopped in front of the storage closet. "I meant to tell you—Gator texted earlier."

Birdie, Bunny and Gator. Their other brother, Moose, had passed away years ago. Since he'd started volunteering at Furever Paws, Matt had heard the Whitaker sisters talk about their family quite a bit. Birdie held Gator in high regard, and as the no-nonsense woman didn't suffer fools, he figured Gator had to be something special.

He'd learned, from overhearing many conversations between the sisters, that the Whitaker siblings had inherited the Whitaker Acres land from their parents, who'd lived in Spring Forest for generations. Gator and Moose had sold their shares long ago, but the sisters had hung on to forty acres, smartly selling small sections of their property and living off their investments.

Bunny smiled. "Oh, how nice. And what did our brother have to say for himself?"

Birdie bit her lip, something Matt didn't think he'd ever seen her do. Bernadette "Birdie" Whitaker could wrestle a crocodile, so when she seemed off balance, Matt noticed. "Well, he thinks we should sell off a parcel of the property, namely the large acreage we use as an outside dog run and training area."

Bunny frowned. "Really? Well, I don't know about that, Birdie. That would leave the shelter with little room for outdoor areas—especially if we expand in years to come."

"I know," Birdie said with a bit of a shrug. "But that was his recommendation."

As always, Matt tried not to eavesdrop but since the Whitaker sisters were talking right in front of him, he couldn't help but listen.

"Gator's never let us down with his investment recommendations," Birdie added, "but I'll talk to him about selling a parcel on the far side of the shelter instead."

"I thought the two of you owned the land outright," Matt said, looking from Birdie to Bunny. "Why would it be Gator's decision? If you don't mind my asking."

During one of their talks about Furever Paws, Claire had mentioned that most of the Whitaker land was undeveloped forest with some creek-front areas. But apparently the region was in the midst of a development boom, and the sisters had been getting offers to buy them out for years, especially by the neighboring Kingdom Creek housing development, where Matt now lived in Claire's house. According to Claire, the sisters had refused all offers; they intended to leave Whitaker Acres as a trust. Now, the Kingdom Creek development wanted to buy land right on top of the shelter. Gator seemed to think that was a good thing.

"Oh, we like to keep our attention on the furbabies and the running of the rescue, not on the business and financial end," Birdie explained. "That's Gator's specialty, and he's proven time and again he's a shrewd financial planner."

He nodded and put away the giant bag of dog food in the closet and shut the door. The rescue, surrounding area and the sisters' farmhouse were all in great condition, so it looked like the way the sisters had chosen to operate Furever Paws was working just fine. Besides, they had been living off their investments for years, so Gator Whitaker had to know what he was doing.

Matt envied what the sisters had built here. They had such rich, full lives, worked at something they loved and were so passionate about, gave back to the community over and over, and lived on their own terms. He admired the Whitaker sisters. They might not think of themselves as businesswomen, but they most definitely were.

"Bunny! Birdie!" a woman called out from the direction of the lobby. "Someone just dumped two dogs from a car and sped off!"

What the hell? Matt glanced at Birdie's and Bunny's concerned faces and followed the women as they rushed out to the lobby. Lisa Tish, one of the volunteers at Furever Paws, stood frowning in front of the door.

The young woman looked to be on the verge of tears. "I was manning the front desk when I saw the car stop up the road. A man got out and practically dragged both dogs from the car, then sped off. I saw the dogs run after the car, and then they ran back to the exact spot he'd left them. They're just sitting there!"

Matt's mouth dropped open. "He dumped them? What the hell?"

"Unfortunately, it happens all the time," Bunny said, grabbing two long rope-style leashes from the counter.

Birdie nodded and let out a deep sigh. "Twice last week." She took a handful of soft treats from the jar on the desk, put them in her pocket, and they all headed out.

Matt could see the two medium-sized dogs, one black and tan, the other mostly brown, standing up the road. That area could get busy, and he hoped the dogs would stay put until the sisters could get to them.

"Hey, pups," Bunny called in a warm, friendly voice. "Got some treats for you."

The two dogs, who looked like hound mixes, stared at Bunny. The mostly-brown one had floppy ears and seemed to have some beagle in him. The black-and-tan dog was possibly a coonhound mix, Matt thought. Two weeks ago he couldn't have told anyone the difference between a hound and a shepherd, and suddenly he could pick out breeds in a mutt.

"These treats are yummy peanut butter," Bunny added, slowly walking a bit farther as the rest of them hung back.

Matt wondered if the dogs would take off scared the way that little gray dog had, or if they'd come running for the treats.

They came slowly toward her for the treats. Relief flooded him. He had no idea why he cared so much about two dogs that he'd never seen before two seconds ago, but hell, he did.

The sisters gave the dogs a once-over. "No collars," Bunny said, "but they do look to be in decent shape. Maybe old hunting dogs that stopped doing their 'jobs.'"

"I'd love to get my hands on that jerk," Matt said, shaking his head. "They weren't useful so he just abandoned them?"

"Like I said, it happens a lot," Bunny said. "I'm just glad folks know we're here and at least abandon them on our property." She turned to Lisa. "I'm glad you saw it happen and called us right away. Otherwise, they might have run off along the road."

Lisa nodded. "I'm with Matt. I just can't believe someone would do this. Dump dogs like that." She shook her head.

Birdie slipped a leash over the larger dog's head. The rope-like leash worked as a collar and lead in one. "Well, that's what we're here for, so all's well that ends well, right, handsome one?" she cooed to the hound. "What a majestic-looking hound you are," she said, patting his side. "Good dog. You look like a Captain to me."

Bunny put the leash over the other dog's head and secured it. She gave him a pat too. "And I'd say you look like a Major."

Matt smiled. "No Corporal?"

"Doesn't roll off the tongue as easily," Birdie said. "But the next cat that comes in will be named Corporal in honor of your service, Matt."

He laughed. "I wasn't fishing."

"Well, you've done so much for us in such a short time that you deserve it," Birdie told him.

He smiled, his chest tightening. How had he made all these connections in Spring Forest? He hadn't intended to. Was Claire right about him accidentally making a life for himself here?

"We sure owe Claire for bringing you into our lives," Bunny added as they started back toward the shelter building.

Matt frowned.

"Now, Bunny, Matt came here on his own, remember? He didn't even know Claire volunteered here when he came to look for a puppy for his niece."

Bunny seemed to think about that for a moment. "Oh, yeah."

"I guess I just associate you two with each other. Matt and Claire. Claire and Matt."

Had the temperature suddenly increased? It was barely fifty degrees today, and Matt felt feverish. There was no Matt and Claire.

Birdie smiled and patted his hand. "Why don't you go up ahead and ready two kennels while I call Doc J and let him know we have two new dogs for assessment?"

"Will do," he said, taking both leashes and bringing the dogs inside the shelter and down the hallway into the Dogs room.

"Hey, Tucker," he said as he passed the chiweenie's kennel. "Some new friends for you to sniff from afar."

Tucker ignored him, as usual, but Matt threw him a treat. The little guy ambled over for it. Someone was going to snap him up soon, Matt had no doubt.

Lisa opened the kennels for Matt, and he ushered each dog inside. "I wish I could take them both in myself, even as a foster mom," she said to Matt. "I used to have dogs, two that I adopted from here long ago, but now that I have young children and one is allergic, I have to get my fix by volunteering here when my kids are in preschool."

Matt smiled. "I get it. Before I started volunteering here, I had no idea just how much I loved dogs. Now, I can't imagine ever not having one. Or two."

She laughed. "Yup."

The door opened and Claire came in, saw him and frowned, then turned right back around.

How had things gotten so bad between them?

Because of you, idiot. Push, pull. Pull, push. You tell her no, then you're naked in bed together. And you wonder why she hates your guts.

Except she didn't hate him. And he was *hurting* her.

He felt like crud. Now he was making Furever

Paws awkward and uncomfortable for her by just being here. This was *her* place, her sanctuary. And he was ruining it for her.

He loved it here too, and had only another few weeks to help out. Hell, maybe he should move out of her house. He probably should. But he couldn't go back to Laura's since Sparkle wasn't 100 percent ready. So where could he go?

His phone rang—an unfamiliar number. "Hello?"

"Matt, this is Jessica Panetta, Ellie's teacher at Spring Forest Elementary."

His heart stopped. "Is everything okay? Is Ellie okay?"

"Oh, yes! I'm sorry, I should have opened with that, the way the school's nurse does when she calls parents. Ellie is just fine. I'm calling because after I met you and Sparkle in the park a few weeks ago, I couldn't stop thinking about how wonderful it would be to have a show-and-tell about puppies and what goes into training them. Kids beg their parents for puppies, but they really don't know the work that goes into training a puppy and taking care of one. I've spoken to the principal, and she agrees it would be a great experience for the kids."

"Wait, you want me to come in and give a talk on training puppies?" he asked, completely dumbfounded.

"Exactly. I envision you bringing in Sparkle and giving a twenty-minute presentation on puppy training and what goes into it. If you like the idea, our principal only requests that you have someone from

Furever Paws accompany you as a second pair of
eyes and hands."

Oh God. Was this conversation actually happening? She had to be kidding.

"I just saw how good you were with that dog," the
teacher continued, "the way she listened to you, how
much work you clearly were putting into the training,
and I knew it would be a truly special extra learning event for the kids. And to be honest, I think Ellie
would enjoy a little spotlight."

His heart dropped. He remembered Ellie saying
she didn't have a best friend when they first met Sparkle. Did she have friends at all?

If twenty minutes of his time would make a difference for Ellie at school, that was all he needed to
know.

"I'm in," he said. "And I'm sure someone from
the shelter will be happy to help me out for the presentation."

"Great!" Mrs. Panetta said. They set a date and
time for the week after next, and when Matt clicked
End Call, he actually had to sit down for a second.

Matt Fielding, talking to a classroom full of kids?
About puppies and training them?

His life was sure taking crazy routes.

*Someone from Furever Paws to be an extra set
of eyes and hands...* He could ask Birdie or Bunny,
but Claire was a teacher and she'd be able to give
him pointers on how to set up the presentation. Then
again, she probably couldn't just leave her own school

to help out at the elementary school, even for just twenty minutes or so.

He could ask. Because it would give him a meaningful reason to spend some time with her despite everything in him telling him to keep his distance. And no matter how he tried, he just couldn't keep away from her.

A couple of hours later, as Hank and Sparkle ran around in the enclosed dog run at the park, Matt sat on the bench near the fence with his phone, reading through the online classifieds from the free weekly newspaper's website, circling possibilities for rooms for rent. Ever since seeing Claire at Furever Paws earlier, the look on her face, the hurt and confusion and sorrow in her eyes—caused by him—he knew that moving out of the apartment at Claire's was the right thing to do. To give them both space, to keep them from constantly running into each other in the yard. This way, if she did want to work with him on the school presentation, she wouldn't be overloaded with his presence.

He read through the ads. There was a boarding-house, and he could always move in there temporarily. Or even an inn or motel, but then again, they wouldn't allow two dogs.

All he knew for sure was that he had to let Claire be.

"Hey, Fielding!"

Matt turned around and smiled. His old neighbor, Zeke Harper, was jogging toward him. Several years younger than Matt, and tall and strong in his running gear, Zeke reminded Matt of how much he used to love to run. Maybe one of these days.

"Hey, Matt, how's the pup training going?" Zeke asked, pulling the wireless ear pods out and putting them in his pocket.

"So good, in fact, that I adopted a dog of my own," Matt said, pointing at Hank beyond the fence. The three-legged old guy was doing great keeping up with the younger pups.

Zeke grinned. "That's great! And I hear that PT I recommended is working out too." He watched the dogs run. "You're really settling in, Matt. Glad to see it."

"Hardly settling in," Matt said. "In fact, the opposite. I'm in need of place to live."

"Didn't you say you were renting Claire Asher's apartment in Kingdom Creek?"

The sound of her name brought her face to mind. Beautiful Claire with the kind, intelligent green eyes and all that silky blond hair. "Yeah, but maybe it's better that we're not that close, you know?"

Zeke nodded. "Understood. A friend of mine has a small, furnished carriage house available right now. Not too far from my place. It's month-to-month, so since you're planning on leaving town, that might work out. And he has a dog himself, so I'm sure pets are welcome."

"Sounds perfect." He put the contact info in his phone. That was a call he'd be making very soon.

For the next fifteen minutes, he and Zeke caught

up, Matt explaining that he now volunteered at Furever Paws and spent a lot of time studying up on dog training and dog psychology so that he could be even more helpful to Birdie and Bunny and the least adoptable dogs at the shelter. He felt a real kinship with those who were always left behind.

"That's really something," Zeke said. "You know I'm a psychologist and volunteer with Veterans Affairs, and I have to say I'm really intrigued by what fostering and training Sparkle and adopting Hank has done for you."

"What do you mean?"

"Well, last time I ran into you, you were saying your life was up in the air and you felt off balance because of it. Sounds to me like volunteering at the shelter, training the puppy for your niece and adopting a dog for yourself have given you purpose. And more too—a real sense of meaning. We already know how much comfort dogs give, but the purpose side of things—that's something I'd like to bring up to my colleagues over at VA."

Huh. Matt had to admit it was all true. His life *did* have meaning now. Purpose. When the hell had all that happened? And there was something else too. Something that had shocked him when he first noticed it. "I'll be the first to say that I went from having a nightmare a night to hardly any, especially since I adopted Hank." He'd had no idea just how much comfort a dog could be.

"You know, Matt, there's someone I'd really like for you to meet. His name is Bobby Doyle, and he's one of the vets I work with at the center. He has an auto body business he's trying to get off the ground, and didn't you say your expertise in the military was with vehicle mechanics? I bet he'd value your input as a former soldier."

"He's all alone?" Matt asked.

"Actually, he has a devoted wife and two great kids," Zeke said. "Thanks to them—and *for* them—he's making great strides." He glanced at the dog run. "I've suggested that Bobby get a therapy dog who is trained to help vets dealing with PTSD."

Matt knew full-well what a great idea that was. "I could talk to Claire and the Whitaker sisters about that. Maybe they know of programs in the area that match dogs with vets."

"I'd appreciate that," he said. "And, in the meantime, I'll give Bobby your contact info and let him know you'd be happy to hear from him."

They shook hands, and as Zeke took off running again, Matt thought about all the man had said. Matt had never paid much attention to purpose and meaning all that mumbo jumbo because his life had been chock-full of both during his army years. And here he was, a civilian, traces of the injury still dogging him every now and then, and he had purpose and meaning up the wazoo. To the point that he was actually asked—him, Matt Fielding—to present a puppy training show-and-tell to a bunch of third-graders.

Once again, how had all this happened without him noticing?

A rambunctious little terrier was being a pain in

the butt in the dog run, so Matt wanted to get Sparkle and Hank out of there. Sparkle was a toughie who gave back what she got, but Hank was a gentle giant who'd let the bully nip his ankles, and he had only three to spare.

He quickly pulled out his phone and called the number Zeke had given him for the carriage house to rent. He made an appointment to see the apartment in an hour. He'd bring the dogs home, then head over.

As he was helping Sparkle up into his car, something occurred to him. If his life *did* have purpose and meaning, then he did have something to offer Claire Asher.

Whoosh! It was like getting a surprise left hook in the stomach.

So why was he still so set on keeping his emotional distance from her?

Chapter 11

"Well, Dempsey," Claire said. "This is goodb—" Tears filled her eyes, and she swiped them away. "I promised you I wouldn't cry, didn't I? And I'm a blubbering mess."

She sat in her car, Dempsey sitting shotgun in the passenger seat. The beautiful boxer mix looked lovely, all fresh from the groomer's and smelling slightly of lavender.

"We were only together seven weeks, and I feel like it's been forever, Demps," she said, her hands on either side of the dog's snout. "But your new mama? She really seems wonderful. She even asked me to meet her for coffee yesterday and tell her every detail about you so she could understand your every nuance.

She wrote down your favorite food and treats, too, and your favorite places to trail walk."

The woman really seemed perfect, the best possible forever home for Dempsey.

"It's time, sweet girl," Claire said, getting out of the car.

Kelly Pfieffer came running out of the house. "Dempsey's here!" The woman was even planning to keep Dempsey's name to make things easier for the transition.

I've been through this before, and I'll go through it again, she thought, forcing herself to smile for Kelly. This was a big moment for both adoptive mom and Dempsey and she didn't want to make this about her.

She waved at Kelly and kneeled down next to Dempsey. "I love you, sweet girl. You're the best. And you're going to have a great life. And I promise we'll see each other at the dog park, okay?"

Dempsey put her paw on Claire's arm, and she almost lost it, but held it together.

Kelly raced over, fawning and fussing over Dempsey, thanking Claire profusely, and then soon enough, Claire was in her car alone.

She let herself cry for a good minute before driving right over to the shelter. Bunny sat behind the reception desk.

"I just dropped off Dempsey with her new mom," she said, tears still in her eyes. "I need a toughie. A foster dog who really needs me."

"Aww," Bunny said, coming around the desk to wrap Claire in a much-needed hug. "It's always so hard to give up the fosters. Especially when we bond with them. But the bonding is what makes them so ready for that forever home. Right?"

Claire blinked back tears. "Right. Dempsey is special, and I know she's in a great home now. Letting her go was rough, I'll tell ya."

"I had one of those heart-wrenchers," Bunny said. "Remember Buttercup? Long-haired dachshund? I was crazy about that little gal. I almost kept her too. But then I remembered my mission—to prepare as many rescue dogs as I can for great new homes. Not to keep every one I fall madly in love with."

"It is really hard to let go of someone you're madly in love with," Claire agreed, her voice cracking.

"Oh, Claire, I'm so sorry Matt is a stubborn fool. A helpful one, but a stubborn fool when it comes to what's right in front of his face."

"Thanks, Bunny," Claire said. "So, who do you have for me? Distract me with a real needy one."

Bunny put her fingers on her chin. "Oh, have I got the pooch for you. Remember the black-and-white shepherd mix that came in two days ago? Doc J has him on medication for a bad ear infection, and he doesn't seem to know any commands. He's very timid. He's praise and food motivated, so I have no doubt you'll do wonders with him."

Blaze. For the white lightning bolt-like zigzag on his otherwise black head. "I'll go see him."

Blaze was in the far-left kennel. He was pressed up against the back of the kennel on a blanket, his head down, and looked pretty scared.

"Hey, boy," she said gently.

The dog lifted his green eyes first, then his head. She held out a treat, and he came padding over very slowly. Claire could have counted to twenty-five in the time it took him to reach the front of the kennel.

"Hi, Blaze," she said, giving him the treat through the bars. "Aren't you handsome? It's no fun to be in here, is it?"

The dog stared at her, and she could swear he was saying, *Please pick me to be your new foster dog. I need you, Claire.*

When she opened the kennel, he ran toward the back, flattening himself against the far side. "It's okay, Blaze. I'm all about love and treats."

"She's telling you the truth," a familiar voice said.

She whirled around to find Matt returning Tucker to his kennel and latching the door.

"I've been walking all the dogs," he said. "I even walked Blaze about an hour ago. Shy guy."

"I'm hoping to bring him out of his shell," she said, turning her attention to the dog as she leashed him and led him out of the kennel. His ears were back, which meant he was scared. "It's okay, Blaze," she said softy as she knelt down beside him. "You're coming home with me, sweetie pie. And I'm going to give you a ton of TLC as I get you ready for your forever home."

"Are *you* okay?" Matt asked as she stood up, and she was touched that he remembered today was the day she had to say goodbye to Dempsey. But of course he remembered and asked how she was doing—because he was Matt Fielding and a great guy, dammit.

She glanced at him and nodded, blinking back the sting of tears that poked at her eyes. "It's never easy to say goodbye. But I'll tell you, it feels good to say hello. This sweetie already has my heart."

He smiled and shook his head. "I don't know how you do it. But I'm glad you do."

His tone was so reverent that she looked at him, and all she wanted to do was fling herself in his arms and be held. It would be a while before Blaze became a cuddler, if he ever did. And Claire could use some cuddling.

"I have a big favor to ask," he said.

"If I can, I will." She *could* start changing that motto. And just say no.

"Ellie's teacher called me and asked if I'd bring in Sparkle for a presentation on how to train and care for puppies. She thought it would give Ellie a little boost in the class too, which is why I couldn't say no, even though I have no idea how to present anything, let alone to kids."

"You're great with one third-grader in particular," she pointed out. "The class will love you. Plus, Sparkle will do most of the work for you by being adorable and keeping the kids' attention."

"I'm hoping so. But here's the thing. The principal says someone from Furever Paws has to be present as an extra pair of ears and eyes, just in case. I know your hours are probably the same as the elementary school's, though. We'd go on at two thirty."

She remembered Bunny's advice—not to run and hide from him. The more time they spent together—

quality time—the more he might see that they belonged together. Unless she was kidding herself. "Actually, I monitor a study hall as my last period of the day. I can easily have someone cover that for me."

"Perfect. And you'll help me figure out what to say? How to structure the twenty minutes?"

"I'd love to. Dogs and kids are my two favorite things." *Add in being with you, and it's heaven.*

He smiled, but then the smile faded. Uh-oh. "Look, I know things between us have been strained and the push-pull is my fault. So, I thought it best if I find a new place to live for the next few weeks."

She didn't want him to go. Closer was better, as much as it hurt. "Matt, you don't have to do that."

"I already did."

It probably was for the best, but it still stung. Like everything these days. She shrugged. "Okay."

"Okay."

Except it wasn't okay. He was running away before he even ran away for good. This time, across town, probably near where he grew up.

"I'll miss Sparkle and Hank," she said, hoping her voice wouldn't crack.

And I'll miss you.

"I owe you a lot, Claire," he said.

"Well," she started, but what could she say? What was there to say at this point?

You need to replace Matt Fielding the way you have to replace Dempsey, her sister had texted earlier, when Claire said her heart was in pieces. New foster dog to dote on—new man to fall for.

Or maybe Claire should just focus on the dog. And the child she wanted. There were some options she could look into. Becoming a foster parent to a little kid. Foreign adoption. The ole sperm bank. She'd always wanted the traditional setup—spouse, at least two kids and dogs—but that wasn't what life had set out for her.

"I'd better get Blaze home before he thinks he's going back in the kennel," she said. "He seems almost excited."

"His tail is giving a little wag," Matt agreed.

"Guess I might not even see you leave the apartment," she said, "since all you have is a duffel bag. No moving van." She was rambling, she realized, and clamped her mouth closed.

"Don't forget the two dogs," he said with a killer smile. "Or the fact that I'd never leave without saying goodbye, Claire. I'll text you about getting together to work on the presentation."

She managed something of a smile, and watched him walk away and disappear through the door into the hallway.

"It's you and me, Blaze." The scared dog looked up at her, holding eye contact. She almost gasped, and gave the pooch a peanut butter treat. "Good dog!" she said, with a pat on his back. "And good sign."

For Blaze. And Claire's entire life.

Two weeks later, Matt looked at Sparkle, sitting very nicely after the *stay* command he'd issued, and declared her done. Her favorite treat, a chicken-flavored soft chew, was fifteen feet in front of her, and though she wanted it, she'd obeyed Matt's command and had for the past three days. She was fully trained. She knew *sit, stay, come, heel* and *drop it*, and a few others that Matt had taught her. Occasionally, she chased her tail, but now it was just cute.

He wanted to call Claire and tell her, to have her come give Sparkle the "Claire Asher, dog whisperer" stamp of approval, but since he'd moved out of her apartment and into the carriage house, he'd avoided her except to get together to structure the presentation to Ellie's class. He volunteered at Furever Paws only on days when she wasn't due in. He missed the hell out of her, but it was for the best, for both their sakes.

The doorbell rang and he answered the door, his niece Ellie flinging himself at him and wrapping her skinny arms around him.

"You're the best uncle in the world!" she said. "Thank you a million zillion times for training Sparkle!" She raced over to the puppy. "Come, Sparkle," she said very seriously.

The puppy padded over, wagging her tail.

"Good, Sparkle!" Ellie said, dropping down to her knees and petting the dog all over. "She is going to make everyone in my class wish they could have a puppy!"

No doubt. Or maybe not. "Well, tomorrow afternoon, when everyone sees how much work went into training her, how much picking up poop is involved…"

It *had* been a lot of work. And he'd loved just about every minute of it, despite the middle-of-the-night potty breaks in the freezing cold. And thanks to the presentation scheduled for tomorrow, he'd been able to get together with Claire twice over the past week. She'd kept the sessions short, making excuses to get home to Blaze, but he couldn't blame her for wanting to keep her distance.

Ellie laughed. "I don't mind picking up gross poop because that's what taking care of Sparkle is all about."

He held up his hand for a high five. "Exactly. So I'll see you at your school at two thirty."

Ellie beamed. "Yay! I'm so excited! Everyone will get to meet my great puppy!"

"Thank you, Matt," his sister said. "For *everything*. Come over anytime to visit Sparkle."

Ellie clipped on Sparkle's leash and headed toward the door. She turned to the dog. "I can't wait to show you my room."

A minute later they were gone, and it was just him and ole Hank. Matt dropped down on the couch, the big dog slowly sinking down on the rug, his head on his paws. "You're relieved that little pest is gone, aren't you?" Matt asked, laughing. Hank lifted his head. "No? You're not. Hell, I'm not either. I loved that little mutt."

The place seemed so empty without Sparkle. Even with Hank there. As the day wore on, he felt the puppy's absence so acutely that he wanted to talk about it with Claire. She'd understand exactly how he felt.

And he owed her an apology for the "you can't get attached" crud he'd tried to feed her. He'd gotten attached to Sparkle. He *was* attached to Hank.

Luckily, he couldn't go see Claire even though he thought it was a good idea. He had a job interview. His old friend Zeke had hooked him up with the veteran he'd told Matt about at the dog park. Bobby Doyle owned an auto body shop and needed some help—temporary was fine—because his best mechanic was out with a back injury. Matt quickly understood what Zeke hadn't said—that Bobby, who suffered from PTSD, could use a steadying presence like Matt around, a guy who'd been injured in a blast overseas and had come back and was piecing his life together. Bobby had built a good life for himself, but despite the family and the business, the man had trouble seeing what was right in front of him. The nightmares made it worse too. Matt had spoken to Birdie about hooking Bobby up with a program that matched therapy dogs with veterans, and Birdie was working on it.

Once Bobby's mechanic returned to work at the end of March, Matt would be leaving Spring Forest. A week, maybe ten days at most. He and Hank would hit the road and settle somewhere and start over. Matt was sure now he'd find work as a mechanic, and lately, he was thinking he might go to dog training school and become certified to work in an animal shelter, maybe even start his own business.

His life was moving forward in the right direction. He wasn't there yet, but maybe he'd get there. Then maybe there could be a chance for him and Claire.

Whoa. He'd had that thought and had always pushed it back down in the recesses where it belonged. But now it was up and out there. He could no longer deny that things were happening for him, that he was building something here in Spring Forest without ever having meant to.

Which meant he'd actually stay?

He looked at Hank. "What the hell, buddy? Why don't I know what's up from one minute to the next? Why is this so damned hard?"

Hank came over and put his head on Matt's thigh. He could swear the dog was saying, "I know, right?"

Eighteen third-graders, including his niece, Ellie, were staring at him as he stood at the blackboard in the front of the classroom, Sparkle on a four-foot leash beside him in the *sit* position. Mrs. Panetta's desk was to his left, and Claire stood just slightly behind him on his right, next to Sparkle's kennel. He'd walked the dog in on her leash, and the moment they'd entered the classroom, the kids had gone crazy with oohs and aahs, so cute, aww, throwing out tons of questions about how much she weighed and how old she was and if she knew she was a dog. Mrs. Panetta had gotten them to shush and explained that Mr. Fielding— man, did that sound weird—would answer all their questions after his presentation.

Ellie sat in the first row, just to the left of him. Next to her was a girl with her arms folded over her chest, who seemed to be sulking. Maybe her parents wouldn't let her have a dog. The boy on the other side of the sulker was grinning like crazy, and could barely contain his excitement about having a puppy in his classroom.

The teacher had introduced him and Claire, so he'd better get cracking.

"Hi, kids," he began. "About a month ago, my niece Ellie was promised a puppy for her birthday, which is coming up in just a few days. So I took Ellie to the Furever Paws shelter to pick one out. Who did she fall in love with? A totally untrained five-month-old puppy that wouldn't stop barking or spinning in circles and chasing her tail, and had no idea that she wasn't supposed to go potty in the house."

The kids broke into laughter at that one. Ellie was beaming, and Matt winked at her.

"Well, my sister, Ellie's mom, wanted a trained puppy," he continued. "So I offered to turn Sparkle into just the right puppy for their house. It was a lot of hard work. Sparkle had to learn her name, to come when called, to stay when told to stay, not to chase birds or squirrels when told no, not to jump up and—very importantly—to do her business, if you know what I mean, outside only."

"You mean pee and poop!" the excited boy shouted.

"Exactly," Matt said, laughing.

He handed Sparkle's leash to Claire, then moved to the far end of the classroom. "Sparkle!"

The dog immediately looked at him.

"Sparkle, come!" She came trotting over, Claire more holding the leash than guiding her. He led her back to the front of the room, then put a treat down on the floor right in front of Sparkle. "Now, this is Sparkle's favorite treat. Peanut butter. Oh boy, does she love peanut butter."

The sulking girl in the front shot her hand in the air.

"Yes, Danica?" Mrs. Panetta said.

"If it's her favorite, why isn't she eating it?" the girl demanded, crossing her arms over her chest again.

"Because I didn't tell her she could," Matt explained. "Okay, Sparkle. Treat."

The dog looked at Matt and then gobbled it up.

Everyone clapped. "Ellie, your dog is so awesome!" someone called out.

Ellie was glowing.

"Sparkle, treat!" Danica said, holding out what looked like half of a chocolate bar.

"No, Sparkle!" Claire shouted. "Stay! Chocolate is toxic to dogs."

"Here, Sparkle!" Danica said, waving the chocolate.

As if in slow motion, Mrs. Panetta, Matt and Claire all rushed forward—the teacher to grab the chocolate before the dog could, and Matt and Claire to get ahold of Sparkle on her leash. But the puppy lunged, jumping up on the girl and knocking her lunch box all over the floor. Her sandwich went spinning—and Sparkle went flying after it.

"Sparkle, stay!" Matt commanded. The puppy stopped and looked at Matt. He scooped her up and put her in her kennel.

"Your puppy is so dumb!" Danica shouted, collecting her baggie-wrapped sandwich and putting it back in her lunch box.

"*You're* dumb!" Ellie shouted.

Oh no. Tell me this is not happening, Matt thought, his stomach sinking.

"Danica and Ellie, you're both going to the principal's office after the presentation," Mrs. Panetta said, directing a stern look at both girls.

Ellie had tears in her eyes. Danica looked spitting mad.

Great. The spotlight sure was on Ellie.

He'd blown this. He'd gotten smug, thinking he knew everything about puppies and training, when he'd forgotten about how unpredictable things could get.

And Claire had reminded him when they'd last gotten together.

"Sparkle will be in an unfamiliar environment," Claire had said. "Lots of little hands will be poking at her, wanting to touch her. We'll have to be on guard and mindful that it may stress her, even though she's well trained."

He'd let Sparkle get too close to Danica, and now both girls were in trouble.

"Mrs. Panetta?" a boy asked, his hand in the air.

"Yes, Tom?"

"I wanted a puppy for my birthday, but now I don't," he said.

"Yeah, what if I got a puppy and it ate my Halloween candy and got sick?" a girl asked.

Sigh.

"That's a great question," Claire said, stepping forward. "And that's part of caring for a puppy. We always have to be really careful about what a dog can get ahold of. It's almost like babyproofing your house. Dogs can chew wires, they can eat things that are bad for them. Having a pet really does take a lot of work, but you know what?"

"What?" a few kids asked.

"Having a pet is also really great. You have an instant buddy, a friend to love and care for, and the rewards are worth all the hard stuff about having a pet."

"I have a dog and he's my best friend," a boy in the back said. "He sleeps next to my bed every night."

"My cat does that," another boy said.

"I hope my parents let me get a dog for my birthday. You're so lucky, Ellie," another girl said.

"Your dog is an idiot!" Danica hiss-whispered to Ellie.

"No, *you're* the idiot!" Ellie hiss-whispered back.

"Girls, that is enough," Mrs. Panetta said sharply. "Well, kids, that's it for today. Let's all thank Mr. Fielding and Ms. Asher from Furever Paws Animal Rescue for coming in today and telling us all about puppy care and training."

After lots of thank-yous, Matt picked up Sparkle's kennel and gave Ellie a quick hand-squeeze, then got the hell out of that classroom. The teacher followed him and Claire into the hallway.

"Please don't worry about things getting a bit out of hand," Mrs. Panetta said. "Claire will tell you— as a teacher, you just never know. But the presentation was great, and I think the kids got a lot out of it. Thank you so much for coming in."

Matt managed a smile and shook her hand. He needed air. Cold March air. Gripping Sparkle's kennel, he headed for the exit.

"Well, it was realistic," Claire said. "And Mrs. Panetta is right. You just never know what will happen. I hope you're not upset about the end."

He gaped at her. "Not upset? Are you kidding? This was Ellie's chance to shine. Instead, some girl tried to poison her dog, and now Ellie's in trouble for calling her dumb."

They reached the door and Claire pushed it open, holding it for Matt who held the heavy kennel. "It happens, Matt. In third grade and in middle school and in high school. All part of learning to get along."

The cool air felt good on his heated skin, but his heart kept pounding with how badly it had all gone down. "I'd hardly call that getting along. Ellie is going to be really pissed at me, and rightly so. I didn't handle things right. Why the hell I did think I belonged in this environment? With kids and puppies? I knew better than that. But I let myself be talked into thinking I'm someone I'm not."

"Oh, Matt, come on," she said, glaring at him.

"I'm not Uncle Matt the puppy trainer, who can lead a classroom presentation," he snapped. "I'm a former army corporal with a slight limp trying to figure things out now that I'm a civilian."

"And you are," she said, touching his arm.

He pulled away. "I thought I was. But I don't belong here, Claire. This is your world. Not mine."

One thing was for damned sure. He *wasn't* staying in Spring Forest. Come the end of the month, he and his Mustang would be gone, Hank riding shotgun.

Chapter 12

"Claire, you know I'm not one to pry, but are you planning to get pregnant by a sperm donor?"

Claire almost spit out the sip of water she'd just taken. She straightened the stack of applications for tomorrow's adoption event and moved them to the counter. How on earth would Bunny know she was looking into options? Then she eyed her tote bag, which had slumped over on the desk. The big pamphlet for "Is Using a Sperm Donor Right for You?" was sticking out.

She sighed. A week had passed since the fiasco in Ellie's class. A week without a word from Matt, despite her texting and calling and even showing up at his place and knocking on the door. She'd peered in the windows, and he didn't seem to be home, so maybe he wasn't avoiding her. She'd heard Hank's nails scrape the floor as he'd come to the door to see who was there, and she'd been almost doubled-over with pangs of missing the old dog. Missing Matt.

She glanced around the lobby. The two of them were alone, thank goodness. Claire shoved the pamphlet back in the bag and hung it on the back of the chair. "Just looking into all possibilities," she whispered.

"I understand," Bunny said. "Believe me."

Claire was about to use the opportunity to ask Bunny about her personal life. She knew Bunny had been engaged in her twenties and that her fiancé had died tragically. Bunny often mentioned the man with a sweet, wistful tone, and Claire had always wanted to know Bunny's story—how he'd died, if Bunny had tried to find love after her loss.

But before Claire could think of a nonprying way to pry, Bunny rushed to say, "Guess things aren't working out with Matt?"

Sometimes Claire wasn't sure if Bunny wanted to be asked about her life or not. Her money was on the latter. "Nope. I tried everything, Bunny. But the man insists, once again, that he's not future material, no one's husband or father, and is planning to leave town at the end of the month. And March is almost over, so…probably Sunday night."

"Stubborn fool," Bunny said, shaking her head.

Claire couldn't help but smile. "Thanks."

Birdie came in from the back hallway, carrying a donation of stacked empty litter boxes, and Claire jumped up to take them from her. "Thanks, Claire. Would you mind logging these in?"

Claire was glad to be busy. She'd walked all the dogs, played with them individually and together in the yard, swept, sanitized, and now she was looking for things to do to avoid thinking about Matt. In fifteen minutes she'd be done here, and would go home to sweet Blaze. The noon dog walker reported that Blaze was a bit skittish on leash when other dogs were nearby, and that was something Claire was working on. She adored Blaze, but Blaze wasn't a cuddler yet. He might never be, and that was okay too.

"Oh, Bunny—Gator texted about selling that parcel of land again," Birdie said.

"I don't think we should, Birdie. It's prime Furever Paws acreage!"

Birdie shrugged. "Gator said he looked deeply into it."

Claire had begun to realize that Bernadette "Birdie" Whitaker had one weakness: her brother, Gator. Bunny, who tended to defer to Birdie in most things, also had one weakness: the animals. So when there was discord about something related to Whitaker Acres, Birdie and Bunny butted heads, which was a good thing. No quick agreements on what should be carefully considered—like selling the land currently used for training the dogs.

"Tell him we're thinking about possibilities," Bunny said, giving Claire a wink.

Claire blushed. She hoped Bunny wouldn't tell Birdie that she was checking out options for having a family. Ones that didn't include a husband. She wasn't quite ready to share that yet.

Because she also wasn't ready to give up on her dreams of a future with Matt Fielding.

The bell over the front door jangled and Richard Jackson, aka Doc J, walked in. The veterinarian, a tall, kind man in his sixties, had a thriving private practice but spent a lot of time at the shelter, offering his services out of the goodness of his heart. If Claire wasn't mistaken, he'd been in more than usual the past few days, fussing over the Whitaker sisters, complimenting their hair and outfits. Considering Birdie often wore paw-muddied overalls, and Bunny liked her Crocs with animal-print socks, Claire thought it was sweet.

"I like your rabbit pin, Bunny," Doc J said with a warm smile.

"Oh, thank you," she said, peering at it on her big blue fisherman sweater. "Birdie gave it to me for my birthday. A bunny for Bunny, she said." Bunny laughed.

"And I just happen to have a bird for a Birdie and a Bunny," Doc J said, handing Birdie a bakery box.

"What's this?" Birdie asked with a surprised smile.

"Open it," Doc J said.

Birdie opened the box and placed a hand on the region of her heart. She pulled out a big cookie in the shape and colors of a robin. "A bird for a Birdie."

"There were no bunnies, or I would have gotten one," he said to Bunny. "But I did get two robins."

Bunny laughed. "You're a peach, Doc J."

Claire watched the interplay between the three and was sure the doc had a little crush on one of the sisters—she just wasn't sure which one. Hey, if Claire had no love life, she wanted others to so she could live vicariously through them.

Her phone pinged with a text. Hopefully, it wasn't her sister with a blind date suggestion.

Nope. It was Matt.

Sparkle slipped out the front door and that moped spooked her and she took off. Ellie's frantic. We're searching on Holly Road. Help?

Oh God.
On my way, she texted back.
Oh no. Holly Road was busy with cars. *Please let them find her*, she thought, rushing out the door.

"Where could she be?" Ellie asked Matt, tears streaming down her face.

"We'll find her," he assured his niece, praying that would be true. "Let's keep looking. Remember to use a gentle voice if you see her and hold out the cheese stick. Sparkle loves those."

They walked down the sidewalk, looking under cars. No sign of the little dog.

A girl around Ellie's age stood on her lawn holding a Hula-Hoop around her waist. As Matt got closer, he realized it was the sulky one from Ellie's class. Luckily, Ellie hadn't been upset at Matt for what had happened. Instead, she'd given him an earful about how Danica was always mean to her and that the principal had given Danica a detention for "not being kind, and starting a problem," whereas Ellie didn't get in trouble at all.

Ellie ran up to the girl. "Danica? Did you see a brown-and-white puppy run past your house?"

The girl barely looked at Ellie. "Yup, I did."

"Did she go that way?" Ellie asked, pointing ahead toward the intersection. It had a four-way stop sign and not a light, thank God, but it was a busy junction.

Danica nodded. "Yup. Straight into traffic and kept going. Guess your only friend is gone, Ellie," the girl said, giving the Hula-Hoop a spin. It landed on the grass, and she frowned and picked it up, giving it another spin. "Maybe she got hit by a car." She spun the Hula-Hoop again, this time working it around her narrow hips. "Too bad, so sad."

Jesus. Matt's sister often mentioned the mean-girl drama among girls of Ellie's age, and he would have sworn eight was way too young for that crud. But he'd seen it firsthand at Ellie's school, and here it was again, right in front of him.

"Danica Haverman!" A woman came around the side of the house with a gardening tool in her hand. "I heard what you said. That was very unkind."

"Her own dog doesn't like her!" Danica said, looking like she was about to cry.

Suddenly Matt realized what was going on here. The girl was very, very jealous that Ellie had a dog.

"I'd rather have no friends at all than be the meanest girl in school!" Ellie screamed.

The girl froze, and then winced and burst into tears.

"We have to go find Sparkle," Matt said to Danica's mother. "I hope they can work this out."

The woman sighed. "Me too. You go inside and straight to your room, young lady," she added to her daughter.

Matt took Ellie's hand, and they went running down the sidewalk in the direction Sparkle had gone. They looked under every car, asked everyone they saw if he or she had seen a little brown-and-white dog. No one had.

All of a sudden, he saw Claire's car coming down Holly Road. He waved, and she parked on the street and got out. "I have mozzarella string cheese," she said, handing one each to Matt and Ellie.

"We have them too," he said, holding up the five he'd stuffed in the pocket of his leather jacket.

"What if we can't find her?" Ellie asked, her tone frantic.

"Honey," Claire said. "Sparkle has a collar with her name and your telephone number on it. Plus, she's microchipped, which means if she's turned into a shelter, they can use a scanner to read the chip and find out who she belongs to."

Matt just hoped that if they didn't find her, someone had picked her up. If that little dog got hit by a car... He was supposed to be watching Ellie for his sister, supervising her with Sparkle. This was on him.

Great job, Fielding, he thought as he got down on his hands and knees to look under a low-slung car. "Sparkle? You hiding behind those wheels?"

There was no sign of her.

"We'll find her. Or someone will," Claire said.

Matt squeezed her hand, and the moment their skin made contact, he realized how much he'd missed touching her. Missed *her.* "Thanks for coming to help."

"Hey! Are you guys looking for a missing dog?" a woman called out from across the intersection.

"Yes!" Matt shouted, and they all went running to the stop sign.

"There's a brown-and-white puppy trembling behind the wheel of this truck."

Oh thank God, Matt thought.

"Sparkle! She's alive!" Ellie exclaimed.

"Let's let Uncle Matt go get her," Claire told Ellie. "She's very used to him, and I think she'll respond best to him in this scary situation she's gotten herself into."

Ellie bit her lip. "Okay. I know you can do it, Uncle Matt."

He put his hand on Ellie's shoulder. He was not returning without that dog safe and sound in his arms. He hadn't ever been able to find the skinny gray dog they'd seen a couple of times, but he was saving Sparkle. Hell yeah, he was.

He waited for a bunch of cars to pass, then ran across the road. He got down again, wincing at the jab in his leg. There was Sparkle, on the inside of the wheel on the far side of the car. Shaking.

"Hey, girl," he said. "Silly of you to run out the door when all the good stuff is inside the house. But I do have your favorite treat. Mozzarella string cheese stick." He ripped off a chunk and held it out toward her. He wished he could grab her, but his arms would have to be ten feet long. And he wouldn't be able to reach her from the other side. Plus, he'd no doubt get hit by a car himself.

Sparkle looked at him and tilted her head, then looked at the cheese in his hand. A big SUV went by, causing her to tremble again and flatten herself against the wheel.

"Yum," he said, taking a bite for himself.

Sparkle slowly moved toward his hand, and when she went for the cheese, he put one arm around her midsection. "Good Sparkle." The dog relaxed a bit, and he gave her another bite of cheese, then he scooped her up. He braced himself against the car to stand back up. "Got her!" he called to Claire and Ellie.

His niece broke into a grin. And seeing Claire smile almost made him drop to his knees.

He attached Sparkle's leash and walked the dog over to Ellie, who smothered her in kisses.

"All's well that ends well," Claire said.

"I blew it," Matt whispered. "We got lucky, but I almost lost that dog on my watch."

"Dogs slip out, Matt. It happens."

"It shouldn't." Just another example that he didn't belong in this world of kids and dogs and people depending on him. He had no experience as Uncle Matt. He'd been winging it, and he'd had no right when a little girl's heart was at stake.

And a woman's. *Stick to your plan, Fielding*, he told himself. *You'll help out with the adoption events, then you're gone Sunday night. Someplace where you'll feel...comfortable, in the right skin.* He just had no idea where that was.

She shook her head and turned to Ellie. "I'm meeting a couple girlfriends for an early dinner, but I sure am glad I got to see you and Sparkle reunited. That's all that matters. That you're back together."

"I'm so happy. Thank you, Uncle Matt!" Ellie said, flinging herself into his arms while holding tightly on the leash.

Man, it was going to be hard to say goodbye to this sweet little girl. And as he watched Claire hug Ellie and then dash off toward her car, he knew he was going to break his own heart again by saying goodbye to her.

As he and Ellie headed back toward his sister's house, Sparkle scampering on her leash just ahead of them, Ellie stopped and said, "Uh-oh."

"What's wrong?" he asked.

"Danica Haverman's back in her yard with her dumb Hula-Hoop."

Matt glanced over. She sure was. "Well, let's see what happens."

Ellie shrugged and they resumed walking.

Just as they neared Danica's yard, the girl dropped her Hula-Hoop and stared at them. She just stood there, not saying anything. Finally, she slowly came over to the end of her yard. "You found Sparkle."

Ellie tilted her head. "My uncle did. She was hiding under a car."

Danica bit her lip, looking at Ellie one second and

the ground, the next. "Can I pet her?" she asked, looking sheepish. "You'll probably say no."

"I'm surprised you even want to," Ellie said, giving Sparkle a protective pat on the side.

Danica's eyes glistened with tears. "I wish I could get a dog."

Ah, Matt thought. He might not understand eight-year-old girls so well, but if he knew his niece, her next move would be kindness.

"Dogs are definitely awesome," Ellie said. "You can pet her. She's really soft."

Danica almost gasped. She bit her lip again and then both girls dropped to their knees, Danica petting Sparkle and Ellie staring at the girl in wonder.

Tears misted in Danica's eyes. "I'm sorry I said your dog didn't like you. Anyone can see she does."

"Well, I'm sorry I said you were the meanest girl in school. You're not. Because mean people don't say sorry and they don't pet puppies."

Danica beamed.

"Wanna come over later and play with her? I taught her how to fetch my socks."

Danica laughed. "Sure, I'll ask my mom."

And just like that, Ellie had a friend.

If only he and Claire could patch things up between them as easily.

Claire pulled open the door to the Main Street Grille, grateful for a little girl time. She, Amanda and fellow Furever Paws volunteer Mollie McFadden often got together for lunch or coffee after adoption events, but she was glad they'd set something up for today, just a regular ole day. Too bad her heart felt like it weighed thirty pounds.

She spotted the two young women sitting by the window. Amanda walked dogs on her day off from running the Grille, and Mollie was a dog trainer who assessed the shelter's newcomers when she had free time. Furever Paws hadn't just brought furbabies into her life, but friends, as well.

"I hear you have a new foster!" Amanda said. "How are things going?"

Claire smiled just thinking of sweet Blaze. "So far, so good. He's on the timid side, but is slowly coming out of his shell."

"Guess who I saw in the park yesterday!" Mollie said. "Dempsey! She was with her new owner, fetching ball after ball. Oh, Claire, she looked really happy. And I heard her new owner say to her, 'you're the best dog ever, Dempsey.'"

Claire laughed, her heavy heart lightening a bit. "Good. I couldn't be happier about that match."

"I wish I could have a dog," Amanda said. "But I live here. One of these days…"

"Well, I know how much Birdie and Bunny appreciate that you come in to walk the dogs," Claire said.

Mollie leaned forward. "Speaking of shelter volunteers, my…friend Zeke is good friends with Matt. He mentioned that Matt now lives in a carriage house nearby. I thought he was living over your garage."

A waitress served the food just then, and Claire's

hearty appetite for her turkey club waned. She still popped a fry into her mouth.

"Just didn't work out between us," she said, taking a bite of her sandwich to avoid having to elaborate. She couldn't talk about Matt or think about him without wanting to cry these days.

She knew he'd added the Sparkle-going-missing episode to the list of reasons why he wasn't meant to be a family man...when to her, how he'd handled it proved that he *was*.

"Sounds like you put 'friend' in air quotes, Mollie," Amanda said, adding a dollop of ketchup to her veggie burger.

They both knew that Zeke was Mollie's late brother's best friend. Zeke treated Mollie like a little sister, while she clearly had feelings for him. But she was gun-shy to act on them for fear of messing up the friendship.

Why was romance so complicated?

The door jangled and in walked Ryan Carter, the new owner and editor of the small local newspaper, the *Spring Forest Chronicle*. He headed straight to the counter, looking around for a waitress.

"Hey, Ryan," Amanda said with a warm smile and a wave. Claire knew that Amanda had developed a little crush on the newcomer. "The counter waitress is just picking up an order in the kitchen. She'll be right out."

He barely acknowledged that she'd spoken.

"Chatty, isn't he?" Mollie whispered with a devilish grin. "Gotta love the brooding types."

"What's his story?" Claire asked. "Single? Divorced?"

"No one knows," Amanda said. "He's a man of mystery, apparently."

But Claire noticed how Amanda's gaze lingered on the very attractive newsman. Yup, romance was complicated.

"Speaking of stories, what the heck is this about the crazy thunderstorm forecasted for Monday night?" Mollie asked, taking a sip of her iced tea.

Claire had just heard about the storm this morning. People were already hitting the supermarkets to stock up on water and flashlights since losing power was a strong possibility.

Dempsey never minded bad weather. But Blaze was a scaredy-dog, and she had a feeling she'd be under the covers with him during the storm.

She picked up her sandwich to take a bite when she glanced out the window and saw Matt across the street, headed into a shop, Hank's leash around the pole out front. Her heart leaped at the sight of both of them, man and dog. She missed them so much.

What she wouldn't give to be under the covers with Blaze *and* Matt when the storm struck.

Chapter 13

By late Monday afternoon, all anyone could talk about was how the thunderstorm forecasted for that evening had turned into a tornado watch. If there was a tornado, it was supposed to miss Spring Forest by a good margin, but you couldn't be too careful. Matt's sister's family had left for a planned vacation to his brother-in-law's parents' place, so they and Sparkle were far from harm. He was grateful he wouldn't have to worry about them. But all *his* plans to leave Spring Forest last night had gone out the window. No way could he leave knowing the town—and the Furever Paws shelter—could be hit hard by the storm. He'd rather stay put for a day or two and just make sure the people and animals he cared about were safe. Then he'd go.

Matt had done some online research on tornado

preparation, and apparently taping windows or even cracking windows to equalize pressure was no longer considered useful. Taking down mirrors from the walls and moving other glass items under chairs, creating a safe space in the basement—preferably with no windows—and having food and water for at least seventy-two hours were all listed as steps to take.

At five o'clock he headed over to the shelter to help batten down the hatches, but when he'd arrived, Birdie and Bunny had assured him their handyman and his assistant had it covered and had handled all the storm preparation for years.

Birdie seemed to be trying her best to be strong for Bunny, even chatting about their nephew Grant, who would be visiting soon. Matt had tried "shooting the breeze" about how he remembered Grant and his sisters coming to visit and staying every summer, and how they'd all—him included—go swimming in the creek behind the sisters' farmhouse. Bunny's face had lit up with the reminiscing, and Birdie had mouthed a thank-you to him for getting her sister's mind off the impending storm, even for fifteen minutes.

His research into helping dogs through particularly severe weather had had him up all night, and this morning he'd bought a few things from the big pet emporium two towns over, including something for Blaze, which he was planning on dropping off at Claire's. He wasn't so sure she would be happy to see him, but he also wanted to make sure she had everything she needed for the storm.

He rang the bell and was greeted by a short bark.

Claire opened the door, surprise lighting her pretty face. "Hey."

"I have something for Blaze." He pulled a package from the bag. "It's a thunder shirt. It's supposed to be comforting to a dog who's afraid of thunder."

Her face softened and she knelt down in front of Blaze. "See that?" she said to the dog. "Matt got you a present to help you through tonight. That sure was kind of him." She stood up, taking the package. "Thank you."

"You probably already have one, but I just wanted to make sure."

She laughed. "I actually have three, in all sizes."

He smiled. "Well, you can never have too many thunder shirts."

"I just spoke to Bunny. They're all set over there. She and Birdie and the staff moved all the dogs and cats to the basement, and two volunteers will stay with them overnight."

"I was just over there. They said they have everything covered. But what about the barn animals?" he asked, thinking of the sweet pair of llamas that Hank liked to visit whenever they went to the shelter together. "The pigs, goats, and geese?"

"The sisters will bring the geese with them into the basement of the farmhouse for the night. They say the rest of the animals will be safe in the barn."

He sure as hell hoped so.

A crack of thunder boomed in the gray sky, and they both looked up. Blaze ran back inside under a chair in the living room.

"I might need *all four* thunder shirts for him," she said. "Thanks again, Matt."

"By the way, I put up a bunch of signs in town about the gray dog we saw—I described him best I could and asked folks to call me or Furever Paws if he's spotted or found, but I haven't had any responses. If only we'd gotten a photo, that would have helped."

She nodded. "Well, I'm sure he'll find some sort of shelter tonight. Dogs have a good sense of weather and hopefully he'll find a safe haven at the first scent of thunder."

That made him feel better in general, but he still didn't want to leave her. "Well, stay safe," he heard himself saying.

She bit her lip and grabbed him into a hug. "You too."

He froze for a moment, then pulled her tighter against him, breathing in the scent of her skin, her hair, so in need of her against him that he'd lost all ability to think.

A streak of lightning lit the sky, followed by another boom of thunder, and Claire pulled away.

"You'd better get home," she said.

I don't want to leave you, was all he could think. If he had had Hank with him, he might have found a way to invite himself in for the night, just to make sure she would be safe.

He forced himself to his car. *I don't want to leave you* echoed in his head to the point that it was louder than the rain beating against the windshield.

By seven o'clock, the rain was coming down so hard, talk of the tornado watch on the TV news freaked him out to the point that he couldn't just stay home. He had to check on the sisters, on the shelter and on the barn animals, who were all alone on Whitaker Acres. He packed up a sleeping bag, Hank's favorite bed, food and water for both of them, his phone and charger, put on his trusty L.L.Bean raincoat and muck boots and headed out.

He drove over to Furever Paws first, the concrete building strong and sturdy in the beating rain. He'd called ahead to let the two volunteers know he was coming to check on them and to see if they needed anything. They said they'd thought of everything but extra batteries for their flashlights, and asked if he happened to have any, so he brought two ten packs that he'd had in his kitchen drawer. He found them safe and sound and playing cards in the basement. Some of the dogs were howling. The tremblers who were scared of thunder were in the farmhouse with the sisters. The cats all seemed okay.

Next he drove over to the farmhouse and found Birdie and Bunny hunkered down in their basement with the special-needs dogs and cats and any ones who'd been particularly frightened in their kennels, all in thunder shirts with extra blankets to cozy up in. The geese were in a large pen.

Three booms in a row were so loud that Matt felt them in his chest. "I'm going to stay the night in the barn," he shouted above the noise. "I'll watch over the animals and be close by if you need me."

"Oh, Matt, bless you," Bunny said.

Birdie grabbed him in a hug.

He raced out to his car, his raincoat soaking wet

in just seconds. He drove the one minute down the
gravel road to the big barn, the windshield wipers on
their fastest setting unable to keep up with the pounding rain and winds. He covered himself with a tarp
and grabbed the sleeping bag and Hank's bed under
it, then darted into the barn, setting up their sleeping quarters on the far side where there were no windows. The rain beat down on the roof so loud he was
surprised the llamas and goats weren't trembling in
their pens. The crazy thing was that the worst of the
storm hadn't even started.

He went back out to the car, backing it up as close
to the entrance as he could, then opened the door for
Hank to jump out. He ran inside, his fur wet, and gave
himself a good shake.

Matt grabbed a towel from his backpack and dried
him off, giving him a pat. "You can go lie down and
try to relax, buddy," he said. "It's gonna be a long
night."

Another crack of thunder exploded, and Hank
lifted his head from the bed. The white noise machine he'd brought to try to counteract the thunder
was useless since the booms were so loud. The llamas
and pigs were a noise machine in themselves; no one
would be getting any sleep tonight, that was for sure.

His phone pinged with a text—from the National
Weather Service. This is a weather alert. The tornado
watch is now a tornado warning. The alert repeated
three times.

Matt gasped. "Oh hell."

Panic gripped him as the winds began to howl.

Another boom of thunder hit so loud that Matt put his arms around Hank. The senior dog didn't seem afraid of the noise, but he'd let out a low growl indicating he sure didn't like it. *Neither do I, buddy.* Grabbing his phone, he sent up a silent prayer for cell service, relief washing over him when he was able to call the Whitaker sisters. They assured him they were fine, safe in the basement with their motley crew of dogs, cats and geese, and she and Bunny were playing cards and having those robin cookies that Doc J had brought. He didn't know Birdie Whitaker all that well, but something told him she kept her fears to herself. If she needed him, he had a good feeling she'd call right away.

Another crack of thunder hit, lightning streaking across the sky. He thought of Claire, alone in the house with the timid Blaze, and tried to call her, but the screen on his phone flashed No Service. *No, no, no.* His chest got tight and his heart started beating too fast. He needed to be able to hear that she was okay. He needed to be reachable for the Whitaker sisters. *Dammit!*

He checked his phone again a few minutes later. Same thing. No Service.

He thought he heard a car door slam right outside the doors to the barn. Hank stood up, staring at the doors. "It's okay, buddy. I'll go check it out."

He unlatched the doors and threw the left side open. Claire's SUV was there, the lights shining. *What the hell?*

He ran over to the car just as she got out.

"I have to get Blaze!" she shouted over the crashing sounds of the storm. "He's in his kennel!"

"I'll get the kennel," he shouted back. "You grab your stuff."

She nodded, and he hurried to the trunk and popped it open, grabbing the kennel, which was covered with a small lined tarp.

"I've got you, Blaze. It's gonna be okay," he said in what he hoped was a soothing tone. He felt anything but soothed. He rushed the kennel inside the barn and set it down, and when Claire dashed in with her bags, he closed the barn door and latched it again.

"Claire, how could you risk it?" he asked, staring at her.

She shoved off the hood of her raincoat, her blond hair dry in a low ponytail. "I couldn't sit at home knowing the barn animals were here alone. I just couldn't."

She knelt down in front of Blaze's kennel and opened it. The dog put his snout and one paw hesitantly out onto the barn floor, then slowly came out all the way and looked around. He saw Hank over on his bed and walked over, giving a sniff, then cautiously put a paw on the bed to see how Hank would respond. Because Hank was awesome, he lay his head on the far side of the bed to make room for the smaller dog, who stepped in and curled up alongside Hank's big body.

For a moment, they both watched the dogs settle, and Matt felt more at ease, knowing the timid Blaze would be watched over by Hank tonight.

"Me too," he said. "I should have let you know I

was planning to come out here. I tried to call you a minute ago, but there's no cell service."

"I'm glad you didn't reach me," she said.

"Why?" He held her gaze.

"Because I might not have come. And then I wouldn't be with you right now. And I need to be with you right now, Matt."

He unzipped her soaked raincoat and helped her out of it, then hung it up on a peg next to his. He got his jacket off, and then, before he could stop himself, he pulled Claire into his arms. "It's going to be okay. I checked on the shelter and the sisters. Everyone's fine. Did you hear the watch has turned into a warning? And that it's supposed to strike over Spring Forest?"

She nodded, her face draining of color. "I heard on the way over. Thank God I left when I did, or I wouldn't have been able to come at all. I would have been worried sick about the barn animals here all alone." She smiled and looked at him. "I should have known you'd come."

"I should have known *you*'d come. Want me to grab anything from your car?" he asked.

"I just brought my backpack with supplies for Blaze and some water and granola bars." She clunked herself on the forehead with her palm. "Oh no, I forgot my sleeping bag at home."

"Guess we'll have to share mine," he said, pointing at the rolled-up green nylon pack near Hank's bed. "If you want," he added. "Or you could have it, and I'll make do with the extra blanket I brought. I saw a stack of blankets on a shelf too."

She glanced to where he pointed. "They're for the animals. Those blankets smell like goat and llama."

"So you'll save me from that?" he asked with a smile.

She nodded. "Thanks for offering to share your sleeping bag."

She was thanking *him*? When he'd get to spend a scary, crazy night with Claire spooned against him, safe and sound? "Blaze looks like he's doing okay," he said, his gaze on the black-and-white dog calmly lying between Hank and the wall.

Claire smiled. "I think Blaze found his safe space for tonight. Thanks, Hank."

His heart was practically bursting with how much he cared about this woman, how much he wanted her, needed her.

Over the next couple of hours, the power went out, so Matt set up a couple of flashlights to provide illumination. There was little to do but listen to the rain pound against the barn. Both of them were too wired to talk much. At around midnight, Claire slid into the sleeping bag with a yawn.

"I don't know if I'll be able to sleep," she said.

Matt slid in beside her. They were so close. To the point he could feel her body heat. "Me either."

When a crack of thunder boomed and Claire almost jumped, Matt laid a comforting, heavy hand on her shoulder and then smoothed her hair back from her face. "It's okay, everything is going to be okay." Her eyes looked heavy, as though he was lulling her to sleep, and he hoped that would be the case. Her lids fluttered closed, her breathing soft and steady, and he realized she had fallen asleep. In his arms.

He closed his eyes, his chin resting against her head. He could stay like this forever. Without the tornado, of course.

A noise unlike any Matt had ever heard raged outside, and he started, bolting upright. He'd fallen asleep too. Claire popped up, disoriented, fear in her eyes as a strange howling wind raged outside. The dogs were standing pressed against the barn wall, Blaze trying to get between his protector, Hank, and the wood.

The tornado. *Oh God.*

The howling was downright scary—from the winds and the dogs now, both of whom were reacting.

"I wish we could do something," she said. "I hate that it has to run its course. Who knows what's going on out there? The damage it's causing." Her eyes were wet from unshed tears.

He reached for her and she melted against him. "We just have to ride it out. I'm gonna go check on the animals."

"Keep your distance, just in case they spook," she said.

"Birdie and Bunny warned me about that," he said with something of a smile. He got out of the sleeping bag, immediately cold and missing being so close to Claire. His flashlight guiding the way, he walked to the far end of the barn and turned into the corral area, immediately spotting the big pink pig with his head half-hidden under some hay. "Good idea, buddy," he said.

In the next pen were the four goats, and they were

all huddled against one another in the tiny house a
volunteer had made for them and given to the Whitaker sisters for Christmas last year.

The llamas, Drama and Llama Bean, were standing and looking like nothing got them down. They
both eyed him and stepped to the edge of the pen.

"It's almost over," he assured them. "Just got to
get through tonight, and tomorrow everything will
be better."

A good metaphor for life and tough times, he
thought. He sent up a silent prayer that Birdie and
Bunny and the volunteers and all the Furever Paws
animals were holding up okay, then he came back
into the main area of the barn.

With the tornado roiling toward them, they'd just
have to huddle together like the goats and hope like
hell the damage was minimal.

Matt lay back down in the sleeping bag, and Claire
did the same, this time facing the dogs. He spooned
against her, his arm around her, and she grabbed on
to his hand. Their flashlights were within reaching
distance, next to their backpacks and water bottles,
in case they needed to make a quick escape. He'd
read that a tornado could last anywhere from a few
seconds to an hour. He'd also heard on one news station that a recent tornado had lasted for *three* hours.

"It sounds like a freight train," she said, her voice
choked.

He pulled himself tighter against her, holding on
for dear life. He'd made a promise to himself and
Claire—without her knowing it—that he wouldn't

touch her, that he'd keep his hands and lips to himself. He wanted to break that promise right now, but he knew come morning, when everything was a wreck, he'd need to be strong for her, the sisters and for the animals.

Besides, he'd have to walk away soon enough. So keep his hands to himself, he would.

Claire's eyes popped open in the dark. Matt was silent and unmoving beside her; he'd stayed up well past 2:00 a.m., a fact she knew because that was the last time she'd jerked awake from the noise and he'd wrapped his arm around her, burrowing his chin into her hair. Every time he'd done that, she'd felt safe and secure enough to actually fall asleep, but she had a feeling Matt hadn't slept a wink.

Before she'd driven out to the barn, she'd put on her old battery-operated watch just in case the power went out, and she was glad she did. It was almost four o'clock now. The winds were howling. She'd heard crashes earlier, possibly trees falling, and she prayed the big oaks on the property wouldn't land on any of the buildings. The tornado had stopped, and she was glad Matt had finally fallen asleep. It was pitch-dark outside, the rain still beating down and the thunder still crackling.

His eyes opened, and he seemed to be straining to listen. "The howling stopped. Still pouring, though."

"We made it through."

He grabbed the smaller flashlight and shone it on

the dog bed. Hank and Blaze were curled up tightly next to each other. "They seem okay."

She nodded. "I'm so glad they had each other for the worst of it."

"Like us," he said.

"Like us," she agreed.

She could barely see him in the dark, but she could feel him, breathing beside her, the very presence of him. They were just inches apart.

"I want to go out there with the flashlight and assess the damage," he said.

"In the morning," she whispered. "The flashlight can't illuminate everything, and who knows what debris is out there or broken branches that could fall any minute."

He nodded. "I had a nightmare earlier. Not the same one I used to have about the explosion. This time it was about you."

"Me? I'm the subject of your nightmares? Great." She tried to inject some levity into her voice, afraid he'd turn away from her and go curl up with the dogs.

"You were running in the dark, thunder booming around you and lightning streaking above your head. Tree limbs were falling everywhere. I was standing up ahead and you were running toward me, but you never got closer. It was so strange. I couldn't move a step toward you. I was scared to death you were going to be hurt right in front of me."

"Was I?"

"I woke up," he said.

"What do you think the dream meant?" she asked.

Because if he was about to read too much into it, she wanted to be able to refute his interpretation.

"It means what it is."

"What it is?" she repeated. "What is it?"

"That I'm supposed to let you go, even if I don't want to."

Now she was glad she asked. "You're not *supposed* to. You're *choosing* to, Matt. *You're* the one standing in our way. Your way."

"For good reason," he said.

"No, for no reason."

"I really love you, Claire," he said, his voice breaking. "I always have. But you've always deserved better."

"I don't get a say?"

He shook his head. "You're romanticizing the past. You always were a romantic."

"Me? Hardly. You're the romantic, Matt. Except in this case, you're turning our would-be love story into an almost-tragedy."

"I'll stay in town long enough to help Birdie and Bunny with any cleanup efforts, but then I'm leaving."

"Great. Hurt us both. Good going, Fielding."

"When you're married to a great guy who can give you the world, you'll be glad I was willing to walk away."

"I don't want the world, Matt. I just want you. I've only ever just wanted *you*."

He shook his head again, but she reached both hands to his face and kissed him so that he couldn't say anything else. No more talking. No more. He was leaving. Their second chance was a lost cause. She would have to accept it.

"Do something for me, then, Matt," she whispered.

"Anything."

"Give me a last night with you. Let's just have tonight and then you can go."

"I made myself promise I wouldn't touch you."

"You get to change your own rules," she pointed out. *Please let that sink into his stubborn head. You get to change your own rules.*

"You have no idea how much I want you," he said.

"Show me, then," she said.

He kissed her, peeling off her thermal shirt. His warm hands on her skin were electrifying. She reached down and undid the tie on the waistband of his sweatpants. And then he moved over her, his hands and mouth everywhere.

"Are you sure?" he whispered in her ear, trailing kisses along her collarbone.

"I'm sure," she said.

And then, after retrieving a little foil packet from his wallet, he made her forget all about the storm, all about his stubbornness, all about the fact that he'd be leaving in a matter of days, once again with her heart.

Chapter 14

Matt opened his eyes, aware of only the silence and Claire's gentle breathing as she slept beside him.

Silence.

He gently touched Claire's shoulder. "Hey, sleeping beauty."

She opened her eyes, then bolted upright. "It's quiet."

"Exactly."

Well, it was quiet if you didn't count the pig oinking in his pen at the far end of the barn. Someone wanted breakfast.

"Let's go see what's going on outside, and then we'll check on the barn animals," she said.

They both shimmied out of the sleeping bag and rushed to the barn door.

"Wait," he said, Claire's hand ready to open the

door. "We need to prepare ourselves. It could be really bad."

"I know."

The dogs padded over, Blaze looking much perkier than he had last night.

"Careful, guys," Matt said. "We'll go out first and make sure it's safe for your paws. Stay."

The dogs listened as Claire opened the door and sunlight poured into the barn. She looked out. "Oh no. Oh God. Matt."

She stood there, shaking her head, looking all around.

Devastation was the only word for the scene outside. Trees were torn from their roots and lying sideways across the property. One had even fallen on the roof, but luckily, it hadn't damaged the barn as far as he could see. The tornado had touched right down on Whitaker land, and had taken many of the huge old oak trees.

"Over here, Hank and Blaze," he said, allowing the dogs out in a safe area to do their business. The dogs seemed careful about stepping over branches and debris.

"Oh God, Matt, the shelter. What if—"

They could see the back of the building from where they stood, but not the front or the sides. They ran over, navigating through the downed tree limbs.

Birdie and Bunny stood in front of Furever Paws, their arms around each other's shoulders.

"Birdie! Bunny!" Claire called.

The Whitaker sisters turned around. Tough Birdie looked like she might cry. Bunny did have tears in her eyes as she shook her head.

"Somehow our farmhouse was barely affected," Bunny said. "We got darn lucky."

"The shelter fared worse," Birdie said. "Right in the path of those huge oaks. There's serious damage to the roof," she added, pointing at where a big section had been blown off and now rested against some trees in the forested area. "And a lot of fencing is gone."

"A few of the storage sheds were blown away—one slammed into a tree and seems to have half pulled it up from the ground."

"But you and the volunteers are okay?" Matt asked. "All the animals are okay?"

"All of us are fine," Birdie assured him.

"Same with the barn animals," Claire said. "And these two," she added, gesturing to where Hank and his shadow, Blaze, sniffed around.

"Well, we sure could use your help walking all the dogs," Birdie said. "Why don't we start with the ones in the farmhouse, and then we'll go see if the volunteers in the shelter basement are awake yet."

The four of them went into the farmhouse, Matt grateful the beautiful white home hadn't been hit. In the basement, they each headed for a kennel, Matt going for the little chiweenie, Tucker. As they stepped back outside, letting the dogs stretch and walk around a bit, he was amazed that so much sunshine could follow such turbulent weather. It was early, barely seven, and chilly, but the day promised to be warmer than it had been lately.

"The fenced play area is sound," Bunny said. "So

why don't we put these guys in there and go see how
the dogs in the shelter basement fared."

"You two also," Claire said to Hank and Blaze,
closing the gate behind them.

Once the dogs were secured, and Matt made sure
that none of the trees were possibly near enough to
come crashing down on the shelter or play area, they
all headed inside the shelter. The section of the roof
that had been damaged was in the lobby, toward the
side where the gift shop had been. Thankfully, Birdie
and Bunny had packed everything and secured it, so
nothing was damaged, except the table where people
would sit to fill out applications; it lay on its side, and
there was some bad water damage from where the rain
had come in. *It could be a lot worse*, Matt thought.

Just as they were about to head into the basement,
the door leading downstairs opened, and two women
stood there. "Boy, are we glad to see you all," one said.
Matt hadn't met these women before yesterday, but he
couldn't be more grateful to them for staying with the
animals. There were five dogs down there, and they all
trooped down the stairs to bring them up on leashes.

Finally, with those dogs settled in the play yard with
the others, Birdie and Bunny hugged the two volunteers,
who were anxious to leave and check on their homes.

With the volunteers gone, Matt, Claire and the
Whitaker sisters stood in the fenced yard, watching
the dogs play. Even Tucker, who usually kept to himself, seemed glad to join the reunion, sniffing at a
gentle shepherd mix's ankles.

"Just based on the roof and the fencing alone, I'm

thinking we're looking at around twenty thousand in damages," Birdie said, eyeing the roof of the shelter.

Bunny shook her head. "Thank goodness for solid insurance. *And* that no one was hurt. Boy, did we get lucky."

Birdie nodded. "And we haven't walked the entire property—more downed trees might need hauling away."

"I hate this," Matt said. "Furever Paws and Whitaker Acres are so special and necessary, they should be untouchable. Even from acts of God."

Birdie put a hand on his arm. "This is how it goes, though, isn't it? Things get damaged and rebuilt, and life goes on."

He felt like she was talking about him. He *knew* she was. But some things were too damaged. Like himself.

Claire stared at him, as if hoping the wise Birdie had gotten through to him, just like she'd been trying to do for weeks now. Why did he feel so stuck? Part of him wanted to grab Claire and tell her he loved her, that he wanted to be with her, build a life with her. But part of him just couldn't. So he stayed silent.

"Let's go take a walk farther up," Bunny said. "See how bad it is up near the road."

So much debris, Matt thought as they surveyed the land. He saw lids from garbage cans that weren't Whitaker property, window shutters from God knew where. And so many tree limbs.

"Oh Jesus, is that a dog?" Matt said, his heart stopping.

"What? Where?" Claire said, looking at him, her beautiful green eyes frantic.

"Under that big tree branch," he said, pointing up ahead. A skinny black dog lay unmoving under the heavy branch. His eyes were open and he closed them every now and then, the only indication he was alive.

"Oh God, it is," Bunny said. "He's trapped. Poor thing looks like he gave up the struggle to free himself. Not that he could, given the weight of that tree limb."

"He's probably injured," Birdie said. "But how are we going to get the limb off him without bringing down the entire tree on him?"

Matt stared up at the rest of the tree, hanging in such a precarious position that could it could come toppling down any minute.

"I've never seen this dog before," Birdie said. "I sure as hell hope someone didn't abandon it before the storm." She shook her head, anger flashing in her blue eyes.

"Maybe the thunder or the tornado spooked him, and he ran off from his home and then got hit and trapped by the limb," Claire said. "I can't tell if he has a collar."

Matt couldn't see either. "I have to help him. Somehow, someway."

"I don't know Matt," Birdie said. "We might have to call in our tree guy with his heavy equipment."

Matt shook his head. "If he can even *get* here. We don't know how bad the roads are. And even if he could get here, the dog can't have much longer."

I'm going to help you, he said silently to the dog as he advanced slowly toward the downed tree, his heart beating a mile a minute.

"If you touch anything, that hanging branch could come crashing down on both your heads," Bunny warned.

He stared at the injured, scared dog and saw himself. Claire, Sparkle, Hank, his sister and Ellie, the Whitaker sisters, Zeke and Bobby—they'd all reached out to him and brought him back to himself. Now he was going to help that dog.

Fear can't stop me, he thought. *Not from saving that dog. Not from life.*

Or from love. Because as Claire said, love is all there is. It makes everything else work.

He sucked in a breath and turned back to look at Claire, to drink in the sight of her for sustenance. She believed in him—she'd always believed in him. And she'd helped him believe in himself. He was getting that tree limb off that dog. End of story.

"I have some experience from my time overseas," Matt assured everyone, moving closer to the dog, his gaze going from the precarious tree limb to the dog's frantic eyes. "We were hit with all kinds of hard stuff in our path."

"Oh God, be careful," Claire said.

"I will," he said. He looked at the dog. "I'm coming for you," he said. "I'm going to get you out."

One wrong move and that tree limb would take them *both* out—permanently. *You can do it*, he told himself. Slow and steady. Then quicksilver. In a flash he thought about coming home to Spring Forest, the shock of seeing Claire. How a little girl's birthday wish of a puppy had completely changed his life.

What if I'd told my sister I didn't know anything about dogs and left it to her to choose a pup? I likely never would have run into Claire. I certainly wouldn't have trained Sparkle. Or adopted Hank. Or volunteered at Furever Paws and met the Whitaker sisters.

I wouldn't be here right now.

Save that dog, he told himself.

"Matt," Claire said—from right behind him. "I'm going to help you."

He was about to say *no, you could get hurt,* but he could see the insistence in her eyes. She was determined. And Claire Asher didn't care about getting hurt—she was front-line material.

Yes. She was.

He held out his hand and she took it.

They walked over as silently as they could, since it was clear that any movement would topple the limb. He kept his eyes warm and on the pooch, who was staring at him, half-frantic, half-resigned to his fate— which probably hadn't been all that great till this point.

He calculated where to best lift the limb pinning the dog and noted a branch hanging precariously, just barely attached to it. "I'll lift and you drag the dog out," he said.

She nodded. "Got it."

"You might get bitten," he warned.

She waved a hand. "Hazard of life."

He stared at her and reached out a hand to her cheek, then turned his attention back to the heavy limb trapping the dog.

"We've got this," she said, holding his gaze.

He believed her.

"On my count, pup, okay?" he whispered to the dog. "One. Two. Three."

Before three had finished echoing in his head, he used every bit of strength he had—and a hell of lot in reserve—and lifted the limb up. Claire grabbed the dog under his front arms and pulled him clear.

His arms about to burst, Matt dropped the limb, and the hanging branch came crashing down right on the spot where the poor stray had been.

His heart was booming. He stood, his eyes closed, his legs buckling, his bad leg unable to deal.

"Oh, Matt," Claire said, rushing over, cradling the dog against her chest. "You did it. We did it. This sweet dog did it." She kissed the top of the dog's head, stroking its clumped, wet fur.

"I'll take him," Birdie said, stretching out her arms. "*Her*, actually," she added, as Claire transferred the dog to her arms. Bunny must have run to the barn for a towel, because she wrapped the poor thing up as Birdie shifted her in her arms. The dog looked so relieved to be warm and drying off.

"I'll call Doc J and see if he can come right away," Birdie said. "Her leg looks injured."

She and Bunny rushed the dog back into the shelter.

"You can take the man out of the army, but you can't take the army out of the man," Claire said.

He grabbed her to him and held her, relishing the feeling of her arms tightening around him. "We're all okay," he said, hearing the wonder in his own voice.

"We're all okay," she repeated, placing her hands on either side of his jaw.

His mind had gone as jelly-like as his legs, so he let himself sit back and catch his breath, let his heart rate come back down to normal. But nothing was normal anymore. Not Furever Paws or the Whitaker land stretched out before him, devastation as far as the eye could see.

And not him.

Claire kept glancing at Matt as they all waited for Doc J to arrive to check on the injured dog. Matt had been very quiet since they'd gone inside to join the others. Now it was just the two of them in the shelter's examination room—and the dog, of course, a female mixed-breed that lay on a padded exam table.

Birdie had said it was a good sign that the dog had accepted a few treats from her, and her eyes did look brighter now that she was safe, though it was clear she was in pain. Right now, the dog seemed content to lay there without being pinned by the heavy tree limb, her rescuers cooing at her, petting her side.

Claire didn't know how she didn't melt into a puddle on the floor, her heart was so overflowing with love for this man.

Birdie and Bunny had gone out to the yard to check on the dogs, and make a plan for what to do with everyone until the roof could be taken care of and all the fencing restored.

"You're going to be okay," Matt said to the dog, gently patting its side. "You're in the best possible place now. Doc J will get you fixed up, and then someone will give you a good home. You'll be fine."

The dog gave Matt's hand a lick as he reached to scratch her ears.

Matt smiled. "No thanks necessary. Anyone would have done it."

"But you did," Claire said. "And whether you like it or not, Matt Fielding, you're going to have to listen to me tell you that you're more of a man than any I've ever known. And I love you. I know you're not a coward, so if you do leave Spring Forest and leave me, it's not because you're scared of commitment or love. It's because you don't love me. I get that now."

His mouth dropped open. He'd been a coward when it came to her. Afraid to let himself *feel* what he truly felt. Afraid to let himself have something so precious.

"I do love you," Matt said, looking into her eyes. "I absolutely do love you, Claire Asher."

"But…" she prompted, waiting for it. Bracing herself, tears poking her eyes and her heart so heavy she was about to drop to the floor.

"Not *buts*," he said. "I just love you. And you're right, I'm not a coward. So why the hell would I leave Spring Forest when everything I love is here? When you're here." He walked over to her and held out his arms. She rushed into them, closing her eyes, reveling in the feel of his arms around her, holding her tight.

"I truly thought I had nothing to offer you, and you showed me that I do," he said. "I'm just sorry it took me so long—and a tornado—to see it."

Claire smiled. "I call that the silver lining."

He reached both hands to the sides of her face and stared at her with so much love, so much intensity in his eyes, it was almost too much to bear. She'd seen that look before, when they'd been very young and deeply in love, no cares in the world. Now there were cares, but the look remained. She called that serious progress. "Eighteen years later, will you do me the honor of becoming my wife and sharing your life with me?"

Okay, now she was crying. "Yes. Yes, yes, yes."

"And, Claire, remember when I said a long, long time ago that if we had a baby I'd want to name him Jesse, after my brother?"

She held her breath. "Yes, of course I remember." She remembered what else he'd said too. *Not* that long ago.

"Let's have a baby," he said. "It's lucky that Jesse would work for a boy or a girl."

"Baby Jesse," she repeated, wrapping her arms around him. She put her head on his chest and stayed like that for a good minute. "Oh, Matt? I do have one request for our new life together."

"Anything," Matt said.

"If no one claims our new buddy here, I'd like to foster her—I'd like *us* to foster her—once she's given the okay by Doc J." Birdie had checked for a microchip and there wasn't one, but protocol meant alerting lost dogs websites and hanging flyers and waiting five days to see if anyone would come looking for her. Then she could be put up for adoption. But she'd need nursing back to health and training—and that was Claire Asher's specialty.

"Sounds like a great idea to me," he said. "I have a good name for her too, if the Whitaker sisters will give up naming rights. Hope."

She grinned. "Hope is a great name. A perfect name for her."

Just then, the black dog on the table let out a little bark as if she agreed. Claire's eyes widened. "She likes the name!"

"Sparkle, Hank and Hope can be our ring bearers," he said. "And Blaze, unless he finds his forever home before then."

"Absolutely," Claire said, laughing. "And all our favorite dogs can be invited. Think they'll sit during the ceremony?"

He laughed. "I don't know about that, but I do know something." He put his arms around her shoulders.

She tilted her head. "Oh yeah? What?"

"That *I* found my forever home," Matt said, just as Hope let out another bark of agreement.

* * * * *